I0670410

Vengeance

Legends of the Starborn

STEPHEN PHILLIPS

This story is a work of fiction. Any similarities to
names, people,places are purely coincidental.

Cover art and story Copyright © 2024 Stephen Phillips

All rights reserved.

ISBN: 979-8-9912424-0-0

DEDICATION

Thank you to everyone who continues to read this series.

CONTENTS

Contents

Chapter 1:
A Stroll in the Stars

The drone of the engines hummed in the background. Jace found it soothing as he scrolled through the information provided by the pirate queen. He and Eislie had been waiting to hear from them since their last meeting on the asteroid several months ago, but they had yet to hear anything. And that was alright with Jace and Eislie. They would have known if the pirates had figured out how to dissipate the charge when exiting the filaments.

Knowing what they did about the pirate queen, they knew the pirates would have let everyone know if there was a breakthrough. Jace looked up from the info pad he held, feeling almost a shutter in his nerves. Something seemed amiss as he turned his attention to the multicolor energy display on the navigation console.

"How far have we gone?" Jace asked.

"Approximately eighty-five point seventeen light years, captain. I estimate our return trip would take almost five months at top speed," the computer responded.

Eislie casually worked the controls while resting her feet up on the ledge of the front console. She turned to Jace, saying, "It's great that Ed's been able to decipher some of the programming from that Lyri ship we found. It's made the adjustments to the engine core systems easier. We don't have to continuously stay in contact with the reactor to stop it from resonating." She sighed. "I wish we had more information on all the other systems from that vessel though, it's been months since we heard anything."

Jace smirked, knowing she was implying their unspoken alliance with the queen of the pirates, Jana, and he looked at Eislie. "I still haven't been able to figure out how those other controls were connected. They seemed to only work in one direction, like it was stopping the energy from flowing back to the console." Jace referenced when they crash landed on the planet and found what remained of a Lyri scout vessel. They didn't hesitate to allow the pirates a chance to take it from them to save it when the Consortium attacked on their return. Like Jace, Eislie had seen the scans of the Lyri ship they'd procured. Even their engineer, Arren had a chance to see them, but none of the setup made sense to any of them. Eislie concluded the same as Jace, that it was as if the one part of the navigation console was only an extension of the reactor chamber, nothing more. The systems it showed were for monitoring and navigation only. How it regulated the reaction while within the filaments was still a mystery.

Eislie shifted, bringing her feet to the floor. "I think we've tested enough for today. We should head back."

Jace nodded and returned to what he was reading. His expression changed as the notes became less technical. Jace noticed a flow in the material and started to scan more thoroughly. He gave a huff realizing what he was reading. He continued to face forward as he said, "Hey, Eis, they've decoded what looks like personal logs along with the drive specifications." Jace held up the pad, showing her the information, he then opened the file their computer had contributed from a previous translation. Eislie sat interested as she readied to exit the filament and switch back to normal space.

As the *Wolfhammer* exited the filament, all the lights aboard brightened for a moment. The ship lurched as they slowed, causing Eislie to slip forward, almost falling out of her seat before saying, "I can't wait till we figure out how not to do that when we exit." She then pushed herself back, cinching her harness tighter.

Jace smiled. He tapped his harness, having already adjusted it in anticipation of the exit. Neither of them liked the effect the ship experienced when leaving the stream. It wasn't only physical; the power systems surged every time they exited. She and Jace had done what they could to protect their ship, improving the *Wolfhammer* and testing when time allowed.

Jace snickered before saying, "Remember that quasi-space we jumped out into a few weeks back?"

Eislie smiled, remembering what had happened. She and Jace exited one of the filaments after a run and were suddenly pulled to the top of the cabin. Jace landed on his back, and Eislie landed sideways beside him, her rear end firmly against Jace's head. It took them both a moment to figure out that they were inside a heavy gravity bubble, and that its influence was

2

increasing. They also realized that the gravity systems were straining to compensate. Unable to move, Eislie ordered the ship's computer to fly them out of the anomaly as quickly as possible before it crushed them.

Jace enjoyed seeing Eislie laughing like that since they'd been together. She even gave a snort as she tried to recover. That's when they both heard the computer join the conversation.

"Captain Tucker, I believe Captain Licessien is still finding the humor in the situation from your statement when I informed you that the time to exit the anomaly would be several minutes."

Jace chuckled, then said sarcastically, "Ed, I have no idea what you're talking about."

The computer paused momentarily before replying, "As per my recording. You said, 'Great, so we're stuck like this for a few minutes.' Then you remarked, 'This gives a new meaning to the term head-butt.'"

They both burst out in laughter, and when things calmed, Jace said, "Not that it isn't cute butt."

Eislie batted her eyes at him before asking Ed to scan the area.

As the computer scanned the area for celestial bodies, it found some that were not in its database and displayed them on the screen. On the navigational display, Eislie could see several nearby planets, all outlier class. These were something new, and no one had cataloged them. The computer noticed the same information and mentioned that fact, prompting Eislie to tell Ed that they didn't want to risk anyone knowing they were out so far. At least not until they had a better grasp of filament travel. "Put that on the private systems and enhance encryption."

Jace watched as Eislie steered toward the nearby filament point. Even though they were no longer on the initial project. However, between what the pirates provided and what Ed was able to procure of the known filament maps from the Alliance computers, they had an extensive amount of information to work with when traveling. That allowed them to test their theories while still making it look like they were out exploring mining locations.

Eislie huffed as she tapped the inertial gravity control, setting it lower, making Jace sigh before they entered the stream. Jace remarked, "C'mon, it wasn't that high."

Changing the subject, Jace asked Eislie after she gave him a silent huff, "Did Callie ever take the job offer we gave her?"

Eislie concentrated as she flew, only nodding.

"So, she's back home?"

Eislie looked at Jace. "No, she's staying on Oppa. That's where she lives. Didn't you know that we opened a franchise there? JESC has been expanding." Eislie seemed to be enjoying telling Jace something he didn't know, especially since he owned half of the company.

Jace grimaced as he looked down at the pad, a tone of annoyance in his voice when he said, "When were you going to tell me?"

Eislie chuckled, "When you found out."

Jace shook his head. "Let's hope we make enough money to keep it open. Your father told me that somebody attacked the *Solace Star* two days ago."

Eislie looked over in horror toward him. "What? Why didn't you tell me? Anyone hurt?" Jace could see the concern growing in her stare.

"Easy, Eis, everyone's fine. I didn't tell you because your father asked me not to. They don't know who it was." Jace stretched. "I just know it wasn't pirates."

Eislie calmed, "You should tell me when things like that happen. I don't care who tells you otherwise."

Jace nodded, "Just like opening a franchise on Oppa, right?"

There was an uneasy silence in the cabin as it filled with tension. The computer kept tabs on them both and knew the indications of their biology and the recent events that happened. It knew that what was happening was about to bring about an argument.

"Captains, I suggest you refrain from any combat within the cabin. Who knows where we would wind up if you damaged the controls."

Eislie and Jace slowly turned to stare at the computer's status screen before laughing. "He's right. I think that's the first real, almost fight we've had."

Eislie nodded, "Yeah, we've been lucky."

Jace felt pressure to say, "Eis, I'm happy Callie has someplace to go, I really am, but it would have been nice to know." Eislie turned to look at him but stopped her from speaking. "And, I should have told you about the *Solace Star*. Let's just drop it and head to where we're going. Okay?"

Eislie looked down in thought before giving a nod. She didn't like fighting with Jace. It seemed out of place between them. Since they met, they constantly interacted well with each other. They did have their ups and downs, but they never really fought. Eislie relaxed as she concentrated on flying but turned to see Jace engrossed in reading the pad he held.

"Something interesting?" She asked.

4

Jace nodded, "Yeah, I just found out why that Lyri ship crashed. You're not going to believe this."

Eislie looked intrigued as he continued.

"This is from the engineer's log. The aft atmospheric stabilizer and filament drive were damaged when we exited near the planet. It wasn't easy, but the pilot brought us down safely. It wasn't the softest landing for most of the crew, including myself. The reactor was damaged from impact, and the restraining coils appear to have fractured. It may take me some time, but I believe we can repair them."

Eislie's eyes brightened. "Anything on how they worked?"

Jace shook his head. "Nah, he just goes on about the crew needing medical help and later that he was unable to repair the flight control systems damaged by a surge." Jace looked up, saying, "They were stranded."

Eislie turned away. "Yeah, on a planet they couldn't breathe on. And everything on it trying to kill them at every turn."

Jace nodded but continued to read.

"We were able to engage the natives. They put us through some sort of test and seemed happy that we were not afflicted. Still need to find out what it was about. I can't help thinking that we've had strange encounters with other people since the Duggor invaded our home."

"You're joking. None of them had the madness. You mean they were never on Earth?" Eislie said.

Jace shook his head. "Apparently not. But he doesn't say much more. Looks like the entry says he misses his partner and hopes the emergency signal makes it to a friendly ship."

"They had enemies even back then, apparently," Jace muttered.

He continued to read and gave a quiet grunt of approval before he smiled. Taking notice, Eislie asked what he found.

Jace looked over at her, "It's the Captain's log. Seems like this might be an archive file for transmission." He returned to reading. "We have hope that the signal made it to the others in the area. We included a warning of exiting before this system to avoid the same damage we incurred. My crew is upbeat, and the natives who we have found are from another planet known as Earth. I have not been there yet. There was a quarantine due to an illness, and most Lyri have been avoiding the planet. But, the Alank warned us not to go. The pathogen the inhabitants are suffering from is more severe than we suspect. We found that the people on this world have exiled themselves from their kind back on Earth. We have offered them access to technology or to give them transport when the others arrive, but they have graciously declined. Their temperament and hospitality toward us remind me of the words the Sages wrote long ago."

Jace paused as he read it quietly, and Eislie watched as Jace looked up in reverence. "Those are wise words."

"Well, tell me, what's it say?"

Jace read the log word for word.

"When the fire of hate chills the heart of compassion, the world is lost."

Eislie turned, a look of quiet contemplation in her eyes, before she said, "Those are wise words. What else does it say."

Jace shrugged. "Don't know. The rest hasn't been translated."

Eislie drummed her fingers on the arm of her control chair. "Ed, how far have you gotten in the translations?"

The computer answered quickly, "Captain, I have uploaded the current information to your information pads. The data is encrypted for your viewing only, as requested. But, as for the additional information, I have not been able to complete anything further since the beginning of this flight. Do you wish me to continue the decryption of the database?"

Eislie looked around. "No, Ed. The safety of the ship is more important. Keep recording while we're in the filament."

Jace gave her a smile. "Who would have thought that the database would be so tough to decrypt."

The computer replied, "The memory was deteriorated. It is not just the encryption but the silicon-based systems for the memory. And, for a vessel over ten thousand years old, it seemed to be salvageable. However, molecular extrapolation and reconstruction of the data is slowing the process. We will have to be reliant on the information given to us by our.... Friends. The copy that we retrieved back on..." The computer paused. "Their people were known as the Alank, but they did not tell us their world's name. Did they inform you what their planet was called, captains?"

The two looked at each other before Jace looked at the computer's interface, "Uh, Ed, it was called *EnKal*." He just realized that the ship never heard their conversation while inside that enclosure where they stayed while being tested for the madness. This new revelation now concerned Eislie.

"They didn't trust us completely, did they?" Eislie said, looking forward as she flew.

Jace shook his head, "I'm not sure of that. They knew we had met the Karazon. I mean the Karazon are descended from the Ergo, just like the

Alank and both were from Earth. I wonder if they didn't tell us because they were unsure what we'd do?"

"About what?" Eislie asked.

Jace leaned back into his chair. "Maybe we'd come back and harm them. Or worse, tell the Karazon about them. That would give the Karazon some leverage against the Alank." Jace closed his eyes, leaning his head back. "Maybe they're afraid of their past and what it might do if they found them. I mean, we found them by accident."

Eislie glanced at Jace. "They're not like Terrans. Some of the Karazon might like what the Alank have done."

Jace rolled his head, giving her a look of discernment. "Really? Eis, they're from Earth. I don't think it'd be a nice reunion."

Eislie seemed disheartened as what Jace said sank in. She liked to think most people were reasonable, even after being treated as they were. But she couldn't help feeling that Jace was right. The Karazon wanted to take them both as trophies, considering them less than anything more than a prize.

The cabin was quiet for the rest of the flight, only interrupted when the *Wolfhammer* exited near the recent mining location they had informed the others about. The fervor only increased as they approached to find an alliance ship now orbiting the planet they were heading toward. They could see damage from weapons fire and outgassing on the giant ship's hull. Jace groaned in annoyance as the comm came alive.

"*Wolfhammer*, we had you reregistered as investigating a mining location on this planet. Where have you been?"

Jace motioned for Eislie to wait as he answered. "Well, we decided to take a little run. Testing out the engines we had to replace the flight control systems from the last time the Alliance saved us." Jace paused. "Oh, wait, that's right. You arrived late. Actually, we lost navigation control and had to fight for control of the ship."

Eislie threw her hands up. "What are you doing?"

Jace gave a sly smile. "Making it seem like we don't trust them for putting us through all that stuff after losing that Lyri ship. Give them a bit of heartburn, you know?"

Eislie looked confused before Jace spoke again. "You guys screwed up our systems when we were back on planet. We're still working the bugs out. The computer took us for a ride after we exited hyperspace. Took us this long to get it under control and back here. It took time to reinstall the original backup we had on board."

Eislie now understood. Jace was covering the recent journey in the filaments, telling them it was the Alliance's fault, and that the computer sent them off course as a ruse. They had only been gone a few hours; a technical issue could account for that. As they waited for the Alliance ship's response, Jace said, "Sorry, Ed. It's not your fault. I want to make them think that our missing was their fault."

"I understand, captain, it is a clever use of misinformation."

Jace chuckled, "Thanks, Ed. Best I could come up with on short notice. Now we have to hope they believe it."

Several seconds passed before they heard the comm again. "Sorry to hear you had navigation trouble with the new system. Can we be of assistance?"

Jace replied, "Nah, got things working again. Glad we kept a copy of the old system. That new one you installed wasn't cutting it. It's probably too new for these ship's systems. We're back on track again, though."

The comm crackled. "Were you aware that there was an Arlain war cruiser in this vicinity? We engaged it only semi-cycles ago. It left just before you arrived. We thought that possibly you were taken."

Jace looked at Eislie, seeing her suddenly very worried before he replied, "No. Wow. Maybe that computer glitch wasn't so bad after all. I hope everyone on board is okay. Any causalities?"

Then, a different voice came on the comm. "Captain Tucker, we were dispatched by Alliance control to ensure you were safe. Did you happen to see any hostiles while you were negotiating your technical breakdown?"

Jace suddenly felt the hair on the back of his neck bristle. "No, thankfully." He looked the giant battleship over before releasing the comm. Jace turned to Eislie, "That's the same class as the *Aranost*, right?"

Eislie nodded. "Yes, Amanar class. It's the best the Alliance makes."

Jace thought momentarily, his mind filling with concern, and he could see the same look in Eislie's eyes. His suspicion she was thinking the same was confirmed when she said, "Someone knew we'd be out here."

Jace tapped the comm again, "Would your captain be up for a meeting? We want to come aboard if possible."

The response over the comm was simple: "Our captain is asking to meet with you as well. Maybe we can help with your technical issues while you're on board."

Jace nodded before responding, "Our ship's good to go, but we'll dock along the port side. We'd love to meet with your captain."

Chapter 2:
Someone Knows Something

The sound of grinding creaked throughout the ship as the clamps closed over the entryway locks. The poly-ceramic hull of the *Wolfhammer* sounded worse for wear, prompting Jace to remark, "Sounds like we need to recoat the hull soon."

The computer came over the speakers, "The hull of this vessel is an ablative style. It will be several standard years of heavy use before it will need service. Unless we are in heavy battle, of course."

"Noted, Ed," Jace said as he opened the inside door.

When the outer door opened, they saw several armed Alliance soldiers, and the captain was behind them. Thankfully, the two saw no weapons drawn.

"At least they're not pointing them at us," Eislie joked quietly, making Jace smile.

As they entered the Alliance ship, the captain said, "Welcome aboard the *Aquaese Coul*."

Jace looked to Eislie, who shook her head, saying, "I have no idea what it means."

Hearing her, the captain responded, "It's old Gilese for a faithful ship."

Jace nodded, and they approached the captain. To his surprise, no one tried to stop either of them. The captain turned, leading them to a nearby room. As they entered, Jace noticed a long table with several empty chairs. The screens around the room were active but seemed to be waiting for their occupants.

"Please sit. I have some information you may be interested in," the captain said, motioning to the chairs across the table. He turned to tap one of the screens, and a file appeared. Jace and Eislie immediately recognized the image of their ship.

"Forgive me; I haven't introduced myself. I am Captain Salis Wehen. I've been following you since you returned with that Lyri vessel a few months back." The captain sat across from them. It was easy to figure out that he was assigned to follow them. And neither Jace nor Eislie flinched when the captain said, "And I have read up on your pasts, both of you."

Jace and Eislie remained unphased, their eyes steady on the captain as he spoke. Salis tugged his short beard before saying, "It's good to see you're safe. It's lucky you had navigation problems." The captain paused. "Although, our sensors did detect some phasing of filament remnants within your shields."

Jace spoke sternly, "Haven't removed the programming from the last time we used it that way. Been meaning to."

The captain felt the two of them staring. "You're not a fan of the Alliance right now, are you?"

"Can we get to the point? The last captain that knew about our pasts tried killing Jace and imprisoning me," Eislie snapped, thinking about when they were saving people on Oppa and the captain of the other ship tried taking them prisoner. He had been involved with their enslavement and was angered at the consequences of its exposure. "It didn't work out well for him."

Salis smiled, "Indeed. I'm well aware of Captain Radit's transgressions. It seems a few from the council were also involved. If you have time, I could fill you in later on what became of the former captain. Right now, there is a more pressing matter. And it concerns both of you and the filament project."

Jace leaned forward, his chin on his palm as he playfully rested his elbow on the table. "Well, captain, tell us what you've got."

Captain Wehen tapped some controls on the table, causing the other screens to light. One was the new head of the filament project, her name absent from the screen, and the others were various high-ranking officials from the Alliance and Oppan space commands. The captain then stood tapping the center screen that had held the image of the *Wolfhammer*. "It's come to my attention that there has been a breach in our security regarding the project. There was a coincidental engagement with a Consortium vessel, and that your ship happens to be in the area." Captain Wehen looked at Jace and Eislie before turning to the screen, "There are also reports of several other ships reporting secure computer break-ins."

On the screen with the Alliance general, they heard, "Breaking into Alliance systems is punishable by imprisonment."

Eislie stood, "So is slavery."

Captain Wehen held his hands up. "Please, this posturing is going to get us nowhere. Besides, if these two had taken the information, they would simply be retrieving what they had procured in the first place, General Isam. I'm sure you are all aware of the laws protecting personal and corporate information."

Jace watched as Isam's screen went blank, and when he returned, his face was a more crimson shade. "I am, Captain."

Salis nodded as he continued, "We're not here to place blame. So, let's avoid doing so." The general seemed to calm. "You are all wondering why I asked for this meeting."

An official on another screen said, "It is highly unusual for a ship captain to request one. But from what you have relayed to us, I feel it is in our best interests to indulge you, Captain Wehen. I'm sure the others on this meeting agree?"

They watched as heads nodded before the same woman said, "Please continue, Captain."

Captain Wehen tapped the screen again, and a video started playing. "This is a recording of the binary system near the Arlain system. For the Terrans here, you would call it Altar. The recording is of a large ship exiting from what we now know as a filament point."

The video played, and everyone watched as the ship emerged from the filament. Although the image was minuscule, Jace could recognize the vessel type given the distance.

"A Wrent class? That's a Duggor ship," Jace said with concern.

Captain Wehen nodded. "It is a Wrent class vessel, but it seems to have been damaged from the stream." The captain enlarged the image, and they could see the smoke and plasma now leaking from the hull of the Duggor vessel just before it exploded.

Salis then showed another. The video was of an Arlain cruiser whose engine inverted as soon as it exited another filament point.

On the Oppa space control screen, the new head of the filament project said, "We've had similar incidences when testing. Most vessels didn't survive, making it difficult to find out what happened."

Captain Wehen sat. "In fact, all ships you've tested have blown apart, haven't they, commander?" Jace could hear the defiant tone in Salis's accusation.

"Yes, all were destroyed," the Oppan representative said.

Salis's demeanor changed as he looked across the table. "In fact, all ships any of you have tested have been destroyed, have they not?"

Eislie and Jace began to feel uneasy, and both turned to look toward the door. They would fight to escape and even order Ed to attack if needed, but their host said something that made them change their minds.

"You have ordered me to bring these two in. Why is that?" Wehen asked.

The sound on another screen came alive. "Because they infiltrated our systems."

Captain Wehen slammed his hand hard on the table. "That's slac, and you know it. Even I could fake a computer break-in." He turned to Eislie and Jace. "And I'm not that proficient in them." The captain returned to the screens. "You want them and their ship."

There was yelling from the screens before Captain Wehen stood. "We'll continue the meeting when you're all done arguing."

It took several minutes before the room quieted, and the Gilesian general spoke, "How are you so sure they did not infiltrate the systems?"

Salis scoffed, "One, because you have all the information from them and on their ship. And two, they would have been careful. I do not think you'd have a way to trace them easily." The captain turned to the two. "You two have been careful in keeping out of the spotlight. In truth, if they thought they couldn't achieve filament travel without you, they would have fought harder to keep you on the project."

There was silence as Captain Wehen's words sank in. "feel free to deny it any time. I would love to hear your reasoning." He sat again, tapping the screen on the table. "All of these accusations are not why I asked everyone to meet. I feel we have a more pressing issue."

Salis played the Arlain vessel again. "This is a Consortium vessel. To our knowledge, they do not have information on filament travel. Yet, we are looking at them exiting from a secondary binary system. Why is that?"

The captain's remark was met with silence, making him speak up, "No takers on as to why they seem to be exiting from a filament point? I'm surprised. I would think all of you would want to know."

"Get to your point, Captain Wehen," the Alliance general growled.

"I was asked to come look for these two given our recent intelligence reports on the Consortium. In fact, I had to give up on my mission to find their former captor to do so;" Salis replied.

"Former captor? You mean Devlin Bosh? He's still alive?" Eislie said as the anger became evident on both of their faces.

Salis nodded as the general commanded over the screen. "Get to the point, Wehen."

The captain took a breath. "Bosh would not have been able to instigate getting an Arlain battle cruiser here. Someone much higher up in their command would have to do that feat—someone with inside knowledge. I hate to inform you, but apparently, you have some Consortium spies within your organizations." Salis looked around. "We're aware that the pirates do, and we catch them all the time. Although some continuously elude us."

"The whereabouts of former Captain Bosh and our security are hardly a matter to discuss with these others," the Alliance general bellowed.

Salis nodded. "You're right, general. It is not a subject we should be discussing with them." The captain then turned to Jace and Eislie, mouthing the words, "We'll talk later" before he continued. "Fellow officers and council members, we have an infiltration problem. And the reason I know this is that even though their flight was public record. The

Consortium knew exactly where and when to find them. That's why we arrived at the same time as the Arlain vessel. The only saving grace is that those two had navigation issues because of the damage we previously caused to their ship's systems. And in my report, the ship they sent was well capable of capturing these two."

Captain Wehen leaned back in his chair, "What I'm getting at is that we have to find out where the leak is." He turned to the screens again, "because if the Consortium gets filament travel before anyone else, we're all in danger."

Several seconds of silence were only broken as they heard, "Thank you, captain. We'll start our investigation from the Oppan representative" before the screen went blank. The others followed suit. The General of Alliance command was the last to speak. "Captain Wehen, what you found is disturbing. I hope you are wrong in your conjecture." The screen then went blank.

Salis said, "He's probably feeding them the info for a few shill," before turning to Jace and Eislie, saying, "You still need help with your navigation computer? I have some good techs onboard."

Jace politely refused, as did Eislie.

"Alright then, let's get you on your way," Salis said as he stood.

They followed him out of the room, walking toward the docking bay. There were suspiciously few Alliance personnel along the path, making Jace concerned. Captain Wehen paused for a moment before opening the door to the exit way. "You sure you don't need any technical help?"

"Nope, we've got it covered," Jace replied, his hands almost balled, ready to fight.

Captain Wehen nodded as he opened the exit way door. Eislie walked through, but as Jace was about to step through, Salis spoke, "What's it like in the filaments? You know, before you arrived here."

"That was months ago. You have everything we reported already," Eislie replied.

Jace looked the captain in the eyes as the man spoke, "Filament resonance dissipates after a quarter cycle. It's in your own words, Captain Tucker."

The small hallway was silent before Salis filled the emptiness. "Bosh is still out there. Watch your backs." He paused. "Listen, I know you've been traveling the filaments, and I'm not going to tell any of them. It'll only make things worse for the two of you."

"That's very thoughtful, Captain Wehen," Eislie said.

Captain Wehen smiled. "So you know, I am loyal to the Alliance. I'm not your friend. But I'm also not your enemy. You two are attempting something much more beneficial."

The captain smiled, changing the subject. "I read the report from the Lyri captain log as well. It seems she was a fan of quoting the Lyrian sages. It's good to see our ancestors had lived somewhat of a peaceful existence."

Jace said, "Until the Duggor showed up, but that's another issue." Jace stopped in the small doorway, "Oh, if you find Bosh, please let us know. We'd like to have a few words with him."

Salis nodded. "You're on my list to call. I want to have a few words with him myself. He sent two of my crew off to be enslaved to the Arlains. But you're definitely on my list to call when I find him."

Jace turned, heading down the gantry way. The captain closed the hatch, yelling, "Safe trip," as he secured the inside door. He turned, walking away, his voice trailing off. "You two better find Bosh before I do. At least there'll be something left to talk to."

Chapter 3:
A Little Time Home, Now and Then

Jace's hand hovered over the control, and he snickered again, thinking about that little gravity situation, and reminded Eislie about it. He joked about Eislie playing with the gravity controls. He thought it was a good idea to increase the gravity in case something like that happened again. Since the incident, they'd been adjusting the gravity onboard before flying the filaments.

"Gilese control, this is the *Wolfhammer*, requesting landing clearance." Eislie gave a happy sigh as she released the comm. Jace snorted as she said, "It's good to be home again."

Eislie flew the ship slowly as they waited for clearance to land. Her mind returned to the information that Devlin Bosh, the man who had imprisoned them, was still alive. She and Jace had wondered what happened to him. They both knew he was on one of the transports that escaped the pirate attack, but through an investigation by the Gilese military, they learned that Bosh never returned to his home on Gilese Three. Instead, they found the building where he had resided cleared out. The investigators noted that it was done hastily, leaving nothing more than hanging wires and the remnants of some broken furniture left behind. Everything else was taken.

Eislie looked at Jace, his eyes focusing on the screen before him. She could tell he wasn't concentrating on the images that flashed within view, but deep in thought. She could sense him pondering and decided to ask, but as she was about to speak, Jace said, "We should let them know Bosh is still alive; he may use some of our crew or family to get to us." Jace crossed his arms before leaning back. "I wouldn't put it past him."

She nodded, looking to the comm, still awaiting a response from the control center, when Jace sighed heavily. "We may want to step back on the filament research for the moment. I think someone knows more about what we're doing than we want them to know."

Eislie agreed, "Probably a good idea. Maybe we can actually focus on business."

Jace smiled. "You know, your parents are pretty good at what they've been doing. I think all that Alliance service was holding them back."

Eislie looked annoyed toward Jace, who only gave a smile back. She shook her head, realizing that he was trying to make a light about the whole situation. When the comm came alive, they both moved to answer, but Eislie was faster and acknowledged the permission from the control center. She leaned back, mouthing the words, "beat you," before sticking her tongue out at Jace, causing him to laugh.

Jace leaned back, saying, "It does feel good to be home."

"Oh, you've finally come around that this is home?" Eislie chided him.

Jace nodded. "It doesn't feel that foreign anymore. It's grown on me."

Eislie smiled as she looked at the monitors, she felt happy that Jace thought Gilese was his home now. Like her mother, he accepted his new adoptive planet after only a few years. As she brought the ship into the dock, Jace grabbed a few things they brought on when they boarded and tossed one pack to Eislie as she moved toward the door.

"Ed, make sure that data from the last run is uploaded to our pads. Encrypt the rest, will ya," Jace said.

"Acknowledged, Captain. Do you wish me to continue to attempt to decrypt the database?"

Jace responded, "Yes, but there's no rush. Given our recent meeting, I think we may want to lay low for a while."

Eislie looked puzzled. "What does that mean, lay low?"

Jace was about to answer when the computer interrupted, "It is a term used by Terrans. It means to keep undercover or hide. I discovered that in several Terran force ship's logs."

"But you last had access to Terran or Alliance systems a while ago, Ed. How did you read them?"

The computer responded, "While you were on the Aquaese, I decided to do…. research."

Eislie rolled her eyes. "He's breaking in again." She looked at Jace. "You're right. He is a delinquent."

Jace chuckled before saying, "Well, he does have us for captains. Can't blame him."

As they closed the door, the computer went to work on the database.

* * *

Jace opened the door to their home, surprised it was just as they left it. The nonrandom cleanliness making Jace say, "I'm surprised to see no one broke in."

Eislie groaned, pushing him aside gently, making him jokingly hop on one foot as if off balance as she threw her pack onto the table. Jace reached out and, grabbing her arm, pulled himself forward gently, hanging onto her as if he was falling off balance. There was some quiet romantic laughter between them as Eislie placed her forehead against his before gently kissing him. However, their romantic embrace was interrupted when the alert for the comm sounded.

Jace and Eislie turned, glancing at the comm on the table, saying, "That didn't last long." Jace smiled. "It's not dinner time, so it can't be a telemarketer."

Eislie chuckled. "We sent them all out into space centuries ago. Garrett probably saw our ship and realized we were back."

Jace walked over, reading the screen to see her mother's name. "Should we answer?"

Eislie pushed him aside as she answered, "Hello, I'm sorry we've only arrived. Please leave your message and hit two to send it into the nearest black hole."

The screen of the comm filled with the face of her mother shaking her head, "You use that every time I call at the wrong time, Eis."

"Mother, what a surprise. We just walked in the door," Eislie said slowly.

Her mother smiled. "I know, sorry to bother you, but Garrett told us you were back."

Jace pointed to Eislie, "You called it."

Eislie looked at him. "No, she called us."

Her mother started laughing. "Eis, he's making a joke. You should be used to Terran humor by now."

Eislie bowed her head. "What is it?"

Her mother sighed, "We have a company meeting in a few hours. We were wondering if you two would like to attend. After all, it is your company."

Jace and Eislie looked away before Jace said, "Maybe we should tell them what we found out at our meeting."

Her mother looked puzzled, "What meeting?"

Eislie spoke this time, "The one on the *Aquaese Coul*."

The expression on her mother's face turned to concern. "Is it bad?"

Jace took the lead this time. "It involves our former jailer. And some information about the Alliance wanting to, uh, request our presence again." Jace looked straight into the screen. "When's the meeting?"

Eislie's mother paused before saying, "About two standard hours, everyone's planetside. You can fill us all in when you get here."

Jace nodded. "Alright, we'll be there."

Eislie made the goodbye short as Jace approached the large glass door overlooking the lake. It was only a minute before Eislie joined him.

"You know, I was hoping to not have to work the next few days. I was looking forward to jumping into that water and relaxing a bit," Jace mumbled.

Eislie put her arm around his waist and pulled into him, leaning her head against his shoulder. He felt her nod before she spoke. "Yeah, do something normal for once."

They stood together for a few minutes, the stillness and silence of the room comforting. The success of the filament tests was something they could accept. But, with the recent finding that Devlin Bosh, was alive, and the Alliance was trying to bring them in again against their will, now became worrisome. At the very least, it was undoubtedly concerning to the two of them. And, with the recent attack on the *Solace Star*, this new revelation may not go over well. Especially given the recent attempts, it meant that they all may be in danger.

A couple of hours later, Jace and Eislie arrived at the office. Flora greeted them while waiting at the front desk for the recent paperwork to be picked up. Things were going well since they had expanded their business while they were planetside. Jace looked around. He and Eislie had only visited the facility a few times over the last year. Both had spent most of their time at the complex on Oppa working on the testing for the filament project. Jace joked that the place looked like it was renovated recently, causing her mother to reply.

"You know that we've actually made some profit since this all began. We've even opened a few locations on other planets."

Jace looked to Eislie, who mockingly turned away as if not to notice what her mother said.

"Really, Eis? You didn't tell him anything?" Her mother scolded.

Jace looked intrigued and leaned in, "So, how many?"

Flora smiled back. "Oppa, Yata, Terlis, so far."

"Wait, Terlis?" Eislie asked.

Her mother nodded. "We opened it two weeks ago. They signed a contract with us to deliver the Sotiral systems, among other cargo. The contract alone is more than half our net income now. And with Yata supplying most of them, we've been busy." She sighed. "We've had a lot of requests for reactional trips, but the ships aren't really set up for that. Not like we can take the *Wolfhammer* out for them."

Jace noticed her looking at them, and he took the hint. "Nope, uh, no, not yet. We need to make much more money before we start doing party cruises."

There was laughter as Eislie asked what was going on; she then looked to see her mother laughing before she muttered, "Great, this is a Terran thing, isn't it?"

Eislie's mother shook her head, "Eislie, he means that we should be on more stable footing before we even consider taking private trips. He's right. We'd need more ships before we even considered personal flights."

Eislie nodded, finally understanding what Jace was saying. Her annoyance with his vagueness was evident when she spoke, "Then why not just say that? Why do you have to be so cryptic?" She glanced toward Jace momentarily before she looked away.

"Eis! What's gotten into you?" Flora said as she tried comforting her daughter.

Eislie huffed and pushed her away. She turned to look at both her mother and Jace, "I'm, I'm sorry. It's just that I don't want to walk away from everything we've done." Her words trailed as she rushed away down the small hall. Her actions made her mother look at Jace with an accusing glance.

"Don't look at me. I didn't do anything. At least I don't think I did," Jace said, confused.

Flora put her hand on his shoulder. "Something happen during the test?"

Jace thought momentarily. "I think it may be the news about Bosh. Oh, and the Alliance suspects we are traveling the filaments. Seems like they ordered us to be brought in."

Flora stepped back. "They can't. You haven't broken any laws. At least I don't know if you have."

Jace caught her words and the subtle joke before he replied, smiling, "At least we haven't, yet."

Eislie's mother chuckled. "You'll find some to break soon." She paused. "She's probably worried hearing the news about Bosh."

Jace nodded as he followed her to the conference room, the dark hallway lighting as they walked down. They turned to enter, seeing Issa and Shasji laughing by the small table with food. Jace smiled, seeing everyone there and Eislie speaking with Garrett.

The meeting was short. Flora updated everyone on the dealings and the assignments for the upcoming flights. Many commented that most of them were based out of Yata.

"They are our biggest client, not to mention we are also bringing in revenue from the Sotiral sales. The Yata government insisted we accept some of the profits. And, with the recent runs, we should have enough to buy a larger ship."

Her statement brought Bensin to say, "Good, then you can retire the *Wolfhammer*. Get a decent ship."

The room fell silent as sets of eyes converged on Bensin as he took a drink, and the weight of their stares not allowing him to swallow. His heart skipped as he looked toward Jace, his green eyes filled with a hidden fire of anger. As he turned away, his gaze was met by Eislie's, her pale blue eyes filled with rage burning as much as the one he had turned away from.

In a desperate attempt, he looked toward the door and could see Larat standing in the way. His heart stuttered, feeling his very soul seared by those around him. He went to apologize and hesitated as Eislie started toward him, only to see Garrett grab her arms holding her back. He turned to see Jace standing tall but shaking his head.

"Wrong thing to say if you want to keep working here," Jace muttered as he looked back to Eislie. "The *Wolfhammer* is a better ship than you are qualified to fly on."

Jace walked over, standing before Eislie, who looked around him angrily toward Bensin. Jace told her, "He's trying to goad us. Probably trying to get something to sue us about." Jace leaned in, whispering, "Might even be trying to get the ship itself."

Eislie turned back, her eyes open with a fear of understanding.

Feeling the tension in the room, Flora said, "Look, everyone, we just found some disturbing news. Eislie and Jace informed us earlier. Perhaps we should let everyone know what you found."

Jace nodded, "Yeah, maybe we should."

He went on to tell everyone about the Alliance, knowing about the recent runs of their ship and that they planned to "lay low" for a little while. He continued with the news about Bosh and informed everyone to watch themselves. "He may try and use you as bait to get to us."

Jace told them that the attack on the *Solace Star* was probably them testing the ship's defenses and seeing who would show if there was an attack. He admitted, "At least that's my theory."

The news wasn't all bad. Larat informed everyone that they were getting a raise in pay since the Yata contract would provide more of a windfall. That news went over very well with everyone. After they finished, Eislie's mother took her aside. Jace could see them talking but couldn't hear. He was about to walk over to find out if Eislie was alright but was stopped by her father.

"Trust me, you'll live longer, avoiding getting involved between my wife and daughter. I learned that years ago," Larat said, pounding his hand down on Jace's shoulder.

Jace turned, "That dangerous, huh?"

His father-in-law nodded, "It'll save you; trust me on this."

Jace agreed and left them alone. It was only a minute before Eislie and her mother parted, with Flora tapping on the internal comm to bring up some music. The music seemed familiar to Jace, but the female singer was one he didn't know. The language was certainly not from Earth.

Jace was startled as Eislie grabbed his arm. "C'mon, I want to dance."

Jace joked, "It's been years since I've danced. You may break out laughing." He feigned resistance as Eislie pulled him to an open floor area.

Flora grabbed her husband's arm. "They'll be fine, she's worried about everyone because that asshole who imprisoned them is still out there."

Larat nodded, "I figured as much."

Flora then looked around, pointing to the speakers. She yelled to Jace, "Hey, you know, this has a heavy metal sound to it."

Jace nodded.

Larat listened. "With this beat, I don't know how you'd dance to it."

His wife laughed before yelling, "Hey, Jace!" As Jace turned, she put her arms up and threw her head back and forth, her lengthy hair flying all around as she did. Jace laughed, then did the same. He was pumping his fists in the air, throwing his head back and forth. Eislie stood stunned by the display. Both he and her mother stopped and were laughing hysterically.

"What are you doing?" Eislie asked Jace. She had to wait for him to stop laughing before he could answer.

"It's how some of us used to dance back on Earth. Among other things," Jace told her, thinking back to his days going to concerts and everything that happened.

Eislie looked to her mother, now hanging onto her husband, as she laughed.

"It's silly, isn't it?" Jace said as he reached out to hold gently onto Eislie's arms.

She nodded, seeing him laughing, and started laughing herself. Eislie pushed away as Jace began "dancing" again to the beat of the music. She stood in wonder and embarrassment as Jace looked at her, "C'mon, we can't be serious all the time."

Eislie paused, looked back at her mother, and smiled, seeing her leaning against her father. She started to mimic Jace and had to push away her hair as it engulfed her face. The display of the two of them made everyone laugh.

Shasji was laughing but walked over near them and started doing the same, causing a loud uproar from those remaining in the room. It wasn't long before most joined them as the music continued. Eislie and Jace moved a bit closer. They did less of the fast movement and held onto each other a bit. Seeing the floor filled with those mockingly attempting the moves Jace and Flora showed them was strange but enjoyable.

But not everyone joined them. Derrit had been gorging on the free food since they started and was standing by Garrett as he watched the display. Their fellow starborn turned to see them all attempting to dance as Jace had. Derrit then looked at the pastry he was eating and tapped Garrett's arm.

"Look at them," Derrit said, getting a nod from his captain. "I don't know about you, but seeing them doing that, I think there may be something in the food."

Garrett looked horrified before looking at Derrit, displaying a practiced look of cluelessness before Garrett started laughing.

Chapter 4:
A Bounty is Forged

The dust swirled around three people standing outside on the landing field—the house nearby, its opulence muted by the wisping debris. The tailored robes adorned with similar regal attachments fluttered and settled as the ship's thrusters extinguished.

On the right of the robed man stood another. He remarked as he straightened his simpler clothing, "That vessel has to be at least a century old. It should have been junked ages ago."

The regal-clothed man snorted, "You show your ignorance. That is an Arlain scout ship. Third reign, rare as they come. I was thinking of offering a fair price and several of my finest slaves for it in trade." He turned to the man who spoke. "Including you, Fellen."

"Lord Malik, please, I have served by your side for ages." Fellen prostrated himself before the man, his simple clothing now collecting dust as he bowed.

Hearing the ship's hatch open, Malik smiled. "Fellen, get up. I would never trade you. You have been a loyal servant. I was merely jesting."

Fellen stood brushing himself off as Malik laughed, "Yes, my lord, your humor, as always, is entertaining." He watched as his master walked toward the ship. Two people exited through the hatch; their uniforms simple but showing elements of status. Malik dismissed them and waited.

They watched as the two whom Fellen took as officers stood at attention. Malik placed his hands together before him. As a third person exited, the noble raised his hands in greeting,

"Devlin Bosh, as my eyes sing. You are not dead." He reached out both hands, and the men clasped hands, shaking them firmly. "It is good to see that the reports of your death are untrue."

Bosh looked to his subordinates. "Yes, it has been a trying few cycles. But I am happy you were willing to oblige my residency."

Malik nodded, "You are welcome in my home, dear friend. After all, where would my wealth be without your endeavors?" The man sighed, "It is troubling that your most prized slaves were the undoing of your profitable enterprise."

Bosh's grip tightened, and it was met equally by Malik's hold. The slave trader knew full well of Bosh's anger toward the two starborn who escaped. And the subsequent alert to the rest of the Alliance caused the release of known starborn prisoners.

Bosh growled, "Those two cost me a lot. I hope that you will indulge me for a short time, Ledger."

Bosh watched as Malik's eyes filled with joyous achievement and acknowledgment. He had been dealing with minor slavers for some time. The need for spide and starborn to mine was something that kept Bosh and, of course, Malik in the Luxury they now enjoyed. And by addressing his friend, as Ledger, a regal who owned many slaves that adored him, now cemented his place within the slaver's heart. Bosh knew how to manipulate, and using old traditions was not beneath him.

Malik broke his hold, raising his hands to the sky. "Ah, I have not been referred to as Ledger for some time. You are gracious in your praise, my friend." He pointed to the two with Bosh, "They are loyal?"

Bosh tapped above the small pattern on his vest, "Completely." He then walked with Malik as he turned toward the house.

"I have procured a small residency for you and an allotment of servants. If they are not to your liking, please let me know," Malik said as he pointed out several statues nearby.

Bosh was far from compliant toward the man. He knew that showing submission would open a whole new problem while planetside. If you showed weakness, you had a good chance of becoming someone's property, or worse, fodder for the game champions.

Malik motioned for Bosh to sit, which he did in his own time.

Although the former captain of the Charon facility was wealthy, he preferred a more minimal estate. It was also easier to pick up and run if needed. He discovered that the hard way when Jace and Eislie escaped from the base. Bosh had to find covert ways for him to access his holdings.

Bosh sat. The chair was comfortable, and when offered a drink, he accepted. The server, barely clad in any clothing, was something Bosh seemed to notice. Malik, seeing this, could not help himself as he pointed to the woman, "Ah, Risel, you have a good eye. She is a most attentive attraction." The man leaned in, "She is one of my favorites."

The man waved the slave girl away and sat forward in his chair, looking Bosh over. "I have agreed to host you, Devlin, but you also mentioned that you have a business matter for me?"

Bosh swirled the liquor in its glass as he sipped, an expression of praise. "Most acceptable vintage, my friend." He looked up over the glass to see Malik staring back in anticipation. "I have someone, or rather people, I would like you to acquire," Bosh said before taking another sip. "In fact, I want them and their ship. They cost me a lot of shill."

Malik smiled, "I must ask their names, but I suspect they have already been mentioned."

Bosh gave a nod. "Them and their ship. I am willing to pay a healthy fee."

Malik's grin was ear to ear. "And what would that be?"

Bosh chuckled before reaching into his pocket. He produced a small wooden box, The silvery metallic clasp holding it closed. He handed it to Malik, warning him not to open it unless he was wearing a Sotiral shield.

"That is an eighth-kilogram of spide. From a new source," Bosh said. "I'm offering seventy kilograms of the crystals for them to be brought to me, not dead, but broken."

Malik handled the small box. He looked at it, a glint of fear replaced by curiosity. "Devlin, would you indulge me for a moment?"

Bosh waved for the man to continue.

Malik asked, "Why broken? If they have wronged you, why not just eliminate them?"

Bosh grinned sinisterly, "I have spent the last few planetary cycles reintegrating my wealth and staying ahead of the Alliance." The man leaned forward. "I will see them dead, but I want them begging me to kill them."

Malik giggled, "Oh, Devlin, you have piqued my interest. Revenge in such an old way. Ah, I like a man who knows how to enjoy a fulfilled existence." The slaver held up the small box. "But this, is it really a sliver of spide?"

Devlin smiled, "I did mention not to open it without a shield to protect yourself."

Malik smiled as he looked at the box. "Is it true what happens to people when exposed to the radiation? I've seen vids, but never with my own eyes."

Bosh gave a single nod.

Malik giggled again. "I wish to see what this can do." The man paused. "Before I agree to your terms, of course."

Bosh turned to one of his servants. "Go back to the ship and bring back a potable extractor."

One of his servants rushed away, and he turned to Malik. "We should find a room with less organic materials. Unless, of course, you wish to really see what happens to them when exposed to spide radiation. And if you are willing to provide a subject."

With Bosh's warning, they adjourned to an empty room. The walls were bare except for hooks and shackles lining one side. Several drains were in the floor.

"This is my training room, well, one of them." He motioned for a slave to stand on a spot, and the man obeyed. The square where he stood lit, and the man could not move his feet. Malik pointed to the man. "Heavy gravity restraints, nearly impossible to escape. This is Olsan. He was one of my champions. However, I fear he will die in the next tournament. I was going to put him out of his misery, but I think he will do."

Bosh's servant returned with the extractor and turned it on. Bosh tapped the controls on his Sotiral vest, and Malik went to open the box but could not.

"Devlin, is there a trick to opening this thing?" Malik sounded annoyed.

Bosh walked up to reach around the man as he held the box and the man's hand against it. "Malik, I mentioned you need to wear a Sotiral shield when opening it."

Bosh opened the clasp and cracked the lid slightly. Malik said with anticipation, "Is it ready?"

Malik pointed the box forward, ordering his slave to extend his arm. And when the man complied, Malik opened the box a little further. Within seconds, the man began screaming as every cell and nerve in his extended arm turned to ash. Malik reveled, seeing the man fall, huddling to scoop the ash now falling to the ground. The slaver beamed with a look of humorous bloodlust before he opened the box entirely and watched the man turn to dust, his screams lasting only seconds.

Bosh reached around Malik, closing the box.

The slaver stood panting, his endorphins surging as the whir of the extractor working filled the room. Malik turned to Bosh, saying, "It is clean, but a painful way to die. Yes?"

Bosh nodded, saying with satisfaction, "Excruciating."

Malik smiled, grasping the small prize and showing it to Bosh. "Is this for me?"

"You may keep it and the portable extractor."

Malik looked to Bosh, "But I do not have a shield for this. I understand it will take some time to procure one. They are much in demand."

Bosh smiled, "Well, I could offer you one from my inventory for, say, a year of residency?"

The slaver gave a joyous clap, "Of course, Devlin, I would be happy to accept your gracious gift for the time." He looked at the pile of dust. "My dear friend, consider your request accepted."

Two days passed while Malik worked to find someone willing to cross into Alliance territory. He also needed them to accept the task of bringing in the ship and crew of the *Wolfhammer*. It was no easy task, and Malik needed more possible candidates. His concentration was interrupted as Fellen addressed his master.

"Sir, forgive the intrusion. The Mistress asks if you have decided on the fare for the gathering?" The man bowed deeply, keeping his eyes to the floor.

Malik turned his head, reaching down to the desk, only to find nothing for him to hold. He gave a huff of annoyance. "Be thankful I do not have my favorite tools, Fellen."

The man dropped to his knees. "As I am always grateful for my service, master."

29

Malik felt a lift in his mood seeing the man begging before him. The slaver prided himself on his ability to break and engrain new followers. He knew all too well that those with the most followers were most loved, which meant status on Arlain. He gracefully walked toward his servant with a flick of his wrist, causing the small chains he wore to jingle. His slave stood in an instant.

"For the Kaial festival, tell the Mistress we will have the traditional fare: steamed meat buns, the Karol spread, and toasted Chiaba." He thought momentarily, and his attitude altered. "Hmm, they may expect those. It may not make an impression. We can add some more current selections, but I'll allow Mistress to decide. You will tell her I said so."

Malik leaned against his desk, the gold-trimmed edges allowing him to side back and forth. "We should find something exotic. The man thought, and his memory could not find the words he sought. In frustration, he went back and tapped the screen of his desk, bringing up a video.

"Tell me of your people. What sweets do they like?" Malik smiled, hearing his own voice from the video.

The man on the screen looked like any Alliance, but he wasn't. He was from Earth. The man was heard correcting Malik when he called it Terra. Malik shook his head and advanced the video. "Where is it? I know he said it."

Fellen waited patiently as his master searched, then in a fit of happiness, Malik tapped the screen again. It was much further in the video, and Malik could hear himself remark how the man would not live long if he continued to fight. He had applied the black flower poison as a last resort, but the man still resisted. "I won't follow you." The phrase brought a frown to Malik's face, but then the Terran spoke again, "Chocolate chip cookie," followed by incomprehensible babble.

The Arlain slaver stood with a happy grin. "That's it, chocolate chip cookies."

Fellen looked to his master. "What are those?"

Malik rushed around his desk. "Fellen, we must have them. I understand they are an Earth, uh, Terran delicacy." The man mused. "In my research, I found that the compound within quickens the heart and induces a euphoria. One enticing of enjoyment, and of love."

The man placed his arm around Fellen, who still looked to the ground. "Fellen, everyone will adore the Mistress and me. I want you to check with any traders in the area. We will fly them directly from the planet if they don't have any."

"Sir? Do we know if the food is safe? These will be the top families of Arlain. We do not wish to harm anyone," Fellen said, his voice quivering.

Malik raised the man's face. "Fellen, we are the superior beings in this universe. Terrans have such a short lifespan and feeble bodies. How dangerous could they be."

Fellen did not argue with his master and nodded.

"Good, now check with our suppliers. If they do not know, we can charter a supply run from an outside source," Malik said, returning to the previous task. He still needed someone willing to bring in Devlin's prey."

"That's it! A charter." Malik sat again, tapping away on his screen. Fellen stayed where he was, not being dismissed, and heard his master mutter, "The Slasta, those assassins will work for any willing to pay." Malik looked out the window. "Eh, I'd have to put out a small fortune if Bosh doesn't deliver. If he doesn't, I'll have him in the games."

Malik looked up to see his servant standing in the room. "Why are you still here?"

Fellen bowed. "I will go tell the Mistress and do as you have commanded."

Malik typed, the display showing a dark background, the sound hissing and crackling. Malik knew the effects of a signal trace disruptor; he had used them to acquire many of his servants.

"Lajar, greetings, and well wishes. I wonder if your master would be available for a meeting?" Malik said.

The figure on the screen shifted but remained silent. Malik was not used to insolence but held his tongue. He knew well the trade of the Slasta, raised as assassins from birth. They knew of thousands of ways to kill many beings, but Malik needed those he sought alive, which would be costly.

"Tell your master I require at least thirty of his followers," Malik said, his voice serious in tone.

The man on the screen gave a shallow nod, and the screen darkened. It was a minute later when another figure appeared. The screen was now a shade of royal blue behind the silhouette.

"You must wish to take control of your planet, Malik Terine," the man spoke.

"How do you know my name? I have not introduced myself," Malik said, wondering.

The slaver could see the man's lips form a slight smile within its shadow. "You have used your personal conveyance comm, slaver. Careless."

Malik smiled, "Let's not be dramatic, assassin. I have a challenge for you."

The assassin looked furious through the screen. "You challenge me?"

Malik huffed, "My apologies. I said I have a challenge for you. I am looking to capture some quarry. I need them taken alive."

"You requested thirty of my best. Can you cover the expense?" The figure asked.

Malik smiled, "I am willing to pay four hundred thousand Lin for your services. But I need them alive."

The shadow on the screen shifted. "That would be a fair offer. Who is the target?"

Malik smiled, "I wish to divulge that in person. And I will pay upfront. Would you be able to meet in three days? Let's say, here at my residence? Tell you what, make it five hundred thousand if you'll meet in person."

The lightness of teeth shone from the dark screen. "In three days, we will arrive. Do not disappoint us."

Malik nodded, "Three days then, and I promise you will not be disappointed."

The screen went blank, and Malik sat back, relieved. "The central bank will not like the withdrawal. But if this works out, I'll increase my wealth over twenty-fold." He stood and leaned on his desk, the look of uncertainty giving a glint in his eye.

Chapter 5:
Is That it?

Jace and Eislie worked feverishly, turning off systems as smoke billowed around their ship. The outer tunnel coils burned through, damaging parts of the ship's hull.

"We have to pull the core! The whole thing is melting down!" Jace yelled as Eislie rushed into the reactor room.

The two were testing the latest modifications and had just reseated the core crystal when things went wrong. They had delayed traveling the filaments, only doing so when needed. But, given the recent news about the Alliance and that Bosh was still free, it gave Jace and Eislie time to tinker with different designs. Unfortunately, this one did not work.

Jace was outside inspecting the damage when Eislie stormed out of the ship, yelling, "What the slac did you do? The crystal almost fractured. It would have inverted right here on the planet."

Jace looked repentant, hiding his frustration. "I don't know what happened. I was reading the specs we had from our last meeting, and this should have worked."

She looked at the scarring on the hull where parts of the tunnel system used to be. The charred remains caused the hull to delaminate along the bottom half of the ship. Jace grabbed a nearby rod and pushed against what remained of the drive system away. He groaned, seeing a chunk of the hull fall to the ground.

"Dammit! Damaged the ship bad," Jace growled.

"Yes, you did," Eislie remarked.

Her comment caused Jace to turn and stare at her, his eyes filled with disbelief and confusion. The silence between the two would have deafened most, but a set of watchful eyes kept them in frame.

I don't think you two were ever supposed to stay on a planet, Arren thought as he started toward them.

The short alien had arrived on Gilese at the request of Eislie's mother. She trusted him since he was competent at working on the *Wolfhammer*. She had asked him to work in the facility on Oppa, but he was more interested in working on vessels than in distribution for the Sotiral systems. Instead, she offered him a position at a local ship repair on Gilese, which he accepted. As he neared, Arren yelled, "What in Tarsis are the two of you arguing about? Ship coils blow all the time. Just fix it."

He watched as the two lovers looked directly at him, causing the old alien to pause. *I've seen a lot in my time. And those two can still scare me.* Arren smiled and continued toward them. "You blew some coils. Let's replace them. He looked at the two before saying, "Or do you want to kill each other?"

Eislie stared at their friend. Arren had helped protect her while she was imprisoned on Charon. She turned to look at Jace when he said, "Wait, did you just talk to us like little kids?"

Arren laughed, "Well, the two of you are certainly acting like children."

Eislie's stare changed to disbelief and then to concern as Jace started laughing. Jace was laughing so hard that he dropped to the ground, sitting as she watched him find humor in the severe accident that they almost had.

"Gods, I love Terrans. They can do the stupidest things and laugh it off." Arren turned to Eislie. "You know I could hear you yelling at him from inside the tool shed."

Jace sat on the ground as he smiled, turning to look at the *Wolfhammer*. "You know, if that blew up, it would have made an awful day."

Eislie looked at Jace. "Yes, it would have. We were inside."

Arren chuckled. "And I was right down there close to it." The short, round alien walked closer. "I've never really seen you two fight. What's going on?"

Jace looked at Arren, "What, you becoming a counselor now, Arren?"

Arren looked at the burned area of the hull and then down at Jace, "Coils only blow if you put too much power through them or if they're hooked up wrong." He looked at Eislie. "And you, if the crystal started to fracture, it wouldn't have gone further, since the coil blew. It's a spide system. You know that."

Eislie felt the sting of his chastised remark and looked at him with disbelief. She then looked frightened and hurriedly tapped her comm. "Ed? You alright?"

Jace looked at her, and all anger faded, and both heard the response.

"Yes, captain, the surge did not feed back into my systems as previously during travel. It seems the coils were effectively working. However, I did detect a possible fault in the port side during power-up. Apparently, it was more severe than I had ascertained. I'm not sure the programming for the system is designed for this configuration, even though it is similar to the ones we have on file."

"You mean I didn't hook it up backward or something?" Jace asked.

"No, captain, the coils should not have failed while testing them, given our current parameters and information."

Jace looked at Eislie, and they both looked at the ship. Eislie said, "If it would have worked, then what happened?"

The three approached the ship only to have Arren grunt and back away quickly, the front of his hand turning to ash. "Shit, spide leak." The old alien stepped back. "It's residual radiation. Right now, a spide suit and portable extractor would probably be a good idea."

Jace leaped to his feet and rushed onto the ship. "Eis, get Arren a jacket. I'll get the extractor."

Within a minute, Arren was inspecting the damage as Jace started the extractor. He poked the hull, causing another chunk of the material to crumble. He seemed to think for a moment before he spoke. "I was looking over those alloy reports from your friends." Arren referenced the information pads on the Lyri ship evaluation from months ago that the pirates provided. "This hull is a different type of material. I wonder if part of the problem you've been having with the surges is because of field dissipation?"

Jace looked at Arren quizzically, causing the short, round alien to smile back as he answered, "The field surrounds the ship, but there is a resonance on the materials of the vessel as well. Let me show you something."

Arren moved to the console near the ship and typed away, causing several diagrams to appear on the screen. "This is what a tunnel field looks like around a ship."

Jace and Eislie stared with interest.

Arren scoffed, "You two can build the damn thing, but you don't fully know how it works."

Eislie and Jace said in almost unison, "Not yet."

Their friend laughed, saying, "I swear you two are perfect for each other. But anyway. The field of the coils moves across the ship's surface, acting essentially as an additional layer. That layer allows you to slide within hyperspace. The drive coils give you thrust."

Eislie pointed at the screen. "What if the filaments are a different type of hyperspace?"

Jace had a realization, "You mean like a different dimensional event? Something different than hyperspace?"

Eislie nodded.

Jace smiled. "That could explain why that beacon we had when we first tested was out of sync. It was resonating to that dimensional time frame."

Arren turned to look at him. "What? What in Tarsis are you two talking about?"

"Never mind, Arren. But I have a strange idea," Jace said before tapping his comm and moving to the terminal. "Ed, can you link this terminal to the modeling terminal?"

"One moment, captain," the computer responded. "I have the data available locally if you prefer."

"One sec, Ed," Jace said as he motioned for Arren to move away from the terminal.

Jace typed away, and within moments, a model of the *Wolfhammer* appeared on the screen. "Ed, can you extrapolate the field across the hull with the new coil design?"

The computer responded, and a new graphic appeared. The field flowed fluidly across the hull.

"Damn, it would have worked," Jace said.

Eislie asked, "Then what caused the coils to blow?"

Arren chuckled, "I see where you're going with this. Ed, can you hear me?"

"Yes, Arren, what do you need?" The computer responded.

"Do you have access to the hull resonance readings from the last trip? Before the surge when you exited, please," Arren asked.

The computer took a few seconds before responding and displaying the data across the screen. Arren then asked for the new specifications of the coils and hull before they blew. The readings were almost identical.

"Okay, so what does that mean?" Jace asked.

Arren scoffed again, "You're not thinking. If the coils aren't the problem, what else do you think it might be?"

Jace stepped back, covering her face with his hands. "Shit, what it's attached to. Like grounding something with a radio."

"What are you talking about?" Eislie asked.

Arren smiled, "He's using old terms, Eis. Let him work. I have a feeling we both want to hear what he has to say?"

Jace moved forward. "Arren, you have those alloy specs handy?"

Arren typed away and provided the information.

Jace used the modeling program and included the information on the alloy. "Ed, if we add the new specs, could you estimate the field coverage and interaction?"

It took several minutes, but the computer completed the evaluation. The calculated data now showed the spike when removing the power to the coils to almost nothing. The three looked at the screen in disbelief. And it took several seconds before Eislie broke the silence, "Oh, slac. Jace, I think you just...." She paused, looking around. "Clear the screen, Ed."

Jace stood tall. "You know we did damage the hull. I think it may be time to redo the outer surface. Maybe some new plating?" He paused. "Ed, what's the total area of the hull?"

The computer instantly responded, "Approximately 583,670 sacos or about 9,725 meters Terran measurements."

Arren huffed. "That alloy would take months to manufacture here. We can make poly-ceramic parts fast. After all, this planet builds ships, but metallics are not their focus."

Jace looked to Eislie. "You know, I never thought about it before. What is the main thing they produce on this planet?"

Eislie sighed, "Mostly fibers, uniforms, cloth, and food. We have a lot of bio farms for food. I thought you knew that."

Jace looked apologetic. "I never really thought about it till now. We need a planet that can make a lot of hardware simultaneously."

Eislie smiled, "I know a level three planet whose main export is ship parts."

Jace looked at her, playfully saying, "Hmm, and where's that?"

"Yata Beta. In fact, we have a ship heading there tomorrow, remember?" Eislie said, smiling at him.

Jace did. He had known a shipment of Sotiral suits had to be picked up, and the *Solace Star* was leaving tomorrow to do just that. The ship wasn't large enough for the entire volume of the plating, but it could handle the weight and size of most of it. They had an additional problem: with their current workshop, it would take months to retrofit the *Wolfhammer*. The Alliance shipyard had the capability, but they wanted to keep them out of this for as long as possible.

Jace turned, looking toward the ship before tapping his comm. "Ed, can you provide full outer specs for a new shell of the ship?"

"What thickness, captain?" The computer asked.

Jace looked to Arren. "Maybe a few semlins, uh, inches in Terran. I wouldn't want to remove any of the current hull. It seems to be protecting the three of you so far."

Eislie hugged Arren, "We'll need to replace the damaged parts, and we can skin the outside. Can you do what Jace is asking, Ed?"

"Yes, captains. I will have that momentarily," Ed responded, and even Jace noticed a hint of excitement in the computer's response.

"I think Ed understands what we just figured out," Jace said, making Arren nod. "You know what'll happen if this works, right?"

Jace nodded, "Yeah, people will want more than a piece of us. Don't worry, Arren. If we survive, we'll give you credit on this too."

Much later, Jace sat in the office, and Eislie spoke with Miriz over the comm. Her friend asked why they needed so much of the quickly fabricated material.

"Eis, we can do that, but why do you need it?" Miriz asked.

"It's for our ship. We needed to replace the outer hull in some spots. But thought it would look patchwork and decided to do the whole thing,"

Eislie replied. Miriz looked at her suspiciously, making Eislie ask, "Do you think it can be done in about a week?"

Her friend shook her head. "Even though it's a simple alloy, the fabrication parts from the specs you sent will take at least three. That, and the demand for Sotiral suits has skyrocketed. We're having trouble keeping up with production."

Eislie thought momentarily. "You just reminded me we need to get a few more for our ship and the *Solace Star*. And we still have the ship scheduled to go out today for the other shipment to Roscin station."

Miriz stared, annoyed, into the screen. "We can spare a few for you and the others, but why do you need the plating?"

Hearing this, Jace rushed over. "Hi Miriz, it's just needed to cover the hull of our ship. What's wrong with that? We're just thinking of our safety." Jace gave a wink. "I blew out the tunnel system on the last modification. It's not like it has any special purpose."

Eislie watched as Jace's greenish eyes stared into the screen. He knew Miriz was clever and would probably figure out what the plating was for, and he was waiting for her to understand. Then they both watched as Miriz leaned back, an expression of surprise on her face. She looked around to make sure no one was in her office. "Is this because of being attacked when you returned from your unexpected trip?"

Jace and Eislie both gave a slow nod.

Miriz sat forward, typing furiously on her keypad. "The quickest I could have the fabrication would be about two weeks."

"That's fine. It'll take me a few days to fix the damage I did today. I'll start working on it right away," Jace responded.

Miriz looked at Eislie. "Did he really damage the *Wolfhammer*?" She watched Eislie nod.

"And she yelled at me for doing it. Not like she stopped me pushing the button," Jace said, making Eislie turn as she stuck her tongue out at him.

Jace laughed, rubbing his face, "we did find out why something wasn't working anyway."

Miriz smiled, "is the *Solace Star* heading out soon?"

Eislie replied, "Yeah, I was going to head out along with it. Jace was going to work and fix what he broke."

Miriz was about to say something when Eislie held up a data card. "Jace and I figured you and I could catch up on recent events with the Sotiral systems and other production issues."

Her friend seemed concerned. "You mean you're not bringing the *Wolfhammer*?"

Eislie looked at Jace, then said, "The repairs have to be fitted, and we wanted to get the new hull done as soon as possible. Besides, we both think it's good of me to see an old friend, see how you're doing after all the drama from a few months ago." She sighed remembering Miriz being poisoned and Jace having to fight the Karazon for the antidote. "Besides, the crew on the *Solace Star* is seasoned, and they know their way around things. They're also people we can trust."

Miriz looked to Jace. "If anything happens, you get in that ship and come get her."

Jace smiled. "Now, that's an order I won't argue with."

Eislie snickered, then said, "You know you never tell a Terran what to do, don't you?"

Miriz nodded, "Oh, I do know that. But I wouldn't give him a chance to slac it up."

Jace pouted in the best facial display. "That hurts my feelings," he said, laughing and turning away, causing Eislie to laugh loudly at his performance.

Miriz joined them before asking, "I have a feeling we have a lot to discuss when you get here."

Eislie nodded.

"Okay, I'll see you in a few days," Miriz said.

Eislie chuckled. "Make it a week. The *Solace Star* isn't quite as fast."

Miriz nodded, "Aright. I'll get the alloy into production. We can finish the fabrication and get your ship back up and running."

Eislie agreed. "See you in a week. I'm planning to wait for him on Yata. We'll show you the new modifications. The *Wolfhammer* could easily outrun most of the racers on your planet."

Miriz looked proud. "I doubt that."

Eislie smiled, "You've never seen our ship run at full speed. I'll take that bet."

Her friend stared back. "Alright, But I get to ride along. And you race against one of our fastest." Miriz seemed to think for a moment. "You're not looking into a Brunell drive, are you?"

Eislie sided her eyes toward Jace and responded in a playful tone, "Why, Miriz, are you suggesting we're gearing up to enter the Zero Circuit? I'm shocked at that accusation."

"Eis, when you get here, you'll have to tell me everything," Miriz said.

Eislie chuckled, "See you in a week."

The screen went blank. Jace spoke, "That's pretty clever. If anyone was listening, they might think we're gearing up for the Zero Circuit instead of filament travel."

Eislie raised her brows innocently. "Yeah, that's what I was going for."

Jace leaned down, kissing her. "You're a terrible liar, you know that."

Eislie smiled. "It's not like we haven't talked about running the Zero. I mean, imagine how much fun it'd be."

"It would be. But I have no idea how to install a Burnell drive yet. Let's figure out the filaments, and then we can go play."

Eislie sighed, "It's going to be weird flying without you."

Jace nodded, "Yeah, I know. But we have to do this just in case people are following us, especially after recent events. I don't like splitting up any more than you."

Eislie stood, kissing him gently. "We'll figure things out. You get the ship running again and head out immediately." She walked toward the door and turned, holding up the data card. "I've got a friend to see. These specs on the outer shell aren't going to deliver themselves."

Chapter 6:
Time Apart

A loud thunk echoed through the hull of the *Wolfhammer* as Jace seated the last of the newly constructed poly-ceramic plates. His torch was tuned to make the connection nearly seamless across the hull. But, as he neared the final seam, it stopped working.

"Arren, you have any more of these torches? Now this one's fried," Jace yelled across to the other end of the workspace.

His intensity was enough to cause everyone in earshot to pop up and look at him. Arren seemed perturbed, and the short, round alien walked toward him with a very annoyed stride.

"I told you before, you have to let them cool for at least a standard cycle before using them like that. The plasma element has to regenerate," Arren snarled, tapping a wrench against the hull of the ship. "You've gone through four of those today. When are you taking a break?"

Jace looked nonchalantly toward Arren, "I don't know. When are you? You've been here almost as long as I have."

Arren was about to speak but waved the wrench toward Jace. "Damn, Terran, I hate when you're right. We've both been working too long."

Jace stepped back and, with humored disbelief, said, "Now I know you've been working too long, Arren. You actually agreed with me."

The short alien shook his head. "If that mate of yours was here, I'd set her all over you."

Jace leaned down a serious stare toward his friend. Jace couldn't hold the face any longer and started laughing. "Yeah, she'd have dragged me home by now. I've almost been working for twelve hours."

Arren shook his head, "No, you've been at it for almost twenty. I know you're in a rush to get the ship up and running, but you have to ensure it's done right."

Jace looked at the ship. "It's better than it was when it was made." He looked to Arren. "But you're welcome to check my work. It couldn't hurt."

Arren crossed his arms. "Oh, my, something's wrong. Did you show humility?"

Jace gave an annoyed glance. Then brought up the welder swinging it down to lightly tap Arren on the head. "Smart ass."

Arren chuckled. "I'm sure things are good. You've burned up a few welders doing it." He looked at the remaining seam before waving for someone to bring another welder. "Finish up. We'll run the testing after it cools a little."

Jace nodded as one of the other engineers handed him a new plasma torch, and he returned to work. As he finished the last part, Jace flipped up his protective visor. With a sigh of relief, Jace glanced over to see Arren watching through those dark round goggles he always wore in the sunlight. Jace could see the smile Arren showed seeing his work. And he knew what Arren was thinking.

You're happy to see us here. You never thought we'd escape that place, did you?

Jace shut down the torch and stepped back. "It's done. How long till we can test?"

Arren huffed, "What? Are you in a rush? Let it cool."

Jace cocked his head, looking at Arren, and sighed knowing the old alien was right. Jace was rushing things. Eislie left over four days ago, but they hadn't heard back from the *Solace Star* since they checked in two days ago. Jace still had to reinstall the tunnel coils, and the trip to Yata would be about a week for its sister ship. Jace wanted the *Wolfhammer* up and running as soon as possible, but he knew Arren was right.

"Sorry, Arren, sort of wanted to get things running," Jace said.

The old man scoffed, "She's only been away for a few days. You'll get there."

Jace laughed as Arren remarked about Eislie being gone. Jace did miss her. The trip he'd have to take would be only a few days with their ship. But Jace was also anxious to install the new outer shell on the *Wolfhammer*. If their theory was correct, it would make accessing the filaments easier. Also, if it worked it meant everyone had access to them.

Jace was about to say something when he spied Shasji hurriedly walking toward them. He could see the bright blue knit hat she wore and waved to her as she approached, yelling, "You look like you're in a rush."

Shasji shook her head, her words quickened by her excitement. "We heard back from the *Solace Star*. They ran into some trouble. But things are alright. And I'm here to tell you that Flora has ordered me to go with you when you leave."

Jace and Arren became interested in her last statement.

She told them, "According to Eislie, they had to run from some Arlains. Those slavers were patrolling the area. Garrett was trying but seemed to be having trouble focusing. Eislie had to take over while Ferren helped Garrett to the medical bay."

"They alright?" Arren asked. She watched as Jace seemed to ask silently.

Shasji nodded, "Yes, but Garrett has some sort of food poisoning."

"Bad food? I thought this was an advanced planet?" Jace scoffed.

Shasji shook his head. "They think they know what it was, they got to him in time. The medical system has him stable. And on Yata had diagnosed it as Torec poisoning."

Arren looked concerned, asking, "Torec? Are they sure?"

Shasji nodded.

Arren looked at Jace., "Check the food stores. If someone slipped those in, they're trying to incapacitate the crew." He turned to Jace. "And scan everything you've got in this ship as well. You don't want to take any chances."

Jace looked at Arren,."It's that bad of stuff, huh?"

Arren nodded, "It'll kill painfully if left untreated, but it takes weeks. Certain people like to use it to inconvenience crews. Maybe hijack them." The old alien looked at Jace, "People of the Tronu system like to use it." Shasji and Jace looked at Arren, their brows up in interest as Arren said, "Bosh is from Tronu."

The old man watched Jace's grip on the plasma welder tighten, causing Arren to say, "Probably had an ally slip it onboard. Seems like he's popped up again."

Jace sighed, "Well, we knew he wasn't dead. I just wish he'd leave us alone."

Arren shook his head. "You cost him a lot. People like Bosh take that personally."

Shasji looked at the old man. "So he wants to kill us?"

Arren chuckled, "Well, I wouldn't take it personally. He probably wants to kill these two and possibly me for crossing him."

Shasji sighed heavily, saying, "So we'd be collateral damage," before she removed her hat. Jace agreed and turned to apologize but instead stared at what was on top of Shasji's head.

Jace looked at her quizzically. "What are you wearing?"

Shasji touched her head and then moved to her ears. "Oh, I was listening to music. I forgot I had these on. She felt the top of her head to make what looked like two small triangles pop up.

Jace looked at her strangely. "Those look like cat ears."

Shasji stepped back, offended. "This is the feral crown edition. It represents the fight of the Hurmann people against the Tas enslaving them on Arlain."

Jace looked at Arren, who only shrugged before he tapped the triangles, making one of them seem to twitch. "Those are cat ears."

Shasji glared at him. "You liked their music. What do you think you were dancing to a few weeks ago?"

Jace looked at her, "What's the artist's name? I have to check them out." He pointed to the top of her head. "I'm sure those are cat ears."

Shasji hit him, saying, "It's Queeks Maco. And these are not cat ears. It's a feral crown," before she stormed away.

The two men stood silent until Arren said, "You know Queeks Maco means nine lives in Arlaian."

Jace smiled before asking, with a hint of sarcasm, "And why do you know that, Arren?"

The old man chuckled, "Because I learned that over a hundred planetary cycles ago. And I know what you're thinking in that Terran brain of yours."

They both laughed as Jace said, "Yeah, those were definitely cat ears."

* * *

Malik sat in an ornate chair, watching Risel move sensuously before him. Her body was only covered strategically as his eyes remained fixed. Moments later, his wife entered. Her hand waved the young servant to stop as she sat beside her husband.

"I think you prefer her to me sometimes, my dear," the woman said.

Malik smiled, his eyes closed, "My dear Yenna, there is no other whom I truly adore." He looked toward the young slave. "Although I do like to indulge."

Yenna glared at him, her stare causing the man to laugh. "It is not as if I don't allow you your pleasures, my dear. Perhaps I should sell those favorites that you carry?"

His wife sighed, "I am a practical woman, but now require your time. We have a gathering to plan. Yet I find you here sitting being entertained."

Malik slumped in his chair. "Yes, of course. My duty to the people." He turned, taking her hand and kissing her palm. "What would I ever do without you and your being? I would certainly be lost."

"I am trying to prevent you from being looked at as a fool." Yenna looked concerned. "I have been told that you have debited several hundred thousand Lin from our holdings. Why?"

Malik nodded as he sat back, "It is for the good of our standing, my dear. And a business cost."

His wife sat back. "I was not consulted."

Malik turned to her, "You do not need to be. This is for the good of this house. And my status."

Yenna sided her eye to him but was interrupted by Fellen approaching.

"What is it?" Malik asked, annoyed.

"Master, I have tried all channels and have been unable to procure the, uh, choc..o..lot chip cookies you requested. I have found no suppliers who can provide them."

Malik pinched his nose as he spoke. "You were given this task. You are my most trusted servant, and you have failed."

Fellen prostrated himself, saying nothing.

Malik rolled his sleeve back, exposing a metallic brace, and was about to strike the man before his wife spoke. "Dear, what is it you were trying to procure? Was this the reason for the Lin? Did you trust it to this feeble thing?"

The slaver turned, his eyes filled with anger, only to be met with a similar stare from his wife. The man turned to look down at his servant. "My dear, I have no reason to explain to you. But you think me such a fool as to trust money to this worm?"

Yenna gave a subtle smile before moving to confront her husband. "Then what was he procuring? What are choc-o-lot chip cookies?"

Malik looked into the eyes of the woman he called his wife, and her heart softened. He took a breath. In his world, showing anger at the misstep of another to whom you dictated plans was a sign of weakness. But he was shrewd and allowed his wife's accusation to fall deafly. He instead looked around her, motioning for another servant to bring refreshments.

"If you must know, my dear, the items are a delicacy from Terra. The food is known to cause a feeling of love and endearment in all who consume it." Malik took a golden cup from his servant and drank. "It was to be our gift. So that everyone would fall to their knees in adoration of us. Or so I think they will."

Yenna looked at his servant on the floor. "Are you certain? I do not wish to be the amusement of our acquaintances."

Malik looked on with a steady gaze. "I have learned this from the Terrans I have tried to break."

His wife remarked, "You've killed most of them. And some even laughed at you as you killed them."

The slaver looked down in despair, "Yes, they did. Even the M'Kay toxin was no match for Terran stubbornness." He turned to look out the large window. "The traditional fare will not be enough to impress. I was hoping to do something exotic."

Yenna sat forward, "And this will not harm our guests. I do not want to be known for trying to kill our..." she huffed, "equals."

Malik turned to her, "How dare you." He moved, grabbing his wife's arms. "Our engineers have made us superior to any other beings."

The slaver grabbed a female servant, a Terran, and held her arm out. He dragged his nails across the tender skin of her arm, causing a trail of red blood to flow. He yanked Fellen from his groundly perch and did the same to him, only to see a clear blue liquid form around the wound and crystalize. And, when wiped away, there was no damage. The woman, however, continued to hold her arm to keep it from bleeding.

"They still bleed. They would die if injured. We are superior, stronger, and more resilient. If Terrans can tolerate these choc-o-lot chip things, then we certainly can," Malik thundered, causing his wife to reel back. She sat silent as Malik looked at the female Terran and then at Fellen.

"Fellen, tend to this one's injuries. Make sure she is healthy." He held the chin of the woman to face his. "She will be one of our attendants. Some of our more deviant guests prefer the fragility of Terrans. Although I do not care for their charms as some of my brethren do." He turned to his wife. "You are by my side for a reason, my dear Yenna. Your wisdom and beauty are but a fraction of your attributes." Malik looked to the skylight. "I would do well without you, but not quite as well, I surmise." Malik sat in his ornate chair, "I should not have trusted this matter to a mere slave. This is something I should have pursued myself."

Chapter 7:
Bounty Errand

Malik walked with several of his servants as he strolled through the activity of the grounds. He had planned to host over thirty of the ruling houses in a show of his wealth and status. All the ruling families had such displays from time to time to show their power. The events also allowed them to provide fodder for those they kept in check to showcase the ruling class's influence in keeping their world among the others they traveled.

The slaver turned to look at the large tent that was in the process of being erected. The entertainment equipment was moved by a substantial individual wearing a mix of metallic mesh and poly-armor. The alien's pale skin contrasted with the dark armor. The slaver didn't recognize the race, but the being seemed familiar as he watched the man move the heavy item easily as he placed it into position. And when finished, the man walked back onto the nearby ship to again appear with another heavy load.

"Such strength. He'd make a fine addition to the games," Malik muttered but then seemed to be trying to remember. "He looks like he's from…."

The slaver seemed to be in deep thought as Fellen stood nearby with a message from his mistress. "Sir, the mistress is asking for your input on the placement of the statues. The gods are displayed incorrectly as per her understanding."

It took several seconds before Malik replied, "Place them in whatever order seems right. No one will be agreeing on which is first anyway." He turned to look at his servant, causing the man to avert his eyes, "Everyone

I've been to, they were in whichever the host felt was more important. No matter how they are displayed, we will argue."

The servant nodded, "The mistress had requested your presence. I was instructed to have you accompany me to her side."

Malik looked sternly toward the man. "Is my wife ordering me to be there?"

"Mistress had requested you to join her, and I am to accompany you till you do so." Fellen bowed, "Or order me away."

Malik smiled. He knew who ruled the everyday house. That was his wife, but Malik ruled everything on their lands. Even the people. The slaver's ego sated as he spoke, "Well, I will help mistress decide where to place the statues." He then placed his hand behind Fellen, guiding him alongside to find his wife.

* * *

"I can't believe I had to take this job. I'm a warrior. I should be fighting to topple planets," the man muttered. "If my funds weren't so low, I wouldn't be here."

The scraping of metal mesh grated as the giant alien placed the bright, shining metal cooking platform on the ground, causing Malik to turn and yell, "That is an expensive piece. Do not damage it."

Malik rushed over to inspect the device to see no damage. He turned to look up at the tall, bulky alien. "You are fortunate there is no damage to this. It is a rare item."

The alien looked at the device. "It is not damaged."

Malik delighted in showing off to other races and smiled before saying, "It is a Terran grill. We will be dining as they do, with animal fare charring out under the sky as the ancestors of Terrans once did. It was my chosen theme."

The alien looked unimpressed, his graveled voice saying, "It is a cooking platform. I have one similar on my ship and used them on the battlefield."

Something in Malik's mind clicked, and he yelled, "Nibik, that's it."

The alien looked on, unimpressed.

Malik motioned for the man to speak, "What is your name?"

"I am Jarrus Tum. Former elite guard," the alien said.

The slaver smiled, "Your voice is damaged from battle, is it not?"

Jarrus nodded once.

Malik clapped his hands together, "You are a former Nibik Warcryer, yes?"

Jarrus stared down at the man before nodding again.

The slaver seemed happy and said, "You have fallen, my friend. How would you like to be one of my champions? I can offer you a contract."

Jarrus palated his contempt for this man, mentioning what he was in a former life, tasting bitter bile in his throat. This slaver had guessed he was a warcryer, those who chanted and gave orders at the tip of their lungs in the battles as they fought. Nibik was once a fertile world, full of life and the people of Nibik. Famous for those who were called to defend and overtake any opponents or those willing to compensate for their services.

Unfortunately, they were causalities of their own hubris when, in their haste to develop a weapon to destroy any attacking fleet, they poisoned their planet—the devastation sterilizing the surface of many of its lifeforms. The great exodus was a dark time for their people. It still stained their memories after decades. Now, the world they knew as home was nothing more than an unlivable rock in space. The new world settled on in their star system, only habitable by the technology they had developed to destroy others.

Jarrus looked to the side. "My time is worth more than for this conversation. Do you have any other duties for me today?"

"I order you to become a champion of mine," Malik said, only to see the furor grow in the warrior's eyes.

Instead of attacking, Jarrus looked to his ship. "If you have no further use of my services, pay me now, and I will depart."

Malik was disappointed but looked over to see his wife arguing with one of the others catering the event. "One moment. I will be right back."

The warrior's stare followed as the slaver rushed over to the woman arguing with his mate, the woman's shrill sound piercing his ears. "I told you we are unable to procure what you are asking. None of our services can enter Alliance space."

"What is the meaning of this outrage?" Malik yelled, trying to assert his authority at this display of disrespect.

Jarrus watched, his eyes as keenly as the warrior he once was seeing the woman reaching behind her. Her hand was deft as it slid something from her sash. He moved forward, not the lumbering hulk that many saw him but as a warrior hunting its prey. He moved closer, his hand reaching out by instinct.

Malik grabbed hold of the woman, spinning her around. If this were any other world or resident not from Hurmann, this would be grounds for enslavement or death. Instead, the woman swung, striking out with a ceramic knife, the blade stopping before Malik's throat by a hair. Jarrus's massive hand held the woman's arm with little movement as she struggled to pull away.

Malik looked to the blade and turned to the woman, only to notice the tattoo on her shoulder as he whispered, "Raakis clan?" He looked at the woman being held and turned to Jarrus. "Release her. You show disrespect to this woman."

Jarrus glanced over, his eyes filled with disdain as he released the woman's arm. He stepped back. The slaver apologized to the woman before accusing her, "You dare to try and injure me in my home?"

The woman stood tall, pointing to Yenna, "I was within my right. I was insulted by this one."

"This is my wife." He leaned in. "You insulted my partner and tried to kill me. I should have your house for this."

"I'm Illain Hufn of Raakis. It would be wise to take a different tone." Malik's threat meant nothing to the woman. She pointed to Jarrus, "And you, how dare you touch me. Filthy servant."

Jarrus felt fire in his chest, the feeling of battle once again filling him as this woman chastised his existence. He shifted, saying, "I can dispatch this one for an additional fee."

The woman started yelling, her words obscene, only interrupted as Malik yelled, "Enough!" Malik turned to Jarrus, "That is disrespectful. You will be lucky if I pay you at all."

Jarrus stepped forward, picking up Malik, his feet hanging in the air. Jarrus said in a graveled, emotionless tone, "I will be paid and leave if you have no further work for me." The warrior knew full well that he would be hunted for attacking any of the ruling class of the Hurmann. However, he had hoped to die someday in battle again. He also knew the pettiness of the Hurmann and that they would hunt down any Nibik they found, or worse, try to enslave them for the games.

Then the warrior felt a sting in his leg as the woman he had restrained plunged the ceramic blade into the thick skin. Jarrus turned his head to look down at the woman staring up at him. The small trail of yellow blood was now highlighted on the exposed white skin. The feeling of battle snowballed until he heard Malik say, "You are right. We have a contract." Malik looked at his wife, an Illain, before speaking. "Perhaps it is the stress of the season. Jarrus, put me down. I do not wish to have you killed."

The warrior didn't move, only turning his head to look at the slaver.

After a heavy sigh, Malik spoke, "Jarrus, if you do not want to enter the games, I will pay you, and you may leave." He turned to Illian, "What was the previous disagreement about?"

Illian stepped back. "We cannot procure the items you requested. None of our trade options are able to enter Alliance space."

Malik's head hung as Jarrus placed him on the ground. "And you have tried all other options?"

Illian said that they did. "These choc-o-late chip cookies, or whatever they are called, are not available to us. We will refund your payment for them. Minus our investigation fee, of course."

"As is sometimes the way of business." Malik sighed as he turned to Jarrus, his gaze meeting the stare of a warrior and the eyes of a killer. "Such a shame you will not fight for me." He waved for the warrior to follow.

The slaver looked down at a tiny trail of yellow, now spotting his floor. "There is a med system in the cabinet over there. You may heal yourself while I transfer the funds. Then you can go."

"No, I will not heal this wound," Jarrus said before taking a piece of cloth from around his neck and tying it around the wound.

Malik looked puzzled, "But you are injured. Not to mention that you are leaving a mess in my home."

Jarrus shook his head. "This wound was a careless mistake. I should have expected the attack. It will heal on its own. A reminder that even an experienced warrior may make a mistake. So, I will remember not to do so again."

Malik shook his head as he grabbed his comm. "An antiquated belief, my friend." He looked at the warrior, "Are you sure you will not fight for me in the games?"

Jarrus shook his head in silence.

The slaver tapped away, "I owe you three thousand Lin." He looked at the warrior. "Do not expect any more. Your service was horrendous."

Jarrus sighed, "What other work do you have on this world?"

Malik tapped away, adding to his notes on the account, "Unless you can find a supplier that handles what I am seeking, then no. Unless you can find a way into Alliance space for a delicacy."

Jarrus checked his comm to see the funds transferred. Then, he turned to look at Malik, "You would pay for this delicacy?"

Malik looked up from his pad, "Handsomely, yes. Do you have a way of procuring Alliance or Terran materials?"

Jarrus sighed, "I brought the Terran grill in for you. I have access to Alliance and Terran facilities. What is the item you are seeking?"

Malik's attitude improved. "Let me show you."

As the slaver typed on his computer, an image and profile of two people appeared. He could see the female from the angle, but the male was obscured. The names Licessien, Eislie, and Tucker, Jace showed on the screen. "Are these the delicacy you are seeking?"

Malik looked disgusted. "We do not eat people. They are another acquisition I am working to find. I have a contract for them already. They are costing me five hundred thousand Lin." Malik liked to brag about his dealings.

The slaver scrolled the screen until a symbol appeared. It was a circle with a blade piercing from the top. Jarrus's people were taught from birth to remember the standards for all opponents. They developed an instant memory for the symbols that differentiated military and political entities. Jarrus had procured people before, primarily for war crimes. He found honor in bringing in those who had committed injustice and watched as Malik showed him the information about the chocolate chip cookies. The slaver's mission was petty, but Jarrus was willing to access and retrieve the supplies in Alliance territory for the large payment he offered. Jarrus's only concern was that his employer needed them quickly, before the first day of the event.

"I've traced a supply to the Talis star system. Even though it is Alliance, the planet is a colder climate. Terrans seem to be the only ones who prefer it." He turned to look at the warrior, "I have no idea why. I have heard they slide down the hills and mountains on flat boards or something."

Jarrus seemed confused, trying to imagine what the slaver was saying before he looked at the man. "There is a station nearby, Roscin. Is that the location with the materials?"

Malik looked up and confirmed that was the case, "My deal with Illain for them was for four thousand Lin. I would pay you that, if you can bring these to me quickly, say within three standard weeks?"

Jarrus looked at his comm. "The station has them, yes?"

Malik sighed, "According to the information Illain provided."

"If I leave now, I can return in time. I will expect payment when I return." Jarrus turned. "I can find those people you are also looking for. An additional fee will be required, of course."

Malik glared at the warrior. "I have others already contracted for that. Just the delicacies for now."

Jarrus nodded and turned, heading out the door. His mind returned to the image of the woman and names on the screen. *If you seek those people, they must be either valuable or dangerous. I would welcome a challenge such as that right now.*

Malik watched as the warrior closed the door. His voice filled with disdain, "filthy alien. Leaving blood on my floors."

He called for his servant, the woman slipping on the yellow blood as she quickly entered. She looked down, then apologetically at her master. "Dulvine, clean that up. You'll find more down the hall." He then waved her to her task.

Malik waited until she cleaned the room floor before accessing his comm. The dark silhouette on the screen was silent as Malik spoke, "I will be here tomorrow. I know you will be punctual. And as promised, I will have payment ready."

The shadow spoke. "You have not informed us of the target."

Malik smiled, "You will have that information when you arrive. And I think you will welcome the challenge when you see."

The slaver watched as the screen went dark, "Once I have them on their task, I can return to this blasted function." He looked at the door. "It is such a burden to be someone such as myself."

Chapter 8:
Watching Eyes

The night was filled with activity as Eislie oversaw the *Solace Star*'s loading. Eislie was thankful not to wear the protective visor but could not sleep, since she had to move the ship closer to the manufacturing facility due to the overflowing vessels in the space dock. She marveled at the machines and people all working to produce the shield systems. Her design quickly became a standard among many Alliance and other worlds. Her friend's company and the planet are now benefiting from the revenue. Eislie turned, seeing a flicker of light, but turned back when she spied Miriz and her new assistant approaching.

"This is some place you've got, Miriz," Eislie said, praising her friend.

Miriz beamed as she moved next to Eislie before saying, "It's your design. I'm just helping make them."

Eislie felt the praise and smiled.

"You were willing to give this all away, weren't you?" Miriz said.

Eislie looked at her friend. "I just wanted to help. I didn't want more people dying because of the radiation."

Miriz leaned back against the railing. "I had to retool almost every plant I own to keep up with demand. I've had to cancel most of my other parts contracts." She watched Eislie looking concerned, and Miriz sighed before continuing. "Most of those were ship materials. I've had most of the contracts locked in for years. At least this will give someone else a chance to prosper."

Eislie bowed her head. "Good. I'd have felt bad if you were in trouble."

"Oh, Eis, I am certainly not in trouble. Even with the thirty-five percent you agreed on, it is more than three times what I made earlier. And the additional profit has allowed you to expand your company as well. You're on five worlds now."

Eislie looked up. "Just offices. My father has been looking for new ships to add to the business instead of chartering them. But he's finding it difficult. Seems like everyone wants us to pay more than what the vessels are worth. The only ones that had a decent price were on Consortium worlds. And I think they've caught on as well."

Miriz laughed. "Well, success will do that. And your other project doesn't help."

Eislie turned to lean on the railing as Miriz was. "Yeah, well, when we figure that out, we're not sure about giving it away."

Miriz stood tall "Why would you? You could put any price on that. If you controlled it, then you could do anything."

Eislie looked down, her mind returning to the discussion she and Jace had in the *Wolfhammer* before discovering that Bosh was still alive. She suspected the same as Jace, that the control panel on the scout ship they had found some time ago was nothing more than to allow the pilot to fly without having to be by the reactor. That thought was in her mind as Miriz said, "You figured out something, didn't you?"

Eislie continued to stare down, nodding only once.

"That's wonderful. If you get it to work, you can be the only ones with that knowledge. You could be the only company with the ability to travel the filaments. That's a wonderful place to be from a business standpoint."

Eislie looked at her and said, "If we're right, maybe. But if not, it may not be that good."

Miriz moved closer, curious to know why Eislie wasn't happy they had almost solved the issue with traveling the filaments. Her concern was evident. "What did you discover?"

Eislie looked at Miriz's assistant, who, for the most part, had remained silent the entire time. "Not here. I'm not saying anything else."

Miriz looked at her assistant suspiciously. "Kelor is loyal. He'd never tell anyone."

Eislie looked at the man. Miriz trusted him, but that wasn't the problem. Others may have been listening, and her longtime assistant Paaz wasn't there. Eislie still felt sorrow for the pain the woman experienced after losing her lover the last time they were on Yata. So, she decided to change the subject.

"By the way, how is Paaz?" Eislie asked, looking caringly toward her friend. She had known Paaz had left after the murder of her lover, Davlen. The memory came of Jace fighting the Karazon named Har, who poisoned Miriz and had tried using the games to force her and Jace to serve him willingly if they lost. Jace was injured after Har had attempted to kill the grand matron. Instead, Davlen stepped between them, saving her. Jace did take from Har the antidote for the poison he used on Miriz.

Miriz sighed, realizing that Eislie wouldn't answer the question she had asked. Eislie's changing subjects so quickly told her that her starborn friend may have discovered something she didn't want to be widely known, even to someone trusted. Seeing those light blue eyes of Eislie staring almost through her, Miriz knew she would have to wait for an answer.

"Paaz is doing better. She's still with her family." Miriz sighed. "Actually, I didn't want to put too much on her."

Eislie looked to the sky, her eyes searching for the stars. "It wasn't exactly a good week, was it?"

That sounded like something Jace would say, Miriz thought before she said, with some concern, "That almost sounded like a Terran response, Eis."

Eislie turned to glare at her, and Miriz could see the stare of defiance her friend returned. Before Eislie said, "It wasn't meant in a bad way. I just meant it wasn't a good time for any of us."

Miriz lowered her gaze. "I didn't mean that in a bad way either, Eis. It's just that…"

She stopped when Eislie hugged her, hearing Eislie say, "I also almost lost my best friend." Eislie released her and stepped back, "I understand why Jace says things like that now. It's weird."

Miriz smiled, "Well, you have been spending a lot of time with him. I'm beginning to wonder if you're starting to embrace your inner Terran."

They both watched as Kelor stepped back, a hint of terror in his stance, "She's Terran?"

Eislie huffed in annoyance, "Part Terran. Why does everyone act that way toward Terrans?"

Miriz stood in surprise at her assistant. The man stepped away from Eislie at her revelation. She turned to see Eislie now smiling.

"What?" she asked Eislie.

Eislie laughed, "He's right. It is fun to see people's reactions to Terrans. I watched him intimidate someone on Gilese just by smiling at them."

Miriz turned to see Kelor shrug. "I didn't know she was Terran."

Eislie approached him, calmly correcting him, "I'm Gilese. I'm only part-Terran. And, if you think poorly of either, this part Terran will have something to say about it."

Miriz watched as her assistant, someone trained to protect her, shuffled back a half step at her friend's words. She would have found it amusing any other time but knew it was something Eislie was teased about not being fully Gilese her entire life. Miriz was relieved to see Eislie step back and lean against the railing. She stood silent, looking toward the *Solace Star*.

Miriz knew a lot about Eislie, having grown up alongside her, and she knew how quickly her friend could rebound from Kelor's comments. She decided to change the subject as Eislie had done to break the silence.

"Speaking of Terrans, how was your trip here without him?" Miriz asked.

Eislie knew she was referring to the fact that she was flying without Jace by her side. "It wasn't the same. A little lonely, even though I was with family and friends."

Miriz chuckled. "Well, have you heard from him yet?"

"He's just getting to the new tunnel coils. He should be done in a day or so."

Miriz looked around. "Well, he did damage your ship. He should fix it."

Eislie nodded. "He damaged our ship, but it turned out to be a good thing."

"What do you mean, a... good...." Miriz went silent, looking up to see the subtle smile on Eislie's face. Miriz paused momentarily. "Does this have to do with the hull plating you asked for?"

Eislie didn't flinch.

Miriz looked around and quietly said, "We just finished the raw plates but haven't started the machining yet."

Eislie smiled, "It's okay. It'll be at least a few days before he gets here. Jace will probably want to look things over before we install them anyway." Her attention was again drawn to a tiny flicker of light off in the distance across the loading area before Miriz tapped her arm before saying, "I can rush the production if it's needed immediately,"

Eislie shook her head, "No. We're not in a rush. We're not even sure it'll work." She then turned to look at the ships below. "Honestly, we're just trying to avoid something. Both of us hope it will protect the hull of the ship. And maybe…." Eislie didn't finish her sentence, her mind wrestling with the fact that, for now, it appeared only starborn could travel the filaments. She didn't want to burden her friend with the fact that all starborn might be even more hunted than they were already.

Miriz took notice, and she dropped the subject altogether. And she looked at the time, offering to take Eislie out for a decent meal. Miriz also knew that more than half the food stores on the *Solace Star* were contaminated, she insisted. Eislie didn't resist, and they headed toward the nearest elevator.

Off in the distance of the loading dock, two people slid back into the shadows of the parts stored around them. One was holding a simple parabolic dish. It shrank as it retracted into the handle.

"It was like she was looking directly at us. You did coat the surface, didn't you?" The one woman asked.

The other woman nodded her head, rubbing her nose through the mask. "It's too bright in here. No one can see things like that."

The first woman sighed heavily before the darkened mask she wore started to fall away to reveal her face as if it were strands from a piece of fabric. The long scar across her forehead and left temple stood now visible, and the fibers retracted into a metal collar.

The other woman flipped back the deep hood she wore to remove her mask with a simple pull, "I have to get my VFM fixed. Only you are in the show now. I feel bad."

The other woman nodded. "Yeah, too bad it was damaged when we went to Rellin last month. Damn, slac had too many guards." She turned away. "I swear some were Slasta."

"It doesn't matter. We took out one of the top five of the ruling families' patriarchs. The others have challenged them. If we do enough, they will tear themselves apart. Then we can continue the revolution."

The one in the metal collar nodded, "It's too bad there's only one of them here. We would need them both on our side."

The other woman asked, "Why do we need them anyway, Eshea?"

"Zarlin, I've explained this before. They are leading a starborn rebellion but haven't moved recently. So far, they made the Alliance show their hypocrisy and are still alive. They're high visibility. And, if we get them on our side, then the Arlain people will see it and rise up with us," Eshea told her.

Both went silent as a security drone floated nearby. Their hoods diffused the visual sensors, but they needed to be quiet when anything or anyone was nearby. They waited for it to clear the area before they spoke.

"Those two are behind the Sotiral suits and brought the illegal enslavement of starborn into the mainstream. With their notoriety and resources, our cause would have a better chance of succeeding," Eshea whispered as she reeled the cord to the device they used to listen.

There was an uneasy silence as Zarlin asked, "Do you know what they were talking about?"

Eshea shook her head, "This thing is supposed to filter out all the ambient noise. We were lucky it worked most of the time. It isn't quiet in here. Too bad we missed some details. It sounded like they found something."

"I thought that too, but the light hair didn't give much detail. Her name's Eesee, right? I didn't read the papers Ral gave me last week. I was too busy trying to write songs. I think she was trying to hide something," Zarlin noted.

"Her name's Eislie, Eislie Licessien. And I got that feeling as well. It was like she didn't want anyone else to know what they found. But that representative seemed to know more than she was letting on," Eshea remarked as she looked behind them. "Her partner is Jacc Tucker, and from what we know, neither of them is someone to go up against. And that ship of theirs is tough. It took out a Duggor cleaver by itself."

"Why don't we just ask them to join us? I'm sure they would agree with what we're doing." Zarlin said.

Eshea seemed to think, "We'd have to find someplace to ask them secretly. It seems they like to do things on their own."

"If we know their route, we could chase them down and talk with them."

Eshea shook her head. "The *Eiger*'s fast, but that ship of theirs seems to change over time. I don't think anyone knows how fast it is."

They scanned the area to ensure no one was around before moving toward the elevator. Both placed the oversized hoods over their heads before entering. "We need to return to the *Eiger* and let Ralla know that only one is here. We may have to move to speak with them separately."

The doors closed on the elevator, and the internal display of the security camera showed nothing but an empty cabin as it lowered to a specific floor. Security glanced at the monitor only to ignore it, and the operator muttered. "Damn idiots keep pressing buttons and walking away. And I get the call when they complain."

Chapter 9:
Underway

Jace's head bobbed as Shasji turned up the music to overshadow the sound of the welder as he worked.

"You know they're performing at Roscin station next week. I'm hoping we can get the *Wolfhammer* going so you can drop me off. I wasn't able to get tickets to the one on Yata," Shasji said, making small talk.

"Queeks Maco, that's a strange name for a music group." He turned to Shasji as she tightly held the tunnel coil assembly against the hull. "But their music is good."

Jace watched as she smiled behind the protective face shield, which darkened as he started welding again. He, Arren, and Shasji had been working to repair the ship for almost two days straight. He pulled away and motioned for Shasji to step back.

"Ed, send power to the coils. Let's see it. I got them tuned."

The ship's computer acknowledged and sent the test signal through the coils. "There is only a point zero, zero, zero, three variation. Well below acceptable limits, captain."

Jace nodded hearing that.

Flora was walking toward the ship. She had stopped by to make sure everyone was still alright and was pleased to see their progress. She was also relieved to overhear the response of the computer. "You should be able to fly then."

Hearing her, Jace turned to see her walking up. She touched the ship. "I don't think she'll be angry at you for damaging the ship now."

Jace snickered before replying. "The ship's fixed. I think I was angrier. I thought I did something stupid." He looked up. The logo for the *Wolfhammer* was no longer complete. Only the W and part of the O remained. The rest was now missing.

Flora smiled back at him, "Nah, that ship's like the two of you. Tougher than it looks."

Jace almost looked embarrassed. But he knew Eislie's mother meant it as a compliment. Being Terran was something they had in common. The way they insulted each other showed a sort of camaraderie that all Terrans had. However, she was there with additional news, and Jace could tell her mood was mixed."

Sensing her apprehension, Jace asked, "What happened?"

Flora looked toward him suspiciously before sighing and said, "You're not becoming empathic, are you?"

Jace shook his head, "Nope. But I've seen that look before. It usually means something happened, or you're about to ask me to do something dangerous. Which is it?"

"The *Solace Star* doesn't have a captain right now. Garrett's still incapacitated. And I know Eislie was going to wait for you on Yata, so they aren't going anywhere for at least a week."

Jace flipped up the protective visor. "That's a problem?"

Flora nodded, "Our contract is to provide the shipment as quickly as possible. But the contract with Roscin station is the real issue, not Yata. If we lose the station contract, we lose a trading hub altogether."

Jace sighed, asking, "How long do we have?"

"A week at most to leave to keep the contract. I've already spoken with Eis. She may take the shipment over. But she also wanted to install the new parts on the *Wolfhammer*," Flora told him.

Jace nodded, "The ship's ready. I just have to head over. But that means we're still short a captain."

Flora looked to Shasji, "Actually, Jace, I wanted to talk to you about that. I think Shasji may have a pay raise coming if you sign off on it."

Shasji seemed surprised as Jace looked at her, asking, "What pay raise?"

Flora smiled, "Both you and Eis mentioned you thought Shasji would make a good captain, didn't you?"

Jace nodded as he smiled. "We did. I'm guessing we're not waiting till we get another ship to make that happen."

Flora nodded, looking at Shasji, "You're already familiar with the systems on the *Solace Star*, and you can fly it." She looked at Jace. "We just need an existing captain and representative of JESC to okay the promotion."

Jace chuckled and looked happily at Shasji. "Well, Captain Yaman, do you accept the offer?"

There was look of happy surprise on Shasji's face as she nearly flipped the visor off her head as she opened it. "Yes! I mean, it's not my own ship. But yes, I do."

Jace laughed before Flora said, "Alright, we just need his signature and the agreement signed by you, and things are set." She looked to the *Wolfhammer*. "Then you can fly Shasji out to take over and do what you planned to do for your ship."

The protective visor ripped from Shasji's head as she lunged forward to hug Jace. He gave an audible "oof" as she impacted and wrapped her arms around him. Jace jokingly said in a fake voice, "Help, she's crushing me."

Flora started laughing as he tried to free himself from the new captain's embrace. She saw tears of joy on Shasji's face as she pulled away, "I've always wanted my own ship."

Jace snickered. "Technically, it's still Garrett's ship. We're working on finding one for you. It's been difficult so far."

Shasji nodded, "I know. But I really want my own ship."

Flora chuckled, saying, "Well, with the latest profits from the Sotiral sales, you may have one soon." She turned to Jace. "We may have to start hiring more crew and captains as well, the way things have been going."

Jace raised his brow. "We're doing good?"

Flora said, "With the recent profits, we've already paid back the full commission spent to buy the *Solace Star*. The next payment should allow us to buy a new vessel outright."

Jace looked surprised. "What? I thought things were tight?"

Flora nodded, "They were, but Miriz transferred the latest payment. And it was well over what we expected. She told me they are having trouble keeping up with demand for the safety systems Eis developed."

Jace chuckled. "Guess she is the smart one."

"I know she is." Flora looked at him. "But you've been the one working mostly on this project. I can't imagine what we'll start bringing in when you figure it out."

Jace looked concerned. "I'm hoping what we figured out so far will allow us to travel without, well, you know, using people."

Flora nodded, knowing what he was insinuating. Eislie had told her that so far, it seemed that only starborn were able to travel the filaments while being in contact with the reactor. She also knew that Eislie and Jace had found a way to bypass that with the recent changes to the reactor of the *Wolfhammer*. She also knew that the massive surge from exiting a filament was the only thing they had difficulty figuring out. And that what they were having made on Yata might be the solution.

Jace looked around before saying, "If what we think will happen when we test this. We can sell the designs or retrofit ships for everyone to use. That would be worth something as well."

Flora touched his face. "Then you and she can do what you want. You won't have to keep mining or hauling freight."

Jace looked to the side as he nodded, "Maybe some people would leave us alone, too."

Both Flora and Shasji knew he was mentioning Bosh and those hunting them for the secret of filament travel. They could see his stare, an almost sad, searching look that pulled at them both.

"We can't stop you. I know you both want to see what else is out there," Flora said.

Jace nodded.

"Come on, since the *Wolfhammer* seems fit for service, we should finish the promotion paperwork, and you can head out. Maybe you can change the way things work. And help everyone." Flora said as she pulled gently on his arm.

As they walked from the ship, Jace muttered, "It'd be nice not to have to keep looking over my shoulder."

Onboard a ship, several Nibik crew members were doing maintenance as Jarrus typed away on the communications console until the screen came alive.

"Long shall be the world and our people," Jarrus said as another Nibik appeared on the screen to say the same.

"It's good to see you, Belon. How has the steady work of merchant been?" Jarrus asked as a more than sarcastic question.

The other Nibik on the screen smiled before replying in a similarly sarcastic tone, "More lucrative than the soldier and errand boy that you have taken on, my son."

Jarrus rolled his eyes as he spoke, "It is tradition and more palatable than tending some small shop on a station. At least I serve our people's memory in that fashion."

Belon responded, "You have not called for pleasantries. What do you want, Jarrus?"

Jarrus looked at his list. There were several items he required. More lighting and statues of gods of different worlds. Foods and supplies from several Alliance planets. He informed Belon about the previous supplies they had procured from the same Alliance worlds as being tainted with Torec and that several of his people were inconvenienced by the stores.

"There were costs to those fouled supplies you provided last time," Jarrus said.

Forcefully, Belon replied, "The manufacture of the supplies is not my concern. They were received as they were allotted. Any quality issue, take it up with the world it is from. I will not refund you any credits." The man looked to the side, saying, "I have others to attend to shortly. What else are you looking to buy?"

Jarrus smiled. "Ah, the true Nibik reveals himself. I am searching for something, something rare."

The other Nibik looked at the screen, "And what would that be?"

Jarrus leaned forward as one of his crew walked by. "Are you able to provide Terran foods?"

Belon turned to the side. "I am. What is it you are looking for?"

"Something called choc-ochit cookies."

Seeing Belon's confusion, he sent a message with the item he was trying to find. His friend read it and knew what he wanted.

"You are searching for that vile food. Why?" Belon asked.

Jarrus looked at the screen, "I have a client looking for them. Why? Do you have them?"

Belon yelled to one of his workers and told him where the food Jarrus sought was. Within moments, a bag of cookies was now in hand.

"They are called chocolate chip cookies, not choc-ochit. However, they taste the same as rancid guin-slac. I do not see how Terrans eat them. Some in the Alliance do as well," Belon said, looking disgusted. "And they consume them with rapid abandon."

Jarrus scoffed, "Terrans are a strange people. Backward but resilient at the same time. Much like our own."

Belon nodded, "They are looked down upon, but seeing them fight is a treat if you haven't already."

"I have seen them fight to the death. Although I found no honor in their battle as entertainment," Jarrus nodded, sounding annoyed.

"I have seen them fight for entertainment here on the station. But never to the death. It is always mutual combat. Where did you view such a vacuous display?"

Jarrus paused, quietly replying, "On Arlain, the Hurmann put them in games. I would have been a poor guest not to partake of the spectacle. My employer had provided several passes." He looked annoyed as he turned from the screen. "I had thought it would be more entertaining. However, I found the display somewhat disturbing."

Belon looked confused. "Was it to decide a battle?"

Jarrus shook his head. "No. It was to provide their master with a win. There was no real need for the battle. Only entertainment provided by death."

Belon sat straight. "As a former warrior and now merchant, I find that disgusting as well."

Jarrus nodded, "The battle served no purpose but to entertain the blood lust of those ruling. The Terran did not prevail."

"Who was their opponent?" the other Nibik asked.

"It was one Terran to two Karazon and a Jesin. Hardly a fair battle," Jarrus said with disdain.

"Three to one? The Terran would have been small compared to those they were fighting. Why was it allowed?" Belon asked.

Jarrus sat tall. "I watched as the Jesin fell quickly at the hands of the Terran, and one Karazon lost a limb. The third was able to kill the Terran with some difficulty."

Belon huffed, "Not as easy to kill as they thought, were they?"

"There was more honor in the Terran's loss than the other's attack," Jarrus sat forward, shaking his head before returning to the business at hand. "I would need several cases of those, uh, cookies. Can you provide them?"

Belon smiled, "If the Hurmann wish to taste guin-slac, you may have as many as you like. I have no taste for the games you described. So, I will offer you these as my offense to that."

Jarrus snickered, "Thank you. I will arrive in a few days. We can meet and reminisce. It has been more than a standard year since I've seen my sister's betrothed's father."

"Jarrus, I will need to register you as an incoming vessel. There is a musical gathering here in a week. They are requiring all vessels to be logged."

Jarrus nodded, "The *Go Ge Go Go* will arrive in about four days. I need to have the items to my client in about three standard weeks." He looked at the screen. "Do they really taste as bad as guin-slac?"

Belon replied, "They do. You may try some when you arrive, but I am warning you. I made the mistake of trying them myself. It started sweet, but the taste was nauseating. Nothing tasted right afterward. It took days for me to get rid of it." He tapped away on the terminal. "Alright, Jarrus, I've logged you in. You'll be assigned a dock when you arrive. I'll have the supplies you are requesting ready. I expect to payment when you arrive."

"I have always paid. After all, it is not wise to cheat family."

Belon nodded, "I look forward to your arrival. Long shall be our world and our people."

Jarrus responded the same before ending the transmission. His mind returned to the battle he had watched, knowing that the Terran was outnumbered, and his mind wondered *if the Hurmann had made a mockery of their world.*

Chapter 10:
Friends Catching Up

Everyone was away from the ship while Eislie remained onboard the *Solace Star*, reading through Jace's message.

Ships fixed. We're heading out in a few hours. See you in a few days. Shasji passed her captain's certification. And your mother insisted that I bring her along so she could take over as captain for the Solace Star.

Eislie snickered, muttering, "Trying to stop me from captaining my own vessel?"

She continued to read.

Not that you shouldn't have your own ship. But then, who'd keep me out of trouble?

Eislie laughed, "You're right, who would?"

Jace's message continued.

I think things will work after we install the new hull—at least, I hope. Just in case, we should ask some friends for help and let them know what we've found.

Eislie thought for a moment. *I wonder if Preston can help. I'll have to see if he's on the planet. Maybe we can get Jana to be ready for a rescue if this doesn't work out right.* She looked around, her mind pondering. *I think she has Preston following us anyway. I should give him a call.*

She continued to read.

I'll call when we're about there. You can decide if you want Shasji to take over command. It'll take me at least a week or two to install the hull anyway. I hope Miriz isn't giving you any trouble about why. By the way, how's Garrett doing? You can let me know when I call. I had to trash most of the supplies from the ship. Right now, I'm waiting for the delivery before we head out. Good news, the booze wasn't affected.

Eislie laughed, then said, "That's good. But it's nice to have food."

She scrolled down to the remaining part of the message.

Found someone looking around the ship. Didn't look like they were carrying any analyzing equipment. I checked, and nothing seemed off on the new drive coils. Seriously. I don't like what happened on the Solace Star. Arren told me who mainly uses that poison, and knowing Bosh is back in business, I'm concerned. Not that I don't think you can't handle things, But I'd be less worried. Besides, it's weird not seeing you in the chair next to me while flying. But that's just me. I'm more concerned about not being able to be there to watch your back. Anyway, I miss you. I'll sign off. See you in a few days. We're heading out in an hour or so.

"Aw, that's sweet. Too bad he had to come across the galaxy to find me," Eislie said under her breath, a hint of longing in her voice.

Eislie reached for the console and was about to change the communication to the secure frequency used by the pirates when she heard someone enter the room behind her.

"Knock, Knock. Everyone decent in here?" Eislie turned, seeing Miriz walking into the control room.

"Hi, Miriz." Eislie rushed over, hugging her friend. "I was just reading a comm from Jace. He's going to be here in a few days. He just finished fixing the ship."

Miriz looked at her, saying, "He damaged it. He should be the one fixing it."

Eislie looked annoyed. "Hey. I agreed to the test too, you know."

Her friend chuckled, looking at Eislie, saying, "Seeing you on another ship is strange. Everything alright between you and him?"

"Yeah." Eislie turned to the comm before reaching over to clear the screen. "He sent me a sweet message. I was just reading it."

Miriz looked around her at the blank screen. "Oh? How sweet of a message that you had to clear it, was it?"

They laughed before Eislie said, "It wasn't that, uh, sweet. But he misses me and was concerned about what happened to Garrett, both of us are."

"Actually, I was here to update you on his condition." Miriz walked toward the hall, connecting the flight deck to the rest of the ship. She peered down the passageway into the rest of the vessel, making Eislie suspicious.

"You alright, Miriz?" Eislie asked.

Miriz looked at her. "Yes. I was just wondering if you were the only one here."

Eislie stepped back, her hand touching one of the tools she always kept nearby while flying. It was also something Jace did when he was alone on the flight deck. He was paranoid that someone would board the ship, and he would have to fight. Eislie started to wrap her hand around the metal tool as Miriz sat in one of the chairs. There was an audible exhale before she spoke.

"Garrett's still under care. The torec poisoning is stubborn. He'll be out for at least a standard month. And that contract with the station is due by the end of the week. You'll have to decide what to do soon." She looked up at Eislie. "Whoever put this in the supplies was definitely sending you a message that they are willing to go after everyone connected to you."

Eislie relaxed her grip. "I may have to take the ship to the station. I'll decide tomorrow. As for the torec, we have a pretty good idea who it was. We don't know how to handle it, at least for the moment."

"Who is it? We'll have them arrested." Miriz stood, then walked over to Eislie.

Eislie shook her head. "The entire Alliance and several planets are still looking for him. They thought he was dead. We just discovered that the Alliance secretly searched for him for months."

Miriz looked confused. "Who are they?"

"We're pretty sure it was Bosh," Eislie took a breath, exhaling to calm herself. "We found out that he took some of his wealth and went into hiding. The Alliance has several ships out looking for him. They don't know where he is." The look of concern on her friend's face spoke volumes in the silence before Eislie said, "One captain asked us to let him know if we find him." She looked down. "I think he has some business to discuss with him, the kind where two enter a room, and one is floating out of an airlock. At least that's the feeling I got."

Miriz shook her head. "I thought I dealt with some difficult people. You and Jace take this to a whole new level. I'm surprised that you decided to come here without him."

"It wasn't our first choice. But things are a little...." Eislie smiled before saying, "secretive for the moment. We think we found something."

With a surprised look, Miriz asked, "What does this have to do with the...." She was interrupted as Eislie put up her hand.

Eislie said, "Ed, how many people are on board?" She looked around, then became annoyed. "Ugh, sorry. Computer, how many people are on board?"

A mechanical-sounding female voice responded, "Two persons onboard. Location Flight Control."

Eislie looked to Miriz before saying, "It's not the same without Ed. Computer, close all entries and exits, and confirm when sealed."

Miriz looked at her quizzically before hearing the computer respond, "Ship sealed, captain."

Eislie smiled. "I'm surprised Kelor isn't here with you. I'm guessing he has other work to do?"

Miriz nodded, "He's new. I can't rely on him completely yet. Not like I did with Paaz and.... Davlen."

Eislie understood the hesitation, knowing Miriz's assistant Davlen had given his life to protect the grand matron. And Paaz's loss when he was killed was also fresh in her thoughts. She thought for a moment before speaking. "I understand. It's hard to know who to trust sometimes."

Miriz huffed, "Like Echoban."

Eislie looked at her friend. She hadn't seen Miriz's partner since they reconnected months ago and didn't think about it. Echoban was always the one who insisted on traveling for her business. That was something Eislie always wondered about her husband. He always seemed eager to help Miriz expand her empire. But now Eislie was wondering where he was.

Miriz noticed the questioning stare in her friend's eyes and gave Eislie a partial explanation. "You won't see Echo around anytime soon. We had a bit of a falling out." Miriz looked annoyed. "It took me over a month to reintegrate what he stole."

Eislie's eyes widened, hearing Miriz say, "That's not what's important now. What did you find?"

Eislie shook off the news and answered, "The new hull should allow us to exit the filaments without the energy surge. At least that's the theory."

"Too bad you haven't been traveling them. I'd love to see what it's like."

Eislie smiled subtly before saying, "Who says we haven't." Her friend looked confused until Eislie said, "How else would we know about the surge when exiting?"

"Wait! How long have you been traveling them?" Miriz asked.

Eislie chuckled, "A few months, here and there. We've been keeping it as secret as possible. We've been managing the surge for the moment. But it's still annoying and hard on the ship's systems. We hope the new hull material will work to dissipate the charging. Right now, we're afraid it'll damage the ship or hurt, Ed."

"He has kept you two alive, so far," Miriz mentioned.

"Yeah, Ed has. He's like us, and we also watch out for him." Eislie smiled. "We trust him, and he's as excited about the filaments as we are. But we all agree that we must be careful. We don't want to be stuck somewhere and unable to return."

Miriz sighed again, then said, "We'll give you as much support as possible. But unless you have another ship that can access the filaments, then you might have a problem."

Eislie smiled, "Thanks, Miriz, but we're not waiting to outfit another ship. We happen to know some others who have something similar already. They just haven't gotten it to work right yet."

"Who has a ship like yours?" Miriz asked.

Eislie looked at Miriz with a sad realization in her eyes. "They don't have a ship like ours. But they are accessing the filaments like we did the first few times. We found a way around some of the issues, but it's hard on the systems. We're hoping that the new shell will fix the problem."

Miriz again insisted on knowing who was accessing the filaments before leaning in, saying, "It's the pirates, isn't it?"

Eislie looked at her, "The less you know who, the better, Miriz."

"You can't give them this, Eis. They'll cause havoc across the galaxy."

Eislie sat hard in the chair behind her before saying, "I'm not sure they will. But right now, the Consortium, the Alliance, and the Pirates all have something on filament travel. And if we don't do something before they figure out what the pirates already know, things will get bad for those like us."

Miriz didn't understand and motioned for Eislie to continue.

Eislie sighed, then explained. "Right now, it looks like only starborn can use the filaments safely. The spide reactors will only function correctly if we're in contact with them."

Miriz reacted strangely to Eislie's statement, repeating, "You can't give the pirates that information."

Eislie stood caringly, grabbing her friends' hands, "Miriz, the pirates already use starborn who are willing to access the filaments. They are not enslaved. If the Alliance or Consortium figure out what we know, then...."

Miriz was waiting to hear the end of her sentence but could see the tears forming in Eislie's eyes as she heard. "There'll be millions of starborn who will end up like Jace and me on Charon, maybe worse." Eislie stood, releasing Miriz's hand before walking toward the port window. "If it's the Alliance, they will lock down and control the filaments. If it's the Consortium, billions will be in danger of being attacked and enslaved. If it's the pirates, you think they'll cause chaos. If we give it to only one side, there will be those who don't have it, who would be willing to kill crews to get at any ship that can travel the filaments. Or worse, to learn about it and how it works. That's why we have to figure out how not to use starborn to travel first."

Eislie walked back, looking into her friend's eyes. "If we give it to everyone, then everyone is the same. No one has the advantage. That way, we save as many people, starborn or otherwise."

It took a moment as Miriz turned away, comprehending what Eislie was saying. "Goddess, no. I didn't realize how serious this was."

She looked back to see Eislie's smile. "Now, do you understand why we're doing this? Why it has to be us?"

Miriz nodded. She understood now the weight that Eislie and Jace were bearing on themselves. The filaments were within grasp of everyone, and it was only a matter of time. She now knew the pirates had been accessing the filaments but needed more knowledge on how to do so. And if what Eislie and Jace found was indeed a solution, then she was right. No one group could hold the answer. Everyone had to have it. She was focusing on the fortune that could be gained, not knowing the consequences. But now, Miriz understood and looked to Eislie.

"Call whoever you need. I'll support you in any way possible."

Eislie smiled. "Thank you, Miriz. I knew you'd understand."

Chapter 11:
Ships Apart

A few hours passed, and Eislie left with Miriz after she invited her for dinner. The crew of the *Solace Star* was still planetside, leaving the ship to the local port crew. Miriz gave the team access as per Eislie's instructions. She had decided to have them load the remaining Sotiral systems and new supplies for the ship. Miriz had hand-picked someone to inspect the supplies before being packed. Linna Tarcin was a trusted associate of Miriz's and was tasked with ensuring nothing was amiss. Miriz didn't want anything happening to Eislie or her current crew.

The small detail moved hundreds of crates of the Sotiral systems on board. When the ship supplies arrived, they were accompanied by the person Miriz assigned. To prevent tampering they were to watch the loading of supplies until they were secured. The woman kept a watchful eye the entire time. Her only distraction was when one of the workers started heading down the hall toward the flight control. He was holding a small box, and she stopped him. The box had the spare control systems parts the engineer had requested when he opened it.

"Mackson, where were you taking these?" Linna asked.

The man returned an innocent stare, saying. "I was told to deliver these to the engineer. I figured they would be on the flight deck."

Linna looked back. "You, Haryn, come here."

The woman moved swiftly toward the two standing at the hallway entrance. "Yes, Inspector, what do you need?"

Linna looked down the hallway. "We are going to follow security procedures on this ship. You will accompany Mackson to the flight deck and make sure he only delivers that package."

Haryn nodded, "Yes, Inspector. I will."

Hearing a loud bang behind her, Linna turned to yell for the rest of the crew to be more careful before waving Mackson and Haryn to their task. The two headed down the hall at a not-so-fast pace. There was silence until they reached the flight deck. Mackson whispered, "Glad it was you. I didn't want to have to explain knocking someone out."

Haryn said, "Only a few of us are on the crew. The odds were against it. It seems like the gods are smiling on us. The Consortium wanted more, but this is a very strictly controlled planet."

Mackson nodded, placing the box with the hardware on a station near the comm. He turned to look at his partner.

Haryn nodded and pulled out a small device, pressing a button on it. It created a short flash, and he watched as several of the ship's controls around them flickered. "Hurry, this quantum suppressor will only last a minute."

"Watch the hall. I'll do what I came here to do," Mackson said before rushing to the comm system and pulling the panel open. As he went to remove a connector, something seemed strange. The connector looked oddly familiar. He reached into his pocket and produced a small device nearly identical to the end of the connector that looked strange. Seeing this, he pulled at the connector, and it released unexpectedly.

"Slac, there's a monitoring device already here," Mackson muttered.

His voice was loud enough for Haryn to hear, and she asked, "What do you mean?" before joining him by the console.

Mackson showed her the devices side by side, and she looked back toward the hallway.

Haryn told him, "Hurry and install ours," as she returned to where she activated the device.

Mackson shook his head, "If it's one they put on, then they'll know we changed it."

Haryn looked at the small device she held and could see it flickering. "Then put them both in. The Consortium wants their comms monitored."

The man did as she indicated but said, "It might cause the comm systems to malfunction. I'm unsure if you can run two of these on the same line."

Haryn shook her head. "Just do it. We're out of time."

Mackson nodded and installed both devices, putting them back in the wrong order. He had to rush to close the panel and returned to face the same way as earlier, just before the small device his partner held released a puff of smoke. However, instead of looking concerned, she smiled. "It is a nice ship." She turned to the man. "I hope it serves the crew well. Please have a safe trip." The man said nothing as she tugged on his arm.

She whispered as they returned to the hold, "Let's hope that doesn't do any damage. The Hurmann back home are paying us a lot to get that on board." The man agreed, and they hurried back to finish loading the remaining supplies.

A short time later, Eislie and Miriz were approaching the ship. They could hear the busyness of the dock crew loading the Sotiral systems, and Miriz turned to Eislie.

"I had someone assigned to inspect the food and other ship supplies that needed replacing." She looked over the crew until she saw Linna. With a quick tap, she motioned for Eislie to follow.

"Linna, I trust you have everything under control?" Miriz asked as she approached the inspector.

Linna turned a concerned expression on her face. "We are almost finished with loading the cargo. And I personally secured the food and ship supplies. I scanned them all myself."

Eislie looked to Miriz, who seemed to be looking quizzically toward the inspector, making Eislie ask, "What's wrong?"

Miriz looked to Linna. "I'm worried about that look of hers. Linna's worked for me for over ten planetary cycles. I only see that when she is really concerned."

Linna smiled momentarily. "I'm concerned about the shipment's mass. We have another forty capsules to go, and I think we're already past the maximum limit on the gravity compensation for this vessel. Are you sure you want us to load the rest?"

Miriz looked at Eislie and could see her smiling.

"All the systems on this ship are upgraded, Engines, power, gravity compensation." Eislie paused. "Hull, not yet. But that may change. It'll haul the mass of half a fleet cruiser. And I don't mean what the cruiser will carry. I mean the ship itself."

Linna looked to Miriz in disbelief, only to hear from her employer, "She has a good engineer. He keeps modifying their other ship as well."

The woman chuckled. "Typical, can't leave things working as they are?"

Eislie shook her head, "Well, he has his reasons. And, I agree with him so...."

Linna nodded, "At least he gets your permission."

Eislie laughed. "Not always. I had to come here with this ship while he's fixing what he broke back home." She turned to Miriz. "Speaking of that, he should be on his way. I'm waiting for a message from him."

Linna looked at the ship. "Why would you put that much power into such a small ship?"

Eislie huffed, "To make sure it can outrun anyone trying to attack it."

The inspector looked at the ship. Eislie's reasoning seemed fair, and she looked to her employer. "We'll load the rest. It should only be a couple of hours. If you like, you can inspect the food stores and other supplies while you wait."

Eislie nodded, then pulled Miriz along.

Inside the *Solace Star*, Miriz held a scanner to a random food package. The display thankfully showed only the contents and nothing else. Miriz said, "Seem like everything's in order."

Eislie agreed, and she turned to head to the control deck. As she entered, she surprised Miriz by saying, "Oh, the spare environmental control systems are here. They must have put them up here rather than in the hold."

Miriz looked concerned. "No one was supposed to be up here. Their instructions were to remain in the hold area. I'll have to have a word with Linna about that."

Eislie looked at the main screen. "Let's see who was up here. Computer, play all instances of people on the flight deck in the last few hours."

On the screen, the video of the last few hours played quickly; there was her and Miriz leaving and the two workers. Nothing seemed out of the ordinary as they watched. Eislie said the video sounded like fairies talking fast, making Miriz look at her strangely.

"Oh, that's from stories my mother used to tell me from when she was young back on Earth. I always liked the one with the fairy ring of wood, The fairy gives it to the man who saved the little girl."

Eislie looked at the screen. "Nothing seems wrong. And the time stamp is good. I'm happy we installed the same system on the *Wolfhammer*." She looked at the comm and checked the messages, only to see nothing. "Hmm, that's strange. I would have expected Jace to have sent something by now?"

Miriz leaned over. "Maybe he hasn't left yet."

"He probably has. must have forgotten to send it." She looked at Miriz. "He sometimes forgets when he's rushing."

Miriz laughed, "Well, He'll be here in a few days anyway." She looked more serious before asking, "You think he'll be here in time for you to stay?"

Eislie looked at the comm. "I'm sending him a message. But, if he left today, it would still be at least four days until he arrives. I don't think we can wait that long if we want to keep the contract."

Miriz nodded, "Send the message and let him know you'll be heading out."

Eislie typed away. As she sent the message, she heard Miriz say, "That'll give him enough time to oversee the hull modification. Maybe it'll teach him not to mess with your ship."

Eislie smiled at her friend's jab at Jace as she looked for a response. She turned to Miriz, "I just thought of something. If he's with Shasji, then maybe they are…."

Miriz looked for her to finish her sentence, only to hear, "No! he wouldn't do that. He doesn't have any backup. Never mind."

Miriz suspected that she was referring to him using the filaments to travel. But she also knew Eislie trusted Jace, and he wouldn't risk his life to try something like that, at least not without her. That was something apparently clear with her friend. Instead, Miriz offered some encouragement. "Well, if he is flying the, uh, you know. Then maybe you should be concerned?" The hint of chiding resonant in Miriz's tone, making Eislie look annoyed at her friend.

"Really, Miriz? I trust Jace. Besides, I'll have to hunt him down if he does that without me," Eislie joked.

The two laughed. Miriz saying, "Well, it doesn't matter. You'll be on your way to Roscin station in a few hours anyway."

The engines of the *Wolfhammer* hummed with a lower drone than usual. They had been that way for several hours. And Shasji could tell Jace seemed concerned. She had been on the crew of the *Solace Star* for almost a year and knew the ship she served on and its idiosyncrasies well. She leaned over, reaching out to tap Jace on his arm.

"Hey. You look like something's wrong."

Jace looked over. "The ship doesn't feel right. Something's off."

Shasji looked at the controls. "The displays all seem good."

He looked at her. "Seems sluggish on the port side. Seems like we're drifting a bit." He seemed in thought for a moment, "I did the checks five times."

"Yes. You did. I was there. You had me check it, too."

Jace smiled, "So neither of us can make a mistake?"

Shasji looked around. She had only been flying on the *Wolfhammer* for the last few days while Jace tested the new tunnel coils and feeds. To her, there seemed nothing wrong. As she looked back at Jace, she could see his mind working. *So that's what that look is.* She thought. She had spoken with Eislie many times and never understood "that look he gets," and when she said, "I usually get worried when I see it."

She sat back, saying, "Maybe we should punch out and take a look."

Jace snickered.

"I'm serious. If the ship doesn't feel right, then maybe something is wrong. Something we both missed. I mean, haven't you or Eis missed something?"

Jace nodded, and Shasji watched as Jace furrowed his brow. She heard him mumble, "That guy was by the port side."

"What did you say?" Shasji asked.

Jace looked to the port wall only to turn back his eyes in concentration, which was broken when he said, "Ed, you have the feeds to all seven couplings online, right?"

"Yes, captain. All feeds are reporting within limits. The new configuration seems to be quite efficient," the computer replied.

Jace tapped the navigation, switching to manual. He adjusted the course and returned to the exact heading before releasing the controls. Jace ordered the computer to release all automated heading adjustments. He continued to stare at the display as the computer acknowledged and waited. Shasji swore he didn't blink but was startled when Jace spoke.

"There, it took almost thirty-four seconds to drift. So, either we have a heavy gravitational body near us, or something's not working right." Jace turned to look at the port side. "Ed? We can run on partial feeds, right?"

"Yes, captain, we would have to reduce power to match the identical feed on the opposite side," the computer replied.

Jace looked forward. "Start with the rear one first and leave them off till I tell you to turn it back on."

"Captain, please confirm what you are requesting. If we disable the feeds, we increase our time to arrive on Yata Beta," the computer responded.

"Do it, Ed. I have a feeling something is not supposed to be there." He turned to Shasji. "I found some guy looking at the ship just before we left. I couldn't find anything wrong, but…. I don't think he was there to get a selfie."

"What's a selfie?" Shasji asked, making Jace groan.

After rolling his eyes, she watched him look around. "Ed, I think we may have an issue. Humor me on the feeds, will ya?"

The computer responded, "Shutting down first feed in five seconds, captain."

The first coil feed shut down, and the hum from the engines lowered. "Power feed disabled, captain. Shutting down the next feed in five seconds."

"Hold up, Ed. Let me adjust course, and let's wait about thirty seconds before shutting down each feed after I adjust," Jace replied.

"Acknowledged, Captain. Do you suspect one of the feeds is compromised?" the computer asked.

Shasji watched as Jace's head nodded shallowly as he adjusted course. "Next feed in thirty, Ed."

There was silence as time passed, and nothing happened. Jace adjusted course and waited again. Jace continued like this several times and was on the second to last feed. Jace was about to alter course but instead waited. Shasji watched as a smile appeared on Jace's face.

He turned to look at her, "Port two seems to be reading correctly, right, Ed?"

"Yes, captain. But I am detecting a drift of almost zero point zero seven. Either the feed connection is bad, or something is delaying the reaction control," the computer replied.

Jace shook his head. "Ed, if it's reading correctly but the reaction time is off, something is between the feeds and the controls. Now I know where to look."

She watched as Jace disengaged the tunnel system, and they returned to standard space. He tapped the display. "Any nearby planets, Ed?"

"No, captain. This area is quite desolate. I presume you are going to investigate the feed issue?" the computer asked with a tone of already knowing the captain's answer.

Jace nodded, "Shasji, watch for anything on scanners while I'm out. No one may be in the neighborhood, but I still don't trust things."

"If you find something, let me know. If you have spares on board, I can put them in the airlock for you. Might make a repair quicker."

Chapter 12:
A Little Walk Outside

Jace grasped onto the ship's hull while the magnetic harness did most of the work as he pulled at the line for the port feed. Upon inspecting the end, there was a small line across the connector. He pulled at it to see if it was sturdy and was surprised when it broke away in his glove. He closed his hand quickly so it didn't float away. He held it up to his visor and could see feed line connectors on both openings.

"I don't think this is a splice," Jace mumbled as he reconnected the feed cable. "Shasji, I think I found something. There doesn't seem to be any damage but let me get inside before we test. Just in case," Jace said over the comm.

"Acknowledged. What did you find?" Shasji asked.

"I'll show you when I come inside. I'm heading for the door now."

Shasji turned as soon as the door opened. "Should I test the feed?"

Jace nodded lightly, kicking the tool bag Shasji placed by the door, just in case. "Might as well know before I take off this suit."

Shasji turned to see the controls already lit as the computer started the feeds once again. She huffed, "Your computer knows what you want before you have to ask." She seemed annoyed, "It's not like the computer on the *Solace Star*. Yours is better."

They both heard, "Thank you, Captain Yaman. It's good to be noticed."

Jace laughed, "That almost makes you sound a bit needy, Ed."

"On the contrary, captain, I enjoy acclimating crew who have not flown on this ship many times."

Jace looked surprised, "Well, Ed, she's going to have her own ship." He turned to look at Shasji. "As soon as we get enough to get another, maybe we can have Ed make some changes to the systems."

Shasji smiled, "I think I might like that." Jace held up the tiny connector, making Shasji ask, "What is that?"

"It looks like a coupler, but I didn't install any couplers on the feed lines. So, I don't think this is what it appears to be," Jace told her as he handed it to her.

Shasji looked at the device, and she noticed it was more significant than a standard coupler. She tried pulling the piece apart and heard Jace say, "Tools are right there. We might as well open it up. I'm pretty sure it's not a coupler." She rushed to get the tool and was startled when Jace yelled, "Wait!" she dropped the pliers she held and stared at him before hearing him say, "Maybe we should make sure it's not an explosive first?"

Shasji held the connector gently and followed Jace as he headed into the med bay.

"The medical systems can detect different compounds. "Ed, can you see if this has any energetic compounds, please?"

"The medical system is not designed to fully analyze that type of device, captain. But you are correct in anticipating the detection of explosive and hazardous compounds," the computer responded.

"I figured as much, Ed. I want to make sure it's not something to harm us first," Jace replied.

The computer went to work quickly and displayed its findings. "The device seems to be a data storage unit, captain. And I do not detect any transceiver parts. This item would have to be retrieved to be useful."

Jace scrutinized the part when he heard the computer's results. He turned to Shasji. "Someone wants to know what our field frequencies are running at. And what power we're using."

He turned to look out the door, then took the small device from the table. "We should get going." Jace was silent as he sat in his control chair. "I've been worrying that they would be pulling shit like this. We're going to have to be more careful."

Jace placed the small device on the console. Shasji turned to look at the console. She looked down at the comm for some reason but saw nothing. She looked back, "Hey, Jace! Didn't you message the *Solace Star* before we left?"

She heard him respond, "Yeah. I sent another two about nine hours ago. They send us a message?"

Shasji looked around before shaking her head as Jace leaned forward. She had worked with her crew, and they had protocols to follow. Flora and Larat had insisted on communication every few hours while on duty. And anyone on the crew of the *Solace Star* was supposed to check in every five hours or so. That was something she followed to the letter, knowing how much these two were getting into trouble.

"They should have responded. Or at least sent us an automated reply that the last message was read."

Jace raised his brow. "Can we reach Yata control?"

Shasji tapped the comm and reached the planet's flight control center. She had a short discussion and asked about the status of the *Solace Star*. The response was one they did not expect.

"Look, *Wolfhammer*, Queeks Maco has been here all week. With all the ship traffic, it'll take at least a few hours to find out."

"Queeks Maco is there?" Shasji asked excitedly, startling Jace.

Jace shook his head. "Yata control, we're trying to get in touch with the crew of the *Solace Star*. We've sent several messages but have yet to hear a response. How soon can you get us the info?"

There was a short silence. "Like I said, a few hours at best. We have a lot of ships coming and going."

Jace sighed, "Alright, let us know when you have the information."

Shasji interrupted Jace, "How long is Queeks Maco going to be there?"

There was an audible sigh heard over the comm. "They are leaving tomorrow for Roscin Station. Caused us enough trouble since they've been here."

"Got it, thanks." She then terminated the call. "Ed, can you increase to the fastest speed possible?"

"Ed, don't do it," Jace ordered, making Shasji look at him with pleading eyes.

Jace sighed again, "We're at least two days out at top speed."

Shasji seemed to think, "Maybe we can use the filaments. It'll get us there faster."

Jace leaned his head back. "No. I still have to run some more tests on the tunnel system for that. Right now, we're stuck using regular old hyperspace. I didn't want to do anything until we installed the new hull plating."

Shasji pouted, making Jace say, "Sorry, we won't be there till after they leave."

* * *

Two days had gone by, and the *Wolfhammer* was a couple of hours out from their destination. Jace walked in to find Shasji sitting in Eislie's chair, her legs draped over the side console.

"Did you sleep up here?" Jace asked, his voice filled with a tinge of humor.

Shasji rolled her head back to look at him. "I'm not talking to you."

Jace chuckled, "Okay, I'll bite, captain. Why are you not talking to me?"

Shasji turned to sit in the chair. "We missed Queeks. I wanted to see them live."

Jace audibly sighed, "You know, you're more than thirty, and you're acting like a child."

Shasji stared forward, "You're just over forty, and you are still a child."

Jace looked confused. "That makes no sense."

Shasji looked at Jace. "You have about six hundred standard years to go. We're both children compared to many in the Alliance."

Jace scoffed, "Back on Earth, forty is almost middle age. More than half your life is done. We don't have this type of medical tech back where I'm from. You have to grow up fast."

Jace could see her demeanor change as she regretted saying what she did. Jace chuckled before he spoke, "You know, I haven't been to a concert for years. I would have liked to have seen them myself. Their music's pretty good."

Shasji turned to see him looking at her.

"You were right. With the filaments, we could have traveled this in no time. I just didn't want to risk the ship." Jace seemed to pause before he

87

turned to look at the navigation screen, "I didn't want to risk your life if it didn't work."

Jace's words sank in, and Shasji started feeling bad for how she was acting. "I'm sorry. It's just that every time I try and get a pass for them, they're always gone."

"Happened all the time back on Earth. You get used to it." Jace looked at the timer and smiled, "We'll be there in a couple of hours. If the *Solace Star* hasn't left, you have my permission to floor the engines. Maybe you'll make it to the station before Queeks does, then you can be there when they arrive."

Shasji smiled at him when she realized that he was looking out for her as well. She had spoken with Eislie many times and knew Eislie worried about Jace putting others before himself. She had heard the stories of how Jace found food for many while back on Earth and how he fought to save the Daak. She suddenly found herself thinking about how he was. *Was this what it's like to be a captain of your own ship? Do you have to make decisions like this? Can I make decisions like this?*

Jace looked over, hearing silence from her, and saw her eyes looking like she was thinking. Unlike Eislie, Jace wasn't empathic, but he did know the look of someone who just discovered something about themselves.

"What's wrong?" Jace asked.

Shasji looked at him, "I'm going to have to start thinking like a captain, aren't I?"

Jace nodded, "Yep. You accepted the job. You'll have to worry about the ship, crew, and anyone or anything you come across. It comes with the territory. I found that out firsthand, by the way." He paused. "You'll have to stand your ground. And also have to know when to tell people to fuck off when they think they know better. But, also listen to them."

Shasji raised her brow. "Do you tell Eis to fuck off when you think she's wrong?"

Jace's eyes widened before he chuckled, "Yes, sometimes." He leaned in. "But I choose my moment to do that. Eis is tough. It's like dealing with someone from my planet."

Shasji laughed. "You and she are a lot alike, you know."

Jace looked puzzled.

She sat tall in the chair. "You both have stood alone against everyone around you. You've helped people. You risked escaping even though you knew someone might kill you. And you've both been betrayed by those you've worked with."

Jace seemed to think, then smiled. "I guess we are."

There were a few moments of silence before the computer interrupted. "Captain, we are approximately an hour from our destination. As per planetary protocol, we are to inform them of our location and time of arrival."

Jace looked at the interface, "We've never had to do that before. Why now?"

Ed responded, "It is a recent update given the actions of the Karazon and several Hurmann instances. It is required for all people of Yata when returning."

"But he's from Terra, uh, Earth. Not Yata," Shasji said.

Jace contemplated momentarily before saying, "Technically, I am a resident of Yata Beta as well."

The computer added, "Captain Tucker has residency origins for Terra, Gilese, and Yata Beta currently."

She looked at Jace in disbelief, "How did you manage that? Most people have one residency, maybe two."

"Technically, Eis has the same. The Daak informed us that they registered her as a temporary origin resident of Earth but never removed it." Jace leaned back. "They did give me a hard time back on Earth, though. They thought I wasn't from there, but it was sorted out. At least, I think it was."

She watched him lean forward, reaching for the comm, "It doesn't matter anyway. I'm not planning on going back to Earth any time soon. Yata, on the other hand, has something we can use."

"What's that?" Shasji asked.

"Resources and manufacturing for specific materials. And they can help me install things," Jace told her before tapping the comm. "Yata control, this is the *Wolfhammer*. We are about an hour out, checking in for available dock space. Also, we have a message into a sister ship of ours, the *Solace Star*, but haven't heard back yet."

There was a silence that Jace broke, speaking to Shasji, "It'll take me a few weeks to install the upgrades on the ship. And we may need help, so when you're done with your delivery, don't head home. Head back to Yata

Beta. We might need some help if this doesn't work. And I'd rather have people I trust doing that."

Shasji looked forward. "And all starborn if possible, right?"

Jace nodded. "Just in case, yeah. I'm hoping this works so we don't have to, well, uh, you know, become part of the drive system."

Shasji nodded, "It wasn't that bad. But I get what you're saying." She looked down. "Imagine how much money we'll make from this. I mean, we'd have transport contracts more than we could handle."

Jace's expression didn't change much, except for a slight sigh before he spoke. "Shasji, we're giving it away as soon as we figure things out and make it safe."

"What? Why?" Shasji questioned his response.

Jace's demeanor changed, "Because if we keep it to ourselves, that endangers everyone we care about. Family, friends, even people and planets we don't know yet."

He turned to see her questioning stare.

"Shasji, people, planets, whoever will hunt down any ship with the ability to travel the filaments. And they'd be willing to kill for it," Jace sighed heavily. "Also, if we can't figure this out, you and any other starborn may find themselves a more permanent part of any ship that accesses the filaments. That's another reason we have to give it away."

Jace could see the fear settling into her, and having been enslaved before, Jace knew what she was thinking. "Shasji, we're doing this to stop any others who figure out that those like us, or any starborn, for that matter, can access the filaments. Eis and I talked about it for quite a long time. Her parents know as well, and we're all in agreement."

Shasji slumped in her chair. "I want my own ship, but I don't want to become part of one."

Jace nodded and was about to say something when he heard the comm come alive. "*Wolfhammer*, this is Yata control. We have you scheduled to come in early tomorrow. Can you confirm your location?"

Jace smiled as he tapped the comm. "We are about forty-two standard out from arrival. We decided to hit full speed to see if we could make the last concert. We almost toasted the engines. I don't think Queeks is still there, though, are they?

The comm came alive again, "Yes, but they are scheduled to leave in about four standard hours. You'll have to catch them next time. It was a great show."

Jace watched as Shasji shifted in her chair.

"Too bad. But we made good time anyway. Could you send us a dock assignment? Also, we had a call into our sister ship, the *Solace Star*, but we haven't heard back yet. Are they still planetside?"

There was a minute as the operator said they'd check. When they returned, the news was what Jace expected. "*Wolfhammer*, the *Solace Star* is en route to Roscin station, due to return in two weeks. We sent a message, but the last we heard from them was while they were in this system. And since we had no response, Yata control issued a search command because they had a comm lead from a nearby vessel on route back. It seems like the *Solace Star* was having comm issues."

"Understood, Yata control. We'll take that dock assignment now. We can confirm when we arrive. Any other messages for us?" Jace asked.

The controller told them there wasn't, and Jace acknowledged. He turned to Shasji, "Well, you might be able to see them, maybe get an autograph or something, but if we want to see a show, it looks like we'll have to wait till they are around again."

Shasji huffed, "Just my luck."

Chapter 13:
A Little Communication Trouble

The *Solace Star* was near a trinary star system when it punched out from hyperspace. Eislie and the crew were working to restore the comms to the best that they could after discovering the monitoring devices.

"You know, Ed would have found these before we even left the planet," Eislie complained. "Issa, Feren, any luck on the rewiring?"

Feren popped her head up from inside the console, making Eislie ask, "How did you get in there?"

Feren huffed before saying, "Lots of stretching. You think I do that stuff for fun?"

"What stuff?" Eislie asked.

"The Eternal Reach exercises. I've been doing them since I had to escape from the *Polastan Acosti* after it crashed. I would have died in the engine room," Feren responded.

Eislie knew Feren had served on a ship, but she didn't know which. She also knew that the *Polastan Acosti* was a high-profile incident. The ship was in Daak territory when the Duggor attacked. They had nearly inverted the reactors trying to escape. The ship was heavily damaged and crashed on a nearby planetoid, one without an atmosphere. The rescue took over three days, since the Duggor scanned the remains of the ship and took only some as prisoners. The rest they left to die. Eislie understood who they assumed who they took were probably starborn. The only saving grace was that a nearby Alliance ship came to their aid after the Duggor ships left.

"I never knew you were in that," Eislie said.

Feren sighed, "I was stuck in the spide radiation field, and that masked me from the Duggor. It also made some of the crew want to leave me behind. I had burns on my arms and body. I wasn't wholly immune to the radiation."

Eislie closed her eyes. "I'm sorry. You got out, that's what's important."

Feren looked at her. "I don't like to talk about it. Kind of like that other place you were stuck in."

Eislie felt her energy drop. She knew Feren was referencing Charon and how she was imprisoned. Even with Jace, she didn't like to talk about it. "I understand," she muttered. "I don't understand how Jace can talk about it so easily."

Feren looked up as if searching. Neither of them had heard from Issa in some time. He had been silent since Eislie asked for an update. She looked around, "Wait, where is Issa?"

Eislie looked behind her, and Issa was nowhere to be found. She motioned for Feren to get out of the console and join her in searching for him. Eislie's mind now thinking *I was able to get Bensin off the crew for this round. Don't tell me that we have another Alliance spy on board.*

They headed to the hold of the ship and ran into one of the crew. "Derrit, have you seen Issa?"

The pilot briefly looked over his shoulder before returning to read the display. He pulled on the nearest strap to ensure everything was secure before replying. "I saw him head into the other side of the hold. Why?"

"He was supposed to be helping me with the wiring." Feren shot back.

Derrit smiled, "He probably headed back to see what other containers were empty." He leaned in, "I think he had plans to sell some of the suits himself."

Eislie raised one brow. "He tell you that?"

"Wanted to cut me in if I helped."

Eislie leaned her head back. "I swear if you were on the *Wolfhammer*, we'd have spaced you by now."

Derrit winked. "That's why I'm telling you."

Eislie tapped the controls of the cargo area and entered. Feren paused. "She really wouldn't space you."

Derrit chuckled, "Probably not, but knowing her, I wouldn't take the chance."

Feren nodded, then followed Eislie before closing the door.

Eislie stood in the darkness, her eyes adjusting quickly. She had to wear a visor most of the time back on Yata, and the lower light was welcome. She could hear Feren behind her and turned to see her in the dim lighting.

"Should we yell for him?" Feren whispered.

Eislie looked around, her ears, listening, and she heard something further down in the hold. "No, let's see what he's up to first." She waved Feren to follow.

They walked only a few meters before Eislie stopped and looked around the corner. She then mouthed the words, "He's right here."

Eislie pointed to the light controls and motioned for Feren to go to them, telling her, "When I signal, you turn on the lights."

Feren nodded and waited by the controls. Eislie walked as quietly as she could and stood only steps away from Issa. She could see him working to unlock one of the shipping capsules. She waved to Feren, who hit the controls, and the room became brighter. Issa nearly jumped to the ceiling when Eislie spoke.

"What are you doing?" Eislie asked, her arms crossed.

Issa stepped back and looked as if he was going to run away until Feren walked up, blocking any escape. He hadn't answered, but Feren spoke for him. "Looks like he's either sabotaging the shipment or stealing. I'm thinking the latter."

Eislie stood silent, waiting for Issa to respond, the cold stare from her light blue eyes sending chills through him.

He waited to reply, then meekly said, "I was just trying to make some extra shill, alright."

Eislie shook her head. "At least have the sense to steal when there are more opportunities to take the stuff. Where were you going to go with the suits?"

Issa remained silent and turned to walk away. "You are not dismissed, Issa. Did you have a buyer for the suits lined up?"

The man looked back and nodded.

"Who are they?" Eislie asked.

Issa remained silent.

Eislie huffed, "Look, tell me who they are. I'm not going to throw you off this ship. Not here, at least. I want to ensure it wasn't the same people who put those listening devices in the comms. Because if they were, they will cross you the first chance they get."

Issa looked at her and turned to answer, "They said they were pirates. And they'd kill me if I told."

Eislie groaned, "Idiot, pirates don't tell you they are pirates. They'd make up a better story."

Issa looked despondent. His captain's logic made sense. "Then who were they?"

Eislie moved closer. "They weren't pirates." She then looked back. "Help Feren get the comms working again. We'll need them. We can talk about this later." Her annoyance was evident.

Issa walked toward the cargo hold inside door. "One called the other, Tallir. That's all I know."

Feren started to follow, then turned and said, "You think your friends can confirm if they were pirates?"

Eislie crossed her arms again, "And you ask that, why?"

Feren smiled. "Hey, I almost joined them. And Shasji told me who you were talking about while you were lost. It's okay with me. I just want to know who I can trust." Feren then followed Issa back to the control room.

Eislie remained behind, her mind processing the revelation that Feren was comfortable working directly with pirates. The concern now was if Feren was like Preston, watching them. That didn't sit well with Eislie. The situation also allowed her to discover the additional listening devices planted on the ship. And she was grateful not to have had the chance to reach out to the pirates while on Yata, and that was fortunate. If she had, whoever was listening would know what she and Jace were up to.

* * *

Aboard the *Eiger*, Eshea put the ship on automatic and returned to meet with the rest of the crew. She could hear Ralla's voice raised, giving one of his lectures on the importance of the work they were doing. The part she heard was one she rarely encountered as she turned the corner.

"I've told you time and again, Zarlin. This nonviolence slac isn't what we need," Ralla said as he sat hard in one of the chairs surrounding the small table.

Eshea paused in the small hallway as she watched Zarlin lightly bang her head against the tabletop. She could hear her words mumbled as Zarlin said, "I'm tired of writing those. I want people to feel good, not angry, when we sing. That's all we sing now."

Eshea chuckled before she spoke, "That's because we need people to fight for our cause, for their freedom. Happy people don't do that. You know that as well as any of us."

Zarlin raised her head. "I know, I'm just tired of being angry all the time. I want something fun."

Eshea was about to speak when Ralla interrupted, "This is war, not some music group. We are bringing our cause to light. We need individuals to understand that most of our people are enslaved."

The room was silent before Zarlin again complained that she was tired of writing angry songs.

Eshea sat and put her arm over Zarlin's shoulder, shaking her gently and making her sway a little in her seat. "We're all tired, but we have to keep going. When we free all the Arlain people from the Hurmann, then you can write any song you like."

Her upbeat tone made Zarlin smile, and Trin snorted, giving a smile. Eshea's actions caused silence until Ralla again killed the atmosphere.

"And you, Eshea, you left here wearing the last working VFM. That was reckless. We haven't finished repairing the other yet. The fiber matrix and voice mod are still not working correctly." He stood pounding the table with his hand. "Without it, Queeks Maco doesn't exist."

Eshea sat back in her chair. "I didn't use the Queeks silhouette. I had another for the vids while we were watching that ship. Besides, only Zarlin and I can wear them for the moment. The voice mods only have a female voice."

Ralla knew she was right. Zarlin and Eshea had similar builds that allowed them to change places when either of them had to work on a mission. The disappointment of her actions, however, made Ralla throw his head back and give a transient growl in his speech. "We lose that mask, we have to stop until we get them both repaired. It's not like there are infiltration units we can steal from back home. Or have you forgotten we all have prices on our heads? They almost got us last time back on Ryus Four."

The attack itself was from a known Hurmann battle cruiser. The *Eiger* was able to respond and damage the other ship. They were moving away as their attacker's engines imploded.

The memory of the attack that nearly killed them made the room again fall silent until Trin spoke. His voice was little more than a whisper due to his adjustment back on Arlain. "I was trained on the masks, Ralla. I'll get the other working soon. We've been busy doing concerts if you remember."

Ralla turned to look at Trin. He knew of Trin's background, a warrior who defeated almost all he faced in the arena. His voice was taken when he spoke back to his owner. Even though medical technology could regenerate and even replace most tissues, the Hurmann found ways to make injuries permanent to punish enslaved people. Ralla unconsciously reached up, touching his left ear, a gesture he'd long put to his subconscious, remembering when it's removal for refusing to obey the slave traders. The Hurmann knew how to remove the genetic memory from the surrounding cells, not allowing them to be regenerated. It took months after he escaped the ship attacked by the Gel out hunting for the retrieval of their own taken by the slavers.

Ralla was silent as he sat. The man he knew as Trin wasn't so lucky. His vocal cords had to be made from scratch. And the only reference to do so was what Trin thought he remembered what he sounded like. After the reconstruction, his voice was never as loud as it should have been.

"We need more songs about the plight of all enslaved by the Hurmann and all other beings who are suffering the same as we have," Ralla said before looking directly at Zarlin. "It doesn't matter if you're tired of writing them. There are so many who weren't as fortunate as us to escape."

Ralla looked around the table before stopping on Eshea. "What did they say when you approached them about aiding our cause?"

Eshea and Zarlin remained silent, making Ralla lean toward them. "You did meet with them, didn't you?"

Zarlin shrank into her chair, but Eshea answered, "We were surveilling them, but only one was there. I told you that." She sat back in a huff. "There was a lot of security, and their ship left before we could approach them."

The groan Ralla made echoed off the walls of the room. "That's a lost opportunity. Who knows when we'll get a chance to catch up to them again." He looked at Eshea. "And you're not even bothered by it."

Eshea smiled. "We'll have another chance. They're headed to the same destination as us, Roscin station."

Ralla sat dumbfounded, asking, "And you found this out how?"

Zarlin smiled, "Queeks was able to get the information." She looked innocent. "Or at least she distracted the security people enough for me to download the info from the nearby system terminal." She held up her hand, the bracelet she wore larger than most displayed before several tendrils slithered from the band into the air.

Ralla smiled for the first time since they boarded the ship. "Well, I guess this wasn't such a slac-up job as I thought it was.

Chapter 14:
Message Sent

The engine room of the *Solace Star* was noisier than usual. Eislie's voice filled the small hallway as she growled, "What the slac? Who worked on this control system last?"

Issa replied, "It was worked on at the last Alliance station we went to. There is some stupid rule that only Alliance repair crews could work on a ship while docked. They told us they detected tritium decay contamination when we were landing."

Eislie stared at Issa, more of a low growl filling her words. "It's a spide system. There's no tritium reactor on this ship." She turned to look back, her hand still inside the panel as she pushed against the wall for leverage. The shiny metal was flexing, and she almost fell back as what she was pulling on broke loose. She showed the small box to Issa and Derrit.

"We installed the new systems ourselves; this should not be here," Eislie expressed in anger.

Derrit wasn't taking any of this lying down and defended their actions. "I'm not spide-proof. I don't like working near the drive or reactor systems, okay?"

Eislie handed him the small box. "You've served on ships before. There are no rules on any Alliance station or planet like that." Eislie looked at Issa. "Besides, you have protection systems onboard. The Sotiral systems would have protected you." Her voice was calmer.

Her back made a thump as she leaned heavily on the same panel she was just inside. She looked up from the floor when Derrit spoke, "How did you know this was in there? Also, what is it?"

Eislie sighed. "I have no idea what it is. I just know something was causing a problem." She seemed to think briefly. "It's probably similar to those things we found in the comms." The two men watched as Eislie dragged her hands down her face, saying, "It was causing us to slow down, and, I don't know, it just felt like something was wrong when I maxed out the throttle."

She looked toward the two after Issa handed her a small rag, "You got something on your face, captain."

Eislie groaned as she turned to see the long, dark streak now down the entire right side of her face. She grabbed the rag from Issa and told them, "Let me put this back together. I don't want to be stuck here too long. Someone might try and board us." She calmed and turned to look inside the panel. "Go up and tell Feren that we'll be on our way as soon as I get this reconnected." She turned to look at the two crew. "If you don't want to be here, you can leave. I won't force you to work on the engines."

Derrit handed the small box to Issa before walking quickly down the hall, closing the door to the engine room as he turned the corner. Issa remained behind, making Eislie ask, "You're staying?"

Issa nodded, "I'm wearing my Sotiral suit. I'm good. Besides, I don't want to be in one place for too long either."

Eislie smiled and turned to again reach inside the panel. "Hand me a clamp crimper. Let's get this ship running again."

The chair's cushion wheezed as Eislie sat hard, making Feren look toward her. The pilot's eyes were drawn to the remnants of grease and dust still on Eislie's face. She motioned to her captain, saying, "You have a little something about here."

Eislie huffed. "Thought I got everything."

Feren laughed silently. "Derrit showed me what you found."

Eislie stared forward, "Yeah, I think it's like what we found in the comm." She turned to look at Feren. "Issa's taking a look at it. Maybe he can at least figure out who made it."

Feren nodded and returned to the flight controls. She was about to engage the engines when an alarm sounded. The ship's computer announced, "Proximity alert. Ship in the area."

Eislie tapped at the controls, and the large navigation screen showed a ship slowing before them. She tapped the comm. "Let's see if short-range works still. This is Captain Licessien of the *Solace Star*. Please identify yourself," Eislie said on the standard frequencies.

The screen came alive, and Eislie recognized a familiar face. *Preston?*

"This is Captain Elis of the *Kitsale Aura*. Do you need assistance?" they all heard over the comm.

Eislie briefly glanced over, hearing the remaining crew rushing onto the flight control as the man continued. "Captain, there have been reports of pirates in this sector. You have to be careful who to trust."

Eislie looked around at her crew. Derrit and Issa were already strapping in, and Feren was already spooling the engines to make a fast escape. Eislie kept her calm.

"Captain, Elis, is it? We've met before, but I can't seem to set the place. However, it is good that you were, uh, nearby," she then winked.

Preston understood her gesture and nodded slightly, understanding that she knew he was following the *Solace Star*. "I believe we have met, captain. I think it was some time ago. But I believe you were on a different ship."

Eislie nodded, "I was. I'm here as acting captain until the replacement arrives. I hope to return to my other vessel shortly."

She looked toward Feren and heard Preston ask, "We've detected you recently in hyperspace. Was there an issue with your engines?"

Eislie sat tall. "There were some unauthorized repairs to our engine control and comm systems on one of our previous stops. We've just discovered them."

Preston looked concerned as Eislie nodded slowly and shallowly. He could see the concern in her stare. "Captain, could you provide a list of the affected systems?"

Eislie tapped away on her keypad, prompting Feren to ask what she was doing. Eislie continued, "We have repaired the drive systems, but our comm is short-range only. Would you mind sending a message to Roscin Station and Yata control for us? Hopefully, they will have the repair parts when we arrive."

The captain of the *Kitsale Aura* looked at the list, and the note Eislie also wrote, "Tell Jace that we found a logger on the comm and engines. He should check the ship."

Preston nodded, "It was lucky that you were able to discover the damage, captain. We can pass your message along. Did you need accompaniment to the station? It would only be a little out of our way."

Eislie smiled, "We'll be fine. Thank you for the offer, captain. We're only seven standard hours away from Roscin. We should be fine. If you could pass that list along, hopefully, we can have our ship back to full working order after we arrive."

Preston nodded, "We will captain, and fair winds."

Eislie smiled, holding back a giggle as the screen went blank. She turned, "Feren, let's get out of here. Issa, you find anything?"

Issa unbuckled his harness. "I was just cutting through the housing of that damn thing. Whoever made it wanted to make sure it survived an explosion."

Eislie nodded, "Get it open. Find out what you can. Derrit, you help him." She looked to Feren, "Let's go."

The *Solace Star* disappeared from the screen of the *Kitsale*, causing one of the crew to say, "Our queen will not be pleased that we did not take that vessel."

Captain Elis responded sternly to the crewman's statement, "I have met Captain Licessien. Our queen currently has an accord with both captains of the *Wolfhammer*."

"That is not the *Wolfhammer*; that is an unknown ship. We could have looted and taken the cargo for ourselves," the man answered.

Preston stood, then walked toward the man. His gait and stance no longer one of patience. He moved to access the comm and sent a message to the station and Yata control, as Eislie had requested. After he was finished, Preston switched to the frequency the *Wolfhammer* used for secure communications and sent the message Eislie wrote. His actions were quick, and less than a minute before, he turned to address the crewman who had questioned him. The man scoffed, "I'm surprised you didn't use your implant." Preston approached the man and paused as the large screen suddenly showed an image of the pirate queen.

"My queen, I take it you've read the message," Preston said.

The queen nodded, then saw the anger now showing on Preston's face.

"Is there an issue, Preston?" she asked.

Preston nodded, "I suspect, even with their prudence, someone that we have not discovered has been watching them. I sent a secure message to the other captain of the *Wolfhammer*. Hopefully, he will understand and act accordingly."

The Pirate Queen nodded, "I do not doubt that he will. You were right not to use your implant. If their comms are compromised, they would know the connection frequency key."

"I suspected that might be the case. However, some are questioning my decision to allow them to leave. What are your orders?" Preston then asked.

The queen raised her eyes. "They are not an enemy. I happen to know that the cargo they are carrying is to help many. I would not deny that of the people. Continue to follow the *Solace Star* and keep me informed. I will have our contacts at the station ready with the repair parts for their vessel."

"Yes, my queen," Preston replied before the screen went blank. Preston turned to the man. "Question my actions again, and you will find what it is like to float freely in space."

The man nodded. Preston ordered the ship to follow the *Solace Star*, and they disappeared quickly into the darkness.

* * *

Jace's hand hesitated as he went to press the comm. His mind ran through the possibility that someone had bugged the comms on the *Solace Star*. The *Wolfhammer* was a different matter. Jace had already checked the comm system, but discovering the data logging system outside the ship was another matter.

He tapped the control to the comm and said, "Yata control, this is the *Wolfhammer* checking in. We've made orbit and just need a landing assignment." He paused, then smiled, saying, "I swear it takes longer to get a parking space around here sometimes."

Shasji leaned forward. "Slacs got to my ship."

Jace snickered, "Technically, it was Garrett's ship. They got to his ship first."

The new captain turned slowly to look at Jace, making him side his eye and laugh. Shasji motioned to him in an animated gesture as to why he was.

Jace turned to look at her. "Eis looks at me like that sometimes when I say something strange. Usually, when I'm trying to make a point."

Shasji said, "Maybe it's what you're saying."

Jace snickered again. "Technically, I'm right. It's not your ship yet. Eis has to bring it back, and it's only if Garrett's not cured." Jace could see the happiness draining from her face, making him say, "We're working on getting you a ship. Take the *Solace Star* out a few times and see what you think. You might not like being captain."

Shasji thought for a moment. "Do you like being captain?"

Jace turned, facing forward, and nodded, "Yep, every day. I wouldn't change my decision."

Shasji leaned back while waiting for the dock control to respond, "Not like you have a crew. Eislie is a captain, too."

Jace nodded, "Yep, it's easier for us. We both know what has to be done. Honestly, I don't know how we work together. Weirdly, it's like we can read each other's actions."

The computer interrupted, "Captain, for the *Takloh*, they worked similarly. It had to do with the interactions of the mental and biofields present. I suspect that it is the same with you and Captain Licessien."

Jace raised his brow and a mischievous glint in his eyes. "Joined at the hip, among other things, huh, Ed?"

Shasji laughed loudly. "You know she'd space you for saying stuff like that."

Jace held back a laugh, and when he said, "Nah, she'd miss me too much." Shasji started laughing loudly, the boisterousness almost overshadowing the comm as the Yata control responded.

"*Wolfhammer*, you are cleared to land. Dock seventeen, stall nine. All non-Yata crew are instructed to process through secure immigration. Required medical checks are mandated for all Yata residents upon arrival as well."

"That's new. I wonder what happened?" Jace asked.

Shasji looked down. "Most level three planets forgo immigration evaluations. Something must be up."

It took several minutes for them to dock the ship. They were immediately met by medical and immigration staff and asked many questions, mainly about the reason for their visit and how long they planned to stay. As Jace was pulled into one section, they put him through an examination like when he arrived at Yata Beta months ago.

The same bright green light shined on him, making Jace rush to cover his eyes. When he recovered, he looked through the window and recognized the operator.

"Hey, weren't you doing this when I was here last time?" Jace said jokingly.

The woman at the controls looked closer at him and shook her head. "Oh, no, it's you again. You know your partner was here a week or so ago. The last time you were here, there was a lot of trouble."

The woman turned to the operator beside her, "It's that Terran from when the Karazon were here.

The other woman leaned over, "Oh, him. I remember him. Maybe try not to cause as much trouble this time."

Jace proudly joked, "I promise nothing."

He watched them laugh before a more somber expression filled her face. "We're doing this because of the black flower exposure. We have many non-Yata coming to the planet for treatment."

Jace unfortunately understood and said, "I'm sorry."

The operator smiled, "Why? You helped many people. We'll get you checked out and on your way. Who is your listed contact?"

Jace gave Miriz's information and asked that Shasji be processed quickly, only to be told, "She is a non-Yata. She must be processed. We cannot rush that, sorry."

Jace nodded, "I'll wait for her then. It's her first time here not on a ship, and I don't want her getting lost." Jace gave a wink. Another flash of green light hit him, causing him to rush to cover his eyes again, "Dammit."

"What's wrong? Are you alright?" the operator asked.

Jace shook his head, "I'm fine. I just realized I left my visors back on Earth. You don't happen to have any more, do you?"

The operator laughed, "We'll provide them after you are processed. It should only be a few minutes longer."

Jace nodded, "Thank you. Oh, and could I get some for my crew? I have a feeling she'll be needing them as well."

Chapter 15:
You Can Never Get a Taxi

Jace waited for Shasji to finish processing. He could hear her complaining that she didn't have that thorough of a medical scan when she joined the Alliance fleet. He had already opened the package containing the protective visors, his mind remembering that he and Eislie hated wearing them all the time while the sun was up.

Shasji stood by the doorway, and when it opened, Jace walked through, placing a visor over his eyes. He laughed, hearing Shasji complain, "Ow, this place is burning my eyes out." He handed her a visor, which she quickly placed over her face. "I was so mad with what they put me through. I forgot what you told me about the starlight here."

Jace nodded, "They told me why they have those procedures in place now. I guess that it's temporary. They'd had a lot of non-Yata coming here to be cured from that training toxin the Karazon use."

Shasji's tone softened, "I guess it's been pretty bad."

Jace agreed, then looked around. "Well, I did call Miriz earlier. There was supposed to be someone here to meet us." Jace tapped his wrist comm. "Ed, any activity on the ship?"

"No captain, just the standard maintenance and lockdown crew patrolling."

"You alert me if anyone tries getting onboard or by the ship, okay?" Jace said.

"Acknowledged, Captain. Am I authorized to dissuade any attempts?"

Jace thought for a moment. "Yes. Just try not to hurt anyone."

"Acknowledged, Captain. I will try to keep damage minimal."

Shasji said, "I would have told him to trash the place."

Jace nodded, "We sort of need the ship to get off the planet. It wouldn't make sense to have it locked down...." Jace paused, remembering the last time they were on Yata, "again. I'm a bit concerned. I called Miriz well before you finished processing. I told her about the monitoring device as well, and she said Kelor was supposed to meet us since Paaz is still on leave." Jace looked around. "We had permission last time to land near her home. Something doesn't seem right."

Shasji started to take a defensive stance, "You think we're in trouble?"

Jace tapped his comm. "Ed, has the ship been locked down at all?"

"No, captain. Should I prevent that from happening?"

"Good, and yes. Something seems off. I can't place it yet," Jace said.

The computer acknowledged the order, and Jace tapped his comm again. As their friend answered, he asked, "Miriz, it's Jace. Wasn't Kelor supposed to meet us?"

Miriz nodded, "Yes, he is. Isn't he there?"

Jace shook his head. "And last time we could park near your place."

Miriz sighed, "It's temporary; too many off-world people were coming in for treatment. We could handle them, but it was taking resources from our people."

"And Kelor is new, I understand," Jace said.

"He's a good man. I trust him. But, he should be there."

There were fewer people than Jace remembered around the processing facility than the last time he was there. "Miriz, were you able to make the stuff we asked about?"

Miriz thought momentarily, wondering why Jace didn't just say what he meant. But she understood that perhaps he was concerned about the project and who might be listening.

"Yes, we have the raw materials. But we have just started the machining. Why? Is there something else you need?" Miriz told him.

Staring at his comm, he said, "I wanted to make sure we could work someplace other than the main dock. You know, take my time on fitting the ship."

Miriz understood his concern. "You'll be able to after a few days.

Jace looked around as the hair on the back of his neck started bristling. And he heard Shasji say, "We know where her place is. We can get a ride."

"No! I do not want you unsupervised. With what you found, I don't want anyone we don't trust taking you somewhere," Miriz insisted. She then tapped away on her comm. Jace could see the disappointment on Miriz's face as she said, "Kelor hasn't responded to my call."

Jace nodded, "We can hang out here until Kelor shows up. Besides, something here doesn't seem right."

* * *

The room was dark. What looked like an operating table was dotted with several blood stains illuminated from above. Two figures were in another room, removing the bloodied clothes they had been wearing.

"Damn hack job. Wish we had time to do a full implant on that Yata," one of them said before the other started rinsing off his hands.

"It doesn't matter as long as it can't be detected." He turned to look through another window. "Nassar is finishing patching him up now."

The other man looked to the table where what looked like an ear was in a small bowl. "I wish we had time to do a full neural connection. Full vision and audio would have been nice. Not to mention, we could have put in an override."

"Jelk, you know that would have taken hours. We had two at most. This was the only way we could do this."

Jelk turned to the other man, "Besides, it took longer than expected to make the bio copy of his ear with the monitor in it." He looked to the table to see the comm of man flicker. "Someone's trying to reach him."

The other man opened the door with the window. "Nassar, how much longer? Looks like someone's trying his comm."

Nassar looked down. "Breng, I'm not one of your servants. You want this done, right? It'll be a couple of minutes. We still have to put him back where we got him. Or do you want him to suspect he was taken?"

Breng looked around. "Just hurry. If they lock onto his comm, we're screwed."

They patched up the man and put him into the back of a vehicle. Jelk took the man's identification and looked at it briefly before laughing. "This guy's name is Kelor Belor. Who names someone that?"

"Don't be a fool, Jelk. Kelor was one of Yata's most influential generals." He snickered. "The guy just happens to have a last name that rhymes." He turned to look in the back of the vehicle where the other was finishing dressing Kelor. "Make sure he has everything we brought him in with. We don't want him suspecting something happened."

The man placed everything back into Kelor's pockets and ensured he was fully dressed. Jelk did one last inspection of the reconnected ear and checked the connected comm. "Comm is linked. We have video." But as he inspected the small screen, he brushed away some of Kelor's hair covering his ear.

"This is not going to be detailed. I hope our employer doesn't mind that," Jelk said, looking over his shoulder at Breng.

"We need to get him back in the conveyance. The two he's supposed to pick up should be done processing by now," Breng said, looking at Nassar as he drove.

It was only a minute before they arrived at the spot where they had taken Kelor from. The official vehicle of the representative displayed along the side. They stopped and pulled Kelor from the back, the unconscious man's arm hitting the side of the vehicle hard. Still, he didn't move.

"That neural sedative works wonders," Jelk said, looking at Nassar.

Nassar had genuine pride when he replied, "I use it most of the time. The person wakes up feeling like they just took a nap. He won't remember a thing."

As they placed Kelor into the driver's seat, Nassar turned his head to inspect the new ear. "Skin looks good. I can't even see where we took it off."

Breng huffed, "As long as it's not noticed. Let's hope they don't do a low-level bio-scan on his head anytime soon. We won't get any information. That vid setup is too easy to find."

They made sure Kelor was seated before Nassar injected the antidote into Kelor's nose. "We have a semi-cycle, maybe less. Let's get out of here."

The men rushed back into their vehicle and drove away. The dust was not even settling as Kelor opened his eyes and drowsily said, "Wha... what time is it?"

He looked at his comm and could see the messages from his employer. Most of them asked if he was alright. Kelor looked around, his sense of duty now kicking in. "Slac, I fell asleep. I wonder why my comm didn't wake me up?" He peered down to see the shadow of the surrounding brush covering the vehicle. As he drove away, he said, "I knew this was too good a place to rest. I'll probably get reeked out by the boss when I return."

As Kelor arrived at the planetary processing center he reached up to touch his right ear. He massaged it, feeling a numbness. "Must have slept on it wrong." He stopped and exited before contacting Miriz.

"Representative Elysse, I apologize for being late," Kelor said, but his eyes were still heavy.

"Everything alright, Kelor?" Miriz asked. She seemed concerned.

Kelor nodded, "I apologize. I pulled off to one of the side roads to wait. The processing center told me that they were running behind. I, uh, must have dozed off."

Miriz initially seemed annoyed but smiled, "Tell that to Captain Tucker. I'm sure he will be amused to hear that. They are waiting inside for you. Please bring them straight here."

Kelor nodded, "At once, representative."

He entered the waiting room, and Jace looked up. Miriz had already sent him a picture of the man, so Jace knew who he was. As Jace walked up to him, Kelor apologized for not arriving until now.

"That's alright. I've been late a few times, too," Jace said, looking over at Shasji as she stood. "Come on, let's get out of here."

Jace was talking with Miriz. She told him Eislie had decided to take the shipment to Roscin station to keep the contract. She also informed him that replacement parts for the comm were already waiting for the arrival of the *Solace Star*.

"You know, even I don't have that kind of influence on the station. I don't know who she talked to over there," Miriz said. "It might have been that freighter that stopped to check things out. According to the logs, the *Kitsale Aura* must have some important people on board. Whoever they were, they know how to bypass purchasing snarls."

Jace seemed concerned. "Who was the captain?"

Miriz tapped away. "This man captains the *Kitsale Aura*." An image of the captain appeared on the screen, and Jace knew precisely who it was.

Preston? Did you go legit? Or is that the ship you are following us with?

Miriz could see Jace's reaction and asked if he knew the man.

Jace nodded, "I think we met him a couple of times. It was good luck that he was nearby. There was a lot of highly sought-after stuff on that ship."

Miriz looked closely at the image. "Should I have him investigated?"

Jace shook his head, "No, I have his info. We'll send him a thank you once the *Solace Star* is at the station." Jace looked at his comm. "How far has the fabrication gotten?"

Miriz sighed, "You asked that only an hour ago."

"Sorry, you're right. I did. It was a long flight. I'm a little tired," Jace said. "The walk outside the ship took a lot out of me for some reason."

Miriz leaned in. "Do you need medical when you get here?"

Jace shook his head. "Nah, they would have caught that when we arrived. I think it's more about what I found earlier."

Miriz nodded, "You inspected the ship when you arrived, didn't you?"

Jace nodded, "Did a good walk around, nothing out of the ordinary."

Jace leaned back, holding his comm up. "Miriz, we were at the ship most of the time. And headed here right after we…" Jace paused, looking at Shasji, "got her captain's certification. We were gone for a couple of hours. Shit, they must have put it on then."

Miriz agreed. "You can thoroughly inspect when the ship is here. That won't be for a few days. I heard back from the center, and they are holding all ships for three days even if the crew is healthy."

Jace looked into his comm. "Any incidences of port crews flying off or dusted back by any ships?"

Miriz looked at him inquisitively. "No, why?"

Jace smiled. "Then they didn't go near our ship."

Miriz thought momentarily. "You didn't order that computer of yours to dust off any crews trying to get in, did you?"

Jace nodded slowly, smiling.

"Goddess, protect them. Jace, all ships are to be shut down while in dock. You know that," Miriz argued.

Jace nodded, "And it is. Ed's crew, he just can't leave the ship."

Miriz looked at him in silence before yelling, "Kelor, how long till you arrive?"

"Approximately ten semi-cycles, Representative," Kelor answered.

111

"Jace, we will discuss your ship and its AI when you arrive." Miriz tried sounding menacing.

Jace smiled, "Oh, I'm sure we will. But I promise I'll be just as stubborn, if not more than Eis has been, regarding Ed."

Miriz smiled, "I'm sure you will. I hope he doesn't do anything."

"Well, Ed's smart. And it's not a secret we reinstalled him. I'm sure the people who know about it will be much more careful when trying to get into our ship." He sighed, "We'll see you in about ten."

Miriz closed the comm, and Jace did the same. He leaned his head back, his eyes closed. The ride again became quiet.

Shasji started looking through a booklet she picked up while they were waiting. She had been to a few worlds, including Yata, but she hadn't spent much time on the planet as a guest. Most of it was in the loading facility of Miriz's company. She looked up to see Kelor scratching his ear and gently elbowed Jace.

She looked at the man, asking, "You, okay?"

Kelor looked back. "Yeah, my ear's a little numb."

Jace seemed to think briefly, "You know you never told us why you were late."

Kelor looked embarrassed, "Well, I knew you were going to be a while until they processed you in, so I parked near the main area nearby."

A smugness seemed to fill Jace's smile, "Aaaaand?"

Kelor smiled as he hung his head in defeat, "It was nice out, so I opened the window and waited…"

Jace nodded, "I'm guessing with your eyes closed?"

Kelor nodded and smiled. "Yes."

Jace laughed, "Well, I can't blame you. It is nice out today." He leaned forward. "And I know how much work Miriz has you doing recently. So, I promise I won't make too much fun of you for taking a little siesta."

Jace leaned back, his eyes closed. The ride of the vehicle was calm and easy. For the moment, the rest of the ride would be full of welcomed silence.

Chapter 16:
Dinner with a Friend

The chair in Jace's room creaked as he sat. Shasji had gone to her room after listening to Miriz and Jace arguing about the actions he had ordered Ed to take if necessary. He had taken a walk to cool down. The discussion about their ship's computer was not something Jace took lightly. The diversion took him a while before he reached his room. He tapped his comm, looking for any messages from the computer or Eislie, but saw nothing. Miriz said she would update him when there was a response from the station.

Jace stood silent as he looked out the window. The large deck surrounding the building was still fresh in his memories from only months ago. Not all of them were pleasant. He opened the door and rushed to cover his eyes as the light stung his senses.

"Dammit, I keep forgetting."

He turned to grab the visor, placing it over his face before walking outside. The dimming light told him what time it was. The deck had a great view of the horizon, and he and Eislie enjoyed the time they spent there watching the stars rise over it.

Jace watched the shadows grow long, and the first stars started to show. His quiet meditation was interrupted when she heard, "I figured you would be out here." He looked over to see Miriz walking toward him.

Jace chuckled, "You coming for another round of arguing?"

Miriz smiled before gently tapping him on the arm. "Eis was just as bad as you when it came to that computer of yours."

Jace smiled. He already knew what Eislie thought about their friend, and Jace was the same. Ed could live as he wanted.

Miriz leaned on the deck's railing. "You know they decommissioned almost all AIs because of their tendency not to obey their masters."

Jace chuckled, "Ed's not a slave. He's curious, smart, determined." He leaned on the railing beside her. "He's also a friend and one of the best people I could have as crew. Well, except for Eis, of course."

Miriz chuckled, "I'm sure she'd be happy to hear that."

There was silence for some time as the darkness grew around them, enough for Jace to be able to remove his visor. He heard Miriz sigh before she said, "It's too bad you need that to walk around in the daytime. It lets people know you are not Yata. And most likely a starborn."

"And what's wrong with that?" Jace coldly asked.

Miriz sighed again, her words full of disappointment, "To me and most Yata, nothing. But those looking for a fight, that's a different matter."

There was again silence between them for a short time before Jace spoke. "I can understand the processing taking time, but the ships being held, that's something I've been wondering about." He was about to say something when his comm made a sound. Jace looked at the message and what Eislie had sent. But as Jace was about to tell Miriz, she never gave him the chance.

"That's Eis telling you they found monitoring devices all over the ship, right?"

Jace looked at her questioningly.

Miriz hung her head down. "I heard back from the crew I have on the station already. They found several in JESC's office."

Jace stood, "Well, someone wants to know what we're up to."

"The delay wasn't implemented until you filed a flight plan here."

Jace smiled. "Sounds like they wanted time. You know to take the one's they put on the ship. At least to me." He paused. "Good thing we put in the quantum monitoring systems in both our ship and the offices as well."

Miriz nodded, "They also found something else." Her statement piqued Jace's curiosity. But when she said, "There was evidence of quantum dampening," Jace became very concerned.

"You mean they have a way to stop quantum recording?" Jace asked.

"I checked with my contacts in the council," Miriz said, "and had a visit by the grand Matron and her guard soon after that."

"When did that happen?" Jace asked.

Miriz turned to him. "Right after I spoke with you. My team called me, telling me what they found. I wanted to see who might use such equipment." She leaned on the railing again. "The Matron was concerned about me prying about such sensitive devices."

Jace looked concerned. "Everything's fine. We didn't even know that technology existed. And she didn't blame me for looking. She was concerned about why I was. When I told her, she offered to have your ship and all of my ships scanned."

"That's not very comforting," Jace said.

"Miriz shifted, "You're right, it's not. Quantum recording was supposed to be a safeguard. But apparently, it can be circumvented."

"Well, shit. Any other good news you want to tell me?" Jace joked.

"All quantum suppressors have a signature."

Jace nodded, "Let me guess. It's Alliance."

Miriz shook her head, "It had a signature known to be used by the Consortium. Specifically, the Hurmann."

It was later when Jace entered the dining room of Miriz's home. Shasji was already seated, waiting for him to arrive. She and Miriz were talking When Jace overheard Miriz say, "Jace told me you're a fan of Queeks Maco. They'll be at Roscin station shortly."

Shasji seemed to sit straight before she answered, "I was hoping to get to see them while they were here, but we weren't fast enough."

Jace chuckled as he sat and looked up to see Shasji looking at him with a gleam of contempt. He knew Queeks was on Yata but didn't want to chance testing the new tunnel coils without Eislie. He was going to say something, but seeing Miriz looking polite, he decided to stay silent.

Miriz looked at Jace, "You know, the last time you were here, I don't think you and Eis were ever out of your room."

Shasji smiled, seeing Jace almost flustered, but she laughed, hearing him say, "Sure we were. I did take a day or two to fix the ship."

There was a moment before Miriz giggled, "Not that I was out of my room much either." She then called over the cook, asking, "How long till everything is ready?"

"A few minutes. As requested, we did not prepare the catlan tonight," the cook answered.

Jace jokingly pouted, "No catlan?"

The cook turned to look at him. "The representative asked for vegetable fare for your arrival."

Miriz snickered, "Please do not consider this an attempt for me to persuade you into somewhat of a different lifestyle. I prefer vegetation as a more sustainable food." She paused. "Besides, Eis told me you eat just about anything."

Jace nodded, "Yeah, I'll eat anything. Except maybe those Alliance starch bars."

Miriz looked over to see the contorted disgust on Shasji's face and her shaking her head. Miriz responded, "Well, I'm sure this will be far better than those. Although I've never tried one of those starch bars before."

Jace smiled. "I'll give you a case." He leaned toward her. "I'd even pay you to try them."

Miriz raised her brow. "They're that bad?" she watched as Shasji silently gave an exaggerated nod, causing Miriz to laugh. *I'll have to try them at least once.*

The food arrived, and Jace told some stories about the drive modifications. And Miriz had hoped Jace would tell her more about the flights within the filaments. Miriz was fascinated and impressed when Eislie told her they had figured out a way to allow the ship to travel without anyone in contact with the reactor. However, when she asked Jace how the plating would work, he changed the subject.

"You said you had the office on the station scanned and found those listening devices, right?"

Miriz nodded, "Yes, there were over thirty. Someone definitely wanted to know what conversations were going on there. Why do you ask?"

Jace looked around. "And how many did you find here?"

Miriz looked concerned. "None, I. . . . never checked."

Jace smiled. "I didn't mean to be insulting, but if we found them in the office, then maybe…"

"I have not had many visitors, but there have been a few. Perhaps my security system would have recorded them, and…." Miriz looked around, remembering that whoever installed the other recording devices also probably used a quantum dampener. "Oh, Jace, I'm sorry, I never thought to check."

"It's okay. I don't think there are any here. Otherwise, they'd have the recipe for this dish. This is awesome. It's actually fresh vegetables. I may have to convince Eis to convert some of the hold to a garden."

Miriz laughed, "Well, she does like being outdoors more since you two have been together."

Jace smiled.

As the three sat around the table, Miriz told stories about her and Eislie when they were younger. She also told Jace about her company and that with the Sotiral systems, she had to move away from ship and storage parts.

"The suits now comprise almost eighty-five percent of our total production," Miriz told him. "And the Yata government continues to purchase more for their use. I can't believe you thought about giving the technology away."

Jace nodded, "Making money wasn't our main goal. Eis wanted to protect people. We've both seen what happens to others in a spide radiation leak." Jace seemed to pull back. "We've both seen it too many times. But truthfully, I'm happy you're doing well from it."

"We're all doing well from it. Remember, this is a partnership. Your company is making most of the profits." Miriz turned to Shasji. "Speaking of which, have you found a ship for your new captain?"

Shasji sat straight again, realizing that Miriz was staring at her.

Jace shook his head. "Finding a decent ship at a good price has been hard. As soon as they find out it's us, they jack up the price."

Miriz sat tall, "I know of some fairly new vessels that might be for sale here on Yata. A few of my former competitors have decided to liquidate some assets. When they return from their missions, of course."

Jace suddenly felt a burden of responsibility. *Did we put people out of business?* There was a moment before he asked, "Anything larger than the *Solace Star*?"

He watched Miriz nod. "I know of at least four Kel class vessels. You could fit three of the sloops in its cargo area. I could negotiate a deal for you, if you like, for a fee."

Jace ignored Miriz's more sensual intonation and looked over to see Shasji almost hopping out of her seat. "Maybe we should talk about it, maybe see them first."

He watched Shasji slump in her chair, her eyes staring with disbelief at him. Her actions made Miriz burst out in laughter. "You are too eager to take on as captain, my dear. I have spoken with Eislie about it already, and she would like you to take on the *Solace Star* for a while. It's a proven vessel. Any new one would have to be broken in."

Shasji now turned to give the same look toward their host.

Miriz smiled, then said, "I think you would need to break in a new crew. I don't recommend that for a new captain. Besides, the *Solace Star* is a good ship."

Shasji seemed disappointed and started to sulk. Jace saw that and responded, "Shasji, I think you could handle the large ship and a new crew. I don't want you burned out doing it."

Shasji looked at him. "Now I know why Eis likes you. You see the good in things and know how bad they can be if you let them," Miriz said.

There was silence as they finished dessert, and Miriz brought up what Eislie had told her about the missing part of the shipment. "Almost a tenth of the cargo is missing. About thirty containers are empty. Someone stole them while in storage."

Miriz looked at her glass, swirling her aperitif, "I don't have any ships available to take the new suits we made. I have most of the orders filled, but the missing items do hurt our reputation."

Jace looked at the now quiet Shasji and seemed to think, "Didn't you say that Queeks was going to be at Roscin in a few days?"

Miriz nodded.

"You know, we can take about thirty-five of those containers in the hold of the *Wolfhammer*. And since the fabrication will take a few weeks, we can take them over, and Shasji can meet up with her crew. That way, Eis and I can return here and do the modifications without rushing."

Shasji seemed to vibrate in her chair. "We could deliver the stuff and, maybe, see Queeks?"

"It would help with my business reputation." Miriz smiled gently, pulling the cover she used to protect her white dress, the cloth tugging open the front of her blouse just a little. She then stood and walked over to Jace, leaning down gently and placing her arms around his shoulders. She pressed against him slightly. "I would be very grateful."

She then gently rested her chin on Jace's shoulder, moving closer only for them to hear the alert of a comm.

Jace didn't react right away but, after a few alerts, said, "It's either yours or mine." He moved his comm closer, "Oh look, it's mine." He tapped it to see Eislie looking happy to see him, "Hey! Miriz, tell you about the shipment yet?"

Jace could see Eislie turn toward Miriz, resting her chin on Jace's shoulder. "Hi, Miriz."

When Miriz said, "I swear to the goddess she is watching you."

Jace burst out in laughter. When he calmed, he said, "Eis, she did tell us about the missing shipment, I've just agreed to bring over what is missing. And maybe Shasji can see Queeks. Can you get tickets still?"

Eislie turned, "Yeah, they're not cheap. But there are still some available."

Jace nodded, "Get enough for everyone." He turned to Miriz. "Maybe we should get things loaded up, dropped off, and come back before you know it."

Chapter 17:
Making Plans

"Praised are the superior," echoed in the chamber of the Hurmann council as they closed the doors.

Malik stood, the contempt of the formalities of his station hidden behind his false stoic stance. The Arbiter motioned for all to be seated, filling the large room with the sounds of sliding fabric, wood, and metal creaking.

"All praise the Hurmann. May our rule guide us to the gates." Malik sighed as he heard for an uncounted time the words of their faith and was reminded by his disgust at how it was used to rule all, even the Hurmann.

The slaver sat tall, his garments displaying several symbols, all marks of his station. Unlike many Hurmann, he was of one of the top ruling families known as the Tas. Malik swiveled his head, looking around to the others nearby, watching several bowing their heads as a greeting and acknowledgment of his station. Malik accepted their actions, even if he had no desire to be there. But to show his loyalty to the Hurmann and their world, Alarn, it was a sacrifice he needed to make. The meeting was the quarterly conclave, and this was the last before the new year. There were things to do, celebrations to agree on, and, of course, a need to confirm his own celebration of the ruling families at the festival of Kaial. Malik was there to invite all worthy to the occasion.

The slaver slumped in his seat, almost dozing off as the formalities dragged on. The only events that kept him from doing so were when the

Arbiter mentioned the current resource counts, including the slaves taken and traded.

"There is also the matter of the terrorists known as Queeks Maco, the so-called reformers of our world who are attempting to turn many against us. They are currently en route to Roscin station in Alliance territory. House Luxin, you were given the task of silencing them. What is your progress?"

A woman stood. "Arbiter, I am Jelai, consort of Garnel of Luxin. I speak for house Luxin at this time."

The Arbiter looked cautiously. "Where is your patriarch?"

The woman bowed. "He is off-world."

The room erupted with loud talking before the Arbiter called for order, saying, "It is tradition to attend each conclave by all ruling patriarchs. What excuse do you offer for his absence?"

Malik watched as the woman took a breath, hearing her say, "He was personally seeing to the apprehension or destruction of the terrorists against Hurmann edicts. We last heard from them in the Ryus Four system."

Ryus Four? And those terrorists are still alive? Malik thought, causing the side of his mouth to twitch upward as he resisted a smile. *If their patriarch has fallen, I may be able to work with that.*

The conclave went on for hours, Malik's mind returning to the planning he still had to do for the party and the other matter he had with the Slasta. He had yet to hear anything from his hired assassins on the capture of *Wolfhammer* or its captains. He began to daydream about breaking them and taking the knowledge of the filaments that Bosh had disclosed. But his mind returned to the dull reality as he heard his name.

"Malik of House Unber. We request you grace us with your petition," the Arbiter said. Malik could almost see a smile on the man's mouth, knowing he had broken Malik from his daydream.

Malik stood, "Praised are the superior." There was a murmur of the exact words throughout the auditorium. The slaver looked around, "First, I give thanks to all who have given and maintained our world."

Many around him nodded again, giving a single clap to set their intentions in agreement. Malik hated the pomp and regality of the Hurmann. He had hoped to one day take the Arbiter's house and claim it for himself. And his mind wandered to possibly using the Slasta to that effect after they had procured the two starborn and the spide. Malik's face became stone-like before he spoke.

"My house has claimed as the third, above House Luxin. We have exceeded the performance and resources from the last meeting. And with the absence of their patriarch, I make my appeal to claim of their station."

There was mumbling and the sound of tapping on screens as all members of the Hurmann looked to confirm his boast. Malik waited as they retrieved the data. And his smile grew seeing many bowing to acknowledge his validity. Malik watched as Jelai glared at him.

"I have made a claim. However, I will abide to a delay if others of the Hurmann wish it." The slaver smiled, knowing well the game he was playing. He showed sympathy for a possible vacuum in power. And that could allow him to gain allies to further his station within the Tas itself.

There was subtle rambling all around before the Arbiter responded. "House Luxin, you have been challenged. However, the initiate has offered a stay due to your circumstances. Under our laws, you may challenge or defer."

Malik turned; his expression emotionless toward the woman speaking for Luxin. He could see the terror and anger growing behind her stare. Malik also knew that if he showed aggression, the entire Hurmann might vote against him. He waited until she responded.

"Uh, House Luxin asks to defer until the return of our patriarch. Would that be acceptable to House Unber?"

The room was silent as Malik felt the power he now held. He took a relaxed breath before saying, "Of course. As patriarch of Unber, I will allow you to defer for one month. After that time, I will renew my claim and be willing to accept Luxin under my patronage."

Malik watched as the woman's hands balled into fists, her eyes hinting at panic before she responded. "Uh, we accept the deferment."

"House Luxin, you have deferred, witnessed by this council and the Hurmann," the Arbiter said before turning to look at Malik. "Malik Terine of House Unber, do you accept?"

Malik bowed. "I do, Arbiter. I will hold to the bylaws for the time limit I have given."

The Arbiter struck the stone hammer against its anvil, creating a sharp clack echoing against the ornate walls. "As a witness, the claim is deferred for one month. House Luxin, you may not challenge the claim once it is renewed."

The duties of the Hurmann continued and were drawing to an end when the Arbiter called for additional business. Malik stood, "I have business to discuss." His voice cut off another nearby. The Arbiter acknowledged him.

"House Unber, state your business."

Malik looked around. "Kaial is upon us. A new year is dawning. In three weeks, I wish to invite all members of the Tas and any member of the Hurmann who are worthy."

There were several cheers around him as a murmur filled the conversations. He watched the smile across the Arbiter's face and bowed, his face giving a smile in return.

"Kaial, a celebration of a new time. As per tradition, all Tas should be in attendance. Members of the Hurmann, not of the Tas, will respond to me, and I will coordinate with House Unber on their application to attend."

The room erupted in talking and laughter as his announcement was repeated. Malik sat, knowing that any others having business for this time would now have to wait until the next conclave.

Several days passed, and Malik was in his study; the preparation for the celebration was taking most of his time. He also had another matter to attend to. The Slasta were arriving later that day. He had reached out to Bosh, who said he would observe when they arrived. Malik had wondered when Bosh was coming since he had seen no sign of the former captain recently.

The head of Unber was frustrated. He needed more time for the preparations required for the festival. The Kaial was once a year and an opportunity to impress new alliances and deter old rivalries. The Arbiter had stopped by with the list of the known members of the Tas who were attending, all with requests on how to be received. The demands were merely a formality; Malik knew they were to test the strength of will of any Tas attempting to persuade other members. It was a game played for centuries, and even though it was one of frustration, it was one that the Head of Unber enjoyed.

"Humph, I can't believe this one. A path of golden should precede my steps as I walk around the room." Malik huffed, then groused in amusement. "I'll give you gold. I'll have one of my slaves piss before you, slac."

He continued to read each request and was interrupted when something hit his desk with a thud. The slaver looked up to see Fellen unconscious across the papers strewn across the desktop. He was about to demand an explanation when he spied the dark blue robes of the Slasta, blocking his view of the door. The silence filled with an audible sound as he swallowed hard before saying, "Uh, welcome. What do you want?"

The assassin in front looked to each side, and the others in dark blue walked silently around and outside the room. It was seconds before the man spoke.

"Malik Terine, I am Tyne of Clan Perig. I believe we have business."

The slaver looked around. For years, he never showed fear in subjugating others, but now Malik felt his bones shivering. Several seconds went by before he answered.

"You are correct." Malik stood, motioning for the man to sit. And as the man silently did so on the chair before the desk, Malik shoved his servant from the desktop onto the floor. He pointed to his trusted servant as the man hit the floor, "Don't worry about that. It'll clean itself up later. Did you receive the files I sent?"

Tyne nodded once.

The head of Unber looked around. "And you understand that I need them alive. They must be brought here, alive."

The assassin again nodded. However, after doing so, Tyne did not move or say anything, causing Malik to fill in the silence. "Is there something else?"

The assassin nodded. "You promised payment on our arrival."

Malik stood, "Ah, yes." The slaver snapped his fingers, but no one entered his office. He was ready to punish his servants when he realized that Slasta were guarding the door from outside. He looked at his unconscious servant and nodded.

"Of course, I would usually have my servants prepare the trade, but I see that you are looking for a more personal assurance." Malik turned, walking to the wall and touching the panel. A loud thunk was heard before it opened, and he removed a large, leather bag with the payment he promised.

"I will give you half now and half when they are brought to me," Malik said as he placed the bag on the desk.

His actions caused the eyes of the man sitting to slit in anger. "The agreement was for payment when we arrived."

Malik felt his throat tighten, seeing three sets of eyes of the Slasta now fixed on him. His instincts for survival kicked in, and Malik smiled, turning to pull another bag from the wall, "You are quite right, my friend; I did promise you full payment when you arrived." He slid the bags toward the man as two who flanked the assassin from earlier moved forward to collect them. But instead of allowing them to move, Malik held them to the desk.

The two looked to the man between them as he stood. Malik smiled, "Bring them to me alive. That is the deal. If not, I expect a refund."

"Insolence." One of the women said as she pulled out a bone blade, only to have the man in the center hold her wrist fast.

"That is acceptable. We have tracked those you are looking for to Yata Beta. We will have them soon."

Malik stood tall. "Forgive me, but if you have them next week, I ask you not to deliver them during the celebration. I do not wish any of my guests to know of this dealing."

Tyne raised his eyes. "And why is that?"

Malik smiled, "There are plans for your quarry I cannot divulge at this time. And I may require your services after."

As he finished speaking, the display on Malik's desk activated. A symbol appeared a single circle with a sword piercing it from above, before a man's voice scrambled and said, "Tyne of Perig, I have been monitoring our mutual friend's conversation. And I must insist that you abide by his request not to have others know of this transaction."

Bosh, are you insane? They could kill me, Malik thought.

The assassin turned to look at the screen, seeing the symbol. The voice filtered and masked, the assassin hinting at a smile. *This is someone who knows how to conduct covert business. Not this fool before me.* Tyne turned to stare at Malik, "If we find them, they will be brought to you alive." He looked to the two by his side, and they removed the pouches with their payment. Tyne gave a shallow bow. "We will try not to interrupt your festivities."

With little sound, most of the Slasta exited, and Malik felt his three hearts start to beat again. He turned to the screen to see the symbol from it disappear. The assassin smiled, seeing the slaver staring at the small display, and spoke, "We have a contract, Malik Terine. We will return with our quarry."

As the man exited, Malik leaned forward on his desk, his shoulders heavy, growling, "Bosh, you slac, if you pull something like that again, I will put you in the games myself."

There was no answer from the screen.

On the floor next to his master's desk, Fellen stirred, "Master, are you alright?"

Malik sat hard in his chair. "I am fine, no thanks to you."

Chapter 18:
Roscin Station

"Have them do a once-over on the hull. That Hurmann ship got a few good shots off before we disabled it," Ralla ordered the station's crew as he walked around the landing platform.

"Ah, Roscin station, it's good to be here." Ralla took a breath. "No better place to spread a message than a place of commerce."

The captain of the *Eiger* looked to see Eshea walking from the ship. He waited till she was closer before saying, "Trin did some good work. Those slacs only got a few shots off before he punctured their hull."

Eshea looked around. "You may want to keep it low profile, Ralla. The Hurmann have been leaving us alone until recently. You don't know if they have agents on the station."

Ralla huffed, "They'd be fools to risk that here. They'd cut off one of the only places that allowed them to trade with the Alliance and others. They wouldn't make a move to risk that." He turned to see the stare of concern as she looked out over the other platforms. He sighed, "Maybe you're right. Keep sharp when you go to see our friend about the masks."

Eshea looked at him. She had been following Ralla's orders since escaping. Queeks was a creation of hers to protect herself and Zarlin. She turned to her thoughts, remembering the time they met each other. Zarlin was a comfort slave for the non-Arlain captives. Eshea had been taken from her duties as a laborer after they discovered she could sing. Terlan of House Besal had become entranced hearing her voice while in the fields. She didn't know many songs, but Zarlin approached her after her punishment for not providing entertainment, that beating gave her a scar across her left eye and cheek. Zarlin spent time healing her that night, and since then, the two had become inseparable.

Eshea looked back at the ship. Zarlin had decided to remain on board to keep the illusion that Queeks needed her best people to tend to her while waiting for the concert. Eshea had already packed the broken VFM, the variable, fiber-matrix mask they used for Queeks image and was heading out to meet with their contact.

"I spoke with Yasa already. He has the parts to repair both masks. If we're lucky, he might be able to hash together a third," Eshea told Ralla.

"See if you can get the third. As much shill as it takes. I don't want to be in this situation again." He turned to look around. "I hope you'll be back quick. I heard the starborn we wanted to talk to arrived at the station. Trin confirmed it with our contact. I want to get them on board as soon as possible."

"What makes you so sure they'll help?" Eshea asked.

Ralla smiled, "They are kindred. I feel it in my bones. They've destroyed Duggor, pirates, Alliance ships, and all those suppressing others. No one causes damage like that on a whim. They'll help us."

Eshea smiled at him, "I better get going then. Don't want Queeks to miss her show time."

Ralla nodded, then turned to head back toward the ship. "Hey! Who's in charge here? I want to speak to someone about getting the ship washed."

Eshea walked past several people, some pointing to her, realizing she was part of Queeks Maco's crew. She smiled apologetically as she headed down the elevator to meet with Yasa.

* * *

Eshea kept her guard up as she exited the lift. She had only one of the masks they used on her. But still felt uneasy about not wearing the one she usually had around her neck. The latest encounter with the Hurmann cruiser was weighing on her thoughts as she entered the location for the shop to meet with Yasa to repair the mask. She stood outside the Artificer Elite shop, and she could see him helping a customer who had a box of parts for some device.

"I don't know what happened. It was supposed to be fixed," she heard. The man was tall and wore a hood, yelling at Yasa as he hit the side of the box.

The altercation went on for a minute or so before she heard Yasa respond, "This used to be a dirt reclaimer, I think. Honestly, you brought me a pile of junk. So, what do you want me to do with it?"

She heard the man complain, "Fix it."

Eshea watched as Yasa smiled back at the customer but couldn't see the other man's face. The hood he wore covered everything. She remembered that some traders would walk around the station like that. It kept those competing against them from knowing for a short time exactly who they were. She heard Yasa say, "You could buy a new one. It'd probably be cheaper. This is nothing more than a pile of spare parts."

Eshea watched the man flip his hood back in annoyance, the paste-white skin almost devoid of hair revealing who he was.

Nibik? God-damn mercenaries. They are one of the last people I need to get involved with today, Eshea thought. She then slid against the wall. *They freely go back to Arlain.*

Eshea became concerned, realizing that Yasa had become a genuine merchant, allowing all customers, regardless of affiliation, to do business with him. *Hopefully, you won't sell out your own people. I need this mask fixed, she* thought before hearing the Nibik growl, saying, "Fine, what would a new one cost?"

She remained in the shadows just outside the shop; she had to tell a man who approached her to slac off when he asked how much her services would be for the hour. The altercation got little to no acknowledgment from the people all around. She waited until the Nibik left before entering the repair shop. She could see his practiced smile as she walked up to the counter.

"How long have you been waiting outside? You could have come in and waited," Yasa said as Eshea stepped up to the counter.

"I saw you were busy and who it was," Eshea said as she looked around. "Tell me I didn't make a mistake coming here."

Yasa chuckled. "You didn't, But I could hear you tell that guy to slac off in here. You should learn to be more diplomatic."

Eshea continued to stare at him, an eerie stillness in her movements. Several moments passed before Yasa motioned to the window and said, "Let me lock the door. We'll take this in back." She turned to watch him as he locked the front door, turning the open display off. Eshea walked along as he motioned for her to follow. She was curious when he said, "Watch your step."

The room was dark as she entered. She could see Yasa move to the side in the dim light and paused where she was. As she lifted her foot, it felt suctioned to the floor as if there was something sticky. Then, her senses filled with the scent of something familiar, something she had encountered during her time as a slave that caused her concern.

She watched as Yasa turned and shook his head, "I said watch your step."

When he turned on the light, she looked down to see the puddle of blue-clear blood that she was standing in. She reached for the blade at her side and went to pull it out of its holder when her eyes saw something. Or, more to the point, someone she remembered. The acrid memory of her past filled her thoughts as she saw the face of Tassier Gil, a consort of one of the members of the Tas and her former owner. The woman's expression was frozen terror, but the Hurmann's eyes were lifeless.

Yasa moved cautiously toward Eshea, saying, "She recognized me. I couldn't let her leave." Eshea stepped back only to have Yasa yell at her, "Stop! The Hurmann don't bleed much, thankfully, but you're tracking it all over the floor." He motioned for her to move forward. "Come this way, I'll get you hosed off."

She looked down to see the blue footprint on the metallic floor and felt the gentle tug of Yasa's hand as he pulled her forward to the drain mat. "I had just killed her when that Nibik came in. I thought he was with her. The Hurmann sometimes use them as bodyguards." He sighed. "I'm happy he was only looking for a cleaner repair."

Eshea pulled her other hand away from her blade. "You had me worried for a moment."

Yasa shook his head. "I killed her only about a quarter cycle ago. I wanted to get her disposed of as soon as possible. The last thing I need is the station investigators in here."

Eshea understood what he meant; Yasa was secretly known by many Arlains who escaped as a point of contact after fleeing. She was sure the station authorities knew as well. However, on this station, all planets not aggressive toward the station were welcome, even those at war, as long as they didn't cause any trouble. It just happened that one of the Hurmann's ruling Tas walked right into his shop.

She lifted her shoe and reached down to grab hold of it to see how much blood was on the bottom, but Yasa yelled for her not to touch it. When she asked why, he told her.

"I had to use a poisoned blade. Since the Hurmann don't die easily, it's the only way to quickly kill them," he told her.

Eshea said, "We could use that to kill all the Hurmann."

Yasa gently pulled her to the drain before turning on the warm water. She became annoyed as her boots became soaked. She became more upset as he threw powder to cover her moistened footwear. As she protested, looked her in the eyes. "The poison doesn't just affect the Hurmann. It affects all Arlain."

Eshea suddenly became concerned.

"Relax, I use it because it takes time to transmit through the skin. But it's almost instant when delivered internally."

She glanced at the woman's face, seeing the terror frozen in her eyes. "That explains the look on her face." She turned to Yasa. "Why was she here? Did she track you down?"

Yasa tossed more of the powder over her footsteps and the pool of blood before answering. "In a manner of speaking, yes, she did track me down."

Eshea gave him a concerned and sorrowful look.

Yasa threw more of the powder on the blood. "She was asking if I had met one of her pleasure slaves. Apparently, she wanted to find him again."

The sorrowful look turned to disgust on Eshea's face as Yasa soaked the floor behind her. She was relieved hearing him say. "Let me get this cleaned up and get rid of her, and then I can get that mask of yours repaired."

It was a short time later as Eshea helped the man move the body of the Hurmann. She looked at the woman, then pulled back. "Did you scan her?"

Yasa shook his head, asking why he should have.

Eshea looked at him. "Her likeness might come in handy if I had it in my mask's memory."

With a bowed head, Yasa told her, "I'd have to pull her voice from the shop recorders. I didn't get a clean one from her before I ended her."

"I can work with that. I'd have to make some adjustments anyway." Eshea smiled, looking at him with a hint of inspiration. "Besides, I am helping you dispose of her. Call it a favor?" She batted her eyes innocently.

Yasa snickered, reaching out to playfully pinch her chin. "Sure, let me get the scanner."

After scanning and unceremoniously shoving the remains of the Hurmann into the fusion reactor that powered that section of the station, Eshea sat nearby as Yasa repaired the mask.

"It's too bad you didn't bring the other with you. I would have uploaded the profiles into your mask for free."

Eshea looked over at him, "We only have the two. I didn't want to take the chance. We need it for our work."

Yasa nodded, his magnifier reflecting in the light. "Queeks was one of my better creations. I think her profile came out great."

Eshea smiled. "Even up-close people can't tell she's fake."

Yasa turned, grabbing a small bag before tossing it to Eshea. "See if that fits. I can have that one updated and running faster than this one. I just have to copy the profiles over."

Eshea removed a brand-new VFM from the bag and placed it around her neck. She tapped it, and the fibers covered her face but only showed as a blank canvas. It looked like material moving as she spoke.

Hearing her, Yasa turned to look at her and laughed. "The electronic emulator on that blank sounds funny when you speak, you know that?"

He turned to go back to work on the mask on the table. "I'm glad I used your voice profile for Queeks, you know."

Eshea nodded, "Yeah, I don't think I could sing with someone else's voice."

Yasa remained focused. "But you are singing someone else's words. Do you have any idea what you're going to do after this is over?"

She thought for a moment before shaking her head.

The shop owner smiled. "Well, when you finally free everyone, come see me. I've been thinking about opening an entertainment location." He looked around. "This shop is nice, low profile. I can get things done under the sensors, if you know what I mean. But I don't want to do this forever."

Eshea understood.

Yasa sided his eyes toward her, "You're not just here for a concert, are you?" Eshea smiled back at him when he asked, "Who you here to see?"

Eshea answered, "Well, we're here to talk to some people about some help."

"Really? Who?"

Eshea giggled, "I would stay out of this one, Yasa. These people have taken down some of the most feared warriors of the galaxy. Even the pirates respect them."

Yasa raised his brows before returning to finish the mask he was working on. "I probably don't want to know, then."

Eshea sighed. "It would probably be better for your health, too." She thought, *I hope for our sakes as well that they agree. Otherwise, we're running out of time.*

Chapter 19:
Plans Change

It was a few hours later when Eshea returned to the ship. She had also stopped to buy some fruits for the crew. The food that she had was palatable, but she wanted actual, non-processed sustenance for a change. She smiled, seeing Trin look into the bag as he took it from her.

"You're a goddess. Did you get any chorkle?" Trin asked cheerfully in his whispered voice

Eshea reached into the bag, pulling out another smaller bag. "Enough for you and Ralla for a week. I got some actual food for us as well."

She turned to see Ralla looking annoyed and heard him say, "I told you to come right back when you were done. Did you go shipping?"

"Relax, Ralla. It would have looked suspicious if I just went to the shop and didn't do any other shopping." She then reached into the bag and pulled out another bag of chorkle, tossing it to Ralla.

He caught it and stared at it momentarily before muttering, "Chorkle. I haven't had this in almost a cycle."

Eshea smiled, taking the bag from Trin. She rummaged around in it and pulled out a single fruit. She took it over to Zarlin, who was busy writing another song. She placed the fruit down on the table. "I got you those pomegranates you like, the ones those Terrans grow."

She watched as Zarlin's eyes focused on the round fruit, and she reached out with both hands, grabbing it gently but securely. Zarlin looked innocently around, cradling the fruit before smashing it against the table's edge and splitting it in half. Some of the berries from inside bouncing along the table Eshea stepped back as Zarlin bit and sucked on the tiny arils. Her free hand picked up the ones that bounced away.

"Zarlin, seriously, you're getting that juice everywhere," Eshea complained.

Her friend looked up innocently, saying, "But they taste sooo good," before slurping into the fruit again.

Eshea let out a guttural laugh as she heard Ralla say, "I thought we agreed not to get those anymore? That juice stains everything, and she's getting it everywhere, again."

Eshea turned to Ralla, "I got the mask fixed and a new one. It took a while to load the profiles. I got a new face as well." She removed the two masks from her pouch. "I have to load the new profiles on the one here, and we'll be set for a while."

Ralla looked at her and approved. "Now we have to see if we can meet with that starborn."

Eshea said, "I wish it were both of them; we're only here for a week."

Ralla agreed, then said, "You said you have a new face. Let's see it?"

Eshea placed the unit over her head and tapped her mask controls, and as the fibers covered her face, the image solidified. Zarlin froze, her mouth whimpering. "Tassier Gil? You took her face?"

Ralla looked at the two sitting, wondering why they were acting as they did before asking, "Who's Tassier Gil?"

Eshea turned to him, the unfamiliar woman's stare on him. "She was our former owner."

"Seems fitting," Trin said.

Ralla asked, "How did you get close enough to scan her?"

Eshea tapped the controls again, and the mask retracted. "Trust me, she was pretty easy to scan."

The captain of the *Eiger* crossed his arms. "Are we going to have a problem later?"

Eshea shook her head. "I didn't kill her."

Ralla looked quizzically at her. "Then how did you get a scan of her? What happened?"

Eshea looked at him, "Right now, she's elementary particles. She was already dead when I got to her."

She looked over at Zarlin and could see her friend's eyes innocently looking at her. She heard Zarlin say, "She's dead? She's really dead?"

Eshea nodded.

Zarlin jumped up, wrapping her arms around Eshea, her hands covered in the pomegranate juice now staining her light-colored shirt.

"Zar, stop. You're getting that juice all over me," Eshea protested but didn't push Zarlin away. She relaxed, hearing Zarlin say, "Eshea, I love you so much."

Ralla looked over at Trin to see the man smiling and heard him say hushedly, "Too bad you both couldn't have been there."

Ralla looked strangely at Trin. The man rarely spoke. "When did you start to become so vocal?"

Trin gave an annoyed stare toward their leader. "Have you listened to the stories they've told us about what that woman put them through?"

Ralla nodded but responded, "Celebrations can wait. Right now, we're all on a mission."

Eshea and Trin watched as Ralla walked away, grunting orders to them all as his voice disappeared within the ship.

"Heartless bastard." Trin's hushed voice was barely audible

However, Eshea heard him and nodded. She looked at Trin, "You and him are the ones who were in battle." She nestled her head into Zarlin. "We were entertainment."

Trin reached out, placing his hands on both, "Hopefully, this will be over soon."

* * *

"Attention, unknown vessel. Under the order of the Arlain planetary forces, you are commanded to identify yourself, or you will be destroyed." Bosh stared at the comm hearing the demand.

The woman at the controls turned to the captain. "Sir, they are demanding that we identify ourselves."

"I'll take it from here, Halli," Bosh replied before tapping the comm. "Arlain control. This is the *Worren*. I am an antique ship dealer from the Loras system here at the request of Malik Terine. I will send you the authorization momentarily."

Bosh turned to the woman. "Send these idiots the files Malik provided. I don't want to be hauled in like some starborn."

The woman acknowledged her master and sent the information. There were several seconds before the comm came alive again. "*Worren*, we insist you provide the captain's full identity."

135

She turned to Bosh, unsure of what to say, and an audible groan of annoyance came from him as he pressed the transmit button. "Arlain control, this is Captain Issacs Jens. All my information has been sent."

There was almost a minute before the controller responded. "*Worren*, the documents you provided are not accurate, you will proceed to landing station 791 for processing, or we will consider you hostile and destroy your vessel."

"That idiot! Get me, Malik on the comm now!" Bosh growled.

The captain looked to the pilot. "Head toward the location slowly. I don't want to be blown out of the sky."

There were several seconds before Malik responded, "Devlin Bosh, do you know what time it is?"

Bosh held back his anger. "Malik, the papers you provided are not working. Care to explain that to me?"

"What do you mean? They are standard authorization documents," Malik responded.

The anger in Bosh's voice grew, "Well, I'm being ordered to a remote dock for a security check. If you want your payment, that will not happen if I'm apprehended or blown from the sky."

Malik paused before responding, "Hold where you are, Devlin. I need to make a call."

Bosh ordered his pilot to slow to a stop, prompting the controller to request why they were doing so. The captain looked around again, sitting forward. "Malik, I've paid you good money for this. You better not cross me."

The controller again spoke, "*Worren*, you are ordered to head to landing station 791 for security… detail… wait, what?" The comm suddenly went silent, causing a crooked smile to appear on Bosh's face.

"*Worren*, our apologies. Your documents have been accepted. Please proceed to the private landing location as per the orders of House Unber. Their private landing facility is aware of your approach."

Bosh sat back in his command chair. "That fool actually did something. He must really want that spide." Bosh pressed the transmit button. "Acknowledged, Arlain control. It is good to see things work more efficiently here than where we came from. Head to the landing site," Bosh ordered his pilot. "I'm going to have a word with that moron when we arrive."

It was only a few minutes before the ship landed. Bosh's crew laying out the exit ramp to see Fellen standing next to his master. Bosh walked out, seeing the Arlain yawning. "Did I wake you, Ledger?"

Malik smiled, enjoying the title Bosh used for him. "A minor inconvenience. It seems that due to the Kaial being near..." Malik looked annoyed, "a single signature was misplaced. It was a simple matter to rectify."

Bosh walked up to the slaver. *If I didn't need you, I'd kill you,* were his thoughts before he spoke. "I am glad it was a simple misunderstanding."

Malik looked at Bosh's ship. "You have fewer crew. Where are the others?"

Bosh said nothing.

"I expected you to stay planetside while we were conducting business. Why were you off-world?" There was a humorous suspicion in the Arlain's words.

Bosh didn't like the slaver's tone but decided to tell him the truth. "Malik, you do want to be paid, don't you?"

Malik raised his eyes. "You have the payment onboard?"

Bosh placed his hand on Malik's shoulder, causing one of his servants to move to remove it. Within seconds, Halli had swiped down using an extended weapon, slicing deep and knocking the man's arm away. Malik raised his hand to signal the others not to approach. He looked toward the woman.

"She is fast. And pleasing looking for a non-Arlain," Malik commented.

Bosh sided his eyes and Halli moved behind him, "She is as deadly as she is beautiful." He leaned into the slaver. "And not currently for sale."

Malik motioned, welcoming Bosh, and they started toward his study, "I have heard from our sources that one of them is at Roscin station right now. The other's whereabouts are currently unknown. But our spies suspect he is on Yata Beta."

Bosh nodded.

Malik guided the captain into his study, "You did not mention if the payment was onboard. Am I to presume that since you are light on crew, they are watching it for us?"

Bosh nodded.

"A prudent action, my dear friend. A prudent action." Malik sat in his chair. "You are wise. You never know who may try to take your possessions."

Bosh smiled, "I wouldn't insult you by accusing anyone, Ledger. Did you have any further information on my prizes?"

There was a silence as Malik smiled back at the captain. "Although your servant is pleasing and deadly, I do have you outnumbered."

Bosh moved his hand to his collar, prompting Halli to do the same before Bosh produced a small tube opening the end. Rotating the small end, he focused the radiation projecting out, burning through the guard on Malik's left, before closing the small tube quickly. And, as the man fell, Bosh said, "I only see one guard, Ledger. Have I miscounted?"

Malik was momentarily surprised but looked to the guard who fell, and a psychotic giggle escaped the slaver's throat. He looked back at Bosh. "It appears you have not."

Bosh placed the tube back into his jacket and gave a slight stretch, fixing his cover jacket, a display reminding Malik that he was wearing a Sotiral shield.

However, Malik could see the exhaustion in the captain and took a moment to insult him. "You would make a fine Tas if you were Arlain."

Bosh gave no emotion as he stared back at Malik.

The slaver nodded. "I have procured a residence for you closer to the citadel. You and your crew may stay there. With the Kaial fast approaching, I cannot allow you to remain here. I'm sure you understand."

Bosh nodded. "Of course. I'm sure the accommodations will be adequate. I will be happy to await your update on any progress of the task I have uh, requested. And I am sure you will not disappoint."

Malik smiled, "Of course, my friend. I will update you on the acquisition and, of course, deliver them to you broken and begging at your feet."

Bosh rose from his chair. "Thank you, Ledger. I look forward to continuing our business." Bosh turned to leave, bringing Malik's guard to move forward, but Malik stopped him.

After Bosh started walking toward his ship, Malik said, "See if the tracker obtained the location of where his ship was. I do not like when someone destroys one of my possessions."

Chapter 20:
Call for Vengeance

A wave of silence moved through the active center of the Arlain space center as several Hurmann walked toward one of the meeting rooms. The current head of operations, Galin of House Toor, led the head of House Luxin, along with several other families with interests and those loyal to the meeting.

"Jelai, the investigators inform us that they have information on the whereabouts of your patriarch but have not told any of us anything." Her representative said as he turned to look at the others. "Although I do not know why the others were summoned."

The current leader of House Luxin did not know either. However, knowing what she did about protocol, she suspected the news was different from what she wanted to hear. They continued to the room at the end of the hall, where two well-dressed guards of the Arbiter stood waiting. As they approached, the guards silently opened the doors.

Galin walked in first, then paused, seeing the Arbiter and four others of the Tas standing at the other end of the room, one open chair before them draped in red.

Jelai stumbled and then froze, seeing the display as she walked in. The sight caused her to fall to her knees, a cry of, "No," filled with despair taking her very breath away momentarily.

As the doors closed, Galin crossed his arms low before giving a silent bow and simple words, "He has fallen," escaping his mouth before standing tall again.

The others followed, repeating the same gesture, before moving to help Jelai from the ground.

There was a short time before everyone was seated. The arbiter took his place behind the red-draped chair. "Jelai, leader of House Luxin, your patriarch has fallen." There were several seconds before he continued. "You may choose a new patriarch or continue to serve as head."

One of the others near the arbiter spoke. "Arbiter, House Luxin has not had a matriarch for some time; her leadership may be in question."

Near Jelai, one of the others stood, announcing, "I will be heard."

Jelai turned to see Yonin of House Fasel and a good friend of her consort, Teris, standing tall. Her mouth trembling as she muttered, "I do not wish to be taken by another house."

Her muted words didn't fall short as Yonin reached to touch her shoulder. "House Fasel will support the matriarch as we did her predecessor."

Jelai turned with a surprised stare, which turned to one of gratefulness before she looked back toward the Arbiter. She was delighted to see all five of them stand. "Jelai of Luxin, we will all support your ascension if you wish to accept."

The woman looked around the room to see all the others standing, the pain of her loss now leaving her as she stood. Jelai crossed her arms before her and bowed, then stood tall. She said, "I will lead our house and bear all responsibilities until my death."

All in the room returned the gesture, and when finished, the arbiter spoke, "Jelai, we are Tas, and with loyal standing alongside Luxin."

She smiled for the first time since entering the room as the Arbiter approached. "We are with you, but now our task will be to keep our alliance."

Jelai now felt the weight of her station. She was now head of house Luxin and all of its responsibilities. Those were minor compared to what she faced next, her mind realizing a fact that she had hoped never to consider. All present were in an alliance with Luxin, but they now faced the rest of the Tas. And any who wished to take away what was rightfully hers.

* * *

"What?" Malik yelled at his wife as she broke the news that Jelai had taken the lead of Luxin upon the death of their patriarch.

"That is what my sources tell me," Yenna retorted, only to look away. "It will make it difficult for you to take their house if others of the Tas support her."

Malik looked to the open window and the statue of one of the many gods they revered for inspiration. His voice was muffled as he spoke softly. "This will not do. With Luxin under my patronage, I could rule everything."

"What were you saying?" Yenna asked her, perfected hearing sure of his words. But she wanted to hear them from him directly.

Malik huffed, "We need a way to ensure that the remaining Tas do not follow the lead of those with them."

The slaver sat back, his eyes forward as his wife moved behind him, her words prodding at his prowess. "You have done well so far, my husband. It would be a shame to lose such power to those more worthy in their strategy."

Malik smiled as a silent chuckle escaped his grinning face, "You take me a fool, my love? I realize what you are doing." He looked toward her. "You are quite right. This would be unsatisfactory for our standing." He pointed to himself when he spoke.

He looked toward his desk. "How many houses are aligned with Luxin?"

His wife thought for a moment. "Yese, Fasel, Drune, Mahul, Dros, and, of course, the Arbiter and House Klin."

"Three of the top ruling. And two with strong followers. This will not be easy." Malik nodded slowly as he spoke, finding inspiration in his thoughts. "What we need is for others to follow us without thought. To weaken their alliance and a reason to unite and serve for us."

Yenna crossed her arms. "And how will you achieve that?"

"After recent happenings, they will again need to call a conclave. They must still cement their allegiance and confirm Jelai as head of Luxin." Malik looked at his wife. "We will need a plan before that happens."

Malik sat, his mind racing. *How do we weaken their alliance?*

His concentration was broken hearing his private screen alert. His wife looked at the screen to see who it was. "Were you expecting a communication?"

Malik shook his head, and before answering, he waved his wife to move aside. *If it's the Slasta, I'll need to find a new wife.*

The slaver looked at the screen to see the crest of the Arbiter displayed, and he felt his hearts beating again. He accepted the message and groaned, causing his wife to ask what it was.

Malik leaned back in his ornate chair. "They are calling a conclave for tomorrow. I don't have time to think of a plan."

Yenna glared at her husband. "You gave them one month. That was foolish."

Malik huffed, sinking into his chair, before nodding, "Perhaps, but it would not be good form to ignore the call to conclave, since I have claim to their house. Nor would it be to go against the confirmation outright. I would look weak if I were to do so."

Yenna remained silent, but as she was about to speak, Malik ordered her to tell the servants to lay out his clothing for tomorrow. She heard him say, "Maybe I'll think of something before they confirm her during the conclave."

There were fewer Hurmann representatives than anticipated when Malik arrived. It looked as if many of the general class were forgoing the confirmation of Jelai as head of Luxin. Malik considered that they had more important things to do preparing for celebrations, probably suspecting that this was nothing more than a formality. Most of the Tas were present, and that was all that was needed. He sat in his chair, his gilded robes less for wear as he waited for the arbiter and the others. Malik's mind wandered as he looked forward. *I have the Slasta. If I had the spide, I could kill all of them and take this world for my own.*

Malik sat, his mind wandering, before seeing a small group of servants moving a large case covered by a red cloth. Its side waved open for him to see the ornately carved wood of the caster box.

"Now I know this is only a formality. They only bring that out when acknowledging a new house or when declaring war." Malik muttered before his eyes went wide with inspiration. "If their patriarch was killed in battle, then…"

Malik stood and then rushed to the aisle. He could see them setting up the display and dispersing the ballots they all had to use to confirm Jelai's place as head of Luxin. He stepped down the stairs gracefully and met with one of those dispensing the ballots. And he made conversation.

"I see we are following tradition. It is good, don't you agree?" Malik said, watching the Arbiter's guard turn.

"I have only seen them use the caster when they declared war against the Alliance. It has been some time," the Hurmann replied.

Malik looked up with inspiration, "Ah yes, war, that's it."

The man gave him a strange glare. Malik smiled, looking back to see the guard staring. "Of course, that is what it was primarily used for, war."

Malik playfully tapped the man's arm, saying, "That is what I wanted to hear. It is good you know our history," before rushing off.

The slaver looked around the room. *Now, who can I use for this?*

He finally had a plan. In their laws, there was always leeway for revenge. And the death of a patriarch was one of those that all could get behind. His mind scheming, he moved to some of the Hurmann who had gathered around the caster. His voice was low, subtle, saying, "Perhaps they are asking for vengeance for the death of the head of Luxin."

Since they were all genetically engineered as to what they would consider perfect, all within earshot heard his muttering. One of the Tas turned to look at him, a cross stare from her eyes. Malik played into her feigning concern. "Am I mistaken? They would have only called the conclave so soon if that were the case." He looked around. "I also heard that Jelai has taken the mantle as head of Luxin."

She snapped back. "You have claim to them. Why would you care?"

Malik's acting was one of stellar quality. "My dear, I surmised that she would take the mantle. That is why I gave her a month. To allow for her placement." He moved closer. "You think me feeble in doing so?"

As the woman nodded, Malik grabbed her by the throat. "My house is strong. I do not fear them or any others. And I would welcome her as head of Luxin. I know she will take reprisals against those who felled her patriarch."

The Hurmann surrounding them heard his words. And they all agreed; he even heard one say, "If he fell at the hands of a lesser being, then we must show that we are stronger."

Malik agreed, and his words inspired others, and he heard, "We must make that known to their house and all who support her. They will act as one. For all the Hurmann."

Malik smiled, seeing one of those he knew to wave the others away. "Tell the others we will confirm, but we will also have vengeance."

Malik stood near the caster and touched its wooden frame. "All that serves me, I will use. Even you."

He returned to his seat and waited until the others entered. The houses that supported Jelai joined as her consorts, and as the Arbiter entered, the room fell to silence.

"Praised are the superior" rang through the chamber before the Arbiter began business. As he announced the support of each house that sanctioned the Jelai's ascension, they moved to confirm her as the new matriarch of Luxin. That's when Malik saw his plan come to light.

The Hurmann and Tas delivered their ballots. When finished, they were pulled from the caster and read aloud. The first few confirmed Jelai, but one with more was read aloud.

"I confirm Jelai as head of Luxin. May she deliver those who accosted her house to our door." The woman read, then looked at the Arbiter, who waved her to read another.

The next was more vicious, claiming that her ascension was a sign for her to bring about vengeance for her patriarch's death. As the remaining ballots were counted and read, an unmistakable message developed. Jelai's acescent now had the tone inferred that she was granted her station to bring in or destroy those responsible for harming her house.

Malik moved closer to Jelai as each ballot was read and reveled to see the faces of those he had inspired and those now in a position to support the house of Luxin. When the official read Malik's ballot, the woman looked up at him before she read. It said, "I confirm Jelai as head of Luxin." That placed a quizzical stare on the faces of the Tas who supported Jelai. Malik was the one who made a claim to her house itself, but he gave only a simple smile in return and was heard saying, "I, of course, will support the ruling of the others if the majority would want conditions."

Malik bowed his subtle grin, hiding the entire plan he now had in play. Yonin, the head of House Fasel, looked around the room. The growing bloodlust on many faces of the Tas and Hurmann was now showing in more significant numbers. The murmurs of revenge now filled his ears.

He turned to one of the Tas supporting Jelai, Bonon of Drune, and whispered, "We must abide by the will of the Hurmann. Their voices cry for vengeance."

Bonon nodded, "Yes, but Luxin has lost at least one ship. They have shown weakness."

The two patriarchs looked to Jelai, their eyes steady as they approached. "Jelai, the people call for retribution of your fallen. You know what you have to do."

Jelai looked across the crowd to see the eyes of the Tas and Hurmann, all searching for revenge. *Gods, they took our best vessel. I will need help.*

It was some hours later, after all the ballots were counted, that the voices of the Hurman were now heard. Jelai was now head of Luxin but was also expected to send reprisal. She knew her house had a slim chance after losing their greatest warship. Jelai would need help, and the ones who sanctioned her ascension were obliged to render aid.

It took only a simple question from Malik as he moved among the Hurmann, "I wonder how large of a force they will choose?"

Malik heard the question grow, the louder it became, the wider the grin on his face became. The supporting Tas, the ones who sided with Jelai's ascension, now banded to show solidarity.

Malik felt victory, hearing them pledge several ships, one large attack vessel, and support ships. The display only made the fires of battle grow within the Hurmann, and when it peaked, there was a genuine call for battle.

One of the lower Hurmann rushed forward, "I will stand among you. We are the superior. They will fall at our feet."

Malik was startled as the remaining Hurmann cheered, his thoughts now, *Gods, what have I done? They want war. This may be easier than I'd considered.*

Several more of the Hurmann pledged fighters, ships, and supplies. The few ships they had previously now became an armada. And the call to attack any harboring the terrorists, Queeks Maco, grew.

Malik could hear the lust for revenge he had started rolling through the Hurmann and the members of the Tas, now afflicted by the very fever. The slaver's mind was working on a way to ignite the crowd further when he heard, "We are the superior." That's all it took for the Arbiter to stand and bring his gavel down.

His words bellowed through the chamber. "We know their location, we know who they are, and we will take our revenge. Queeks Maco and wherever they harbor will be nothing but dust when we are through."

Malik cheered with the others but then moved through the crowd to a more secluded area where a few Hurmann sought quiet. He turned to peer into the chamber, the celebration of war now on full display. He sat quietly away from the others, the column nearby, hiding the victorious grin that showed his sharpened teeth as the leading Tas ordered the ships to make ready to leave. "Now I need to see what others I can bring to my side," escaped his lips before approaching one of the Hurmann nearby.

"Friend, it is glorious, is it not?" Then he heard the man say, "If they succeed, it will be."

Malik feigned a surprised look, his mind knowing full well the lower caste of the Hurmann who thirsted for greatness. His eyes hid the delight as he heard, "If they do not succeed, then perhaps those of us who are stronger should take their place."

Malik smiled, placing his hand on the man's shoulder, his single talon tapping friendly against the metals the man wore. "Then perhaps if they do not, you may get your chance."

Chapter 21:
A Little Business

Eislie was waiting to get tickets when Zarlin noticed her online. The member of Queeks Maco rushed away, tapping her comm to inform Ralla. Zarlin moved to an unseen spot and quickly activated the Queeks mask. She was ready to begin playing her part as Eshea accompanied her. They both decided to meet with Eislie under the guise of meeting their fans as they greeted many walking down the line of people waiting for tickets.

The two wore disguises, which were purposefully not very good. It was something Queeks Maco was famous for, and many fans played along to get to meet them. Their faithful fans knew it was something the singer had done that made Queeks famous among many. The two moved along until they finally reached Eislie, who was with Derrit, when they stopped. Zarlin, playing Queeks, removed her glasses, looking at Eislie, saying, "I know you."

Eislie stepped back, almost ready to fight, but did nothing, seeing all the security around.

"You're one of those starborn," Zarlin said.

Eislie responded angrily, "So?"

Zarlin smiled back as Ralla approached. He could hear the distaste in Eislie's tone and began thinking. "Damn, no wonder the Alliance is afraid of them. She could probably kick all our asses by herself." He looked at Zarlin, thinking *Eshea would have been better for this.*

Zarlin crossed her hands over her heart. "Such fire, such strength. I do not call you starborn out of disrespect. After all, all stars grant life and warmth. I simply meant that you were someone I recognized as a healer.

You and your partner have shown the galaxy the plight of those enslaved like we have. We see you as kindred."

Good save, Eshea thought before speaking. "What Queeks meant is that we would be honored if you, your partner, and your crew would join us backstage after the show."

Eislie looked around. "Well, he's not here yet. We had an issue with our ship, but he'll be here in a few days." Derrit was ecstatic as Eislie thought, *can't wait to tell Shasji.*

Zarlin looked down the line. "Are you waiting to purchase tickets?"

Eislie nodded.

Ralla whispered to Eshea, "Maybe we should give them the tickets and passes. It would be good publicity." Zarlin repeated his words as she leaned in to tell her the same, adding, "See how many they need."

Eshea smiled cheerfully, responding, "Queeks wishes to give you a gift. How many are on your crew?"

Eislie thought for a moment. "Six, but if my best friend comes along, it'll be seven, uh, eight."

Eshea said, "One moment," then looked to Ralla, and he nodded before using his comm. Zarlin moved to a fan beside Eislie and quickly signed something. And then to another before Trin came rushing toward them through the crowd. He handed a small bunch of bands to Eshea. And Zarlin looked back, taking them from her before giving them to Eislie.

"From one free soul to another. Please accept these for the show." Zarlin said using Queeks voice.

Eislie thanked Queeks, her words full of a similar sentiment.

Eshea smiled, "I speak for Queeks when I say we look forward to you enjoying the show and joining us afterward."

* * *

Jace was at the workshop looking over the first of the newly machined shells they planned to use on the *Wolfhammer.* Miriz remarked on seeing his expression, "You look like a child seeing a new toy."

Jace turned to look at her, "You know what they say? It's better to grow older than up."

Miriz snickered. She could understand why Eislie and he were together. She had spent time alongside her while on Gilese. Jace was different than most she had encountered, not a feral warlike Terran nor a compliant Alliance. He showed the measure of an explorer, looking at wherever he was with curiosity and wonder. But the resilience and strength it took to deal with those around him.

Miriz moved closer, wrapping her arm around his before gently pulling him along. "You know, if you want to get there in time, you'll have to leave in a few hours."

Jace nodded, tapping his comm, "Ed, how's the loading going?"

There was a moment before the ship's computer responded, "The hold is at two-thirds capacity. I estimate the loading will be completed in approximately two standard hours."

Jace smiled, looking at Miriz when she said, "He could probably make the trip on his own, couldn't he?"

"Ed? He could if he wanted to. He showed that initiative when we were taken prisoner while evacuating Oppa," Jace said, then looked away. "Of course, we know he wouldn't abandon us."

Miriz leaned into Jace for a moment, and she held a little tighter onto his arm. She was surprised he didn't pull away, but his next question confused her. "How long have you been friends with Eis?"

"A little over thirty standard, why?" Miriz asked before thinking for a moment. "You know we have a couple of hours. There are things we could do instead of watching machines work metal."

Jace sighed and smiled, "You've known Eis her entire life. I'm surprised that you didn't stay on Gilese." Miriz gently pulled again on his arm, but Jace only shifted. Her smile softened when Jace said, "You know she was happy to reconnect with you after a few years, get back a part of her life that was more normal after she was stuck on Charon." The stare in Jace's eyes made Miriz feel a little defensive. It was the stare of someone who knew what was going to happen. Jace's following words caused her to pull away. "You know, sometimes I enjoy the teasing, but I get the feeling you two were a bit competitive occasionally. Maybe even rivals once or twice."

Miriz suddenly frowned, "You're not playing fair" before she pulled again on his arm with a little more force. Jace moved, but it was at his pace.

"I don't mind the teasing. It's good for my ego," Jace said with a sarcastic smugness.

"Words like that can get you in trouble here," Miriz shot back playfully.

Jace laughed as they disappeared around the corner of the building toward the loading facility.

The ship was nearly loaded when they arrived, and Miriz had asked to come along. She had wanted to ensure the facility at Roscin station was up to her standards. Miriz had other business there that she wanted to take care of personally. She had been on Yata for almost two years and never left. She felt it was time to take her own journey to see Eislie and visit one of her more remote facilities. She also hoped to convince Jace to travel the filaments since she had never done so.

Kelor was waiting nearby, watching Miriz's things. As Shasji walked up, she saw the cases Miriz was bringing on board and remarked, "What, only three cases?"

Jace looked at her, shaking his head, saying playfully, "Play nice, Shasji."

Kelor said nothing, only giving a subtle smile, seeing the humor.

The new captain was shorter than Miriz and looked up at her. "She has been fawning over you the entire time we've been here. I'm surprised Eis hasn't decked her."

Jace laughed, "Miriz did the same when we were here last time."

Miriz looked hurt. "I can admit that Jace is definitely worth the effort." She moved closer to Shasji. "Besides, you think you have a better chance?"

Shasji looked at Jace, "Maybe, but I know better." She moved closer to whisper to Miriz. "Eis would space me the first chance she got."

Miriz stood tall, laughing, "Actually, I know Eis, she wouldn't, but she'd make it look good. It'd make you think twice."

Seeing Shasji mock Miriz as she helped Kelor with Miriz's things as Jace closed up the ship was humorous. "Ed, warm up the engines. We're leaving as soon as we have clearance."

The computer acknowledged the command and sealed the doors as Jace walked in.

Miriz sat in Eislie's chair, her hands on the controls waiting to lift off. Jace sat in his command chair and turned to look at her while Shasji leaned against the back of his chair. They heard Kelor grumble as he strapped into one of the other seats. Jace said nothing, but that didn't stop Miriz from understanding his silent question.

"I have flown ships before. My main business was in parts, remember?" Miriz remarked.

"What do you think Ed? Should we let her fly?" Jace asked before pausing. "Oh, and Ed, add Miriz and Kelor to the crew, please."

"The computer responded. Mirizali Elysse and Kelor Belor added to the crew, captain." The computer paused. "Are you familiar with Toklah vessels, Mirizali Elysse?"

"Call me Miriz. Plot a course to Roscin station. When we have clearance, we'll leave," Miriz commanded.

There was a moment before Ed responded, "Captain, may I suggest that crewmember Miriz have limited access to ship functions."

Jace and Shasji burst out laughing, seeing the expression of rejection Miriz gave.

"I'll take it under advisement, Ed." He then tapped the controls and changed the flight system to his command chair. "Eis and I share the flight controls, well, most of the time."

He pulled on his harness, strapping in as Shasji sat and did the same. Jace smiled. "This isn't a standard ship. You've met Ed before. I'm surprised you tried ordering him to do something."

Miriz shot back, "I hear you give orders to him all the time."

Jace nodded, "And Ed makes suggestions when I do as well. He doesn't blindly follow them."

Miriz sat back, tightening her harness "So, is that how he keeps you out of trouble."

"It is not always effective," Ed replied, causing Jace to laugh again.

"You're right, Ed. But you do your best," Jace said, then turned to Miriz. "Ed's not a computer on one of your ships. He's crew, and you're not captain, Miriz. Right, Ed?"

"Correct, Captain. I will follow the command structure as I see fit," the computer responded.

Miriz smiled, "I guess I'll just be along for the ride."

A few days passed since they left, Jace did most of the flying. He and Shasji had taken turns piloting. Jace allowed Miriz a few hours after she requested to do so. She remarked that the ship was more challenging to fly since it required more involvement by the crew. While Miriz was busy, Kelor spent most of the time watching the cargo.

Jace remarked, "It's not going to just vanish from the hold."

"I swear that computer of yours changed our course. I had to adjust things the entire time," Miriz complained as Jace sat in his command chair.

Jace looked at the computer's control center, saying, "The ship can fly itself. You sure you weren't just imagining things?"

Miriz looked confused and angrily toward him before turning with a huff. Jace smiled and looked at the computer interface, "Ed, how many times did you change course while I was resting?"

The computer responded quickly, "The pilot on duty had made several dozen adjustments."

"Why so many? You don't need your sensors recalibrated again, do you?" Jace asked, concerned.

"No, captain, I made the adjustments to prevent the representative from accessing the ship database, comm, and from other activities," Ed replied.

Jace looked back toward the hallway, "The comm I can see her using. She's got a business to run. But what was she doing looking through the database?"

"Captain. I do not believe it was malicious. I have noticed with you and Captain Licessien that you tend to fidget when not stimulated. Although it is less with my captains, representative Elysse seemed much more prone to distraction, and it was also to prevent her from disturbing you, captain. Was that not the correct action?"

"Wait, did Eis tell you to do it?" Jace asked, somewhat annoyed.

The computer paused. "She had left previous instructions, yes."

Jace seemed offended. "Wow, she doesn't trust me?"

"As per Captain Licessien, I am to inform you that, and I quote, 'tell Jace I do trust him, I just wanted her not to bother him.'"

Jace sat back in his chair, his shoulders shaking as he quietly laughed. "She ordered you to mess with Miriz?"

"Yes, captain." Jace noticed the seemingly amused tone in the computer's response.

Jace smiled ear to ear. "Sounds like Eis is getting some payback from years ago." He looked around. "If I don't tell her, you tell Eis. I appreciated that. Miriz is a handful sometimes."

"I will inform Captain Licessien if you fail to do so, captain."

Miriz stood, her footsteps louder than usual as she walked away. Jace wished her a good night as he took control of the *Wolfhammer*.

Sometime later, Jace shifted in his chair and was staring out at the energy ribbons passing by. Something was soothing to the way they traveled. He and Eislie had said it was as though you could feel the space around you moving. He spent a few minutes mesmerized by the light show before he turned to look around. Jace moved his head as if listening. His actions didn't go unnoticed by the computer.

"Is everything alright, captain?"

Jace looked around once more before saying, "The drone of the coils is almost gone. I think the new ones made the ship quieter." He sat forward. "I never noticed until now."

"We are also traveling using less power, captain. It's almost a 27% drop from the previous iteration."

Jace had noticed the lower power usage back on Gilese. "That's quite an increase." He looked around, asking, "Can you extrapolate how much of a surge would that have caused if we used them within the filaments?"

The computer responded, "Models indicate that the control systems would have incurred a surge of approximately 139%, above their threshold for remaining operational."

"Oof, I'm glad we didn't use the filaments to go to Yata. I would have had to rebuild everything." Jace looked at the interface control. "Would your systems have been affected?"

"Yes, captain. Although I would have shut down to prevent the surge from crossing into my main interface."

"Ed, I don't like ordering you to do things, but if you suspect something is wrong, you tell us," Jace said sternly.

"Of course, captain. But do you not think it is wise sometimes to take risks?"

Jace smiled before saying, "Of course, Ed. But you're crew and a friend. You're just as important as anyone."

"The new shell design should dissipate the charge exiting. It may also be why the alloy was used for the Lyri ship." The computer paused. "May I ask you a question, captain?"

Jace nodded before the alert on the comm sounded. He looked at the display, and the computer read the message, "Captain Licessien wishes to inform you that she has a surprise and will wait till all crew are awake to contact you. Safe flying, see you soon."

"I wonder what she has?" Jace smiled. "You said you had a question, Ed?"

"Yes, captain, I have noticed that you mentioned others to be the same as yourself. I have noticed that you do not look down on many unless they harm others. Why is that?"

Jace sighed before answering. "Ed, no matter who you are, if you are alive and think, you're no different than the being next to you. Their lives all have the same weight."

"That is an interesting concept. Why have you destroyed some of them?"

Jace wasn't surprised by the question. He knew he had to do things to survive. Hurting someone to escape or protect others was part of existence, even if you didn't want to. "You're right, Ed. I've had to hurt others, reluctantly. And I don't take that lightly. I may believe that everyone is the same, but a balance must be maintained. If others try to harm anyone, Eis, Miriz, family, or friends, that upsets that balance. You're included in that too, Ed."

The computer remained silent before alerting Jace that Miriz was entering the control room.

"Hey, Miriz, you should be getting some sleep," Jace said.

Miriz walked up. Tears were in her eyes, and she moved closer, kissing Jace with care before pressing her forehead to his. She pulled away and knelt. "What you just said, have you told Eis?"

Jace nodded, "She knows."

Miriz shook her head. "She is so lucky."

Jace smiled, "I see it as I'm the lucky one."

Miriz gently held his hands. "I'm serious. If you and her ever split, I'd be willing…"

She was interrupted when Jace laughed, "Miriz, you never know what the future holds." He leaned closer, "And right now, you should get some sleep. Eis has a surprise for us but wanted to wait till everyone was awake."

Miriz pouted. "Maybe you can tuck me in?"

Jace sighed, giving a suspicious stare. "Go get some rest, Miriz. Captain's orders."

Miriz stood and saluted him before saying, "Can't blame me for trying."

Jace sat back after watching Miriz disappear around the corner. He turned to look at the display, "Ed, remind me to ask Eis what it was like with Miriz while on Gilese. I have a feeling it must have been a really fun time."

Chapter 22:
A Leader's Dilemma

The drone of hyperspace engines filled her ears as Jelai rested in her room. The Hurmann called for vengeance at the dispatch of the former head of House Luxin. The conclave demanded that they deal with those who had destroyed one of the formidable vessels of the Hurmann. She wasn't the only one forced by honor and station to be there. Her allies, Houses Fasel, Drune, Mahul, Dros, and, of course, the Arbiter's house, Happ, and House Klin, were to provide vessels and fighters for the attack.

Jelai's mind raced as she considered the consequences if they failed. The Hurmann would demand compensation for their weakness. She also had the claim of House Unber, which Malik never rescinded. *If we fail, we are lost*, Jelai thought as her fingers crushed the over-cloth draped on the chair where she sat. The red fabric was a testament to her fallen husband.

She sighed as she looked at the miniature image of her fallen husband. Most marriages were of station. But, between them, there was something more. She felt a more significant loss, finding that he died at the hands of a lesser species, made her loss sting worse.

"Queeks Maco will pay for their disrespect," Jelai muttered before leaning back in silence.

It had been a few days since they left Arlain, and would be a few more before they reached Roscin station, the current known location of Queeks Maco. Jelai's mind formed many ways to torture the singer for killing her love. Her ruminations were interrupted, hearing a general alert throughout the ship.

"General alert. Quasi space detected. Returning to standard space for evaluation."

"Quasi space? This is an open area. There should be no anomalies," Jelai muttered, concerned.

The leader of Luxin stood and then headed out of her room to see what was happening.

Reaching the control deck, she ordered, "Status, what is the situation?"

One of the crew turned, crossing her arms before her midsection, and bowed. "Matriarch, we have detected a large quasi-space area. There is a heavy gravity body nearby, but it does not seem to be the cause of the anomaly."

Jelai looked at the screen. She had been fortunate to learn much about navigation and the ships they held in her free time. She and her husband had worked together to fortify themselves against the others of the Hurmann. A matter to prevent them from claiming House Luxin. But now, that planning was likely in jeopardy. She turned to the woman, "Show me the scans."

The officer complied and brought up the details. "Matriarch, the anomaly seems to be near the heavy gravity well, but it is not a part of the heavy body system. Initial scans show debris. Some materials appear to be manufactured."

Jelai turned to the woman. "You suspect a ship?"

The female office nodded before saying, "It was massive, whatever it was. We are, however, too far to discern the possible design. We can only ascertain some of its make-up are manufactured elements."

Jelai looked back at the screen. "Have we returned to standard space?"

The officer nodded. "The other vessels have joined us as well."

"Good, then dispatch three deep scouts and recalibrate for returning to hyperspace immediately. They can continue once they have determined the ship and what may have happened. They can join us later."

There was a look of disagreement from the officer before Jelai glanced at her. "They will not miss their chance to exact revenge for the murder of my husband. And if they discover that it is those responsible for his demise, our people can bring what remains of their bodies for us to display." The anger and force in her tone were enough to make the ship decking creak.

The female officer turned her eyes down, "Yes, matriarch." She turned to bark orders, "Ready three deep space scouts. Order them to examine the anomaly and join us at Roscin station when finished."

There was a sudden rush of activity as they readied the scouts, with Jelai tapping the comm to reach out to Yonin of Fasel. His part of the fleet had accompanied them to support Luxin in the attack on the station. Yonin was not surprised when she called.

"Yonin, I'm dispatching three ships to investigate the anomaly. We should continue once we have recalibrated. I do not wish to allow those terrorists to escape because we were late," Jelai said.

Yonin huffed before answering, "Yes, I agree. They can join us once they ascertain the vessel type. But I recommend we leave immediately."

* * *

Shasji, Jace, and Miriz were looking at the screen, and Eislie's image appeared as Kelor entered the control room.

"Hey," Eislie said.

Jace responded with a simple "Hey" back, which annoyed Miriz, who said, "You two are definitely aligned."

Jace chuckled, hearing Eislie say, "She's not giving you any trouble, is she?"

He shook his head. "Nope, and Ed seems to be helping with that." Jace looked at Eislie. "I think we need to have a chat when we see each other."

Eislie's expression was playfully annoyed, "Oh, and why is that?"

Jace looked to Miriz, "Well, your orders to Ed were definitely keeping Miriz busy."

"You're not playing fair, Eis," Miriz said before pouting playfully.

Eislie looked at her friend, "Oh, I'm not?"

Jace stepped in and said, "You know I noticed that Eis has been messing with you ever since I met you. I'm not the most observant person, but I can tell something is going on between you two. And I want to find out about it."

Shasji leaned forward. "Be careful. You might be getting in over your head."

Jace looked at her and then at Miriz before looking at Eislie. They were all staring at him. Even Kelor seemed to look away as he sat back. Jace said, "You know, I'm outnumbered here. I think a strategic withdrawal is in order."

Over the speakers, they heard, "As per my psychological protocols, that would be a prudent course of action, Captain Tucker."

The laughter they all let out was broken, when Jace said, "Eis, everyone's here. What did you want to tell us?"

Eislie took a moment before she stopped laughing and leaned forward, only to hold up a bunch of wristbands. She held them up to the comm. "This was the surprise."

Miriz leaned forward, "What are those?"

Eislie smiled triumphantly, "Backstage wristbands for Queeks Maco, courtesy of the band themselves."

There was a loud shriek from Shasji as she leaned over Jace, who was reeling from her scream of joy. "Really? You spoke to Queeks?"

Eislie nodded, "Yes, and we all have them. Even you, Miriz. I got one for Kelor, too."

Jace shook his ear. "Ed, can the med unit repair a busted eardrum?"

"Of course, captain."

Miriz chimed in, "I may join you." She then gently pulled Shasji back from the screen. "Shasji, let's find out what Eis has to say."

"We're all invited backstage. And Queeks gave us premium seating." Eislie could swear she could see Shasji vibrating as she moved closer to the screen.

"Anything else? What time? It will be at least a day before we get there," Shasji said before turning to Jace, "Maybe we can use the filaments."

Jace's demeanor changed. "Uh, no. I just reviewed the readings. We'll probably blow most of the systems if I don't modify some things before we test."

"Is it that bad?" Eislie asked.

Jace nodded, "Ed confirmed the readings. The new shell should solve the problem. At least that's the theory." He then looked at the screen. "We probably shouldn't be talking about this over the comm right now. At least not after everything that's happened recently."

Eislie nodded, "Tell me when you get here."

Shasji said, "We could use lower power. That might help."

Over the speakers, the computer responded, "That would not be advisable. The charge is exponential. It depends on how long we are traveling within the filaments. It is independent of the power used to enter."

Shasji looked at the computer display, then heard Jace say, "That's what we found too." He moved closer. "The way we have it set up now, touching the reactor won't help. It'd probably kill whoever was there."

Shasji seemed depressed as she understood. "So we can't get there any faster?"

Jace smiled, "Oh, we can. I can up the engine feeds. May have to let them cool a bit before docking, though." He looked at the screen. "When's the show?"

Eislie responded, "Two days from now. What's your travel time currently?"

The computer responded, "Current travel time remaining is fourteen hours forty-nine minutes, standard, approximately, Captain."

Jace looked at Shasji. "We'll be there in less than a day and still have time. No problem."

Eislie turned and stared at Jace, annoyed, "Did you just say that out loud?"

Miriz looked at the comm screen, "What are you talking about? He just said we'll have time before the show. No problem."

Eislie turned to Miriz, "Every time one of us says something's going easy, we get pulled into some, uh, situation."

Jace sighed, "We're due, Eis. You know that normal day thing I mentioned months ago?"

Eislie rolled her eyes.

Miriz looked at them both. "What's this all about? Are you telling me you believe in fate now?"

"No!" was heard from both Eislie and Jace. Their response caused Shasji to step back.

"You know it would be nice to have a normal day where something doesn't go off the rails," Jace said.

His statement brought a quizzical look from Miriz and Shasji before Miriz asked him to explain what he meant. "It's nothing. It just seems to be some weird coincidence when one of us says it's easygoing. Something impossible seems to pop up."

They spoke for a few minutes, and then Eislie disconnected. Jace increased the engine output and asked the computer to monitor the feeds.

It was a couple of hours later when the computer gave an alert. "Quasi-space detected, transitioning to normal space."

Jace was trying to get some sleep but joined Miriz at the controls. "Where, Ed?"

"Ten arcs, bearing -134,170,16," the computer responded.

"Minus 134? That's impossible," Miriz said.

Jace agreed, "Yeah, but it is quasi-space. Wait, where are we, Ed?"

"We appear to be near a heavy gravity body. We are at a safe distance, but I recommend caution, given the conditions. Negative space may be the reason for the unusual location reading."

Miriz scoffed and was about to make a joke but looked over to see Jace staring, concerned at the display. His next question made her understand. "Ed, any sign of Duggor?"

"Negative, captain. However, the remnants of a ship seem to be in the bulk of the anomaly."

Jace looked to Miriz. "We found something similar when we went to see her father. It was a Duggor Wrent class that inverted its reactor and blew the engines."

Miriz became very concerned. "Can we outrun them?"

Jace nodded, saying, "For the most part, yeah. I've upgraded the drive systems. I just don't want to test them out here near that thing. We almost were stuck in one a while back." He pointed to the heavy gravity well near the quasi-space area.

He then smiled, asking the computer the remaining time until arrival.

"We are approximately seven hours from our destination if we resume our previous speed."

Jace chuckled. "It'd take a little over two days for any normal ship from here." He turned to Miriz, pointing to the holographic screen. "You still think we can't outrun those racers of yours?"

Miriz smiled back. "I may have to see if I can procure a Burnell drive for you two."

There was another alert. "Captain, several ships seem to be approaching at the edge of our sensor range. However, they are too distant for me to identify."

"Maybe we should look for survivors," Shasji said, finally entering the control deck.

Jace thought momentarily. "Any life signs or transmissions, Ed?

"None detected, captain. However, the vessels I previously mentioned have adjusted heading and are now on an intercept course."

"Activating tunnel drive. Let's get out of here. I don't want to find out who they are," Jace said before they headed out.

Chapter 23:
Station Arrival

Jarrus exited his ship. Per station rules, he had to check in with the docking crew and have them inform the party he was there to see. *Such rules are worthless. Why must I wait? I could be searching for those people my employer was looking for,* Jarrus thought as he waited for Belon to arrive. He was relieved that he didn't have to wait long.

"Ah, greetings to you, my son. I take it your flight was uneventful," Belon said before the docking crew moved to continue their assessment of his vessel.

It was unusual for a Nibik to greet another in such a manner. Jarrus found displeasure that he was welcomed so informally and attempted to correct the misjudgment.

"Long shall be the world and our people," Jarrus said, only to see Belon smile.

"I see you still follow the old ways, my son. I do not hold that against you. Long shall be the world and our people," Belon replied.

Jarrus again found his remark distasteful but followed his soon-to-be father-in-law toward the exit way. There were several moments before he said, "You dishonor our people. You have adopted the ways of these others."

Belon looked forward. "I am more than twice your age, child. You dare speak to me about honor. I fought in the battles to protect what was left after our misjudgment."

Jarrus's pace hesitated. He was about to turn and strike the old Nibik but stopped as he saw the returned glare of bloodlust hinting from the eyes of the older man—Belon's stance filled with remembrance and fire of past battles.

"If you strike, you will find that I am not easily slain. The only reason I would not kill you is that your younger brother is to be joined to my granddaughter."

Belon stopped, his head turning away slightly back toward Jarrus's ship. "The *Go Ge Go Go* is looking well. It does not seem to have seen much battle. I do not hope that perhaps its captain has neglected its namesake."

Anger filled Jarrus's voice as he responded, "Ge Go would not be displeased with its accomplishments."

Belon nodded, "Then that is all I wanted to hear. Forgive any perceived disrespect, son. Life outside our world can be more challenging than it appears."

Jarrus stopped to look back at his ship. He knew well the legend of Go, Ge Go, the general that slayed the head of the Pauren empire, but only after Nibik fell victim to its own hubris. Most Nibik now live not on their home world but others nearby. Belon motioned for him to follow "Come, we can talk as we head to my shop." He turned, Jarus hearing him say, "And you can take those obnoxious treats from my storage for your employer."

"By the way, who is your employer again?" Belon asked.

Jarrus spoke quietly. "It is one Tas of the Hurmann."

"Slavers? Are you procuring slaves for them?" Belon said, his voice a low, angry growl.

Jarrus shook his head. "No. They pay well, but I have been procuring items they cannot."

Belon moved closer, looking at Jarrus closely. "We have never enslaved people. Make sure you do not."

It was a short while before they reached the shop. The sign above was written in Nibik and several other languages. Jarrus was confused as to what it read.

"Why does your sign say, Chamber of Sliver?" Jarrus asked.

Belon leaned back on his counter, a gentle chuckle escaping him. "It was supposed to read Chamber of Silver. I missed the issue until two days after installing it."

Jarrus stood tall. "I would have beaten the sign maker."

His father-in-law replied, "I intended to do just that. However, that error had set my shop apart in those two short days from all those with a similar name." He pointed around the shop, the contents more for ships and battle than just garments and supplies. "I took it as a sign from the divine. I had to slightly change what I was selling. That is why I have not returned to Nibik for the past few seasons. I have been too busy."

Jarrus looked behind him to see someone trying the door. The sign on it clearly showed that it was closed. He turned back to Belon. "The Divine had given you a path you had not taken."

"Indeed, it had," Belon said before leaning back against the counter again. "Speaking of the Divine, the feast of Erak is soon. With this shipment of yours, would you make it back in time to celebrate?"

Jarrus shook his head. "I can return possibly toward the end. It will give me time to atone and enjoy some festivities. Some of my crew have voiced their displeasure."

Jarrus felt proud that the older man mentioned the feast. All Nibik were duty-bound to return and celebrate during the same time each year. It was the time they celebrated their faith as a people and their survival. Most Nibik attended, but there were sometimes reasons when they couldn't. Being in battle was one. The inability to travel was another that was also allowed. Damaged ships were always a possibility.

"Your atonement for your absence would have to be given," Jarrus said with a slight tone of judgment.

Belon nodded, "As it should. And I could see my daughters and their families. Although their mother does visit from time to time."

"You should go. Take a trip to our homeworld." Jarrus's words became more subtle.

"My atonement would cause me to be away from this place for some time. I fear I would come back to nothing." Belon looked around. "I am too old to fight for our people now. I serve many Nibik who roam the galaxy while here. I am their reminder of our ways and that there is a life beyond the battlefield."

Jarrus smiled for the first time since he arrived. "That is a noble and honorable calling. Perhaps you would allow a surrogate for the feast."

Belon nodded, a smile of appreciation growing on his face. "I would be honored if there was."

Jarrus felt a kinship toward Belon, knowing that he still valued the ways of their people. He approached the man and touched his shoulder. "I would bring any messages you have for family. And explain the reason for your absence."

Belon grabbed Jarrus' forearm and shook it with assurance. "That, my boy, would be an honor for me. And for that. . ." He motioned for Jarrus to follow. He opened the storeroom door and showed Jarrus what he had come to collect.

"These will be yours for the taking. No charge. After all, you are family." Belon opened one of the containers and removed a box of cookies before handing it to Jarrus. "These are what you came for."

Jarrus inspected and noticed a peculiar scent. "Ugh, this smells terrible."

Belon motioned to him. "Terrans eat these with voraciousness. You had discussed interest in trying one, didn't you?"

Jarrus tore open and lifted one from the package. His senses were now fully aware of the smell of the delicacy. "These are rank. Terrans really eat these?"

Belon seemed to have a mischievous grin hidden as Jarrus brought one to his mouth and slowly bit down on the small, crispy, cake-like morsel. As he chewed, Belon let out a hearty laugh, seeing the expression of disgust Jarrus was now showing.

Jarrus spit the cookie to the ground. "Vile! I can't believe Terrans eat these."

Belon was still laughing, only able to blurt out, "They eat them without abandon."

The captain of the *Go Ge Go Go* looked at the man. "No wonder Terrans are hard to fight. They must train themselves by ingesting these horrid. . . things."

Belon took the box from Jarrus, tossing it into the garbage. "I do not know how they eat them either. I had to endure five of them when the Terran military and Alliance were here to buy the last shipment I had brought in."

"Five? You deserve a banner of honor for enduring that. I will explain that to your daughters." Jarrus looked around, using his sleeve to wipe the taste from his tongue.

Seeing this, Belon moved to the nearby cabinet, taking out a bottle. "Here, these Tauren spirits will kill the taste."

Belon watched as Jarrus sat against the boxes of cookies. "I will have my people load your vessel."

Jarrus stood, "I will transfer the funds. How much will it be?"

Belon shook his head. "My son, you have endured enough today. And you are willing to be my surrogate for the feast. It is the least I can do for you."

* * *

"Roscin Station, this is the *Wolfhammer*. Can you confirm that dock assignment again?" Miriz asked as she worked the comm.

The reply was filled with static and overlapping conversations, "*Wolfhammer*, Dock 71, section 3. You are to remain. . . . ship. . . and crew."

Jace looked over. "I didn't get any of that."

Miriz worked the comm again, "Repeat, Roscin control. Your transmission is dropping out."

"*Wolfhammer*, change to comm. . . 7, beta. I repeat, 47, beta."

Miriz snitched comm frequencies. "Roscin control, can you read us?"

"*Wolfhammer*, we can read you. This concert has been overloading the general comm channels. Please head to dock 71, section 3, and wait for your assignment crew. Once we process you, we will unload your vessel. You may depart after finished."

"They're going to hate me telling them we're staying for the concert," Miriz joked.

Jace chuckled, "They'll probably make us move and dock somewhere else."

Miriz informed the control that they were staying for a few days, to the annoyance of the station controller and his response. "Fine, stay there. I don't have time to find you another dock right now."

Miriz shook her head as she closed the channel. "Sounds like they're having a bad time with this concert."

Jace looked at the screen. "There's a lot of ships here. You know, if I were a criminal, this would be a great place to score stuff." He snickered at Shasji. "Keep an eye on your wallet."

Shasji smiled back at him as he piloted the ship to its landing spot.

It was only a few minutes after they landed before the assignment crew arrived. Miriz took complete control as the cargo door opened. She and Jace were busy with unloading when Eislie tried to sneak up on Jace. She watched as he turned his head slightly, his eyes focused on the new loader entering the ship, but turned away toward Miriz. Eislie readied to grab him, wrapping her arms around him, trapping his arms. She was surprised when he didn't fight and was disappointed to hear him say, "Oh no. I seem to be trapped by a horrible assailant. I don't know what to do."

Eislie leaned against him. "Not even remotely believable. How did you know I was there?"

Jace lifted his arm by bending at his elbow since Eislie held him tightly. "New loader, shiny surface."

She looked around him to see the gleaming metal. "That's cheating. You could see me."

Miriz looked back as Jace turned and gently kissed Eislie. "Are you two going to get a room? Or maybe wait till later." Jace laughed as Eislie tightened her arms around him, and he lifted her from the deck. Miriz sighed, "I swear you two are unbelievable." She pointed to Eislie. "I can see her. Gilese are known for not caring about open signs of affection."

"What's that mean?" Jace asked playfully.

Miriz moved closer. "It means that they do not put much abandon toward open signs of affection, body, or romantic gestures."

Eislie spoke up. "And neither do Yata."

Jace thought he understood but silently asked for an explanation.

Miriz was happy to explain. "It means they are not embarrassed as much if they are found unclothed. Perhaps in a field at night while looking for their lover."

Jace looked at Miriz, then at Eislie. "Is she talking about you or her?"

Eislie rolled her eyes but said nothing. On the other hand, Jace had a somewhat devilish grin. "Although that might explain the swimsuit you wore while we were on Earth."

Miriz looked at Eislie. "What is he talking about?"

Jace noticed a man standing beside him, seeming interested in their conversation, and asked, "Can I help you?"

"Sorry, sounded like an interesting story," the man said.

Jace looked at him. "Private conversation. You mind?"

The man walked away, and Jace continued, "She was wearing this fine two-piece. And I don't mean quality. It barely covered anything." Jace pulled Eislie gently toward him. "Not that I disapproved. Anyway, this guy came over while I was getting drinks and started hitting on her."

"He stuck you?" Miriz asked Eislie.

Eislie shook her head, "No, I thought he was going to help me with the sun protectant, but instead, he just wanted a feel."

Miriz looked shocked, but Jace continued the story. "You should have seen her. She went to elbow the guy while I was walking back. She stood her ground and asked the guy, 'Who do you want to fight first him or me?'"

Eislie pointed at Jace, saying, "And he almost got arrested again. For just being there."

Miriz laughed, "You two are perfect for each other." She then looked at the crates being moved. "This is fun, but we should head to the office. I still have a ton of paperwork to do for this shipment. And we should probably get everyone together. You know, for that surprise you had for us all." She then looked at Shasji, walking toward them with what looked like a headband with cat ears. "What is she carrying? Wait, are those cat ears she is wearing?"

Jace laughed, "Don't let her hear you say that too loud. She calls it a feral crown."

Miriz shook her head but turned to see one of the workers wearing something similar.

As Shasji approached, she held out her hands. "I got these at the shop. I figured that if we're going backstage, we should show that we love them."

Jace took one and looked at it. Eislie reluctantly did the same. Jace laughed, then put the thing on his head, saying, "I've worn weirder things."

Eislie soon followed before Miriz placed the band on her head and said, "Well, we're all wearing cat ears now. Should we head to the office?"

Shasji took offense and started to say, "It's a feral cro. . ." her words stopped as Miriz placed her finger on Shasji's lips. "They're cat ears, my dear. There's nothing wrong with calling them what they are. Now, let's head up to the office." She paused. "Kelor, make sure these are all counted and get to where they are supposed to." Miriz turned to Jace. "We should get the paperwork for the current delivery processed, the shipment offloaded, and your new captain instated."

Chapter 24:
Deadly Eyes are Watching

When they arrived at the office, Jace nearly walked into a man who wore a short cloak covering his shoulders. He shrugged, knowing that different people from other planets had different ideas of fashion, and continued on his way. As Jace entered the room, he looked around. He could hear Miriz confirming the update from Kelor on the unloading, and he looked up to see the logo for JESC clearly showing along the support across the ceiling. And on his right were four of the Sotiral suits on display. He snickered, reading the sign underneath them, "Non-functioning, Display Only."

As they entered the central part of the office, Jace quietly mentioned that he had received the message from Preston that Eislie had asked him to relay about the monitoring devices. And that Miriz had had the office searched to find similar monitoring devices.

The place was much like the office back on Gilese. White walls and simple furniture, although the two longer chairs Jace noticed, were more on the softer and fluffier side. He pointed it out to Eislie, who said, "Yeah, I bought those. Everything here seemed to be too formal."

Miriz walked around talking to one of the staff she had hired to run the office and nodded as she spoke with them. Miriz had helped run JESC along with Eislie's mother while Jace and Eislie continued to explore the galaxy and work on the filament project. Miriz dutifully inspected the stack when she took the paperwork for the current delivery. After she was satisfied, she brought them to Eislie.

"Flora said they had a similar incident with a delivery to Oppa. But only three containers were missing."

Eislie looked over the report before handing it to Jace, who scanned it, saying, "You think it's someone who works for us?"

Miriz nodded, "You have any suspects?"

Eislie answered, "Well, Bensen was on the crew to Oppa. But we removed him from the one to Yata and here." She looked around. "We still think he's working for the Alliance."

Miriz agreed, "On Oppa, I'm pretty sure it was him. But on Yata, we didn't use Alliance loaders. Whoever took the containers took them secretly."

Jace looked at her. "It's a little too coincidental. That and what we found on the ships and office were about the same time."

Miriz walked over, whispering between Jace and Eislie, "I have it on good authority that the suppressors used in the first place were likely Consortium."

Eislie lowered her head. "Someone wants to know what we're doing so they can take it."

Jace agreed.

Miriz sighed, "Did they have the parts to repair the comm systems?"

Eislie nodded, telling her that there were three shipments of the parts. Miriz seemed confused, wondering how someone had tripled the order. Eislie tapped Jace, telling them she used the ones marked "ARR2270.9," figuring Jace ordered them.

Jace raised his brow, "I didn't order anything. Miriz said she was already doing it." But then, he thought about the earlier message from Preston. He remembered that the frequency they used to communicate with the pirates was ARR 2270.9. Jace looked at Eislie, saying, "Hey, Eis, we should use those parts. It may have been another friend who put them on order."

Eislie looked puzzled before Jace shook his head, saying, "I'll explain later."

Jace walked over to one of the new seats and felt its cushion slowly settle around him as he sat. The wheezing air escaping it reminded him of the furniture back home. "Eis, I think you have a thing for this kind of furniture."

Eislie looked playfully annoyed, then heard Miriz mutter, "Terrans."

Jace snickered as Eislie flopped down next to him, causing the chair cushions to wheeze again and whistle. Miriz joined them gracefully, sitting on the arm of the chair next to Jace. "We should check the installation of the new comm parts. Make sure there are no additional items added."

Eislie and Jace agreed.

Miriz tapped the paperwork referencing the new captain of the *Solace Star*. "We can do the same for the *Wolfhammer* after it's unloaded. But right now, we have some important business to attend to."

Most of the time, Eislie, Jace, and Miriz were the only people speaking. The rest of the crew, Feren, Issa, Derrit, and Shasji, had so far been quiet. Although seeing them all looking at their comms every few seconds let Jace suspect why.

Jace shook his head. He had removed the headpiece Shasji had given him earlier. "Hey everyone, the conversation's over here."

Miriz snickered, seeing them all look in his direction.

Jace motioned for them to move closer. "I know you're excited that there's a famous band here and all, but someone has been messing with things in the office and our ships. It would help if you were looking for things that seem off. Not glued to your comms on what's happening with Queeks."

Feren noticed the tone Jace used when speaking. She had been on ships where the captain used it as a warning. She closed her comm and tapped Shasji's arm. "We should probably be listening to him."

Shasji followed suit, and eventually, Derrit did as well.

Miriz stood. "Good, now that we have everyone's attention, I have an announcement." She started reading from the paper, then paused, looking at Eislie, "Sorry, I'm used to doing this for my company. This is really your responsibility." She then handed the paperwork to Eislie, who watched Jace motion for her to continue what Miriz had already started.

Eislie looked over the paperwork before walking up to Shasji, saying, "I am stepping down as captain of the *Solace Star*. It's your command now, Captain Shasji Yaman."

Shasji happily accepted the documents and smiled as Feren playfully tapped her. "Congratulations."

Derrit scoffed, "Maybe you won't be as tough as Eislie was."

Jace smiled. "Be thankful Eis was captain, not me. She's the nice one."

Derrit looked as though he made a mistake before realizing Jace was joking. He nodded. Tapping Shasji on her shoulder. "Yeah, don't be like him."

There was gentle laughter around the office, and when done, Shasji was nearly crushing the paperwork close to her as she thanked Eislie.

Miriz sat down again. "Now that it's official, let's celebrate a little, then head down and go through the ships. Make sure the repairs are to *our* specifications."

* * *

"What's the feed show?" Nassar whispered as Jelk watched the small screen of his comm.

"He's looking at paperwork. He's nowhere near those two," Jelk replied.

Nassar said, "Breng had to get himself locked up. The idiot was carrying that neuro sedative on him when we processed in. I just hope he doesn't turn us in."

Jelk was more optimistic. He had worked with Breng on other jobs. The man was a brilliant surgeon and medic, but he did have his failings. Even back on Arlain, he was under scrutiny for his activities. But Jelk knew Breng wouldn't turn them in, at least not since they were paying him.

"Relax, Nassar, Breng's good. He won't expose us. He'll come up with a good explanation for the authorities."

Nassar looked at Jelk's comm. "He better. Because if these starborn leave while he's in lock-up, we're leaving him here."

Jelk nodded, "Loyalty to our paying clients comes first. He knows that."

The two returned to listening to their vid feed from Kelor; they didn't notice the two figures a short distance behind them.

"It seems we have others looking for our quarry," Tyne said, stopping the other assassin beside him as she moved to eliminate the men they were watching. "No, it would cause a disturbance and alert the security forces. Even they will have to check in with someone. It may make our actions more visible." He then looked at the small screen of the distant comm to see a moving image. Tyne reached into his short cloak, his actions fluid and silent as he brought something to his eye. He placed a device that latched onto his face, allowing him to see farther into the distance.

"They have a live feed. It's showing containers and that control room that look like they are from the ship we have been hunting." Tyne turned to the woman. "Restig, they have a transmitter on one of that ship's crew. See if you can find the feed."

The woman moved to the side, tapping away on her enhanced comm. "I have it. But it is encrypted. I'm only able to get a partial image."

Tyne stood motionless. The only movement was his jaw. "It's enough for us to track them and that crew member. It will make our mission much easier."

The woman returned to his side as she looked at her comm. "Masih has confirmed that the two we seek are in their office. They appear to be readying to leave. What is our next move?"

Tyne looked around. "Once they have unloaded the cargo, the command will order them to move their vessel. We should be on board and take them then. We'll tell Masih to follow them and meet us when they arrive."

Restig acknowledged his order.

The two assassins crept into the darkness and headed toward the dock, leaving the other men to themselves.

* * *

Jace slapped the button on the elevator as they entered; he turned, smiling, as he looked out the door, but someone caught his attention, causing him to mutter, "Is that the same guy?" He then looked around. "There's a lot of Alliance around now too."

Hearing him, Eisle asked what he said, to which Jace replied, "Nothing. I still have to get used to all these people from different planets."

Eislie shook her head.

They spoke about Shasji's new assignment, and when finished, he heard Miriz quietly whispering with Eislie, making the hair on the back of his neck stand up. He was about to ask, and Eislie must have sensed his intention because she gently grabbed his hand. "We have to do something for my mother's birthday next month. Miriz has an idea."

Jace turned. "Wait, your mother's birthday is next month? I thought it was three months away."

Eislie shook her head, and Jace sighed. "This weird month thing the Alliance has still got me all screwed up."

Miriz chuckled. "At least you didn't forget Eislie's."

Jace bowed his head in shame. "Actually, I did twice."

Miriz feigned being offended. "How dare you." She turned to Eislie, "Never forgive him for that."

The two friends laughed as Eislie said, "I messed up his once or twice, too. Thankfully, Ed reminded me."

"That's because you asked him to remind you." Jace smiled, looking at Eislie. "Wish I would have thought of that."

The sound of friendly laughter was heard as the elevator doors opened, and they walked into the dock. Kelor had finished the unloading and was waiting by the ship as per Miriz's instructions. He waved to them as he waited by the closed bay of the *Solace Star*.

"Everything go smoothly?" Jace asked Kelor as he walked up.

Kelor nodded and followed them onto the ship, "Yes, and I was checking on the new comm in the *Solace Star*. According to your computer, they also installed a new comm on the *Wolfhammer*. They used that box of parts you recommended. I don't know why they didn't use the ones we procured."

Eislie asked the same question, to which Jace replied, "They were from a different source. I believe our friends from the *Kitsdale Aura* provided the ones you used."

Miriz became concerned. "I had the parts specifically scanned. You can't trust something another captain ordered."

"That captain is a friend, Miriz. We know who he is." Jace turned. "You wouldn't remember him. But he's someone we trust."

Miriz looked at Eislie, seeing her nod before turning to Jace, "You think they may have added something additional?"

Jace looked around, then gave a shallow nod, "I think they might have some enhancements that will allow us to communicate in the filaments. At least, that's my theory. I mean, so far, she's kept her promise."

Eislie nodded. "Ed, did they do anything else?"

"No, captain, I scanned the comm systems, and Captain Tucker is correct. The new comm is an enhanced type."

Jace looked around, a smug smile on his face. "They want us to figure out this as much as anyone.

Kelor looked around. "Who are you talking about?"

Miriz closed her eyes. "You two are going to be in a lot of trouble one of these days if you are implying who I think you are."

Kelor looked at his employer for clarification. "Kelor, it is best you don't know. That way, they can't use it against you at trial."

"She's right," Eislie said, smiling. "Let's do a once over on the systems for both ships. Make sure no one else did anything, and then we can head back and relax for a few hours."

Chapter 25:
A Little Trouble Onboard

Almost two hours later, Jace sighed with relief as he pulled himself from the engineering space of the *Solace Star*.

"Looks like everything's that supposed to be there." He turned to Eislie. "We should replace the comms in our ship while we are here as well."

Their computer listened to the conversation and responded, "Captain, the new comms would have to be integrated into the current systems. It should not be an issue, provided they are authorized."

Miriz asked Jace, "You're letting the ship's computer decide what it wants?"

Eislie put her arm over Miriz's shoulders. "Ed gets to decide what works best in the ship. He has to use them all of the time."

Jace smiled as he walked from the vessel. "You know, if Kelor's done unloading the ship, maybe we should go take a look. Check out the *Wolfhammer's* systems. Make sure no one's added anything while we were gone."

Miriz was about to say something, but Eislie interrupted, "No, Miriz, he's not just being a paranoid Terran. If they were monitoring the ship before, they may try again while we're not there."

Miriz shook her head. "I'm sure that computer of yours would alert you."

Jace's smile eroded. "He didn't last time. Whatever they used, he wasn't able to catch them."

Miriz looked to Eislie concerned. "He's right. Your computer didn't know there was a monitor attached inline."

Eislie agreed and activated her comm. "Kelor, how's the unloading going?"

"We're finishing up. Everything seemed straightforward for this shipment. There hasn't been anyone other than myself and the three loaders here the entire time. It was an easy job."

Eislie looked concerned, remarking, "I can't believe he just said that."

"Now we have to check things out." Jace chuckled. "Not being superstitious or anything. It just seems to be our luck."

Eislie grabbed hold of Jace and gently pulled him along, heading toward the *Wolfhammer*. None noticed the movement in the shadows as a man moved from his hidden spot to follow them. The only sound heard was a whisper into his comm. "Targets heading to dock 71."

Eislie laughed as Jace said the last ship they passed looked like a hippo, seeing its weird, rounded edges. Miriz had to look up what he was talking about. She, like Eislie, had never seen a hippopotamus before. The boisterous fun allowed two quick-moving cloaked figures to edge closer to them before being joined by a third. In the shadows, the three met.

"They are entering their ship. We must act now," Restig said. Masih looked to Tyne for direction.

The assassins' leader looked cautiously around. "They are not preparing to leave. We must be patient for this hunt. Our target must be taken alive and intact as per our contract."

Restig looked to the ground. "Yes. But what if we force them to leave?"

Tyne turned to look at her, his eyes steady, causing her to hesitate to breathe. "You will obey, or you will die."

Restig nodded once in compliance but noticed a softening in her master's stare.

Tyne looked to his right, "I will check on the security forces. Your instincts have not failed since you were bound. Perhaps they are correct in the timing."

As he moved away quietly, they heard him say, "We will act if appropriate." Tyne disappeared into the dock, leaving the two to watch the crew of the *Wolfhammer*.

The assassin quickly moved to survey the area, pausing to see Alliance guards now nearby. He moved to a location out of sight and could see the guard tap his comm before opening a door and entering the room. The assassin inspected the area and found no other guards. He stopped, hearing several of the station's crew now entering the area across the room. Their laughter and words drove the silence from the entire area.

The group was now preventing him from exiting without being seen. He knew he could kill them all, but that would alert the station security to their presence, and they would undoubtedly have to fight for their prizes. For now, the assassin waited until he could move unencumbered.

By the ship, Restig looked at the video feed she had tapped. "That one," she pointed to Kelor. "He has the transmitter."

The two waited for some time and watched Jace emerge from the ship. She watched as one of the dock crew approached, yelling at them. She heard Jace yell back, "You know, you could have told us they wanted us to move the ship as soon as unloading was done instead of yelling at us."

The two assassins heard the banter from afar and broke from the transmission. Restig became concerned as she heard, "Alright, we'll lift off in a few minutes. Keep your shirt on."

The man beside her tapped Restig's arm. "We can't wait for Tyne. They're leaving. We should attack now." Restig agreed, and the two headed silently toward the *Wolfhammer*.

"Alright, we'll move," Jace complained to the dock worker as he walked onto the ship. Hearing the man say that he would charge them additional fees if he complained again made Jace turn to confront him. As Jace was about to argue, the man watched as the co-captain of the *Wolfhammer*'s face grew pale with fear as he turned to see two people now holding blades to the throats of Eislie and Kelor.

There was a moment of silence before Jace growled, "Let them go."

The two made no effort to remove the blades from their spots. Miriz looked more closely and gasped, "Bone blades." She moved toward Jace. "They're Slatsa."

Jace spoke through gnashed teeth, "Who are Slasta?"

The dock hand looked at him. "Hired assassins, killers."

Jace's voice carried a warning as he spoke, "You hurt her, you pay. Let them go."

Restig held herself tall as she responded, "Our employer wants you and her alive. The others are ours to decide what to do with."

Eslie sided her eyes to look at the woman holding the blade to Kelor's throat and could see the video display on her wrist. She watched as the images moved as Kelor did. "Kelor, you're working for them?" Eislie blurted out.

Her outburst caused the man to shift, and the woman's blade touched his skin, instantly causing injury before he pulled his head back from the blade, "No! I don't know who these people are."

Jace yelled, "Eis, what's the screen show?"

She told him about the display, and Eislie could see the small stream of blood now dripping down the same side of Kelor's chest. She then remembered that he complained a few days ago that his ear was numb, and she looked toward Jace. Her eyes let him know she felt no deception from Miriz's assistant. Eislie then watched as Jace's eyes grew narrow. She had been close to him for most of their time together, and she knew he was working on a way to end this.

Jace looked to the floor and then to the ceiling before looking toward the controls. He then placed his hands up. "Alright, we'll get ready to lift off."

Jace sat in his chair and tapped away at the controls. Eislie observed that he spent more time setting the inertial gravity and began to realize what he was doing. They had fought over that same thing some days ago. She turned slightly to look at the man holding her as Jace said, "Everyone ready?"

Eislie responded, "Ready," before forcing her elbow sideways, moving the assassin's blade away, only to feel heavy and pulled suddenly to the ground. She and Jace had been flying the filaments and had encountered quasi-space anomalies on occasion. Those experiences from evading and escaping being near a heavy gravity body allowed her to keep her balance. And, before the man could react, Eislie pushed back hard as Jace released the gravity, throwing her entire weight against the assassin and slamming him into the wall behind.

Kelor was fast to catch on. One reason Miriz had hired him was that he was a former security force member. With adrenalin pumping, the man never felt the blade of the assassin as she sliced across his face, cutting across his ear as he pulled away. The dock hand joined in, striking her squarely, causing her to fall unconscious.

Jace quickly grabbed some of the wire he had stored in the control room. He unreeled the wire by slamming it down on the edge of the rear console and snapping the spool in two. He handed one half to Eislie, and they quickly trussed both of their attackers up. Jace made sure to twist the arms of each into an unnatural position to make it difficult to move their hands.

Jace moved to question Kelor but was alerted to the people now rushing onto the ship by the computer. He recognized them as soon as he saw their uniforms.

"Great, the Alliance security is here. What, you waited until we took them down before jumping in?" Jace's tone was part anger and annoyed sarcasm.

Tyne had returned following the security team only to find no trace of his underlings. He could hear the loud arguing from the ship and watched as both of his fellow assassins were brought out unconscious and bound.

These two may be more difficult to take than I realized, Tyne thought. *If those two do not escape, I will have to kill them if they are not already dead.*

"The security forces now know we are here. I may have to call in others." Tyne moved further into the shadows, and he muttered, "I have never failed to take my quarry. I will not allow that to happen now."

Miriz held a towel to Kelor's face and removed it as the medics started working on his injury. She turned and walked over to see what Jace was yelling at security about and watched as he pulled off the comm of the woman who injured her assistant.

The medic gently tugged at a thin filament holding the part of Kelor's ear that was severed, causing her to ask, "Did you have reconstructive surgery done like this for a reason?"

Miriz overheard the woman's remark and returned to look at what the medic referenced. She inspected Kelor's injury before asking the medic to do a deep scan. The results showed a conductive polymer and a larger device implanted inside Kelor's skull—the filament terminating in a lens.

"Jace! Eislie! Get over here," Miriz yelled and pointed to the injury as they arrived.

"That's the transmitter. It's in his head," Miriz said.

The medic confirmed her statement. Jace looked angry but remembered that Kelor said he slept on his ear wrong. And he complained that it was numb when they met. He also realized that he wasn't showing any signs of pain from the injury.

"Kelor, did you know that was there?" Jace asked.

Jace watched as the man's expression turned to fear. "I don't even feel it. That woman took off half my ear, and I don't even feel it."

Kelor looked at his employer to see the concern in her eyes. "You mean you don't even feel anything?"

Kelor shook his head. "I don't even know what, this…. wait, did you say this thing is in my head?"

Eislie looked at Jace, whispering, "I think he's telling the truth."

The medic waved over some of the security forces. She had only seen something like this one time in her service. "Commander, I need you to look at something." She then handed the officer her scanner and showed the device's image. Jace could see the stone look on the officer's face twitch.

"Stabilize him and take him to secure medical." He then stood and pointed to everyone. All of you are going to have to be scanned. This is now a security concern."

Jace looked at him. "When it's done, at least two of our crew have to be in the same room." The commander walked up to Jace, about to say something, before Jace said, "If you like, scan me now while everyone's here."

The commander motioned for the medic to scan him, and she did so quickly. She found nothing unusual about him. Eislie volunteered and was cleared. Miriz hesitated, then allowed the scan to continue. She interrupted the woman as the medic moved toward her left side. "I have an antitoxin scan unit near my liver."

The medic stepped back, hearing her admission.

Miriz looked at Eislie. "I had the implant put in just in case something like what happened before, well, you know."

Eislie looked at Jace, and he could see the surprised stare of his love and was pretty sure of what she was thinking. *She's afraid it will happen again.*

Jace's eyes looked away as he nodded. Eislie knew he understood what she was thinking. But Jace turned to see the commander staring. And Jace began to wonder something. This officer did not detain them.

"Commander, you don't seem surprised we took down those two in our ship." Eislie could tell when Jace suspected something was happening, and she moved closer to him. Then, before the commander responded, Jace said, "You know, you haven't told us your name."

The commander stood tall, "Two captains, this ship is the *Wolfhammer*, and you took down two suspected Slasta on board your vessel." The commander sighed. "I was already warned about you two. We have a mutual acquaintance, Captain Wehen."

Jace shook his head, "I see. I don't suppose you're on a list to find a specific someone, are you?"

The commander looked around. "I've been asked to question you on any updates for a particular individual if that's what you are requesting. And to assist if needed. I am Commander Emdras."

Eislie looked to Jace and watched him shake his head. "We should talk later. After things cool down." Jace sighed, "Eis, we should have everyone scanned. They did it back on Yata, but they've been here a few days. Miriz agreed and told him that it'll be mandatory for all employees of JESC.

Tyne overheard the exchange, "It seems our quarry is also hunting someone. I'll have to be more careful. I suspect the one who has hired us may be the one they are searching for. That would make these two much more dangerous. I should contact for reinforcements." Tyne disappeared into the darkness and set out to collect his fellow assassins.

Chapter 26:
The Hunt for Bosh

An image of Tyne faded from the screen. The screen no longer illuminated the man at the table, his hooded form agile as he rose and turned to face another who was standing silently nearby. Tyne had reported to his superiors of the recent failure and that he would personally correct the issue. He also alerted them that the targets he had been tasked to retrieve were possibly looking for their true employer.

"Leader, his news is disturbing. It seems that our true employer may be the target of those that we have been asked to acquire." The man spoke softly but with a tone that chilled anyone nearby.

Their leader rose from his desk, and his dark eyes pierced the dim room. "Have we discovered the true one behind our employer?"

The man along the wall responded, "Yes, we have a location."

Their leader seemed to be in thought. "Garmon, with recent events, we will need to meet with the one behind that Hurmann fool. I do not like to be without accurate information." He then ordered them to find the one behind Malik and bring him to the Chamber of Ash.

Garmon paused, "Will all be called to attendance in the chamber if the one behind our employer is found?"

Their leader nodded, "With the capture of two of our own from Clan Perig, we must discuss several actions."

Garmon acknowledged him and headed out quickly to fulfill his order.

When Garmon arrived at the dwelling, several Slasta were already waiting for him. "Garmon, we have not seen anyone leave except for that female Gilese earlier."

* * *

Halli handed Bosh his drink before returning to her duties, only to be stopped when Bosh asked, "Were you followed?"

When she answered that she wasn't, Bosh was confident. He had been off world several times since arriving on Arlain and was welcoming the feel of planetary gravity. He tapped the info pad Halli had left before sipping his drink. As he was reading, he heard an alert from his computer. Bosh confidently sipped again before tapping the other display. It showed the housing Malik had procured for him and what looked like several figures outside the door. Bosh's face showed a subtle smile. "Looks like I was right, that fool Malik doesn't know what he's doing."

He watched as they entered the dwelling and saw the assassins run throughout the apartment. Bosh tapped his console and said, "You are very good at your profession. Although I presume that the location you are now walking into may not be what you expected."

Bosh had moved his residence, fearing just such an incident. It took him a few days and a lot of Shil to arrange the transaction to move to a more secure location. The Slasta looked to the terminal, displaying the same image Tyne had described, the sword piercing a circle from above. Bosh's voice encoded to be challenging to trace. One of the Slasta approached and removed his hood. Garmon stared at the terminal. He now realized that the man they were really working for enjoyed his anonymity and realized that Bosh was the brains behind the contract. "You would be a worthy adversary. However, you and the one who employed us have forgotten to inform us of those seeking you."

Bosh's eyes slit, his mind now thinking, *The Alliance is still looking for me?*

Garmon heard no response from the terminal. "I take it you were unaware of the recent findings."

Bosh sat back, still processing the new information. He moved to tap the screen again, "I was not aware. Do you have further information or any update on the acquisitions?"

Garmon's mouth hinted at a grin. "If you were not aware of our quarry searching for you, then you have nothing to worry about."

Bosh felt a chill but remained calm. "Did they say who they were looking for?"

Garmon wasn't surprised that this man called his bluff. "They did not. However, it appears you have withheld information about our targets that allowed two of our own to be captured."

Bosh huffed, then replied, "I would make a statement about you not knowing your craft, but I am well aware of the Slasta and their attributes. Forgive the transgression. I will have our contact provide you with more information on the abilities of your targets. I did not trust our contact enough to divulge the information previously. You will have the information shortly."

Bosh watched as the man stood tall, hearing, "Do you mock us?"

The former captain felt the man's stare through the video feed. "No, I do not. The lack of information was a miscalculation on my part. I will prepare the additional information shortly." Bosh then ended the transmission and sent a signal that caused the terminal in the dwelling to short out, destroying all information on it.

Bosh sat back and was about to sip his drink. As he held the glass up, the ripples bouncing from its sides were only quelled as he gulped the entire contents down.

The Slasta stepped back and smiled, "You would be a worthy opponent." He then turned to the others. "Find out as much information on our targets. This one we cannot trust. If he wants these two, I suspect they may also want him."

* * *

Jace shook his head, hearing Issa and Ferren complaining about being medically scanned again. They had endured it on Yata, and now, at the station, they were very understanding after being informed why.

"You mean they put the transmitter in his head?" Ferren yelled.

Miriz nodded, looking to Jace to see him with that smug Terran stare he had when he knew he was right. She had seen it on many Terrans and didn't care for it. She was about to say something when Eislie tapped her, saying, "Don't worry about that. You get used to it."

Miriz looked at Eislie, "You're part Terran. You must be used to it."

Eislie turned with a look of, I can't believe you just said that. "It must be rubbing off. After all, you had that unit implanted." Eislie wasn't making fun of her friend. She was truly concerned. When Miriz was poisoned when the Karazon tried to force her and Jace to go with them, it left lasting scars, even if they weren't physical.

Miriz smiled, looking more vulnerable. "It's not a cure, but it'll keep me functioning till I can get help. I had to rely on both of you not to get killed to survive the last time. And you had to take down assassins to save Kelor this time."

Eislie could feel her pain in Miriz's words and hugged her. She then pulled her along to where everyone was waiting. They all heard Jace as he spoke.

"Okay, now that everyone's been checked out and safe," Jace trailed off, "at least for the moment. I'm just thankful they didn't implant explosives in anyone."

Issa spoke up. "Historically, the Hurmann did that with slaves during the Alliance skirmishes decades ago."

Jace looked at Issa, his greenish eyes burning a hole through the man before he asked, "Really? And you know that, why?"

Issa looked around, "It was part of my history classes while studying for my ship assignment." He looked around to see others staring at him, "You mean you never knew about the Hurmann and the Consortium? I thought it was required learning."

There was a silence as most people in the room shook their heads. Miriz then stated, "Usually, interplanetary policy is only for the officer core. Did they give you additional leadership training?" Miriz was thinking that since their business was growing, she was considering Issa for possibly becoming an additional captain. Then she asked, "Were you passed over because you're a starborn?"

Issa looked around and nervously laughed, "Um, not exactly. They sort of used that to bust me down to the lower levels."

Jace looked at him and shook his head, but Miriz became concerned and now worried about their company's reputation and hers. "Why were you removed from the core program?"

Issa looked around the room to see the stares of his fellow crewmembers. He could see Jace shaking his head but not the same look as the others, asking why he was disgraced. After a few prodding questions, Issa finally decided to give them an answer.

"Being a starborn was what they used. Honestly, I'm just barely a starborn. I was at this party with some officers. And things got a little out of, well, you know," Issa said.

Miriz didn't want to let things go; she had her reputation and that of both companies to manage. She pressed him for more information, "what happened? Tell us now."

Issa looked to see Miriz with a determined glare, and Eislie looked at her confused. He heard Jace say, "It doesn't matter as long as you didn't kill someone at the party or something."

Issa laughed, "Not exactly, but I think the Alliance vice general made more out of it than it really was."

Hearing the vice general mentioned now did it for Miriz. Someone that high in the chain of command could be a problem for all of them. "What happened?"

Issa looked sheepishly toward the floor and then at Miriz, "Well, his daughter was there as well, and we sort of used his office for uh. . ."

Hearing that, Eislie looked at Jace to see him think, and then a large smile crossed his face before she asked, "What?"

Jace did his best not to laugh. "Miriz, I think I know what happened. I guess it involved removing clothes, maybe a few positions, a few different pieces of furniture. Tell me if anything rings a bell."

Eislie started laughing, causing Miriz to look at her. She heard Issa say, "You're not far off."

Then Miriz realized what Jace was saying, and it hit her. "You mean with the Vice General's daughter in his office?" When they heard Miriz say, "By the goddess, are you serious?" They all laughed.

It was several minutes, and Issa endured several additional prodding questions from the rest of the crew before things calmed. Jace was speaking with Eislie about something; no one knew exactly what it was. But Shasji remembered talking with Eislie earlier, about Bosh still being alive and that the Alliance was hunting him. He also mentioned to Shasji that the current commander of the Alliance security force was possibly an ally in that measure. Eislie could see the hatred in the man's eyes when he inferred about Bosh to them earlier. As the room quieted, Shasji found out what they were talking about.

"Alright, everyone, listen up. We're here to enjoy ourselves today. But when the concerts are over, we have some work to do. Most of you know what happened to us and what we've done to stop starborn from being taken. We've confirmed that the person who ran the facility is still alive, and that Garrett's incapacitation was due to him or his allies."

There was a drone of displeasure in the office as Jace tried to be serious. "Look, I know this all sucks, but you're going to have to be more careful now. We'll all have to check things, including supplies, regularly for the moment."

"You want us to watch our backs?" Shasji yelled.

Jace nodded, "Yes, and each other's. That's why Eis and I have decided to set up a permanent crew for the *Solace Star*. Since Garrett will be out for the foreseeable future, Shasji will be the permanent captain of the ship."

Jace watched as Shasji was about to interrupt but stopped her. "Shasji, before you say anything, Eis and I agree. The ship is small, but after what we have to finish on Yata, it may be the easiest to adapt."

Eislie said, "You understand what Jace is implying, right?"

The new captain of the *Solace Star* thought for a moment and remembered that she had asked Jace to try the filaments while heading to Yata. She looked at Eislie with her eyes wide. "You mean, my ship might be able to. . ." She didn't finish her, sentence understanding the mixed company and that the office might still be monitored. She pulled her hands together, quietly jumping in place. "I'm in."

Miriz looked confused and approached Eislie, who whispered about the shell they were going to test for riding the filaments. She finally comprehended what Jace was saying. Her only response was, "It is larger than yours, and with that capability, it would make it a valuable asset."

The rest of the crew needed help understanding, except for Feren, who said, "I'm in on that. Let's do it right after the concert."

Jace chuckled. "Well, we have to test and ensure it works first. If it works, the *Solace Star* will be the second. It is a larger ship."

Miriz leaned on Eislie's shoulder. "You may want to set their ship up first, just in case you need some help."

Eislie shook her head. "We have some friends that might be able to help without endangering anyone here. We'll be asking them for assistance before we test anyway."

Miriz snapped back, "How do you know they won't cross you?"

Eislie was confident that the pirates had similar interests, and she knew that Jana, their queen, agreed to release the findings to everyone. Eislie also knew that whatever they would do was, at the very least, weeks, if not months, away. She knew, as did Jace, that what they were doing was farther along than any of the others attempting filament travel, including the Duggor, who have been working at it for almost a thousand years.

That fact was something that Jace and she had never understood. The Duggor had taken Lyri but could not travel the filaments without inverting their reactor or engines. The systems he had designed were similar to the Lyri and the Duggor, but so far, an entire race had yet to figure out how to make it work. For now, Eislie wasn't concerned with the ship modifications and knew they had a chance to enjoy themselves.

"Look, everyone, all of this can wait. I know everyone has been working a long day, but I think we should all get some rest. Everyone go take a nap, relax; the concert is later tonight, and we have been invited backstage, so let's take the rest of the day off," Eislie told everyone.

Miriz protested, but Eislie told her, "It's our company. If we want to give people the day off, we can. Besides, not much is going to happen while the concert is going on anyway."

Chapter 27:
Hurmann Attack

The Hurmann fleet was nearing the station, the large ships readying for battle and recovering slaves as spoils. Jelai looked over the plans of the station. It was the obligation of the highest ranking of the Tas leading the fleet to provide a battle plan for their success. Her deceased husband, Garnel, was a brilliant tactician, she had much to learn from his affairs while he was plotting, but a solution to the attack was something that eluded her. She had also read correspondence from home about the actions of House Unber and that a group of Slasta had been noticed around his compound.

Yonin was at her door, and she allowed him to enter. "The others are waiting for your orders."

Jelai turned to look at him. "I still have not found a good option. I can see why we have not attacked in the past."

Yonin had supported House Luxin since they were granted their own line, and he respected the woman before him, not only for her husband's actions but for her support of many actions against the Tas she helped quell. "Would you like some help?"

Jelai shook her head slowly. "I have realized that this may be a pointless action on our part. The station is heavily defended. I fear we have been sent on a fool's errand in the guise of vengeance."

The Hurmann tapped the screen. "I have been studying the plans as well." Jelai looked suspiciously toward him, causing Yonin to say, "I would not hold my own against others against my house if I were not a prudent head." He paused. "I also would not have defended against others such as Malik of House Unber. The one who convinced the others that we should take this initiative."

Jelai agreed with him and shared the information that the Slasta were at Malik's compound. That news made Yonin say, "Perhaps it is for the security of the festivities."

Jelai turned to look at the head who supported her house to remain independent. "According to the financer, he withdrew a large sum of five hundred thousand Lin. That seems excessive for security."

Yonin looked at her. "Five hundred thousand? With this many houses of his opposition away, he might be looking to take over the Tas."

Jelai nodded, "Perhaps my mind has been focused on that instead of this mission." She then leaned back. "We should not focus on taking the station. Just the elimination of Queeks. We could claim it a mercy to the rest of the survivors that we only punish those who have attacked us."

Jelai offered him a seat, and Yonin accepted. "Yonin, I believe we have been sent here to allow Malik and his supporters to take control of the Tas and the Hurmann council. I will inform the fleet of our plan to attack and destroy that ship and Queeks Maco. The takeover of the station will be a secondary. I plan to cite my concern for things back home with the other heads of the houses. Do you think it prudent?"

Yonin smiled as she asked. He had to rely on others with more knowledge and experience to become the leader he was. He agreed, and they quickly called the standing heads of each house to a meeting.

"Do you have proof of this conspiracy?" Tem of Drune asked.

Jelai nodded. "Yes, hard evidence. The only reason I have not acted is that the cost may be for security. At this time, we do not know Malik's true intention."

Tem nodded, "It is a sound conclusion." He turned to the others, seeing them all agree. "Should we head back?"

Jelai stood. "No! We attack, but we focus only on Queeks and their ship. Show those who support them that we are the superior. We allow those on the station to live. Some may understand it and possibly consider joining the Consortium."

Lyl of Dros spoke. "It may make us look weak, allowing those many to live."

Jelai's eyes showed no fear, "we attack those closest to Queeks. Most of their followers will be nearby anyway. They will be the payment for our victory. We will show them that we are the superior."

Lyl nodded, "There have been rumors among some of our loyal that you have not been a strong, effective leader. How should we approach this?"

Jelai stood gracefully. "I'll show you." She turned to face the monitor and ordered her servant to contact all ships. "Show them everyone in the room."

As the monitor lit, Jelai spoke. "Praised are the superior. Today, we will exact vengeance for the loss of one of our own. In a few hours, we will be at Roscin station. I have briefed all the heads of the houses on the attack plan. Our focus will be the terrorist group known as Queeks Maco and anyone within their immediate circle. We will cut the head from the body and leave the rest to rot. Its stench will remind those less significant that we take only what we desire."

There was a brief pause, and even from her own ship, she heard cheers of support. She turned to look at the others before she continued. "Today we are Arlain, separate houses moving as one. A day where we choose our victory and allow those lesser to suffer for their existence. Victorious are the superior."

Jelai motioned for her servant to end the transmission. And Jelai turned to see the surprised and supportive looks of the houses within her sight. She smiled, hearing from Tem, "I stand corrected. Long stand the house of Luxin."

* * *

Jace felt silly wearing the cat ears that Eislie put on his head. Shasji was already in the crowd and was dancing among the others in the area before the stage. He was watching Miriz as she stood near the wall. He walked over to see how she was doing.

He could barely hear himself over the music already playing. "Hey, Miriz, you look lost."

"I don't usually go to these types of events. I'm usually sitting in box seats," Miriz replied.

Jace laughed, "This is the best way to enjoy a concert like this. C'mon, live a little, Miriz." Jace looked at his jacket. "I can't believe I agreed to wear my crew jacket to this thing. How did you convince me to do that, anyway?"

Jace laughed loudly, hearing her say, "Easy, I convinced Eis. She convinced you. Besides, it's good advertising."

Eislie was looking for Jace and saw him speaking with Miriz. She pushed through the crowd to reach them. "What are you two doing over here? The party is out there."

Jace laughed. "I'm trying to get her out there." He turned to Eislie, "Or should we leave her here?"

Miriz yelled back jokingly, "You two are insane, you know that?"

Jace replied, "I never claimed to be sane."

Eislie jumped in, "That's true, he never has."

She watched as her friend Miriz laughed but sensed something was wrong, so she asked.

"It's Kelor. They found a lot of damage from the implant. They will have to reconstruct the entire auditory and nervous systems on his right side. They can't do that here," Miriz told them. "They want to send him back on a medical transport. They're prepping him now."

Eislie could see the concern, and felt a tinge of responsibility, saying, "You 've lost Paaz and Devon and now Kelor since we've been around." She turned to Jace. "Seems like we're playing too rough."

Miriz grabbed Eislie, "This isn't your fault. Don't blame yourself."

Jace grabbed Miriz, and Eislie knew what he was doing as he pulled her away. "Miriz, she's not blaming herself or me. It's the people hunting us."

Miriz pushed him away, "You don't understand, Paaz and Devon were only my assistants for about a year. The others before met similar ends."

Jace looked surprised. "Jace, running a multiplanetary business can be dangerous. And it seems whoever you have hunting after you two is making that worse."

"Miriz. Look, go see how Kelor is doing. We only wanted to see you have some fun. You don't have to be here," Jace said

Miriz looked to Eislie and moved closer to Jace. "He understands more than he lets on, doesn't he?"

Eislie nodded, and she watched Miriz caress Jace's face before she kissed him passionately. Her actions caused Eislie to glare toward her, and as Miriz pulled back, Jace was standing there with a look of annoyance. As she said, "Nothing?"

Jace looked at Eislie, "Eis, at least give her a ten-second start."

Eislie stood there, "One, Two…"

Miriz turned. "I really am concerned about Kelor." She then looked at Jace. "I had to try Eis."

Eislie continued counting and laughed as Miriz walked away, Jace saying, "You know, one of these days, you're going to have to tell me what this competition thing is all about."

Eisle grabbed Jace. "Maybe when you're older. Come on, let's go dance."

Jace jokingly gave a fake temper tantrum, "But I wanna know now. Waa," before he started laughing. Neither saw the person watching them through a stage section, who disappeared as they walked away.

Trin had been watching Jace and Eislie. He saw the whole interaction. He whispered to himself, "Lucky bastard, he has two Gilese women vying for him. That has to be fun." He was quiet as he approached the dressing room where Eshea was getting ready. He entered, and Eshea called out to him.

"Hey, Trin, help Zarlin get the instruments set up. I don't think the station people did it yet," Eshea yelled, then looked around. "Have you seen Ralla?"

Trin's whispered voice was steady. "No, I'll help Zarlin in a minute. Those two starborn and their crew are here. I saw something you might like to know."

Zarlin entered. "Trin, come help me with the instruments the station crew didn't do slac."

Trin turned to see Zarlin happier than usual. Of course, she was always delighted doing concerts. She loved the attention and that she could sing what she wanted. But Ralla insisted that Eshea sing when it fit their objective. But Ralla did allow her to pick songs that weren't just for the cause. He turned, tapping Zarlin on the shoulder. "Hey, that starborn has two Gilese vying for him. Did you know that?"

Zarlin looked at him, "What do you mean?"

Trin now had the attention of Eshea as well, and he told them that the dark-haired one kissed him right in front of the other. "The light hair didn't seem surprised, just annoyed."

Zarlin looked at Eshea. "He has two Gilese courting him? That has to be interesting."

Eshea chuckled, informing them, "The dark-haired one is Mirizali Elysse. She's Yata."

Zarling looked at her, "Wait, he has a Yata and a Gilese vying for him?"

Trin spoke up, "Apparently."

Zarlin looked down. "Oh that poor man."

Eshea laughed, "Don't be too worried about him. The male is a Terran."

Zarlin looked confused and then at Eshea. "I wonder how that's going to work."

Eshea laughed, "I don't know, but maybe we could ask that before we ask them to join us."

Trin and Zarlin could be heard laughing through the closed door as Ralla walked back toward the dressing room. He was going to complain about the instruments, but overheard Zarlin say, "Let's get set up. That crew didn't do slac."

Zarlin finished setting up the microphone and the other instruments. Trin tested the percussion a few times. He always checked since he would be playing them anyway. He watched as Zarlin put her arms out and bowed to the closed curtain. He chuckled, seeing her action. His voice was audible but quiet as he yelled, "What was that for?"

Zarlin turned with a smile before walking over to him. She looked over the percussion, asking if he remembered the last set on Yata. "They unplugged your setup."

Trin nodded, "You didn't answer my question. What's with the bow?"

Zarlin looked toward the curtain. "I just like when people enjoy my songs. I don't get much credit for them since it's Queeks singing them." She sighed. "Do you ever get tired of just singing angry songs?"

Trin placed his arms around her and spoke. "You, me, Eshea, we've all had to endure. Well, even Ralla. You and Eshea kept each other safe. I met Ralla, and he helped me get my voice back. We've all suffered." There was silence before Trin said, "I do. I don't want to play angry songs my entire life. I want something nice, upbeat, softer as well."

Zarlin smiled, hugging Trin in return. "I'm just tired of doing angry songs. And Eshea told me that a friend was willing to offer her a singing job. I mean, I can write and play instruments, sing." Zarlin hesitated. "I just wish this whole thing was over."

After a few seconds, he pulled away and looked her in the eyes. "So, do I. I know you and Eshea would be great together. You'll have that soon, hopefully."

Zarlin smiled at him. She noticed he never said what he would do after this was all over. And she wasn't going to push. Trin had been private from the time they met. She knew he was good with the ship but needed to know what else he could do besides the percussion. She looked down, seeing him smile.

"Come on, we have less than an hour to showtime. Let's make sure everything's working." Trin handed her an instrument, and she happily played a few chords. She heard the cheering from beyond the curtain as they tested the instruments.

Chapter 28:
The Show Goes On

Jace was leaning against the wall. There were seats, but you risked being sat on by those dancing when they didn't see you. A smile was across his face as he looked over to see Miriz sitting in what looked like a penalty box. There were others with her. He walked over, hopping the divider, only to be met by several armed security. Jace immediately took a defensive stance, his eyes scanning the five individuals surrounding him.

He heard one of security say, "This is for authorized fans only."

Jace pointed to his head, "Why do you think I'm wearing this stupid set of ears?"

Miriz responded to his joking, "Jace, show them your wristband before you get yourself thrown out."

Jace held up his hand, then mockingly waved his other hand as if modeling the band that was given to them by Queeks earlier. Eislie returned with some drinks and started laughing, seeing Jace mockingly showing off. She sat beside Miriz, hearing her say, "He is going to get himself ejected." She handed the drinks to Miriz, releasing them so quick that Miriz almost dropped them. Eislie stood and headed toward Jace, scolding him, "Will you stop? You're supposed to come in through the entrance, not jump the fence."

Jace threw up his hands, making one of the guards move toward their weapon. The guard relaxed, hearing Jace yell, "Nobody told me that. I would have used the door."

Eislie excused herself as she pushed through the guards, grabbing Jace. "Before you get yourself thrown out, get over here."

Jace huffed but joked, "Can't argue with her, she won't let me." His statement made a couple of the guards snicker.

"What were you doing out there anyway? Please tell me you weren't out there doing that weird dance Eis told me about. The one you did back on Earth," Miriz said as Eislie dragged him to their seats.

Jace was about to make a remark but didn't. There was something about the crowd, or maybe he felt like he was being watched. But he answered, "No, I was watching over Shasji and Feren. I think Issa went off somewhere."

"Issa went to go find Derrit. We should ask Shasji to join us. According to security, all guests are brought backstage at the same time. So we all have to stay here," Miriz said.

Eislie agreed, "Apparently, the crowds get really bad during the concert. This area is for VIPs, and it's protected."

Jace looked around. "Okay, should I go get Shasji?"

One of the security team looked toward him. "I would hurry. We don't allow anyone in this area after the concert starts."

Jace nodded and rushed to where he jumped the fence before Eislie yelled, "Remember, use the door. Don't jump over like you just did again." She turned to the guard, "Maybe he'll listen."

The female guard laughed, then shook her head.

After a few minutes, Jace returned with Shasji and Feren. Issa and Derrit had returned as well. He was out of breath, saying, "Just made it. They were getting ready to close the doors."

Jace sat as the guards closed off the section and the platform raised for them to get a better view of the concert. When it started, everyone was impressed.

The show went on for almost three hours. The music was great, even by Jace's standards. At first, he didn't understand some of the lyrics because they were in the Arlain language. He had to ask Ed to update his translator remotely, although the computer seemed distracted. When Jace asked, Ed responded. "I have been monitoring the concert. It seems to be very informative." Jace was not as surprised as he thought he would be at the computer's observation. Jace was telling Eislie what Ed had told him when someone tapped him on the shoulder.

"Captain Tucker, Captain Licessien, my name is Ralla. Are you enjoying the show?" The man asked. Jace told him it was great, as did Eislie. The man then asked, "We'll be taking everyone backstage shortly. Would you and your crew be able to wait a little before meeting Queeks Maco? Uh, to allow the others to do a quick greeting and signatures before you. They wanted to meet with you all separately."

Jace turned to Eislie and shrugged. "Sure, we'll let everyone know."

Ralla acknowledged him and told him to wait until one of the production crew arrived. He called over one of the female guards, who was looking somewhat apprehensive. Ralla spoke with her, and she nodded hastily. As the show ended, the crowd cheered, and the curtain closed. As the platform they were on moved toward the stage, The guard remained by them.

Shasji rushed forward, but Eislie grabbed her, saying, "Hold on, we're going in last."

"That's not fair. I thought we were meeting Queeks?" Shasji argued.

The guard responded to her complaint, "You will be. The meeting for you is for the extended VIP, according to Ralla." She turned away, almost blushing. "I can't believe I actually spoke with Ralla. I mean. I, uh. . ." She looked to see Jace chuckling. As he tapped Eislie, she heard him say, "Check out, fan girl."

The guard laughed, however, when Shasji said, "She's not holding a fan," and watched as Jace smacked his hand to his face as he bowed his head. She thought she heard him grumble, "Can't make a joke if no one gets it."

Almost an hour went by before Ralla appeared. He motioned for them to follow, and the other fans had already departed by this time. Queeks was sitting on a rather plush chair while the others sat nearby. They all gave the crew of the *Solace Star* and *Wolfhammer* a hearty greeting.

There were several minutes while the others met with the band members and asked questions, autographs, and even videos to show others back home. Jace and Eislie remained more toward the background, as did Miriz. Jace remarked, "It's too bad Kelor was in medical. I think he would have enjoyed this."

Jace's remark didn't go unnoticed as Ralla approached, "We can visit your friend later if you like."

Jace smiled, but being from Earth, he was having second thoughts. Something in his mind told him this wasn't just a meet and greet. He looked at Eislie. Like him, she didn't have much of a smile. Their stances caused Miriz to ask quietly, "What is it?"

Jace gave a smile but looked around the room. The rest of the crew were being entertained. And so far, they were, more or so, left alone. That told Jace this meeting was about something else. His questions became clear when Ralla steered the conversations toward the plight of the Arlain people.

"We have been gathering allies for our cause and hope to free all people held and enslaved. Much like you two were."

Jace sighed. "So, that's what this is about?"

His statement silenced the room, his crew looking offended by his remark. Miriz even apologized. "He's Terran. They're very cynical."

"Don't get me wrong. I loved the concert. The music was incredible." Jace looked around the room before sitting in the long chair behind him and putting his feet on the table. Miriz scolded him for being impolite. But Jace said, "I'm sensing an ulterior motive here."

Ralla stood. "We are simple people, Captain Tucker. We have no other motives than to explain the plight of our people."

Eislie sensed something and looked back at Jace. She then moved and sat down next to him. Miriz remained where she was. Jace looked at Eislie, saying, "You think I'm wrong?"

Eislie shook her head. "No, they definitely want something."

Ralla crouched down before them. "We are just happy to have you here, like kindred souls."

At that moment, Miriz joined them and sat next to her friends. The rest of the crew joined them on their side of the room when Miriz said, "With what he said, I don't have to be a paranoid Terran to know they want something now. Uh, no offense, Eis."

Eislie gently punched Miriz, and Ralla was about to speak when Jace interrupted. "So far, you've been doing most of the talking. Those two, uh," he pointed to Zarlin and Queeks, "have not said much, but they have been watching us." Jace looked at Trin. "The other one, uh, Trin, was it? I understand. Shasji told me what happened to him." Jace paused. "Personally, I would have, oof." Jace was interrupted as Eislie elbowed him hard. "Yeah, that would have been too dark for this situation." He pulled his foot off the table. "Sometimes you have to listen to others."

Ralla was about to speak when Queeks interrupted. "Ralla, the rest of the crew, I can see them not understanding, but these two have already endured enslavement. Maybe we should just ask them."

Ralla glared toward Queeks before composing himself. He remained silent as if contemplating words when Eshea deactivated her mask. There was an audible gasp as most of the crew realized they weren't meeting Queeks in person. Jace remained where he was as the crew became upset.

"My name is Eshea. I am, well, most of the time, I am Queeks Maco. Or at least play her."

Jace looked to Zarlin. "I'm guessing that mask works on more than one person."

Zarlin looked surprised. "How did he know I play her too?"

Trin gave a hushed laugh. "You're the only other woman in the group. I don't think me or Ralla could pull off the outfits."

Jace laughed, then pointed to Trin. "You know, him I like. It's an honest man who can make fun of himself."

Eislie looked angrily at Jace, making him gently grab her hand. Before pointing to Trin, Zarlin, and Eshea. "Those three I get." Jace then pointed to Ralla, "You, are a different matter. They've seemed to have made peace with their past, somewhat at least. You, on the other hand. . ."

Trin spoke, "How do you know I'm an honest person? You know nothing of my past."

Jace was about to speak, but Ralla interrupted, "Trin had a varied past before he was enslaved. He was also convicted wrongly of crimes against the Alliance."

"Why would you offer that? Do you think it'll sway anything?" Jace stood, walking toward Ralla. "Trin's right. I don't know about his past, and those Alliance files on me aren't very accurate either. You have no idea what I had to do in the past." Jace breathed. "Look, right now, I still like you people, so just ask what you need to ask. Don't bullshit us."

Ralla seemed offended but then stood down. "You are right. We didn't mean to conceal any motives. We did ask you here to ask for aid."

Jace chuckled and heard Eshea say, "We understand that you may not agree, but we have to ask if you'd help us."

Jace looked back at Eislie. She nodded, and Jace said, "Okay, what do you want?"

From that moment, Eshea did most of the talking, Ralla looking somewhat discouraged by what Jace had mentioned. Eshea had worked with Terrans before and knew they preferred a more straightforward approach to diplomacy. Miriz did as well. So, when Jace said, "For me, personally, I, we have some business to finish up. It may help more than what you are doing. But I might consider it later. Right now, however, we have other obligations."

Ralla stood tall, asking, "The plight of our people is not a concern to you?"

Jace walked over, his voice stern. "Do not put words into my mouth. I think it's terrible what's happening on your world. But do not say that I don't give a shit." Jace moved closer. "I just happen to see another option that might help more than just your people right now."

Ralla shot back, "Terrans, they only think of themselves."

Eislie rushed forward, slapping Ralla across the face, "They do not. If you think that, you have no idea what we've done to help people."

Eshea rushed over, pushing Ralla back, seeing the shock on his face. Zarlin joined her, as did Trin. Zarlin gently placed her hands on Eislie's shoulders to comfort her. She had known many Gilese slaves and understood them. Feeling the tension in her muscles, Zarlin then looked Eislie in the eyes and realized. "By God, you're Terran too, aren't you."

Eislie replied calmly, "Partially. So, when you want to insult a Terran, make sure there aren't others in the room."

Jace turned to Eislie, "You okay?"

She glanced at him and nodded. "This is getting too tense. Maybe we should call it a night."

Jace looked back at Miriz to see the others near her, wondering what was happening. He felt bad at what they just witnessed. "Everyone, look,

I'm sorry you had to see this. We didn't mean to break any ideas you had about Queeks. If you want to be angry at me, then go ahead."

Eshea spoke up, "You've done nothing wrong. We shouldn't have disguised this as a fan meeting. We should have told you what it was up front." She turned to the crew of the *Solace Star*. "Please forgive us, and don't blame your captain."

Jace chuckled. "You do make good songs. I enjoy them."

"Thank you," Eshea said in a genuine tone of thanks.

Jace nodded. He turned to leave, again apologizing to his crew, only to hear Ralla say, "You will deny the plight of fellow slaves?"

Jace turned. His face showed no anger as he said, "That statement tells me two things. Either you're desperate, or you are trying to bully us into joining you. Which is it?"

The crew of the *Solace Star* understood what Jace was saying and watched as Zarlin asked, "Ralla, what are you doing? We don't force people to join us."

"Shut up, Zar, you're too innocent. This is war," Ralla replied.

Eisle stepped between Zarlin and Ralla. "Oh, now you're just being hurtful. Do you care more about your cause or the people who are your friends, Ralla?"

* * *

Outside the station, several cruisers appeared from Hyperspace, "Mistress, the concert is still in process. It is on the lower portion of the station. We can be in position to attack in forty standard seconds."

Jelai looked across the bridge of her ship, servants and allegiants all ready to fight. She had to decide now to prove that she was fit to lead House Luxin and that she was strong enough to rely on her allies. She gave the order, "We are fortunate. Focus on the location and attack, obliterate everything. Leave nothing in the concert area alive."

Chapter 29:
A Very Bad Day

Tyne cleaned the thin ceramic blade on the guard's sleeve. His former associates now lay motionless, the bodies breaking down into elemental components in their cells.

"Find the light of death. You will be honored," Tyne said tossing a second dose of the molecular decomposing solution all their people used when captured. "It was unfortunate that they did not allow you to take your own. Our quarry did not allow that of you."

Tyne moved quickly and with stealth out of the detention area, his work there finished. He now had to find a way off the station. The transport they used was now grounded. Its core crystal was removed to prevent it from powering up.

The assassin moved through the dock unnoticed by most. The occasional maintenance robot turned to investigate as if something had shifted. Tyne came across a ship loading some cargo. It had a small crew, and a race he had recognized.

Nibik? They were on Arlain when we arrived. Perhaps they are heading there. Tyne thought.

Tyne heard one of them yell, "Get loaded up. That concert is ending soon. I want to leave before they do."

Good fortune follows me, it seems, Tyne thought. The assassin moved to follow one of the loading crew into the ship's hold. From there, he repositioned to a secured room without being seen. *After we are underway, I will take this ship.*

Jarrus thanked Belon for the cookies and sealed the room to prevent the stench of the choc-o-chip from tainting his ship. "I will be happy when these are gone." The captain of the *Go Ge Go Go* turned, heading to the control room.

"Let's lift off. I don't want to be here any longer," Jarrus ordered as he looked around. "I want to deliver this cargo and return in time for the Feast of Erak."

The crew acknowledged his order, and they started liftoff procedures. When they had reached the outer station, Jarrus ordered them to set course for Arlain before their sensors detected a fleet of ships entering the system. Within seconds, they watched as the large cruisers fired on the southern part of the station. They also watched as several ships launched from the station were quickly destroyed. Jarrus knew the capabilities of his vessel and knew his ship was severely outgunned. "Keel, move closer to the station and cut power to minimal."

"Jarrus, we should fight," Keel shot back.

The captain growled back, "We have cargo for these very same. And this fight is not a worthy cause. Our deaths would be useless." He thought of the season they were now entering for his people. "This is time for atonement. We will aid those who are innocent."

The crew talked amongst themselves and agreed with their captain. Jarrus was correct. This was a time of atonement. If they were to die, it would be in aiding others, even enemies. They flew closer to the southern half and cut power.

"Use thrusters only; if there are survivors, then we will aid them. The Hurmann may attack, but we will only defend those we assist," Jarrus ordered.

"Then we will be atoned. Such is the way of our people," Jarrus heard one of the crew shout. Jarrus felt the pride of the season and the fire of battle balanced within his chest. His senses became sharp, seeing what remained of one of the individuals at the concert as they floated by. *If they are in one piece, we will bring them on board.* Then, one of the crew saw what looked like a person wearing a safety veil float from the station. Jarrus immediately ordered them to retrieve that person.

* * *

Jace felt the wall buckle as he hit it, his senses ringing as the air started to thin. He quickly pulled his safety veil over his head and sealed it. He felt his body lurch to the side as the outer wall gave way. Eislie and the others were already out the door of the meeting room. Jace remained behind when Eshea asked him to consider their offer to join them.

Jace turned, he could see out into space when the rest of the wall gave way. What remained of the concert area was now exposed to the harshness of the elements. Jace could see Eshea and Zarlin holding onto the railing above the step. Trin had been holding onto one of the cabinets that seemed mounted securely to the floor. Ralla was by Trin grasping for a hold of any kind.

Jace watched as several pieces of debris flew in from the doorway. And he noticed Shasji holding onto something. When Jace looked closer, it was someone. Eislie was holding her hand and reaching for Trin. Jace held onto the railing and pulled himself closer to Eshea and Zarlin, grabbing a wire from one of the instruments as he shuffled toward them. He looked over to see Eislie looking at him, Jace nodded then tapped his collar to activate his comm. "I've got these two. See if you can get him through the door."

Eislie acknowledged him. She securely planted her feet against the deck before stretching to reach Trin, his hand was barely clasping hers. Trin got a better grip and held his leg out toward Ralla. Jace watched as their leader, Ralla grabbed Trin's outstretched leg. Jace tugged the wire before wrapping it around Zarlin and Eshea and pulled them along against the force of the escaping atmosphere.

They all moved toward the doorway where Eislie stood. Her hand braced against the door as Jace pulled the other two forward. He had found a solid handhold and tied the wire wrapped around his arm to it as he pushed them toward the door. Shasji held the door open, preventing the emergency system from closing, but it was temporary. The shelf she was using to secure the door was starting to slip. Jace quickly pushed Eshea and Zarlin forward, and Eislie grabbed hold of them. After they were through, Jace moved forward.

Eislie reached out to him, and Jace looked behind her, seeing something large heading right for her. He motioned for her to duck, but she turned and was struck hard by the item. Jace tried grabbing her as she was thrown by, but Jace felt the impact of another item, causing him to let go. Jace's body spun around, and the last thing he saw before losing consciousness was Eislie floating out into space.

Shasji watched as a Nibik ship moved to stop Eislie from floating away. *Good, they'll get her on board,* Shasji thought before seeing Jace hanging limply by the wire he had secured earlier. And she reached out to try and pull him in. The shelf she used to block the door shifted then split, its jagged metal tearing through her veil as it gave way. She felt her lungs expand and the breath fighting its way out of her. She didn't have time to think as the pain of the decompression caused the blood in her lungs to seep through its walls. She watched as a spray of her vital fluids started to escape her. The shelf shifted out, and the emergency door started to close. Feren pulled them through just before it closed. Feren turned Shasji over to see the blood running from her mouth.

All she could yell was, "Medic!"

Jace woke with a start, his head still pounding. He pulled his arm up to feel his muscles screaming at him. He sat up to see them working to stabilize Shasji nearby. Miriz grabbed Jace and held him tightly. Jace gently pushed her away as he asked, "Is everyone alright? What happened?"

Miriz seemed to be holding back tears as she stared at Jace. He turned, looking around before grabbing his head. "Ow, Where's Eis?"

Miriz couldn't hold her tears as she said, "They're still looking for her."

Jace moved to get up, but one of the medical personnel grabbed him. He pushed them away before Miriz attempted to hold him down. "Jace, it's been too long. Her veil was probably breached when that thing hit her."

Jace pushed her away. "No. She can survive if her veil was sealed." Jace slammed on his comm. "Ed, can the ship launch?"

"Yes, Captain, the station has asked all available ships small enough to aid in searching. Are we going to do so?"

Jace's voice filled with resolve. "We're going out as soon as I arrive. See if you can find Eis's comm signal."

"I have been trying for the entire time you have been unconscious. I have yet to lock onto it. The ship is ready now. We will launch when you arrive, Captain."

"You read my mind, Ed. Let's go find her," Jace said, pushing anyone who was trying to hold him back away.

Over four hours later, Jace swept through the area by the station. They had retrieved three bodies. He was upset that he was unable to do anything for them. Jace's head was pounding as he worked the controls. "Ed? Anything?"

A noticeable delay occurred before the computer responded, "No, Captain. I found no life form readings or the Captain's comm signal. Even with my sensors on full, I do not detect her signal."

"Keep trying, Ed," Jace replied, moving the ship to take another pass before hearing the comm alert.

Jace hit the comm hard and was disappointed hearing Miriz ask, "Jace, any luck?"

He answered, his voice cracking, "No."

Jace grabbed his head. It was still pounding. Miriz, seeing his actions, said, "You were struck hard. The medics need to evaluate you when you come back in Jace."

Jace remained silent. The pounding in his head was like a heavy beat as he looked to his side to see the empty chair. His breathing became studded as he whispered, "No, I'm not giving up," the plea for help hidden in his words.

A tear fell from Miriz's eye, "Ed, your Captain is injured. I know you don't like me, but I'm ordering you to bring him back now."

There was a moment of silence, before Ed replied, "Captain, Mirizali is correct. You are not in a fit condition to fly. I am returning you to the station. If needed, I will continue the search."

Jace ordered Ed to keep going, but as he fought against the computer, Jace felt the world start spinning and he fell unconscious.

Jace opened his eyes as the ship touched down. He looked at the empty seat and heard the computer say, "Captain, please seek medical aid. I will continue to search for Captain Licessien on my own."

Jace begrudgingly stood and headed for the airlock, punching the inside hull hard, his injured arm screaming in pain as he pulled it back. "Ed, find her, please."

The computer instantly responded, "I will continue to search until you order me to stop."

Jace held back tears. "Thanks, Ed," before exiting the ship.

The dock crew jumped on board to remove the bodies they had retrieved, and as Jace walked through the gantry, he watched as Ed took the ship out again. Jace's footsteps were heavy as he walked into the station.

Jace had found where Miriz was and that she was now watching over both Kelor and Shasji. Feren had gone to help with the recovery, and Jace would have liked at least one of the crew to help, but all were already allotted to other ships or injured. He walked into the room to see Shasji under a regen field, and Kelor sedated. He had known that they did that to prevent him from experiencing pain until they could take him back to Yata for treatment.

Jace's foot squeaked as he stopped in the doorway. Miriz rushed over to hold him. She quietly told him that she had already called Eislie's parents, who were already on their way. Jace held Miriz tightly, his body shaking as he quietly sobbed, repeating, "I couldn't find her."

Miriz held him tighter, and she felt Jace shift. "I couldn't find her, Miriz. I… couldn't… fin….”

She felt Jace's entire weight and fell to the ground with him. She pushed him back. His eyes had rolled back into his head."

"Jace! Wake up!" Miriz yelled. She shook him, but his body was limp. She pulled him against her, yelling, "Medic!"

The medical staff helped him up. Jace's vitals were erratic, and they started working on him immediately.

Chapter 30:
What Happened?

On the Nibik ship, Jarrus inspected the two he had saved. The male had already succumbed to the ravages of space, but he recognized the woman with light hair from the files that Malik had allowed him to see. *This must be them,* he thought. He ordered his crew to heal their injuries but sedate them both, before remembering the male was already dead. He then informed the crew that these two were wanted by the same people who requested the cookies. Many crew members did not understand his implication. "We are not slavers."

Jarrus agreed but watched as two of his crew fell to the ground, their bodies unmoving. He then watched as a figure moved to behind another. Jarrus heard, "You only have a seven-person crew, now five. That female on the ground is the one I seek. Give her to me, or I will kill all of you."

Jarrus moved forward only to see the assassin kill another of his crew. "This is my ship," the captain growled.

Tyne's eyes never wavered. "You will take me and her to the coordinates I provide. If you want to remain alive, you will comply." Jarrus growled as the assassin moved closer, telling him, "I don't need any of you to fly this ship. But you have ordered her healed, and we do need to heal her injuries. I'm sure we can come to an appropriate arrangement."

The Captain of the *Go Ge Go Go* ordered Eislie to be healed, then asked, "What of this one?"

Tyne scoffed, "That one is not the one I am hunting. Besides, that one is dead already. Dispose of the body in any way you desire."

Jarrus motioned for one of his remaining crew to take Eislie to the medical bay, and Tyne watched them take her before ordering, "You will sedate her as the captain ordered. And Captain, if any move against me, you and all your crew will find death. And I will take your ship."

Tyne then moved to the controls, holding a blade to the pilot, "Get us underway, now."

* * *

Jace opened his eyes to see the dim ceiling above. He recognized he wasn't on the *Wolfhammer* and looked around to get his bearings. Jace turned his head to see Miriz sitting in a chair nearby. His movements caused the sensor in the bed to alert the staff that he was awake. Jace went to move only to find himself restrained to the bed.

Jace pulled at the restraints only to have one of the medical staff stop him, "There was trouble with the gravity. We restrained all patients as a precaution. The woman moved to free him and checked his vitals. "You're almost back to normal." She looked at Miriz. "She's been there since they brought you in two days ago."

"Two days?" Jace said, then went to get out of bed.

The medic pushed him back down. "You still need to heal. Your injuries were severe."

The commotion woke Miriz, who stood, helping push Jace back onto the bed. "Jace, stop. You still need to heal."

Jace stopped struggling and lay back. His face showed sadness, and his strength was all but gone as he lifted his arm. "Ed, what's your status?"

"I am operational, Captain." There was a long pause before the computer continued, "I regret that I could not... find Captain Licessien."

Jace's voice cracked. Noticing the computer's hesitation, his mouth quivered as he said, "That's okay, Ed. That's okay. We did our best." A tear ran down his face as Miriz laid her head across his chest to comfort him.

A day later, when Jace appeared in Shasji's room, Miriz returned to watching over them. Feren was there, and she got up to hug him as he walked in. Miriz did the same before Jace asked, "How's she doing?"

Miriz smiled, "She's better. She experienced severe decompression syndrome. Almost two-thirds of her organs were compromised."

Jace looked to Feren for an explanation. "It's an excruciating way to go. Most of a person's organs embolize. She's lucky she survived."

"She's tough." Jace looked at Miriz as she looked up at him. Then Jace sat in the nearby chair as if his energy had just drained away. He said, "I don't know what to tell them."

Feren looked to Miriz for an answer to what he was saying, and she crouched down, holding his hand. "I think Flora was just as upset finding out that you almost killed yourself looking for her."

Jace looked at her, then leaned forward, his hands over his face. "It doesn't feel like she's gone." Miriz looked puzzled as Jace said, "I mean, she could have been vaporized during that attack. But we should have at least found her body, or something."

"Don't! Don't do this to yourself, Jace. You'll drive yourself insane." Miriz's words were filled with warmth and sadness and mild anger, "Besides, you almost killed yourself. You had internal bleeding in the brain and spinal column. If you weren't a stubborn Terran, you'd be dead."

Jace chuckled, looking at Shasji. "Chalk another one up for Terran stubbornness."

It was a day later, and Jace was waiting near Shasji's bed. He had just spoken with Eislie's parents, who told him they would be there in a couple of days. The ship they were on was needed to help with a distress call from another that the Duggor had attacked. Jace understood and told them he'd still be there when they arrived. Jace had just sat down after handing Miriz something to drink. Her status allowed her some comforts on the station due to her business.

Jace looked up to see Eshea in the doorway with Zarlin. He waved them in.

"How is she doing?" Zarlin asked.

Jace told them she was doing better and thanked them for stopping by. "I'm sure she would be fawning over you if she knew you were here."

Eshea gave a gentle laugh, knowing what they all had been through. She, like Zarlin, felt sorry for trying to pressure them into joining their cause days earlier. She told them that the *Eiger* was destroyed, and they were arranging transportation.

But that wasn't why they were there. Zarlin looked at the floor when she spoke. "We heard what happened to your partner. We're very sorry."

Jace held his composer as Zarlin said, "She died because you were saving us. Even after we insulted and tried to make you join us."

Eshea nodded and was not offended when Jace put his arms around them. Miriz could see the pained look behind his eyes as the two women

210

held onto him. Eshea pushed away. "On our world, we would owe you, our lives."

Jace shook his head. "I don't believe in any of that." He chuckled. "Besides, if I did, many people would owe me."

His joke made most in the room chuckle, and then they all looked over, hearing a low groan from Shasji and seeing her stir.

Jace commented, "Maybe she will get to see you after all."

Seeing Shasji open her eyes, Jace smiled and snickered, hearing her say, "Queeks?"

Jace pushed the two forward and watched Shasji smile. "No one's going to believe that Queeks was here in my room." She lifted herself only to say, "Ow, so that's what decompression syndrome feels like." She looked at Jace. "I don't like it."

Miriz said, "You sure you're not part Terran? That's something Jace would say."

Shasji chuckled, "I think I've been hanging around the two of them too much. By the way, how's Eis doing?"

The color drained from Miriz's face, and she turned to look at Jace. She watched as he sighed, "Uh, Eis didn't make it? She, uh…."

Shasji shook her head. "You mean they couldn't save her when they brought her on that ship?"

"What ship?" Jace's voice filled with an authority that caused everyone to move away.

Shasji could see the look of hope in his eyes as she said, "It was a Nibik vessel. I didn't see its name before I passed out."

Jace slammed down on his comm, "Ed, you get that?"

"Yes, Captain, I am already working on finding the information."

"You mean Eis might be alive?" Miriz said.

Jace looked at her, a spark of hope now back in his eyes. Eshea watched as the entire crew of his all looked to him for a course of action. Then they heard his comm come alive.

"Captain, the Nibik did not give a destination, but there are only two places they visited while on the station. The shops were Artificer Elite and the Chamber of Sliver.

Artificer Elite, that's Yasa's shop? Eshea recognized the shop name. Yasa had known her for some time, even before she escaped.

"Chamber of Sliver sounds like some dungeon thing," Jace said as he looked around. "Can we find out where they are on the station?"

Eshea knew the location of the one shop and its owner. She moved aside and quietly tapped her comm. "Ralla, it's me."

"Where are you? Trin and I are still working on getting transportation. We need to get off the station," Ralla responded.

"The *Eiger*'s gone, Ralla. Right now, the Hurmann think we're all dead," Eshea shot back. "But that's not why I'm calling. Did you stop by Yasa's shop today?"

Ralla answered, "Yeah, we picked up some weapons. Concealed stuff just in case we run into any Hurmann."

Eshea looked at Zarlin. "Zar, Ralla is still working on getting transport." She returned to her comm. "Listen, Ralla, I'm going to help someone find one of their lost crew, Eislie Licessien. I'll be back later. If I need to, I'll find transportation on my own. We'll rendezvous on Gan 3 like before."

"Good. If we help them, then they'll owe us. We can get them on our side," Ralla responded.

Eshea sighed, "I'm not interested in that, right now it seems she's been taken by the Hurmann."

"What? Eshea, we need to keep going. The Hurmann can't think that they've won. And if they catch you, they'll kill you. I'm ordering you to return to the room now. You need to get back…" <click>." Eshea closed her comm

Zarlin watched as she moved closer to speak with Shasji. Eshea could hear her apologize for deceiving them initially, but they meant well. Eshea could see Jace's resolve and knew she had to help the man who saved her and Zarlin, so she stepped up. "I can take you to the first one. I know the owner. But the other, I don't know."

Jace moved to talk with Eshea and watched as she yelled over to Zarlin. "Zar, Ralla wants you back at the room soon. I'm going to help them."

Zarlin shook her head. "If you're helping, I am too."

Eshea moved closer and hugged Zarlin. "Not this time. Right now, I know I can help them with something. And honestly, it's not really a place you need to go. It's down in the lower levels, by the reactors."

Zarlin seemed to freeze for a second, something Jace noticed. He stood beside Eshea. "I'm thinking she has been near something similar."

Eshea nodded, "Her other owner put slaves who misbehaved near the reactors. They're not spide, but they can cause stray radiation burns."

"Sounds like you have some real winners running your planet," Jace muttered.

Eshea looked at him strangely, saying, "They're always winning."

Jace muttered, "What I said means something completely different where I'm from." He then turned to Shasji. "Shasji, how soon can you captain the ship?"

Shasji smiled back. "I'm mostly okay, but I'd like a few more days."

He turned to Miriz. "Miriz, the *Solace Star* needs a minimum crew of three. I think you should get Kelor and head back. Feren and Derrit can help." He looked around. "By the way, where is Derrit?"

Feren said, "He's been helping out with the repairs on the station."

Jace sighed, "I hate to take him away from helping, but we need to regroup. Miriz, I'll order him back. Get them on the ship and return to Yata Beta. I'll let Eis's parents know." He looked at Eshea. "Take me to that shop, we'll start there."

Miriz yelled after Jace as he left the room, "Where are you going?"

"To see if I can get a lead on where Eis was taken," Jace replied as he disappeared around the corner.

He could hear her yell, "Be careful."

Eshea and Jace headed down to the lower levels, Eshea muttering she hoped Zarlin would return to the room and that Ralla wouldn't be too hard on her for not returning with her.

Jace remarked, "If he's your leader, he'll understand, but from what I can tell, he's nothing more than a zealot with a sense of revenge."

Eshea defended Ralla. "He's a good leader, but I think he's too involved with the cause to see what it's doing to everyone."

When they arrived, Eshea noticed the shop was closed, but she knew that Yasa would sometimes do other business. She tapped her comm. "Yasa, it's me. You open?"

Within seconds, Yasa appeared and opened the door. He looked at Jace and asked, "Who's he?"

Jace said, "I just want to ask you some questions if you have a minute."

Yasa reached behind him, and Jace watched his movements before pushing him backward, taking the weapon from the nearby stand that Yasa was reaching into. He could see the spikes on the thin, whiplike device. "Oh, nasty. But, I'm not into that sort of thing." Jace then snapped the item down against the table.

Yasa turned to Eshea to see her surprised at Jace's actions. "Why'd you bring security down here?"

"You think I'm security." Jace laughed, "Listen, I need some information on a client you may have had here. I'm only looking for information."

Jace watched as the man slowly shifted his hand further behind him and brought the whiplike weapon down on the counter, shattering the small glass top. "I don't care if you have a weapon back there; I am only looking for information. Let's not make this harder than it has to be."

Eshea looked at Jace to see the determination in his stare, "Yasa, if you shoot him, you'll only piss him off. This man took the brunt of the debris while saving me and Zar when the room depressurized. I don't think a shot is going to stop him. We're only here for information."

Yasa crossed his arms.

Jace relaxed a little, "You supposedly had a Nibik in the shop a few days ago. I just wanted to know if they mentioned where they were going."

Yasa huffed, then said, "What's it worth to you?"

Eshea moved forward to plead for Yasa to help, but Jace beat her to it. "You're trying my patience. They may have taken my wife as a hostage. Do you know where they were going or not?"

Eshea had been in battles, and she heard the tone Jace used. She realized that if Yasa was about to attack or tell them to leave, she may have to clean up what was left of her friend. Instead, she heard his response. "The Nibik is a slaver?"

"Don't know, don't care, right now I need information. Do you know or not?" Jace said, his fists clenching tighter.

Yasa looked at Eshea to see the fear in her eyes, and he said, "Uh, no, he only came in to have a cleaner repaired. I sold him a new one. That's all."

Jace looked at Eshea. "He's telling the truth." Jace sighed. "We have one other lead. Let's see if they know anything." Jace turned to leave but paused.

He looked at Yasa, "Listen, if you hear anything, you can reach me through JESC Salvage."

"Wait, that company makes the Sotiral suits, right? Is there a reward?" Yasa said.

Eshea looked at him disappointed. "Not the time to be greedy, Yasa. We're trying to save someone. The Nibik may have taken her."

"Oh, Eshea, before you go, I have some information on a former Hurmann you might like to know," Yasa said, causing Eshea to remain behind for a few seconds.

She followed after Jace. "Did that computer of yours find the other shop?"

Jace looked at his comm. "Yep, it's about two floors down. We'll know soon enough if they know anything."

Chapter 31:
Atonement Help

Belon looked up to see two people walking into his shop. He recognized the races. One was Arlain. The other was possibly Gilese. When the man spoke, he knew right away he was dealing with a Terran.

Ed had confirmed that only one Nibik vessel had arrived and departed. So Jace knew if he had been there, the shop owner might know at least something. "You have a minute for some questions? A Nibik ship docked her a few days ago and left. We know one of the crew was here. Do you happen to know where they are headed?"

The shopkeeper remained professional and asked why he needed to know the information. Jace was already starting to lose patience. "They may have taken someone I care about."

"What? That's impossible. We're not slavers," Belon defended.

Jace looked the man straight in the eyes, "One of my crew saw them take two people onboard, and we've checked with security. They were never returned to the station. Also, neither of their comms can be reached. I'm asking nicely, please. Do you know where they went? I only want to talk to them."

Belon suddenly looked disgusted and fearful. He then looked at Jace, asking, "Are you certain?"

Jace sighed, "I believe the person who saw them picked up. I want to find out for sure."

Belon leaned on his counter. "Jarrus, my soon-to-be son-in-law, had mentioned he was working for someone, but as a courier, not a slaver."

Jace became hopeful. "Did he tell you where he was going?"

The shopkeeper shook his head, "No. He did not. It's just that he needed choc-o-chip cookies. Vile things."

Jace gave a hungry growl. "I haven't had those in years. Now I want some. You don't have anymore, do you?"

Belon looked disgusted before he moved forward, placing his hands on Jace's arms. The alien, much taller than Jace, asked, "Was it someone special?"

Jace nodded. "One might have been an employee, the other I'm aligned to."

Belon stepped back. "I ask the divine for forgiveness for my son."

Jace again became impatient. "Look, do you know where his ship might be? We're limited on time."

Belon looked at Jace. "No, I do not, but he is trying to return for the Feast of Erak. And to atone for sins."

"We don't have time for this. where do you think we can find him?" Jace asked.

Belon sighed sadly. "It seems the divine is tasking me to atone for my past actions myself." He looked at Jace. "The feast starts in two days but will continue for two weeks. He was trying to return before the end."

"So, in two days, he'll be back?" Jace asked.

"It will be at least a week. But Jarrus was hoping to return before then. He was my proxy for not attending." Belon shook his head. "It seems I must help you to atone for his sins."

Belon pointed to the small side room, "Those cookies are in there on the near wall. I will guide you to where we need to go myself. Perhaps someone of his crew's family may know where they had gone." Jace seemed annoyed as Belon said, "Forgive me, I wish to aid you. If one of my family has done such a heinous act, we will all need to atone for their actions."

It was a few minutes as Jace, Belon, and Eshea headed up in the lift. Jace was talking into his comm. "Miriz, I've got a lead. I'm heading out now. Get the others on the *Solace Star* and return to Yata in case I need backup."

"But Jace..."

Miriz was interrupted when Jace said, "No, Kelor and Shasji are your priority. Tell her parents I'm going after her. I'll contact you when I have more information." Belon looked to Eshea as Jace said, "Ed, warm up the engines. I've got a lead."

"Yes, Captain, I will file a flight plan, and we will leave when you arrive," the computer responded.

At that moment, Eshea's comm alerted her. "Eshea, where are you? We have transport."

Eshea seemed annoyed as she answered, "Ralla, I'm helping the starborn. I'm not coming back to meet you. We'll rendezvous at the agreed location when I can."

"If you're helping him, then make sure he knows he'll owe us. Maybe he'll change his mind," Ralla said. Eshea's comm was loud enough for Jace to hear.

"You can tell Ralla to go fuck himself," Jace griped.

Belon looked at Jace, "Do not let anger take you, my friend. We will find your answers. And hopefully, your love as well."

Jace muttered jokingly, "If you're going to spout philosophy the whole time, I may throw you off the ship. By the way, how far are we going?"

Belon replied, "To Nibik. It is about a week and a day flight time. I'm sorry it is so far to find answers."

Jace chuckled. "That's about three to four days the way I fly."

Eshea looked at Jace. "How fast is your ship?"

Jace shrugged, "I don't know. Since the last upgrades, we haven't tested them at full. Guess we'll see how fast it is." The doors to the lift opened, and Jace rushed toward the ship.

When he arrived, Miriz was standing by the entrance of the *Wolfhammer*. The computer opened the door as he walked up. Miriz stood there silently, only looking at him.

Jace broke that silence. "I have to try to find her, Miriz. I can work faster alone."

Miriz looked at the two now appearing behind him "You need people onboard you can trust."

Jace looked at Eshea and Belon, "I'll have to trust them if this doesn't pan out. I'll need you and the others to, well, you know."

Miriz threw her arms around Jace. "You bring her and yourself back, safe, okay?"

Jace pulled her gently against him, "I will."

Miriz let him go. Tears were in her eyes when she said, "You know, her mother said not to try and stop you. She threatened to go after you both if you don't make it back."

Jace smiled, "Well, you know us crazy Terrans."

Miriz gently kissed him. "I'm serious. You both better come back."

Jace nodded, then motioned for the others to board the ship. "We'll meet you on Yata."

As he walked onboard, Jace turned. His eyes were not full of that confidant Terran stare Miriz complained about. He tapped the hull of the ship before closing the door. Miriz remained standing nearby as the ship lifted off. "You both better be there."

* * *

The latches snapped against the hull of the *Go Ge Go Go*, and Tyne held a blade to the pilot's head. Jarrus was reserved and compliant, knowing full well that the Slasta who was onboard would keep his word in finishing off the remaining crew. Instead, he ordered them to place their cargo from the station near the airlock on the bridge. The scent of the chocolate chip cookies nauseated the remaining crew of the *Go Ge Go Go*. Tyne, however, was smiling, thinking, *that is an intriguing fragrance.*

Tyne turned as the cabin door opened. He nodded slightly, acknowledging his fellow assassins as they entered. Jarrus kept his eyes on the woman as she approached him. She turned to the small piles of boxes; its scent noticed by her. She approached Tyne, then looked back at the cargo near the airlock.

Tyne said, "That is something else our employer is seeking."

219

"Have you confirmed the targets?" the woman asked as she turned to look at him.

Tyne kept his answers short. "The female is confirmed. The male is dead, but he is not the one we were hunting."

The woman turned her head, her eyes giving silent orders to those who followed her. "And your apprentices?"

"They have found the light and will be honored." Tyne bowed his head, knowing that his apprentices accepted their deaths without question.

The woman also bowed her head. "Remember them, and never fail again."

Tyne raised his head and faced forward, "May I find the light of death if I do."

Moments later, when the other assassin returned, Eislie was draped over his shoulder. The other had moved most of the waiting cargo into their ship. The Slasta commander pointed to the airlock, and the others took Eislie on board.

She then glanced at the Nibik captain.

Jarrus could see the void in her eyes, the coldness of death itself. He felt fear for a moment, but, being a warrior, he began to growl.

The commander turned to Tyne. "Leave this ship with the dead."

Tyne turned to the woman. "They are Nibik. I have a better idea." The woman turned to face Tyne, only to hear him say, "They provided me a means of transit and our prize. Perhaps we can compensate them for aiding us."

The woman's expression showed a hint of anger, only to be softened as Tyne said, "Their honor will also be tainted from now until they die. Torment for such as these."

The commander smiled as she motioned for Tyne to enter the ship. She followed, saying nothing as she closed the door, silencing the cursing from the remaining captain and crew of the *Go Ge Go Go* behind her.

It was two days later when Arlain came into view. Eislie remained sedated but healed by the crew of the *Ember Line*. Tyne was onboard finishing his communication with their clan when he turned to see the commander glancing at him.

"You will remain on this world while others retrieve the male. We have information that he has taken his ship and two others. According to our station informants, it is suspected to be a pleasure cruise."

"Yes, Commander, I obey. I will remain here until our mission is fulfilled. And will return home until I am allowed to take on new apprentices. As per tradition."

The commander acknowledged him and ordered the comm to alert their contact on Arlain. Within moments, Malik appeared on the screen. The assassin's systems did not allow them to see the full image as they spoke.

"Using a secured line? Who is this? Show yourself," Malik ordered.

The commander became annoyed, a short sigh escaping her before she answered, "This is Liw of Perig. We have one of your requests with us."

Malik became silent before a salacious smile appeared. "I see. When will you arrive? Did you bring the cookies?"

Liw's groan of annoyance was audible before she said, "Yes, and we have the female you asked procured."

Malik looked confused before he said, "Female?" Then his eyes showed joy. "Oh, yes, that one. Did you procure the other, or is he dead?"

Liw sighed again, her lips forming words that only the closest could hear, "We should kill this fool and leave." She responded, "The male was incorrectly taken, but we have the other target's current location. For now, you have the female."

"Why did you not capture the other?" Malik griped.

Tyne moved forward, his eyes asking for permission to speak from the commander, which she gave.

"Your attack on the station had caused them to be separated. I procured the female. However, the male was not nearby," Tyne said with confidence.

"I did not attack the station. Who would be willing to do such an inept undertaking?" Malik said.

Tyne sighed, his voice just a whisper. "You are right. We should dispense with this one and leave. They were Arlain warships that attacked the station. Was it not your people who ordered that?"

Malik thought for a moment, his breathing slow. "The conclave, the order for vengeance." He turned to the side. "My own plan may have cost me the other." He turned to see the Slasta still connected. "You do have one of them, correct?"

"Yes, and we are in pursuit of the male. He will be brought to you shortly," Liw answered.

Malik nodded, his hands together in appreciation. "Splendid. Please bring her in discreetly. I have guests arriving shortly. When do you anticipate the other's capture?"

Liw turned to Tyne. "We will accomplish what you have tasked us. We do not fail."

Malik was about to ask again but remembered stories of others who questioned the Slasta and their methods. Instead, he sat back. "Then I will await your success."

Liw ordered communications terminated. She looked to Tyne. "You will convey the prisoner to our employer. And you will remain to make sure he does not decide to turn on us."

Tyne bowed a smile across his face, accepting her order.

Chapter 32:
Detective Work

Jace piloted the *Wolfhammer* quickly. He had wasted no time and didn't sleep until they reached Nibik. Belon remarked how quickly they arrived. "It has only been nineteen standard. How fast is this ship?"

Jace responded. "I wasn't running at full power."

As the planet came into view, Jace asked Belon, "Who do we contact to land, or do we just land?"

Belon looked at Jace. "You should learn patience, young Terran."

Jace's face turned red with anger, causing Eshea to step in. "Belon, it is not wise to annoy a Terran, especially when your own family caused the situation for this visit."

Belon looked at the planet the Nibik now called home. "You are right. Forgive me. I am sorry. Only Nibik are allowed on the planet during the feast. I could bring you as guests to observe. I would have to clear it with the authorities."

Jace handed him the comm. "Call whoever you have to. And if they say no, that's tough shit for them because no matter what I hear, the answer will be yes, understand?"

Belon's hand almost trembled as he heard Jace threaten him—*such fire, and not Nibik.*

There was a short discussion before Belon raised his voice. "It is a matter of atonement. They have been wronged, wronged by family. I have left all my obligations to atone for our disgrace."

There was silence on the comm before they heard, "Permission granted, may atonement be given."

Jace exited the ship, saying, "Ed, same protocols as always."

They all heard the ship say, "I understand, captain."

Eshea looked at him. "What protocols?"

Jace calmly said, "I die and can't get Eislie back. The ship blows. Reactor and engines."

Belon was horrified. "That will kill thousands. You cannot do that."

Jace continued to walk, only saying, "Where's the one we need to talk to, Belon?"

The Nibik was still in shock. "I have not found him yet. Let me search." As the Nibik stood at a terminal searching for his soon-to-be son, he turned to Jace. "Would your ship really detonate?"

Jace looked at him. "I die. The rest of you do as well." He turned to Eshea. "Sorry, nothing personal."

Eshea turned, leaning against the wall. "If it's my time, then it is." She looked at Belon, "Did you find him yet, old man?"

The Nibik didn't ignore her prodding. "It was your people who attacked the station I called home. Why are you with this Terran?"

Eshea shifted. "They may have been from my planet, but my people, never. As for why I am helping this man, he saved my crew, me, and someone I love."

Jace put his hands on each of their shoulders. "This isn't a therapy session. Don't make me hurt both of you. Did you find him yet?"

Belon looked repentant and sighed, "I am sorry for what my family has done, but yes, I have. He is a short walk from here. However, they will not allow you inside. It is tradition."

Jace pulled him away from the terminal courteously, saying, "Screw tradition. They took someone I care about, and if you think your tradition will stop me..." Jace's voice became a growl.

The Nibik stared into Jace's light eyes, the green hiding a fire even a seasoned warrior would fear. It was the strength of a soul ready to do anything for another. He stood tall. "I am an old warrior, and you are right. I will bring you to see them. I will accept any fate, even if I am to be forsaken for this," Belon said, motioning for them to follow.

As they entered the hall, thousands of Nibik were seated at long tables, food mobbing on conveyors as they feasted, drank, and reveled. Jace remarking that it could have been a scene from a meeting of the Norse gods on his world. The comment brought a remark of gratitude from Belon. "You honor us. That is not something we deserve, Terran. But I am grateful that you can see that within us now."

Belon pushed away those watching the doors, proclaiming a matter of atonement for the two non-Nibik for being there. When he found Jarrus, he called them to follow. As Belon approached, he noticed that the crew of his soon-to-be son's ship had joined him.

"Jarrus!" the old warrior bellowed, causing many nearby to quiet. War criers were known to be of a line. Jarrus was one, as was Belon in his prime. Jarrus showed a mix of surprise and happiness as his soon-to-be father approached. He stood to greet him.

Instead of an embrace, Belon struck with both fists, knocking Jarrus back into his seat. The old warrior stood silent, anger in his stance. He said nothing as Jarrus stood again, seeing the Terran and Arlain walk up behind his father-to-be.

"You struck me? Why?" Jarrus asked, almost sounding hurt. "I informed your wife and family as you requested."

The old warrior looked to see those from his crew nearby ready to defend their captain, "Where is your entire crew? They will all need to atone for your actions if they did not go against you."

Jarrus stood. "My crew…. My crew did not move against me. They…"

One of the nearby crew stood, "Elder, whatever the charge, let us hear." He looked around, hearing, "We were disgraced in battle."

Jarrus stared angrily at the crew. They survived, but they now needed to regain their honor. Jarrus was being proud and stood his ground. "I did nothing so as to save you all." As Jace calmly walked into view, Belon looked to his side, as Jace said, "I heard that you picked up two people at the station, two Gilese."

"You dare speak," Jarrus growled.

Jace had enough of the formalities and rushed forward, pushing Jarrus onto the bench. The surrounding Nibik all stood but paused, hearing Jace yell, "Did you rescue two people or not?"

Jarrus bared his teeth as Jace stared at him and answered, "We did. A man and woman."

Jace calmly asked, "Where did you take them?" His voice sounded hopeful.

Jarrus said nothing.

But, as Jace asked again, one of Jarrus's crew replied, "The man was jettisoned. He was dead. The woman was taken from us."

"Where did they take her?" Jace pleaded, but even Belon noticed the Terran was losing patience.

Jarrus responded by sitting tall. He pulled out a knife. "Best me, and I will tell you."

Belon was confused by Jarrus's actions, "Jarrus, we have wronged this one. Why do you challenge him?"

Jarrus looked at Belon, the Nibik's stare filled with resentment for himself. He took a breath, "The Slasta took her. One killed four of my crew. They did not kill us all."

Jarrus held out the knife. "This is how I wish to atone. I offer you my life."

Belon placed his hand on Jace's shoulder. "He has lost those under his charge." Belon looked at Jarrus. "This is not their way, Jarrus."

There was a long silence before Jarrus held the knife out again to Jace. Jace looked at Belon and then back to Jarrus; Jace said, "I don't have time for this," before grabbing the knife from Jarrus and driving the blade through the alien's arm into the tabletop—the hilt snug against the Nibik captain's arm. As many stood silent in shock and the yellow blood flowed from Jarrus's injury, Jace looked at him. "Alright, I win. Tell me where they took her."

The Nibik tried pulling the blade from the table, but Jace had driven it in with such force that he couldn't. The captain of the *Go Ge Go Go* sat helpless, staring back at Jace. And watched as Jace calmly moved forward, "I'm waiting for an answer."

Jarrus looked around and saw Eshea moving forward. Jarrus pointed to her, "They took her to her world. Arlain."

"Ar..lay..in. Okay, do you know who they took her to?" Jace asked, his voice steady.

Jarrus nodded, "Malik, of House Unber."

Jace stood and looked at Eshea. "Do you know Malik?"

She nodded, "He is Hurmann, Tas, the ruling class. One of those I'm fighting against."

Jarrus looked at the woman. "You are Arlain. Why would you help this one?"

Eshea moved forward. "I am a former slave. I fight for my people's release. And, for this one, I own my life and that of my crew. All worthy causes to fight for."

Jarrus said, "He said she was a criminal they were searching for."

"She is my wife! And we were both held as slaves. Both hunted, and you delivered her to slavers again." Jace growled.

His outburst caused the whole facility to go silent. That quiet was only broken by one of Jarrus's crew, "Then our lives are yours."

Jace looked at Eshea, asking her if she could get him onto the planet, and she agreed. Jace motioned for Eshea to follow as he started to leave, only to hear, "Our lives are yours. We will help you fight this battle or die" from Jarrus and his crew.

Jace stopped, his voice lower but resolute, "No, we have a better chance of doing this without you. And if you think I'm going to kill you, you're wrong. I hope to make it back alive." Jace looked at Jarrus. "If I don't succeed, I may need the help later." He looked at Eshea, "Come on, let's go."

Jace looked around the room before looking back at Jarrus and Belon, "Thank you both. And thank you for telling me the truth. I know honor can hurt, but truth and doing the right thing are sometimes stronger than honor."

The room was silent as Jace and Eshea exited, all Nibik looking at them with a stare of praise. A respect that they had only given their own in battle. Jarrus looked down. "I will repay them for the wrong I have done." He looked up at his father-in-law-to-be. "Thank you for guiding them here, Belon. You have shown me that I still have much to learn."

"Ed, do you have Arlain in your database?" Jace asked as he rushed toward the ship.

"Yes, Captain, I was already plotting a course. We will be ready to leave when you arrive."

"I have to show you something when we are on the ship. I think I have a plan," Eshea said. Hearing that, Jace sped up his pace.

The *Wolfhammer* was in hyperspace. Eshea sat in his seat while Jace sat in Eislie's. Eshea shook her head. "I thought this was your seat."

Jace calmly said, "It is."

"Then why did you choose to sit there?"

Jace smiled. "Just keeping this one warm for her." He tapped the controls. "She's going to hate that I changed her settings."

Eshea laughed. "You must love her a lot to know that."

Jace nodded, "So, what did you want to show me, and you said maybe a plan?"

Eshea pulled the VFM and locked it around her neck. She tapped its controls, and Jace watched as the fibers slid along her face until the image of Queeks was solidified.

"I don't think Queeks Maco will get a warm reception, from what you've told me," Jace joked.

Eshea chuckled, "This is a VFM, an infiltration system variable fiber mask. And it's more than just Queeks." She tapped the controls, and the fibers rearranged to show another Arlain. "This is Tassier Gill. She is one of the ruling Hurmann as well. Yasa told me that she hadn't been reported as dead. Her crew have all been eliminated. She was also known for her more, uh, primal tastes that took her from her house for weeks at a time."

Jace raised her brow. "Primal? I'm guessing…." Jace made a few hand gestures.

Eshea laughed. "She has a thing for Terrans. She finds them, um, stimulating."

Jace looked humorously quizzical. "A Terran fetish? That's not something I'd thought I'd ever hear. Let alone think about." Jace sat back. "Alright, that might get us in. Then what?"

Eshea turned forward. "There is a celebration happening, Kaial, a celebration of a new time. Where my people honor the gods and their fortune." She sighed. "Although the Hurmann mostly use it for showing their power and wealth."

Jace scoffed.

Eshea relaxed in Jace's command chair. "It is unfortunate that we are over a week away. Even with the speed of your ship."

Jace sat forward. "Maybe not." He looked at the computer's command console, "Ed, you can speak with Eshea here. Can you extrapolate the damage if we used the new system to travel the filaments?"

"One moment, Captain."

"Filaments? I heard they were working on them, but can this ship do that?" Eshea asked.

Jace looked at her, "Ed, give me a couple of scenarios. The faster we get to Eis, the better."

"Yes, captain, I am also interested in retrieving Captain Licessien quickly. But the modeling will take a few hours."

"Thank you, Ed. Let me know what you find. I'm going to take a short nap. I've been up for almost two days. I'm getting ready to crash," Jace said.

He motioned for Eshea to follow him. She accompanied him to one of the rooms on the ship and opened the door. He walked her inside. "There's a shower, some food, a bed. If this doesn't work, it'll be a couple of days. Might as well be comfortable."

Jace moved outside the door. He watched Eshea smile before he tapped the frame, closing the door. Eshea walked over and heard, "Ed, seal the door. It will only be opened in an emergency, my command, or when I am on the control deck."

She heard the computer confirm the command.

"What? You can't do this to me. I'm not a prisoner," Eshea protested.

Jace tapped the internal comm. "You're not a slave or a prisoner. I just can't have you on the control deck without me. You've shown you have skills, and I'm thankful for them. But it's only while I rest. I suggest you get some rest as well."

"Jace, you can trust me," Eshea pleaded.

"Eshea, I do trust you. But I can't risk you'd side with Ralla on me changing my mind and helping you just because you helped me.

"I wouldn't, I swear," Eshea replied.

Jace responded, "Eshea, What Ralla would do is use this against us, make us indebted to him. I have a feeling he's done that to you already. In truth, if he has, then it's no different than enslaving you again."

Eshea stepped back from the door, "Ralla wouldn't, he didn't. I, uh...."

She heard her own words, and her mind began screaming. *He kept saying we owe our people, we owe him. Oh gods, Ralla, you, you....*

Eshea stepped back sitting on the bed. She heard Jace say, "It's only for a few hours, get some rest. Hopefully, you'll see I'm not doing this by choice."

She felt her hearts fill with sadness. She whispered, "Has Ralla been keeping us, using us? He won't let us leave the ship without coming back. And Zarlin, he won't let her write her songs, only his. Oh, gods, Jace."

Jace gently pounded the door. "I'm sorry. If this makes you rethink helping me, then I'll let you off anywhere you want. Just tell me."

"No, Jace, I owe you my life," Eshea said.

Jace's voice was low and studded, "You owe me nothing. None of your crew owe me anything. I just need help to get Eis home. You can leave if you want. I'm not going to stop you. Just know that I, we need help."

"Crash? He's exhausted," Eshea whispered, only to hear Jace say, "Yes. I am."

Eshea felt a tear roll down her face. She understood why he locked the door. This was to protect the ship, to protect himself. And he made no argument against her other than that. As her tears fell, she began to understand and composed herself. "I understand. I'll try and get some rest. I'm tired as well." She lay back on the bed. "Oh gods, please help us win this."

Jace turned to walk to his cabin, the streaks of tears down his face, "I'm sorry, I didn't want to do this, but I'm too fucking tired."

Chapter 33:
A Delivery and Gathering

Tyne and the others moved quietly along the corridors of Malik's compound. Several dozen Tas had already arrived for the celebration. They moved through, trailing a long, covered box between them. There were three in front and three behind as they approached the room that their employer insisted on.

When they entered, Malik's voice loudly instructed several servants to hurry in constructing a device. Tyne looked to the side, and the extended shelves along the wall holding various forms of torture slid to the side to reveal a more intimate chamber. If the Slasta had not worked for people like this Arlain, he would have been appalled by the display.

Tyan stood silent only momentarily before he spoke, startling his employer. "We are here."

Malik turned around, bringing his hands to his midsection. "You are silent even when you are expected. Please bring her in."

The Slasta pushed the long box inside the room and removed its cover. Eislie could be seen sedated but unharmed. Her condition caused Malik to ask, "Why did you heal her?"

One of the other Slasta responded, "She is worth more alive to you."

Malik looked annoyed. Then his mood seemed to brighten. "Oh well, I guess it will allow me to inflict more damage while I break her." He then ordered his servants to take Eislie from the cart and place her into the apparatus.

One slave started to remove her clothing but was stopped by Malik,

"Not that I find their people repulsive, but I can use that to inflict fear. Leave her clothed."

The servant pushed Eislie ungraciously into the device, her back slamming solidly against its frame, but she didn't wake. Malik looked to Tyne, only to be told, "She is heavily sedated."

Malik scoffed, "You fear a single Gilese female."

Tyne spoke with disgrace, "This female and her mate subdued two of our better assassins."

Malik turned, a glint of fear in his stare as he said, "Make sure her shackles are secure."

There was a flurry of activity briefly before Eislie hung in the frame, her arms above her head and to the side. The restraints holding all parts of her body secure. Tyne moved forward and administered the antidote.

Eislie's eyes fluttered, her senses all coming back to life. She felt the pressure of the shackles that now secured her. Eislie's eyes darted around before she started to struggle.

Malik smiled, then looked to Tyne. "You may leave." He motioned to his servants. "All of you may leave. I want to start this one alone."

The slaver followed the others before waiting at the small room's door. He tapped the controls, and the shelves slid back to conceal its view and sound. Just before it closed, Malik was heard saying, "My dear, the one who wants you as his wishes you broken but unharmed. I do enjoy a challenge."

Eislie screamed as Malik held the sonic device to her chest. Its pressure waves resonated within her skeleton—the sounds causing micro fractures to avoid significant damage but inflict severe pain. Malik pulled the device back as Eislie's head hung down, gasping for breath. He turned to criticize her, but when he returned, the fire behind Eislie's stare startled him.

Malik looked disappointed. "Gilese slaves usually succumb by now. It looks like I'll have to use other measures."

Eislie yelled expletives at him, threatening to kill Malik when she was free. Malik looked back in disbelief. "You are going nowhere except where and when I tell you."

The slaver again used the sonic device, and Eisle gnashed her teeth before screaming in pain. Malik had a sadistic smile, but that quickly changed as his comm alerted him.

"What is it?" Malik growled.

"Husband, we have guests to greet, and you are in playing." Malik heard his wife chastise him.

He heard Eislie snicker.

"You find something funny?" Malik asked, the sadistic grin returning to his face.

Eislie said nothing, but her eyes were defiant before she spit on him. Malik hastily wiped it from his face. "You know, I have more than one of these holders. Actually, I have three. When your mate arrives, I'll have him strapped up, and you can both watch as I break each of you."

Malik then moved a chair with a small wide arm before Eislie. He placed the sonic device on the wide section, "I have things to attend. But I will not leave you bored, my dear."

He then turned on the sonic device, and Eislie could feel the pain throughout her entire body. She watched as Malik walked away. "I'll be back in a few hours, my little toy. Enjoy yourself."

Malik greeted the latest of the Tas as they entered, his servants putting on a grand display and obediently showing the ruling class to their assigned rooms. But one of the guests noticed his lack of attention.

"Is everything alright, Malik?" the man asked,

Malik clasped his hands together. "My mind was elsewhere. A project I was working on. I am deciding how to accomplish a task to provide a greater windfall for my house." He then watched as one of his servants inspected the delicacies he had set out for his guests. The Terran slave hovered over the cookies he had procured. He watched as she tried to take one covertly but was stopped by another Arlain slave. Malik's wife had also been observing.

"No one has touched those things you brought in; did you taste them before setting them out?" Malik's wife asked quietly.

"I had not the chance. Perhaps I should. It would be a disaster if these were harmful." Malik muttered, walking over and glancing at the servant who was eyeing the cookies earlier. He picked one from the tray and tasted it. As the flavor hit his taste buds, he spit it out. "These are rotten." He looked to his guests. "My dear guests, apologies, I had not realized that these were set out." He handed one of the cookies to the same slave as before, ordering, "Eat it."

The girl brought it to her mouth and bit gently. She found its sweetness and flavor intoxicating but dared not let her master know. She spit it out as he had. Malik grabbed more, shoving it into the girl's hands.

233

"You will eat all of these."

She bowed her head and hesitated. She then put one whole cookie in her mouth and began to chew. She frowned as best as she could, but the flavor was incredible. She fought back a smile as she ate another.

Seeing his slave obediently following his orders, he demanded one of his other servants to remove the cookies and distribute them as punishment. Many of the Arlain slaves found them disgusting, but the Terran and Gilese did their best to hide their enjoyment. Hearing another of the Tas announced as they entered by his servants, Malik reveled in his superiority and then approached his wife. "Well, that would have been embarrassing. Shall we greet our new guests before we retire for the evening?"

Unnoticed by Malik's staff, one of the servants slipped away, her short golden hair visible as she changed clothing to resemble one of the new families that had arrived. She froze, seeing a member of the Slasta nearby. She waited until she could complete her change before heading out of the compound. Slaves were not allowed to leave, but members and their servants of the arriving Tas were. As the woman made her way toward the ships of the ruling Tas that now dotted the landscape, she slipped into one of the nearby alcoves. With a quiet grace, she tapped her comm.

"Master, I have audible confirmation that Eislie Licessien has been brought to the compound. I am not able to find her to confirm visually. What are your orders?"

Bosh tapped his comm. "It's not like you to be ineffective, Halli. What is the hindrance?"

Halli looked concerned as she breathed, "I have searched the compound, but I only found evidence of her being brought in. The Slasta I questioned provided the information indirectly."

Bosh raised his brow. "Questioned? You did not leave any evidence to alert them that you were there."

Halli smiled, "No master, I said I was sent as a pleasure slave by Malik."

Bosh chuckled. "And were you?"

Holli smiled, "Of course not, master."

The former captain sat back in his chair. "Halli, return to me. And make sure you are not followed. I do not trust our associate."

Halli confirmed and closed her comm, the evening darkness allowing her to slip away and return to her master.

On the *Wolfhammer*, Jace tapped the controls to the cabin where Eshea was staying. It had been a few hours, and what little sleep Jace did get was worth it. He knocked on the door. "You can come out now. The computers got the requested data, and I don't want to force you to come along."

Jace was walking away and heard the door to the cabin open. He turned to see Eshea rubbing her eyes. He heard her complain, "I'm used to taking short naps from being on the run, but how are you so full of energy?"

Jace scoffed, "I'm not. I'm pissed, scared, and just really pissed at where she was taken."

Eshea looked at him confused. "You said, pissed, twice?"

Jace chuckled, "Don't worry about it. C'mon, Ed's got the data I need. And I want you to decide."

She followed Jace to the control room. "Ed, bring up the data. And tell me how much damage we'll do if we run the filaments."

"The filaments? This ship can travel in them?" Eshea was still surprised.

"We could before, without damage. But we made some modifications and, well, let's say we have to be a little more careful at the moment." Jace sighed, "We were working on a solution but haven't had a chance to install it. Theoretically, we can do it, but . . ."

Eshea looked concerned. "What?"

"It'll probably damage the tunnel coils and maybe the outer hull if I'm not careful." Jace sat hard in his command chair. "If we do this right, it'll take less than two hours to get to Arlain. But, if I screw up, we'll be floating dead in space at best." Jace looked at her. "I was hoping to do this with Eis first. But if I blow it, we might die. So, I wanted to give you a choice. I can thank you for helping me this far and drop you off, or. . ."

Eshea smiled, then sat in the other command chair. "Captain, you risked your life to help me and the people I cared for. You're not getting rid of me that easily. Besides, you need me to get anywhere near that compound." She then tapped the mask, and the fibers formed into the image of her former owner. She smiled, her voice the same as the woman the mask now showing. "If the gods have brought me this far, then it is time I returned home."

Jace shook his head a smile on his face before he looked at her again. "Last chance."

Eshea turned forward. "Computer, how do I say 'let's go' in Terran?"

She heard Jace laugh, then say, "Ed, plot a course of jumps. And find me the nearest filament point."

"Yes, Captain. If we keep travel under half a cycle, we should not experience as severe an energy buildup." The computer paused. "I have plotted a course, Captain. We will have to make five jumps. I estimate travel time will be 1.78 standard hours. Although there is a concern."

"What is it, Ed?" Jace asked.

"Captain, the nearest filament path exiting in the Arlain system is a less than stable route as per the data that we have," the computer told him.

Jace looked at Eshea. "You sure you want to go with me? Just asking."

Eshea nodded, "I'm not afraid of a rough flight. You've never flown with Zarlin before."

"Ed, how soon to the nearest point?" Jace asked.

"Approximately 7.23 standard minutes, captain," Ed responded.

Jace looked at Eshea. "Well, you've got seven minutes to change your mind." He then steered the ship on a heading to the nearest filament point.

Chapter 34:
Arrival at Arlain

The structure of the *Wolfhammer* groaned as Jace did his best to keep them in a straight line. "I thought you said this was less stable. Not this bad, Ed."

"I was wrong. Zarlin's flying is much better," Eshea remarked.

Jace snickered. "Reactor status, Ed. Now!"

"Resonance is increasing but within our current safety parameters. I do not detect any sign of inversion," Ed responded.

They felt the ship jolt heavily, making Jace ask, "How soon till we punch out, Ed?"

"Estimated three minutes and fourteen seconds," the computer said before alerting Jace to something that it detected. "Captain. I am detecting a large build-up of filament energy across the hull. If we were to exit now, it would damage the systems."

Jace looked around. "I thought we'd be okay with short runs. Are you telling me that that isn't the case?"

"Apparently, Captain, the more unstable the filament, the more the charge increases. That was not in our data," Ed responded.

"It's okay, Ed." Jace then looked like he had an idea. "Ed, that ship we were in, they disconnected the drive feeds. Eis was hurt when I turned it on. I wonder if that's what damaged their engines before."

Jace remembered the Lyri ship he and Eislie discovered months ago. He had turned on one of the external power feeds, and the line near Eislie exploded, the stored energy from the arc injuring Eislie severely. Eshea looked toward him perplexed, making Jace say, "We found a ship. We based some of the designs of the new systems here off those. Eis got hurt when I turned the feed line on to see what it was, and…" Jace was interrupted as the ship lurched to the side. "Ed, can you fly if I go back and pull the feeds offline."

"No, Captain, I would need to remain online, and with the increased power build-up, it may damage my systems," Ed responded.

Jace looked to Eshea, then stood up. "I'll need a countdown. Can you fly?"

Eshea nodded.

"Good, I don't have time to transfer control. You sit here, keep us on course, and when Ed shuts down, give me a count from then on the exit time." Jace tapped the controls and synchronized it with the computer's time. "Ed, shut down and disconnect. Eshea, when that reaches ten, start counting down; when it reaches zero, punch out."

Jace rushed to the back and opened the engine room door. He kept it open, yelling for the time to Eshea. She informed him, and Jace waited until she started counting down. When she reached zero, Jace cut the feed lines as they exited. As Eshea hit the controls to exit, not all of the lines were disconnected at the same time. At first, it seemed to go smoothly, but then there was arcing throughout the ship. Jace heard the unfortunate sound of some of the tunnel coils blowing on the outside. He rushed forward to see Eshea trying to stabilize their trajectory. When they exited, the blown coils sent them into a spin. Jace grabbed the controls and quickly brought the *Wolfhammer* back under control.

"Ed, you still with me?" Jace yelled.

There were a few seconds before he heard, "Captain, I am functional. I am waiting to confirm other systems, but we have damaged some drive coils."

Jace motioned for Eshea to move, and he said, "We did, Ed. I heard them. I don't know how bad it is yet." Jace then tested the controls. "Port side's a bit sluggish, same as last time, but it seems we can still fly." Jace appeared relieved. He looked over to see Eshea muttering something. He smiled before asking, "You alright?"

He heard Eshea say, "I am surprised you haven't frightened your enemies to death with your flying."

Jace chuckled, "Actually, we have scared a few." He watched her sigh in relief before asking the computer how long until they would arrive.

Finding the time short, he asked Eshea what the protocol for their planet was on unknown vessels.

"It's complicated, but if you have video comm, they can confirm Tassier's identity, which may allow us to bypass things," Eshea told him.

Jace then asked, "Do we need to identify our ship?"

Eshea nodded, "Do you have a logo on this vessel?"

Jace sighed, relieved. "We used to. I sort of blew it off when I damaged the ship previously."

"That is fortunate. It seems the gods have set our path for us. Now I have to convince them that you're my slave," Eshea said.

Jace groaned, "Anything else I need to know about?"

"Well, Tassier has a liking for Terrans. You did damage the ship. If we play this right, I can get us in quickly. We will have to identify the ship. But *Wolfhammer* is well known," Eshea told him

Jace hung his head and seemed to be thinking of something easy to remember. "How about *Wolvesbane?* Is that a common name?"

Eshea looked curiously at him. "What does that mean, *Wolvesbane?*"

Jace smiled. "It's a flower on Earth, and it sounds like no one will know what it means. Besides, the W and O are sort of still showing, it'll make sense."

It took a short while, and they were able to land. Eshea looked at Jace as he was about to follow her out the door. "You can't go out there like that. Servants have a uniform for Tassier's house."

Jace seemed offended, saying, "I'm not going out there naked or anything. What do I need to wear?"

After a few minutes of going through the limited clothes Jace had on board, they agreed on a simple dark-cover shirt and dark pants. Eshea watched Jace huff as she said, "And we need to put a collar around you."

"I don't exactly have collar-making materials onboard," Jace grumbled.

Eshea found what looked like a robe. It was something Eislie had picked up. The cloth was of fluffy material, and Eshea put it on, its dark color somewhat attractive to her. She then grabbed some of the strapping from the cargo area and sliced it into a piece long enough to fit around Jace's neck. Jace offered to tape it together with duct tape. The silver looked like the control box all Tassier's slaves wore. "There, you should pass now as long as no one is too observant. Shall we go, oh, maybe get killed?"

Jace waved his hands to the airlock. "It's now or never."

Outside, several guards of House Unber stood ready, along with one servant and three members of the Slasta. As Eshea exited, the VFM, hid her identity faithfully. Her acting and knowledge of Tassier Gil allowed her to convince those guards who she was instantly.

"You're fortunate. You are one of my favorites," Eshea turned, yelling at Jace as they exited. The robe flowed wistfully as she continued forward, stopping as her chest touched the guard standing in her way. "How dare you. Where is your Master? I will speak with him."

The guard looked at her, his eyes fixed on hers. Malik's servant accompanying them spoke. "It is late, and Master is resting. I am Tosk and am empowered by him to greet you and to ascertain if you are to enter."

Malik of Unber does not trust his own, I see, Eshea thought before looking back at Jace and sighing. Her acting seemed not up to the task. Jace discovered, however, that she did not disappoint.

"Wake your Master. I am Tassier Gil of House Trop."

The slave didn't falter. "Please provide your invitation or leave."

Eshea shook her head and sighed, then growled angrily, "I have just returned from off-world. I am not returning to my dwelling just to return here again."

The servant spoke defiantly to who appeared to be Tassier Gil, telling her, "We have been informed that Tassier Gil was off-world and that she was to return. That was made clear in her response." The servant then looked at Jace to see his eyes looking over the guards and those blocking his path. She walked up to him. "This is the only slave you have brought?"

Eshea was starting to become worried that they would have to fight, but Jace helped by saying, "Do you wish me to vanquish these things before me, mistress?"

By the gods, thank you for playing along, Jace, Eshea thought. "No, save that for the games. They are merely obeying their Master's orders."

She then overheard one of the guards whisper to the other, "According to the information we have, she has a fetish for Terrans. He's probably not just for the games."

Eshea turned to Jace and gently stroked her finger under his chin, "Besides, I don't want too damaged, for tonight."

She then turned to see one guard whisper to the one in charge, "Identity scan confirms Arlain linage, and her image matches the files."

The slave turned and spoke with the head guard, asking, "I heard she enjoys Terrans. Is that true?"

The guard nodded.

Tosk glanced at Jace and then turned to look at the Slasta before hearing, "How dare you turn you back to me, slave" from Eshea.

Tosk turned quickly to face forward and stood compliant as Eshea said, "It would look poorly on your master's house if I am forced to return home for such a trivial document." She looked to be thinking. "Perhaps I will see if any of the other Tas have not yet arrived. I am sure they would like to know how they will be treated if they have not."

Eshea could see the fear of the slave's stance at the thought of her Master's personal loss due to her delaying a member of the Tas. Tosk turned to the two remaining Slasta and could see they didn't find any fault in the situation and dismissed them. *If the assassins are not afraid, then we should allow her,* Tosk thought.

The servant looked at Eshea. "Tassier Gil, I will inform Master that you have arrived when he is available. Will you please follow us to your accommodations?"

Eshea continued to play her part. "You will show me my room. I do not follow a slave."

"Uh, of course. I meant no disrespect." Tosk was becoming intimidated by the woman before her and bowed as Eshea walked past her.

Tosk hurriedly moved a step behind the woman she knew as Tassier Gil. The slave moved but paused as they nearly passed the room her Master had assigned. Tosk gave a meek utterance, and Eshea turned. There was an almost caring, frightened expression as she did. The servant seemed puzzled until Eshea spoke, "Ugh, this is the room your master has chosen?"

Eshea looked over the door, its gold trim and anointments very regal, even for a member of the Tas. She continued her act, looking toward Tosk, giving her a burning stare of annoyance. Jace was becoming annoyed with the formal act and wanted to start looking for Eislie, so he moved forward. Jace pushed the door open so that all could see inside. Eshea glared at him only to hear him say. "This room is well suited for me. I thank you." He showed kindness toward the servant, then turned to Eshea and whispered, "This is pretty close to the exit and the ship."

Eshea looked toward the short hallway and nodded, "You were always good at making suggestions." She then caressed his shoulder, sighing. "It may be interesting." Eshea gave a salacious grin before turning to Tosk, saying, "Please notify your master that I have arrived when he is available." She then pushed Jace into the room and said, as she closed the door, "No rush."

Jace looked around the room. He checked the windows, seeing them open to the courtyard. And he looked up at the causeway that overhung the windowed area. He rushed to the door, looked through the small pin windows, and saw that the others had already left. There was a moment while Eshea looked around, and she watched Jace's expression turn from unhappy to distant anger as he said, "I thought my people were fucked up. You know that."

Eshea's expression turned solemn. "I know. That's what I've been fighting against." She leaned her face into her hands. "Gods, this was a crazy idea. How will we get out of here when we find her?"

Jace sat on the bed. "As long as we can get to the ship or activate my comm, we'll have a chance."

"You're sure of that?" Eshea shot back.

Jace nodded, "Yep, because I just realized I'd probably be fighting my way out of here anyway. And if they hurt her, or worse, I.....” Jace went silent.

Eshea looked at him. She realized what he was saying and knew from that moment she needed to stay out of his way. "We're here. It's still early for the night. And given it's quiet, I think Malik may have sated the Tas who arrived already."

Jace nodded, "Yeah, it is quiet. I'm not complaining. Fewer people to deal with while we search." Jace looked at her. "Any ideas where to start?"

Eshea stood and looked out the window. "This place seems pretty similar to where I was. My guess is he has her in the training area. It's usually toward the back, away from the living and guest areas." She looked back. "Let's hope we avoid running into any Tas who enjoy being near that place. There are some sick people, after all."

Jace moved next to her. She looked up to see the weapons also mounted on the edge of the building. "He even has anti-ship guns. This slaver likes his security. Did you see those guards?"

Eshea nodded, "They were poorly trained. At least I was able to intimidate them. What worried me were the two behind them. Those people were not Arlain."

"I noticed them, too. They seemed to be looking through us. It was creepy," Jace said.

Eshea agreed. "They were Slasta. Hired assassins, I'm sure of it."

"You mean the same people who tried ship-jacking us?" Jace raised his voice.

Eshea placed her hand on his arm. "Lower your voice. We don't want them rushing in here thinking you're attacking me. They'll kill you where you stand."

Jace calmed. "You have any ideas on how to get back there?"

Eshea nodded, "Give me a few minutes. Acting like that woman who owned me is making my head hurt."

Chapter 35:
Searching

Malik had entered the room to find the device he had left now silent. "Slac quality, these torture devices." He lifted Eislie's head to find her asleep. "How dare you slumber while I break you?" He slapped Eislie's face, causing her to wake suddenly.

It took a moment before her eyes focused, and Malik could see the streaks of tears that had dried on her face. And he saw the look of fire now attempting to burn through him. "Oh, my, you have the stare of a Terran, my feeble little toy. I didn't know any Gilese had that kind of fire."

Malik moved toward the chair with the small table attached. He then tapped his comm, and the outside door slid open. Eislie could see an older woman holding a tray with two bottles. She watched as Malik motioned for her to enter and picked up the clear one before opening the top and drinking. "Ah, refreshing. Did you know the spring water here is eloquent and satisfying? It is a treat on to itself." Malik held it before Eislie. "Seeing your tears tells me you have lost some yourself."

Eislie was thirsty. She had been unconscious for over a day, and hanging in this contraption was no better. Her mouth moved toward the bottle before Malik pulled it away and drank again. She silently cursed him, hearing him say, "As I said, it is thirsty work, breaking new slaves."

She watched as Malik sat and his servant placed the tray on the small table. The slave then moved behind her and used some controls to lower something. Eislie turned to see a thin, flat, box-shaped device and glared at the woman, growling, "Get me out of here. You know this is wrong."

Malik laughed as he called the woman to him. "You are wasting your time. My slaves love me with their entire being." He moved closer, looking at Eislie directly, only to see her staring back defiantly. She heard him chuckle. "The pain of the resonator did not break you. And that defiant Terran stare, I know, has something to do with it."

The slaver happily grabbed the amber bottle and held it to Eislie's face, opening it. The fumes were acrid and disgusting to her. Malik, on the other hand, took a full breath. "Ah, the smell of victory. I always break Terrans with this. If they don't die, of course. You see, I was informed of your questionable heritage by another."

"Who? I want to know so I can kick their ass," Eislie growled.

The woman watched as her master stepped back from Eislie. He said, "You'll find out soon enough, and serve him and his every whim when we're through."

Malik then moved behind her and poured the liquid into the device lowered earlier. She heard him chuckling to himself before hearing, "This, my slave, is Urom venom. It excites the nerves. It will cause all of your senses to become heightened to the point of excruciating pain." Malik suddenly appeared close to Eislie's face. "Some say it has aphrodisiac qualities."

Malik hit the controls of the machine. Eislie heard the mechanics of it move closer.

"Your wife must need a lot of it to even be near you," Eislie declared defiantly.

Malik raised his hand to strike her but stepped away. "Well, well, you nearly made me lose control." He motioned for his servant to move closer to him before he walked toward the wall and removed something from the cabinet. When he returned, he was holding a small woodgrain box, the very one that Dosh had gifted him earlier, the very one that contained a sliver of spide.

He held it up like a treasure, "You know I haven't used this since your soon-to-be new master gave it to me. And I've been dying to try it again."

Malik placed the wooden box on the table and rushed to put the shield suit over himself. He then activated it and pulled his servant closer. He moved closer to Eislie, his hands near her right hand. "Perhaps you will be better off understanding that none of your body is yours any longer." He brought the box up and opened it. Eislie looked panicked for a moment before she saw the familiar glow of spide illuminating her hand. She then turned to see Malik confused.

Malik held the box open. "No! This is not working?" He then turned to his servant, about to say something, only to hear her scream, which was quickly silenced as he watched her burn. Malik stood in disbelief as half his servant's body fell to the ground, and the ash of the other half fell nearby. He stood dumbfounded before closing the box.

"She was one of my oldest and most loyal slaves." He turned to glare at Eislie. "She was a true follower. She never questioned." In disbelief, Malik again started the device behind Eislie. "You will know what it is like to serve. This device will break you. The venom is most effective when a current is passed through your spinal nerves." The slaver again confronted Eislie. "You made me destroy one of my favorites. How dare you?" Malik looked at the box containing the crystal and then at Eislie, seeming to find inspiration in his thoughts. "That's why he wants you and the other."

"Who?" Eislie yelled.

Malik smiled. "You will find out soon, my dear, and you will serve him willingly when I am through."

Malik slammed the controls, and Eislie felt the sting of each needle as they pierced her skin, moving deeply near her spine as it started to inject the venom, the searing pain causing her to scream.

"It's been over an hour. How are you still resisting?" Malik muttered to himself before looking at the vitals the machine was taking for Eislie. *She'll die if I don't stop.* He seemed to think, *Then, I won't be paid.*

Malik tapped the controls of the machine, stopping it. He heard the cries of pain turn to whimpers before Eislie fell limp and silent. The restraints and needles were the only things holding her in place. Malik moved behind to find the reservoir for the venom empty. He looked at the bio readings for her again.

"I'm impressed. Not many can last as long as you have." Malik pulled one of the reservoirs from the machine and poured more from the amber bottle into it. He reattached the long needle but became distracted as Eislie lifted her head. He moved around, pulling her around to face him.

"I understand the current that each needle produces is excruciating. It burns and gnaws at your nerves. The venom allows each moment to feel like an eternity," Malik said, only to watch Eislie close her eyes and fall unconscious. He stepped around and placed the tube with the needle on the table. He turned to look toward the door. "She is being difficult. I will have to think about how to break her if this is not working. I may have to do this with more damage." Malik thought momentarily, then muttered, "I wonder if Bosh will still pay if I damage her too much."

The slaver then tapped the controls and opened the door before walking out and closing it behind him, his words trailing off. "A little refreshment and some time to think of what to do next." Eislie heard him yelling at one of his servants, "Bring me water." And he did not see the tears falling from her eyes as she whispered, "Jace, please hurry."

* * *

Jace and Eshea were walking through the compound. Eshea had understood the layout, and they were working on making it to where she thought the training room was. They had checked several areas and had yet to find anything.

"Are you sure you know where this place is?" Jace was becoming impatient.

Eshea understood she was facing death just being back on the planet, but she had promised to help him. She was hopeful and started toward the long hallway that connected the building to the location in the back and stopped suddenly, seeing a lone figure in the darkness of the courtyard. She moved closer to Jace, "That doesn't look like a guard. It could be one of the Tas."

They moved closer, and both Jace and Eshea noticed how the man moved, thinking the same thing, *This has to be an assassin.*

Eshea pulled Jace closer. She had hoped to make the person think she was enjoying walking her pet, and she was beginning to think it was working until the man stopped. Within seconds, they heard only fabric moving through the air as a blade nearly stuck Jace in the back. He had turned in time to allow it to glance off. Jace lunged at the man, his knee contacting the man's groin. The grunt of pain was silenced as Eshea drove a blade up through the assassin's chin into his brain stem. The night was filled with the quiet sound of a body falling to the ground gently as Jace grabbed him.

He looked at Eshea but said nothing. He only heard her say. "They find his body, and we're not making it out of here alive."

"We're running out of time." Jace looked around and spied what looked like a large water drain for the courtyard in the small area. "Hold onto him for a sec."

Jace jumped into the bushes and pulled at the grate. It moved without much sound. "Thank god for landscaping," Jace said as he rushed back to grab the man's body. He hauled the dead weight and shoved it into the drain with some effort. There was just enough room, which Jace found when replacing the grating. "That should give us some time. Let's keep looking."

Eshea found it disturbing that what she had heard about Terrans finding killing so easy and then returning to the task at hand was true. She said nothing as Jace pulled her along toward where their destination was. It took moments before she stood in a frighteningly familiar room.

Gods, I don't want to be here. She thought as memories of her time with Tassier Gil now flooded her psyche. Seeing Jace desperately looking around, she was disheartened. He said, "I thought you said this is where they trained slaves?"

Eshea nodded, becoming increasingly unsure, "It is, but sometimes they have more than one."

She looked down the hall and watched as a servant exited from a door a short distance away. She felt inspired and rushed out the door, "You there. Where is your master?"

The young woman froze and then looked at the ground as Eshea approached her. The girl said nothing as Eshea moved closer. Eshea felt something familiar about the girl as she neared and was startled as Jace appeared suddenly by her side. The girl remained staring at the ground as Eshea spoke.

"Answer me. Where is your master?"

The girl hesitated, "He, he has asked me to fetch water for him."

Eshea looked at Jace, "You have not answered my question."

The girl briefly looked up, and Eshea felt panic fill her as she recognized the person standing before her. Her words were unconscious as she spoke. "Naree?"

Jace could see the heartbreak in Eshea, even through the mask of her former owner. She turned to him, whispering, "It's Naree."

Jace pulled her closer and hid Eshea's face from the girl, whispering, "You know her?"

Eshea nodded, "She's Zarlin's sister. Tassier owned both of us. I didn't know where she was sold to."

Jace felt more anger at these people than anything he had previously. But he was there to find Eislie, and no one would stop that. "Pull yourself together. Maybe she knows where Eislie is."

He felt Eshea nod in agreement, and as she pulled away, turning to Naree, "Look at me, do you know me? Where is your master?"

Naree looked up and recognized her former owner. "Mistress, it has been some time. How may I serve you?"

Jace felt torn hearing that. His thoughts were uncensored: *These people are fucked up.*

Eshea held her composure. "I ordered you to tell me where your master has taken a new servant. A light-haired woman. Have you seen her?"

Naree nodded, "He is training her."

Jace couldn't wait any longer, moving toward the girl. "Where is she?"

Eshea gently pushed Jace back. "She will tell us. She does remember who I am."

The girl nodded, "Master has asked me to bring him water. I must obey."

Eshea placed her hand gently on Naree's shoulder. "And you will, but tell me where I may find him so that I may inspect the new slave."

Naree moved to the door. "Master is there. Please, I must get water for him."

Eshea leaned into Jace. "I can't leave her here. If we leave, she's coming too." Jace didn't have any argument and agreed.

As Eshea went to touch the door, she hesitated and turned. "Bring back the water quickly. Now hurry."

They watched as Naree rushed away, and Jace heard Eshea's voice break as she said. "He has her completely obedient to him. If we have to kill him, it'll destroy her."

Jace agreed. "We'll get her out too. Just help me get Eis first."

Eshea nodded, and she opened the door, saying, "Keep your face down. I'm hoping he's not going to recognize you."

Inside, Malik was sitting in a comfortable chair. He praised his servant for returning quickly, only to hear Eshea say, "Malik of Unber."

Malik rose quickly, the familiar voice of Tassier ringing in his ears. "Ah, my guest, I see you have arrived. I still owe you several Lin for the slaves you provided. Have you come to collect?"

Eshea walked toward the slaver. She fought every instinct not to kill him where he stood. She reached her hand out. "Malik, I heard you have a new acquisition. Perhaps I may see them?"

Malik looked puzzled as she neared. "I have told no one of any acquisitions."

Jace could see him moving to access his comm and rushed forward. Jace threw his entire weight into the slaver and picked him up, slamming Malik into the ground. He grabbed Malik's head and smacked it against the stone floor.

"Wha?" Malik said before he went unconscious.

Chapter 36:
Now or Never

Malik felt a hand slap his face and opened his eyes. It took a moment before his vision focused. He went to grab his comm, only to find his arms tied securely to the chair.

"What is the meaning of this? You dare attack another of the Tas in his own house?" Malik growled

Malik's protest was met with a sharp blow to the other side of his face as Jace stuck him. Eshea had moved toward the wall, examining the instruments the slaver used on his beloved servants. She remembered having been tortured with similar tools for days until she finally accepted her mistress. She picked up a thin metal rod, its sharp point and taper used to pierce flesh slowly. Its radius grew more significant as it went in, causing close bones to separate excruciatingly. It was used primarily on Arlain slaves, not Terrans, because they would bleed out if it were. She picked it up, and the memory of its function still haunted her.

"Where is she?" Jace growled as he struck Malik again.

The slaver tried to shake off the stupor, but when he did, his eyes found only the green of Jace's stare and the fire behind them ready to erupt.

"Wh…. Who?" Malik tried to delay as long as possible. He recognized Jace from his file and knew Terrans could be fierce and determined—something they were prized for. Malik also learned it's what made them dangerous.

The slaver looked back, causing Jace to follow his gaze, only to see nothing. Malik, on the other hand, was misdirecting him. The Slaver had extended his claws slightly, a genetic enhancement he insisted on, and worked at severing the wires Jace had used to restrain him. Malik felt the bonds loosen slightly and faked still being set to the chair.

Eshea had returned to Jace's side, holding the rod she had taken from the wall. "You can use this on him. Pierce it between his wrist and the base of his hand. But do it slowly."

Malik looked up. "You are not Tassier. She never tortured her slaves. She would always delegate that task."

Eshea lifted her collar and tapped the controls to her mask, making Jace look at her. She looked stoically back. "If I am to die, it will be as who I am."

As the fiber mask retracted, Eshea's face became visible. And the expression on Malik's face turned to anger. "You're Eshea Alon. Queeks Maco is dead. How are you here?"

Eshea stood tall, placing her hand on Jace's shoulder. "You never killed Queeks. She is alive and well thanks to this man. He saved us all from being blown out into space."

Jace turned his head slightly before noticing the bonds on Malik's arm snap and his left-hand lifting from the chair. Jace threw all his weight down as he slammed Malik's arm against the metal frame before reaching back, demanding, "Give it to me. Now!"

Eshea passed him the rod, and in one motion, Jace brought the point down, piercing Malik's arm. The slaver howled at the pain as Jace reached down and, with all of his pent-up rage, bent the rod to pin Malik to the chair securely. Jace looked back, yelling, "You got another one?"

Eshea returned with a similar item, and Jace thrust it into the slaver's other arm, doing the same. Jace then struck Malik's face dead on before growling, "Where is she?"

Jace stepped back, awaiting the slaver's response, only to hear the door on the room's far end open. So far, they had the luxury of the room being soundproof, but as Malik heard the door, he went to yell. Jace used both hands to hold the slaver's jaw securely shut, lowly growling, "Take care of whoever it is," to Eshea.

Eshea only approached the door to see Zarlin's sister entering with the water. She rushed over quickly, closing the door behind her. She turned to see the confused look Naree was giving her before the girl ran to place the tray with water on the nearby table.

A hidden happiness seeped through as she said, "Eshea, are you here now? Are you serving here?"

Jace had released Malik and heard him yell, "Slave, defend me. Call the guards, now!"

Naree looked confused for a moment before she ran toward the door. Eshea was not about to let them be caught and grabbed the girl. Eshea was much stronger than when she was enslaved and held Naree tight. "Jace, I've got her. Get him to talk."

Malik was astonished as Eshea brought the girl next to Jace. "I've got her."

Jace handed Eshea some of the wire, saying, "Make sure she doesn't get free."

"She's Zarlin's sister, I won't hurt her," Eshea protested.

Jace sighed, "Just tie her up. We're not done with this guy yet."

Jace looked at the table nearby and noticed the small wooden box. He picked it up and inspected it. He looked at Malik. "Nice box, looks like it has something important in it. Or is it one of your toys you like to use on people?"

Jace went to open the box but was unable to. He brought it over, "Is there a trick to opening this?" Jace's voice seemed a little too passive-aggressive for Malik, but the slaver knew the contents. He surmised that if Jace were to open the box, he might be rid of him, so he answered. "Bring it closer. This device allows you to open it."

Jace recognized a Sotiral generator circuit and brought it closer. And as he was near, the lock shifted, but the lid remained closed as Jace held it. He was starting to lose patience and forced the small box to open. There was an audible snap as the lid cracked slightly, facing only him, but nothing happened.

Naree yelled, "I know where she is. Don't hurt master."

Malik was about to order her to be silent, but Jace hit him hard enough to stun him momentarily. Naree rushed to the wall and motioned to a lock. Eshea then pulled at the lock, and the wall moved away. Jace became angry. "You son of a bitch. I should kill you. She was right here?"

Fearing her master was about to be harmed, Naree rushed toward Jace, hoping to knock him away. But as she did, she knocked the small box from his hand. She fell to the floor only to have the small box land nearby, and the lid opened slightly. The girl screamed as her hand and part of her arm turned to ash.

Eshea rushed to help but felt the effect of spide radiation and pulled back. Eshea cried out, "How do I save her?"

Jace calmly picked the box up and closed it, Eshea seeing nothing happen to him. Malik looked on with a comprehending stare. Eshea said, "She's in shock. Her hand and part of her arm are gone." She looked up at Malik. "You torture people using spide?"

The slaver didn't seem to care. Jace said, "You know. Don't you?"

"My slaves are loyal. They would die for me." The slaver grinned. "And yes, I do. You and that female would set quite a price."

Jace huffed and gave a very Terran smile, one that all beings who knew Terrans never hoped to see. Malik's face displayed a grave understanding that something bad was about to happen, and he felt Jace's hand pull down on his jaw, opening it, and he nearly choked on several of his own teeth as Jace shoved the small box inside the slaver's mouth.

Jace's tone sent shivers down the Malik's spine, "You open your mouth again, and you and they die." Jace pointed to the now-open hidden door. "She and I walk out of here, leaving the rest of you dust."

He turned to Eshea. "Is she stable?" Eshea nodded. "Good, help me get Eis."

As Jace entered the room, he saw Eislie hanging limp in the machine. When Eshea saw it, she exclaimed, "Oh gods, he used Urom venom on her." Jace rushed forward to see the needles sticking into Eislie's back. The restraints were digging into her flesh. She was breathing, but only just.

"Let's get these out of her, then see if she'll wake up. Then we'll get her other restraints off afterward," Eshea said, and they worked quickly.

Outside the room, two members of the Slasta were about to enter. "Drom has not returned from his patrol. Let's inform Malik before we have everyone alerted."

The other Slasta scoffed, "Drom had other business on this world. Perhaps he has taken off to pursue it."

"Keh, the guild does not allow personal endeavors other than those sanctioned. We are to keep them separate."

The woman smiled. "Noss, you know full well what you're saying. I am well aware of your other contracts. You inform Malik, I'll do one more pass to make sure he's not here."

Noss pushed the door open and entered as Keh walked again into the courtyard.

Jace and Eshea worked quickly at removing the probes piercing Eislie's spine and Jace moved around to look at her. His hands gently cupped her face as he pleaded. "Open your eyes, Eis, open them. Let me see those pretty blue eyes of yours. Please."

Eshea fought back tears as she started working on the other restraints. When Eislie's hand became a fist, Eshea looked down to see Eislie lift her head. She could see the torment as the two looked into each other's eyes, before Eislie started sobbing. Jace placed his forehead against hers. "I'm sorry. I'm sorry, I didn't get here faster."

Jace pulled back, and Eshea watched as he forced his fingers under the metal of the restraints. The metal snapped at his assault. Eislie fell forward onto him, and Eislie weakly said, "Get us out of here."

Jace picked Eislie up in his arms and was about to start toward the door when he saw a man standing over Zarlin's sister. The Slasta turned to see them staring back at him, and instinct took over. The assassin rushed forward, making Jace dodge, but he was unstable trying to hold onto Eislie. He placed her down as gently as possible before the Slasta used a thin blade to pierce Jace's back.

Jace cried out in pain but then turned and pushed the man. His anger and need to escape giving him strength to overpower his assailant. Noss lost his footing and knocked over the chair with the table and its contents to the floor. Jace moved in and kicked him across the face. He watched as the man slumped to the ground.

Jace wasn't sticking around and returned to Eislie, but as he lifted her, the assassin picked up the tube with the long needle that had fallen from the table and thrust it into Jace's back. Malik had already primed the charge, and the venom flowed into Jace. It took only moments for Jace to feel its effects. The searing pain of everything attacking every nerve in his body, even the weight of Eislie in his arms, was tearing at him. Jace let out a primal scream and turned, snapping the needle in his shoulder. He then reached out his free hand, and when it contacted the man's face, Jace's hand clawed through the assassin's cheek, getting hold and spinning the man's head around. The assassin's head flopped around as it snapped from his spine before he hit the ground with a thud. Jace grunted as he lifted Eislie securely, hearing Eshea yell for him to follow. The effects of the venom and his wounds were starting to make themselves known.

As they ran through the hall, they could see the other Slasta now returning. She tapped her comm, "Tell our true employer that we have both his prizes, and he should see them both shortly." Keh knew that Devlin Bosh was their employer, even if Malik thought he had kept it secret. She recognized Jace, but she was less foolhardy than her partner and rushed away to get the others. Jace and Eshea kept going.

Eshea paused for a moment. She threw Naree over her shoulder, but given Eislie's injuries, Jace was not going to take that chance. Eshea watched as Jace's consciousness seemed to waver, and she asked, "Are you alright?"

Jace grunted, complaining, "That thing injected me, and I was stabbed. Do you think I'm alright?" He hit his comm. "Ed, warm up the engine. Eis is hurt badly, and so am I."

"Captain, there are guards near the ship currently."

"Then get over here. I don't care if you have to land on these fucking people," Jace snarled.

Eshea now understood why others feared Terrans when you attacked them. Next to her was a man who killed a trained assassin by nearly tearing his head off. And he was carrying someone after being stabbed and injected with toxin. But then she remembered the anti-ship weapons they had seen earlier. "Jace, the guns. If the Slasta are there, we might not be able to get away."

Jace said nothing. He only headed for the exit, hoping to find relief as the *Wolfhammer* was landing. The back door was still opening, and Jace rushed inside with Eislie. He slammed on the door's controls, making it close as Eshea stepped in. Jace took Eislie to the med bay and placed her on the table. "Ed, do what you can. I'm getting the ship off the ground."

Eshea placed Naree on the other table and started the healing process before Jace could stop her. Jace almost fell into his seat, feeling the effects of his injuries. But before he tapped the controls, the ship shook violently, and the computer sounded an alert. "Grav drive is offline. Primary external feeds are damaged.

"Override, Ed. Let's get out of here." Jace yelled.

The computer did as instructed until another volley hit them, causing the power in the ship to surge. Jace heard the warning again. "Grav drives offline; the internal feeds are not reconnected, Captain. We cannot lift off."

"What? Are you fucking kidding me?" Jace yelled and rushed to the engine room. He had forgotten to reconnect the internal systems he had turned off to save the ship when exiting the filaments.

Jace worked feverishly, bypassing the internal feeds he had taken offline earlier to stop them from overloading when he felt the ship lurch several times. The computer reported that the ablative shell of the ship was beginning to fracture.

Jace returned to his chair and hit the power to the drives, but nothing happened. He slammed the controls repeatedly, causing the console to deform. "Why isn't it working?" Jace was sounding desperate.

"Captain, the grav system is offline, and all external feeds are damaged. We only have the tunnel system partially connected." The computer almost sounded worried.

Eshea sat hard in the chair next to Jace. "You mean we can't take off?"

"Ed, what's still working?" Jace asked, his words truncated from the pain he was experiencing.

"Grav drives and shielding are offline. The tunnel drive is partially functional. We have only a short while before the hull is breached. Flight engines are functioning at extremely low power, but once outside the gravity well of this planet, we should be able to use them for limited propulsion."

Jace's breathing was becoming heavy as he fought back the pain of his injuries and the venom. He turned to look back toward the med bay and then to Eshea.

Eshea looked at him, "There must be some way we can lift off. We can't use the tunnel drive on the planet. It'd tear out a chuck the size of a stadium if we did. Not to mention kill everyone in the area."

There was a sound and an alert on the comm that lit. The computer said, "We have an incoming transmission."

On the screen was a face that boiled Jace's blood. "Bosh." The growl of anger in Jace's tone startled Eshea.

Bosh smiled, "You look a bit worse for wear, Terran. My friends told me you'd arrived."

"Fuck you, Bosh. They tortured her, so I'm not in a good mood right now. What do you want?"

Jace said nothing else as the ship rocked against a new barrage of weapons fire. Bosh's eyes stared out from the screen. "They didn't break her, you know. And in a few minutes, they'll take you both." Bosh's eyes slit as he grinned. "And I'll break you both myself."

Jace sided his head toward the door. "Why can't you leave us alone?"

Eshea looked to Jace, seeing his eyes, tired but determined. She could see Bosh staring back as if trying to force Jace back.

"You cost me a lot of Shill, and I want payback," Bosh said, sounding victorious.

"Shill? You're still thinking about money. They are trying to kill us. They fucking tortured her, you asshole."

Bosh became angry. "I had a good life until you ruined it, Terran."

The expression on Jace's face went from anger to genuine disbelief. "You still think this is about money? You enslaved us. The Duggor hunt us. And everyone in the galaxy thinks we're shit. Why won't you just leave us alone? We're not hurting any of you."

Bosh gave a victorious smile as he watched the *Wolfhammer* shake. "It doesn't matter; you can't escape. I have reports that they damaged your drive systems. You're going nowhere." Bosh leaned forward. "I've won. That small army outside will do anything for the price I've offered them. And they are all there just for you."

They all heard the computer warn, "Outer hull fracture detected. What are your orders, Captain?"

Bosh boasted, "Even if you could escape, there'd still be an army after you."

Jace's head swiveled, his eyes looking for something, his mind racing as he tried to comprehend why the former captain of the prison was still hounding them. Then Bosh said, "I'll make you watch as I break her. Then she can watch you die, Terran. I'll take everything from both of you."

Jace's eyes fixed on the monitor, his face emotionless until he spoke. "You've already taken too much, Bosh." Eshea could feel the anger from the man in the chair next to her, watching him tap the controls. "You said you have an army out there just for us? Call them off."

Bosh shook his head slowly for effect as a grin covered his face.

Jace looked into the screen his eyes piercing through the electronics. "Call them off. Leave us alone."

Bosh gave a simple response, "No."

Jace closed his eyes, and Eshea could feel the tension in his arm from where she sat. When Jace said, "If you don't call them off, then I'll take them away from you. When we meet again, Bosh, it'll be the last time. Just leave us alone."

Moments later, Jace activated the tunnel drive on the *Wolfhammer*, opening a hyperspace tunnel. Eshea heard Jace give an order. "Ed, head to the coordinates I've programmed, best speed. This order can only be rescinded by a captain."

Eshea was still in shock at what Jace had done. She looked around as Jace sat back. She could see him fighting back emotions, his lips shaking as a tear rolling down his face. She heard him mutter, "Just leave us alone."

Eshea felt her heart breaking as she watched the man next to her calm and his breathing slow as he lost consciousness. She attempted to wake him, but Jace opened his eyes only long enough to push her away.

"You need medical attention. We have to get you into the med bay," Eshea said. "You have to tell the computer to give me control."

Jace shook his head, rolling it against the back of the chair. "Med bay's full, and I won't give you control of this ship. We're not soldiers in your fight."

Eshea looked him in the eyes. She saw the sadness and realized he knew exactly what he had just done on the planet.

Bosh felt the ground shake and the feed to his display darken before he heard alarms all over the city. There was an emergency comm alert about an incident involving a ship and what looks like the activation of a tunnel system on the planet's surface.

"We estimate that hundreds were killed." The announcer paused. "Uh, I've been informed that the residence was of House Unber and that most of the ruling class was in attendance. It is not confirmed, but it appears that many of the Tas and their families are thought killed or missing."

Bosh quickly stood, his chair falling backward and his eyes wide in fear. "He used the tunnel drive to kill them." Bosh looked to his side. "He killed my army." Bosh paused. He then ordered, "Prepare my ship to leave. Now!"

One of Bosh's servants asked if he was alright. Bosh turned to the man, the look of evident fear now pouring from his face. And his servant knew that his master had just made a terrible mistake.

Chapter 37:
Safety

On a small transport, the remaining crew of the *Eiger* and Queeks Maco watched the emergency transmission from their home planet. The incident on Arlain had all the remaining members shocked in disbelief at what happened. They all knew Eshea was with Jace back on Arlain, but she would never undertake such an action. Their bewilderment was short-lived.

Ralla yelled, "Increase speed. If the Tas has been destroyed, we only have a limited time until chaos starts."

Trin nodded and accelerated as Ralla went to look for Zarlin.

"Zar, you have those files that starborn left?" Ralla yelled as he rounded the corner. He paused, seeing the many screens around the room, lit, displaying scenes of destruction from their world.

"That's horrifying. You think Eshea did that?" Zarlin asked.

Ralla said nothing as he moved to look closer at the carnage on display. He only shook his head. Zarlin looked up to see his mouth open in genuine disbelief at the devastation. She clutched the blue shirt that was Eshea's close. "She wasn't in that, was she?"

Ralla heard her plead but didn't have an answer. He found himself muttering, "I have no idea."

The two stood in horror at the damage caused by the tunnel drive. Zarlin's eyes looked to the ground. "Maybe they killed her."

"Who, Eshea?" Ralla asked.

Zarlin shook her head. "No, that woman, the light-haired starborn, Eislie. Maybe he did that because they…."

Ralla turned slowly to look at her, his seasoned stare gone, filling her with a terrifying fear. His mouth tried to form words for a few seconds. "We, we only have a few hours. Uh, get those files on curing the effects of the black flower to our contacts quickly. We, um, we'll deal with what happened later."

Zarlin nodded and tapped away at her keypad. "It would be so sad if they killed her. They seemed so happy together." She wiped a tear from her eye as she worked.

Ralla turned, his feet seeming to trip over themselves. He steadied himself against the wall, his head down and eyes wide, whispering, "Gods, what would they have done to us if I forced them to fight?"

Then the leader of Queeks heard the ship's comm. "Ralla, I have Hasner on the comm. The Tarnen want to know if we're underway."

Ralla pressed the comm, "Tell them we'll rendezvous with the other ships and watch for the files on helping free our people from their dependency the Tas have inflicted. If we work this right, and with the disarray on the planet, we'll get a foothold in only a few hours."

* * *

A medical technician awakened Jace as she was treating his wounds to stabilize him. Eshea had done her best to stop the bleeding while they were in hyperspace. She stood nearby as the medical staff examined Naree's arm and newly regenerated hand. Jace shifted in his command chair, feeling the pain of the needle still stuck in his shoulder.

"Easy, remain still. I'm still evaluating your injuries." The medic seemed surprised as she said, "You have a fragment of metal lodged in your upper chest and shoulder."

Jace heard the woman and felt the sharp pain as he moved and pointed back toward the med bay. "Ow, Eis, how's Eis?" Jace's words sounded slurred as he spoke.

The medical technician looked back. "They've taken her away. She'll be fine. Now remain still while we stabilize you."

Jace's eyes became heavy, and he mumbled, "Please be alright," before passing out.

Another technician asked, "How bad is he?"

The woman shook her head. "thin stab wound, A large metallic object lodged in his chest and upper shoulder. And the one called Eshea told us it was from something that injected about a half-liter of the same toxin the woman had in her."

Overhearing the medical staff, Eshea looked back at Jace, saying, "I don't understand how either of them is still alive."

Jace groaned as he woke. He opened his eyes to see Miriz seated across the room. He drowsily looked over to see Eislie sleeping in the bed next to him before asking, "How is she?"

Miriz raised her head quickly, realizing Jace was awake. She held back tears. "You're worried about her?"

Jace nodded, his face angry but sad. "They hurt her bad, Miriz."

Miriz took a breath. "Apparently, you hurt them in kind."

Jace said, "I'm not proud of what I did. I wasn't letting him take us again."

From the corner of the room, Jace heard, "That is good to hear."

Jace rolled his head to the other side, his eyes took a moment to focus, and he said, "Grand Matron? I'm sorry I didn't see you."

The Grand Matron walked toward him. "We know you would have tried official channels to get Eislie back. The Tarnen council has been speaking with us about your statement. They do not like people taking military action into their own hands."

"Tarnen council?" Jace asked, confused.

The Grand Matron acknowledged him and explained, "They are the new ruling body of Arlain. Almost all the Tas were killed in the incident. Activating your tunnel drive on the planet killed not only the army attacking you but most of their ruling class. The Tarnen have a preliminary government in place." She sighed. "Some want to bring you in for attacking their world."

Jace sat up, his breathing and words interrupted by pauses of pain from what remained of his injuries. "They kidnapped Eis, tortured her, and they think they're in the fucking right? That asshole put a price on our heads. And if those bureaucrats think I'm going to sit and wait for them to get off their asses...."

Miriz and one of the medical technicians gently tried to get Jace to lie back. But, the Grand Matron walked forward and placed her hand on his chest to assist. Jace slowly lay back, his face wincing in pain as he calmed. "Those bureaucrats have taken control of that planet. They were merely questioning what had happened to warrant such an action," the Grand Matron told him.

Jace looked toward her. "It was us or them. I didn't want to do what I did." He paused. "If I hadn't, then there would still be an army after us." She watched as Jace held back frustrated tears. The Grand Matron steeled her emotions and placed her hand on his shoulder. Jace looked forward. "We weren't harming anyone. We just wanted to explore the universe. Why won't they leave us alone?"

The grand Matron leaned down so Jace could hear her whisper. "You did what you had to do, right or wrong. You are alive. She is alive." She placed her hand on his head and motioned for another man to approach.

The man wore the same clothing as the planet they were on, and when he spoke, there was no sign of anger or malice. "I am Farh Celos, the representative of the new ruling council assigned to Yata Beta, given the evidence your computer provided. And, I may say in great detail and quantity, it seems. If the evidence is true, and you were on our world, what you did would be considered a localized dispute between private parties."

Jace looked up at him, confused. "A what?"

The Gran Matron nodded, "You were threatened by an individual under the protection of the house you destroyed. Interestingly, what you did is not severely punishable under their laws."

An expression of distasteful disbelief came over Jace's face as the Matron continued. "I'm afraid they have officially started proceedings for you and Eislie to be reprimanded for interfering in a military action by mistake."

Jace's eyes opened, stunned, stammering, "W....what?"

The man smiled. "There will be a punishment. I'm afraid you won't be able to return to the planet for the next few months. I have to apologize for that inconvenience."

Jace's mouth fell open, and the Grand Matron gently used her hand to close it before she turned to leave. "Do not worry, captain, you may both stay here to recuperate. I'm sure the ambassador will understand if you do not show up planetside for the next few months for your trial on Arlain."

Jace sat silent as the grand Matron and ambassador walked from the room. He turned to Miriz, asking, "What just happened?"

Miriz sat before holding his hand. "Well, you saved Eislie, overthrew a government, rid the galaxy of a bunch of slavers, and in the process gained some folk hero status back on said planet, so I've been told."

Jace looked to Eislie, "Please tell me I have brain damage. I don't understand what's going on."

Miriz smiled, "Then I'd be lying."

Jace again looked at Eislie.

Miriz looked over. "I was on my way back to Yata when I heard your wonderful computer broadcasting an emergency message. The *Solace Star* was able to relay the message to a nearby Yata cruiser. And your med bay stabilized Eis, even with the damage to your ship's power systems." She held his hand tighter. "It was smart of you to order your computer to send the beacon. We found you and her just in time."

Miriz gently kissed Jace on his forehead. "She had severe internal injuries she's healed, so now she's just resting."

Jace sat up and pushed Miriz away. Jace moved to the edge of the bed placing his feet on the floor. He let out a quiet groan as he put weight on them.

"You're not healed yet. You should be lying down," Miriz protested, grabbing onto him.

Jace pushed her away, but she held onto him as he moved to lean on the edge of Eislie's bed. Jace reached out, gently nudging Eislie's face, making her open her eyes.

He smiled, quietly saying, "Hey."

Eislie smiled back, reaching out to him, and returning his words, "Hey."

Miriz heard him groan as Eislie reached out and tightened her arms over his shoulder. Eislie placed her forehead against his. "You should be in bed. You're not healed."

She looked at Miriz. "He is so stubborn."

* * *

In a darkened room, seven hooded figures sat around an oval table. The one at the head removed his hood as a light shone down on him. The others remained in darkness. The man's voice was quiet but commanding as he called the meeting to order and confirmed the grim news.

"The House of Perig has been silenced. It has been some time since we have had to call a gathering to decide on the fate of only two individuals."

"How many were lost?" The man to the right of him asked, his hood barely moving as he spoke.

From the head of the table, the man replied, "73, all Oficios."

A woman on his left said, "You honor them with that title? Were they all Oficios?

She watched as the man nodded slowly, confirming her question. "They were under Bramaic's watch. Her blood was taken with theirs."

The woman nodded before she brought her hands up, crossing the palms back to her face. "Then the light of death has them. They will be remembered and honored."

The one at the head of the table motioned to the side, and someone approached. The person knelt to hear his master's words. The two nearest sat straight, nodding in agreement at the man's whispered commands, while the others began to discuss the recent loss of an entire guild to a single target. There were words of revenge and anger, of unfathomable distress that a single half of the chosen prey, gravely injured, had taken the blood of so many of their trade. And to do so while facing the very man who set the guild on them in the first place. Their words of disagreement became louder. "He could not have done anything after being wounded. The serum of pain would have been excruciating."

Silence engulfed the room as a man returned from the shadows to place a small wooden box before the man at the head of the table. All the others looked at him as he opened the lid.

The man looked up at the others before speaking, "We have not provided one of those to anyone outside our houses since High Master Koth. I have never seen one bestowed on anyone during my time."

"You are correct, Master Taar. We have not needed to use this in almost an eon. We are feared throughout the galaxy." The man sighed. "But, what is fear when its prey will not run?"

All in the room nodded. "Then we must all agree. I call for a quorum."

Everyone at the table sat tall, hands flat until they spoke. Silence prevailed until broken as the man slid the box down to the woman beside him. It was a moment before she slid the box to the next person and held her hands up. She then pulled a ribbon from her sleeve and wrapped her wrist, covering the Banaa she wore. Its leather and knotted thread bearing the name of her first kill was now hidden beneath her palm.

"I, Master Rau, pledge by my first kill. And confirm our prey worthy."

The man beside her did the same, covering his Banaa. "I, Master Taar, confirm."

Each table member continued as the one before confirming and covering the sacred symbol. When it was time, the one sitting at the head of the table did the same. "I, High Master Koth, a descendant of my namesake, confirm."

All sat silently for a moment before the one known as Koth shifted the box to the side before placing his hands on the table beside it. "We all agree. However, I have not chosen a messenger. Would any like to provide one?"

Rau stood, her voice determined, "I will bear that honor. I will send my best to deliver our message."

The man at the end rose, closed the box, and handed it to Master Rau. "Then send our message. That we will allow the full guild to continue until they have complied."

The woman gave a shallow bow of her head and turned to disappear into the darkness.

Koth turned to face the rest. "I need another to retrieve the one who set our fellow guild to their demise."

There were plenty of volunteers for Koth's new call to arms.

Chapter 38:
A Message and Warning

A day later, a man was forced into a darkened room and pushed into a single chair. When they removed the hood covering his head, the only thing visible was the ring of light that surrounded him. The image of fear and surprise illuminated on Bosh's face would have sent most running. As his eyes adjusted, the former captain looked around straining to see the ornate architecture subdued by the darkness that permeated the room. His only light was what was encircling him.

From his career, Bosh learned many things and knew where he was. Soon after his eyes adjusted fully, he muttered, "The theater of the Vhit Atira. The Chamber of Ash?" He had only stories and minimal information about the assassin's guild known as the Slasta, always using others to hire them for him. But now Bosh found himself in their very theater of death.

Bosh's head snapped forward as he heard, "Devlin Bosh, do you know why you were brought here?" The voice in the darkness was forceful.

The captain gulped before saying, "You're going to kill me?"

His answer was met with laughter before the voice was heard saying. "It would be fitting, but an outsider has already claimed you."

"What do you mean, claimed? Who?" Bosh asked in fear and anger.

The voice continued. "You placed a price on the head of your quarry. Our guild worked as your hand. And that quarry took the hand and the body that wielded it under your request."

Bosh looked around in the shadows as he heard, "It was carried out by the same individual you threatened while facing them. And we are aware of the conversation. We had monitored everything in Malik's compound."

Bosh thought, *The vid feed.*

"Our guild paid with their blood, and your prey claimed you before doing so."

Oh gods, Tucker said it would be the last time he saw me face to face. Bosh thought. "Then why am I here?"

Within moments, the voice he heard came from a man who moved closer, allowing the circle's light to illuminate his cloak. "Your hunters will be given one standard year to claim you and return your blood to us."

Bosh tried sounding strong. "And if I kill them first?"

The man said nothing.

"Answer me!" Bosh ordered.

The man moved closer the light illuminating the edge of his hood. "You have the blood of seventy-three of our own on your hands, Devlin Bosh. It will be only two fewer if you do."

The realization of what the man said finally sank in, and Bosh's words uttered involuntarily, "Oh gods, I'm marked for death."

Bosh could see the teeth of the man as he smiled. "Devlin Bosh, you will be set free, and your hunters informed of their duty."

There was anger in Bosh's words as he said, "I was taking revenge for them destroying my life. Who are you to judge me?"

The man spoke. "I am Koth of Tuins, messenger, host, and your judge. Remember my name."

Bosh heard movement around him as the man motioned to others in the darkness. When the hood was placed over Bosh's head, it took only seconds for him to lose consciousness. Rau approached Koth, "My messenger will be at her assignment shortly."

Koth acknowledged her statement.

* * *

Jace was arguing with Miriz as she again chastised him for going to save Eislie alone. The Grand Matron sided with Miriz as they faced off.

"No one was ready to go. Why would I wait? Eshea was ready. I just took off," Jace defended himself.

"Jace, they could have captured you. We wouldn't even be having this conversation," Miriz countered.

The altercation lasted for a few minutes, and Jace moved on to argue with the Arlain representative only to have Eislie tug on his arm. She said nothing as she leaned against Jace, causing him to calm. She felt relief as he started to joke with Farh before he returned and apologized to the grand Matron and Miriz.

But as Jace was listening to Miriz again chastise him for going in alone, his eyes focused on a woman entering the room. Eislie felt the sudden tension in his arm, and she followed his gaze to the very same woman. The room started to quiet as the rest of the others noticed the reactions of both. When everyone was silent, Jace asked, "Who are you?"

The woman wore a long dark cloak, her face hidden by wrapped fabric, her eyes the only things visible. She stood alone and produced a single blade. As she moved forward, one of security tried to grab her, and they watched as he fell to the ground after a single strike from the woman's weapon. After a few others met the same fate, no one interfered. Jace and Eislie watched the woman closely as she approached.

Jace sighed before he said, "If you're here to kill us, that's pretty low. I mean, hitting someone in a hospital, that is. Who are you?"

The woman raised her head, saying, "You noticed me as I entered. You are worthy of the praise of my masters. I am not here to kill you. I am a messenger."

Jace said nothing but was not in the mood for games and watched as the woman slowly swiped the blade around to keep everyone away. She approached Jace, who was ready to fight but held back. The woman looked at him and saw that he and Eislie were prepared to fight. "The Vhit Atira have sent me. I am to give you this."

She held out a thin box, and Jace grabbed it before looking at it. "What is it?"

The woman stood silent, saying nothing, motioning for Jace to open the box. Inside, he could see a white blade made of bone and metal. Jace held it up, and Farh recognized what it was. Jace was surprised to see the man scurry backward away. "Gods, a bone blade."

Jace looked up to see the grand Matron covering her mouth and whispering something beneath. He also watched as Miriz looked at Eislie. Jace looked to the assassin, "Is this supposed to send us a message?"

He then heard the representative from Arlain say, "It's a bone blade. You do not ask questions; just accept it."

Eislie and Jace both turned, their eyes steeled on the man, causing him to step back. The assassin noticed the display and smiled, "Your enemies cower from a single glance." She looked at the pair squarely, asking, "Where are you and your ancestors from?"

Jace smiled. "That's a bit complicated. I was born on Earth, uh, Terra, but apparently, my ancestors are from Earth and Lyri."

The woman looked to Eislie. "Like him but even more complicated: Gilese, Terra, and Lyri."

The assassin looked to the Grand Matron, asking, "Are they citizens of this world?"

Miriz stepped forward. "Yes, under my watch and protection. I owe them my life."

The assassin nodded slowly. "The bone blade is given to quarry who have killed members of Atira, the member guilds. It is given in respect."

Jace was suspicious and asked, "Why?"

"Do not ask any questions. Accept the gift!" the Grand Matron yelled, causing Jace's eyes to narrow in defiance as he looked toward her. The assassin's smile broadened, looking at the Grand Matron, who said, "he is not familiar with the guild, or their ways."

The woman nodded, "We are aware of this. I was sent to bestow this gift and its message to them, and them only."

Eislie moved forward. "Then tell us the message."

The assassin acknowledged her. "Grand Matron, you would do well to remember the meaning of this gift. And while you do, I will explain." The assassin held up her left hand, showing her Banaa, the tattoo, the name of her first kill. "By the founders of our clans, this blade is a promise. For as long as you live, no member of the Atira or Slasta will kill anyone on any world you or your ancestors are from. That honor is also extended to any who aided you. You will never be hunted by any of us again. But, to do this, the blade must taste the blood of the one who called the guild to hunt you within one standard year. That will be your responsibility."

"Oh, okay, I know who this is for," Jace looked at Eislie, who nodded quickly. "Then we accept. Thank you."

The assassin nodded and turned to leave but was stopped by some guards, making Eislie say, "Uh, Matron, you may want to allow her to leave. For your guard's sake, please." The Grand Matron agreed, waving them away.

The assassin turned. "I will let my masters know that you have accepted." She then walked toward the door, and they all watched as the assassin disappeared into the crowd of the medical facility.

Jace closed the box. "Looks like this has Bosh's name on it."

"You're not killers," Miriz protested.

"At least not intentionally," Jace muttered, still regretting having activated the tunnel drive on the planet's surface.

The remainder of the day was thankfully less eventful. It took several hours for them to return to Miriz's home, where the *Wolfhammer* awaited them. Jace was inspecting the outside of the ship and was just about to enter. Eislie was walking toward the ship and yelled to Jace that she just received a message from her parents and that Miriz said that dinner would be ready shortly before Jace opened the rear door and entered the ship.

"Captains! It is good to see you both well," the computer greeted them.

Eislie laughed. "Ed, you sounded like you missed us."

There was a moment before the computer replied, "I have been looking forward to the new upgrades and the new hull. Our previous adventure seems to have made our ship worse for wear."

Jace seemed confused. "Ed, you alright? You seem kind of, I don't know, chipper."

Eislie looked at Jace strangely, making him joke, "For the… oh, look it up. I'm getting tired of explaining Earth sayings all the time."

She understood what he said, and the computer noticed, "I believe Captain Licessien understands. It seems she is playing a joke on you."

Jace looked at Eislie, who smiled back. "My mother uses those phrases a lot. I know what they mean."

He grabbed Eislie and pulled her close. He made her rock on one foot as he pulled her into his command chair. She sat herself across his lap.

"You know, it's good to be back," Jace said.

"Yes, Captain, it is good to see you both back," Ed responded, and even Jace noticed the intonation in the computer's response.

Eislie looked concerned. "What is it, Ed?"

The computer took longer to respond. "On our trip back, several systems went offline. Including the med bay. I rerouted all functions possible to reactivate them to save Captain Licessien."

Jace pulled Eislie a little tighter. "How close, Ed?"

Eislie turned to Jace, knowing what he was asking. And she dreaded the answer. She felt the caring in the computer's response. "It was too close, captain, for both of you. If Eshea had not followed my instructions, I do not believe we would all be speaking."

Eislie gently kissed Jace before he said, "Thanks, Ed. We owe you a lot."

"No, Captain, you have given me more than any others I have flown with. It was my duty to help you both." The computer paused. "But the hull does need repair, and I understand that it will take some time to fabricate the new shell."

Eislie snickered, "Sounds like you want some repairs. We'll get them done as soon as we can, Ed." She then looked at Jace and said, "We should thank Eshea for saving you as well."

Jace agreed but commented, "Too bad she went home to Arlain. It's not like we'll be stepping foot there any time soon." Jace seemed to think. "Hope she's good with just a video message."

Eislie kissed him harder. Then, as she pulled away, "Speaking of messages, my father said they are on route to Yata. The *Solace Star* is fully crewed and heading here to see us."

"I'm not planning on going anywhere for a while. Besides, we have to make the new hull parts and the shell for the ship." Jace said, then seemed to think. "You know, I think a little time off is just what we all need. What do you think Ed?"

The computer agreed.

Jace lifted Eislie's legs and lifted her from the chair. She placed her forehead against his as he carried her toward the doorway. "I think a little rest, some home cooking, and not being chased by everyone would be great, don't you?"

Eislie and the computer again agreed with Jace, and as they were about to exit the ship, Eislie grabbed the protective visors from the table and placed Jace's over his eyes while the computer asked one more question.

"Captain, we used the filaments to reach Captain Licessien in time. Do you think the new shell will solve the issue of the charging on the hull and allow us to travel the filaments freely?"

Jace thought momentarily. "I hope so, Ed, I hope so." He looked around at the ship and into Eislie's eyes before saying, "I guess we'll all find out together."

MORE STORIES FROM THE AUTHOR

It's been a long, arduous journey for Jace and Eislie, but they finally figured out how to allow everyone to travel the filaments safely. It's too bad for these two that some still want to keep that knowledge for themselves. What's worse is that the Duggor have decried all starborn to be captured after several of their ships are destroyed visiting the mysterious planet Reothes. Now, Jace and Eislie have to avoid capture once again.

It seems these two can never catch a break.

After nearly dying, again, they discover what happened to a race of beings thought lost long ago, and learn the origin of the Lyri themselves. While meeting these new allies, Jace and Eislie discover a secret about the planet Reothes and possibly a way to end the war with the Duggor for good.

Join the crew of the Wolfhammer again in:

Legends of the Starborn

REVENANT

Will they find a way to end the war and stop those hunting them?

For more stories, please visit.

www.wolfhammer.com

ABOUT THE AUTHOR

Stephen has experience in technology, engineering, and sales spanning over 30 years. He has been writing science fiction and fantasy for far longer—his work primarily for role-playing and short stories personally, using his knowledge and imagination within his life. He is always known to have a story to tell, and it's usually sprinkled with a hint of adventure. Through his character's eyes, you find that life can be an adventure, and it's always better with a bit of science and magic.

The Legends of the Starborn series is his jump into the science fiction genre and something very familiar. The universe can be a big place, and many universes even more so.

For more stories, please visit:

www.wolfhammer.com

or

www.afairyslight.com

www.ingramcontent.com/pod-product-compliance
Lightning Source LLC
Chambersburg PA
CBHW051534260626
47170CB00003B/923